It Can Happen to You

It Can Happen to You

Lynn Crymble

HARPER
WEEKEND

Harper Weekend

It Can Happen to You

Published by Harper Weekend, an imprint of HarperCollins Publishers Ltd.

First published in Canada by HarperCollins Publishers Ltd in an
original trade paperback edition: 2009
This Harper Weekend trade paperback edition: 2011

HarperCollins books may be purchased for educational, business, or
sales promotional use through our Special Markets Department.

HarperCollins Publishers Ltd
2 Bloor Street East, 20th Floor
Toronto, Ontario, Canada
M4W 1A8

www.harpercollins.ca

Library and Archives Canada Cataloguing in Publication information is
available upon request.

ISBN 978-1-55468-308-6

Printed and bound in the United States
RRD 9 8 7 6 5 4 3 2 1

For Christa

So, what do you know for sure?

—H.P.

One

Penny stands with her hands on her ample hips and squints in the glare of bright sun. A trickle of sweat runs down her cleavage. On a scorching day like this, there are only a few souls scouring the bark-mulch aisles of the Maple Leaf Garden Centre. Most gardens are in full bloom by now, having made their debut at least a month ago. Penny is late for the party as usual.

"Christ, is it hot." She feels light-headed and hungry and sticky and premenstrual.

From her purse Penny takes out this week's *Thrifty Gardener* flyer and holds it over her eyes. Of course she has forgotten her sunglasses, which is not helping her hangover. Last night she finished off a third of a bottle with a penguin on it and then moved on to some other animal. A wild horse, or was it the painted turtle? She prefers the classic bin label. In fact, she might just swing by the liquor store on the way home and pick up her favourite Shiraz.

Her stomach, however, has other ideas and roils and splashes and gurgles loudly at the thought of more wine. As if to dissociate herself from the sound, Penny quickly rounds a corner, where she finds herself among rows of wilting dahlias. She plucks at her shirt, which clings too closely in the heat. A woman at the opposite end of the aisle glances at her, then quickly looks away.

She can't believe she's even considering more wine at a time like this. Her head is pounding. Not only has she forgotten her glasses, but she hasn't even brought her hat. She's quite good about sun protection and rarely leaves home without the large straw Panama that she brought back from Italy all those years ago.

"Shit!" she says under her breath, and this time a young woman with a watering hose replies.

"Can I help you?"

"Oh!" She didn't intend anybody to hear her. She turns in the direction of the voice and almost stumbles over her own feet.

"Oh! Nothing. Nothing!" She struggles to maintain her composure and reminds herself not to ramble. She has always been socially awkward and has never been able to put her finger on why. It is not uncommon for her to elicit awkward reactions from strangers. Penny recognizes the odd look spreading over the woman's face as the words pour out of her mouth.

"I forgot my hat and sunglasses at home. Can you believe it? On a day like this! And if that isn't enough, I'm hungover." She almost emits one of her anxiety snorts but musters enough self-control to excuse herself and scuttle off into the next aisle without making eye contact.

Why can't I just be normal? Why? And it's so hot! I'm probably going to have a heart attack right here next to the petunias. Here lies Penny Stevens. She was short and fat and forgot her hat. Rest in peace.

Penny forces herself to take a deep breath the way she learned at a recent meditation workshop. She doesn't practise on a routine basis, but she is proud that she regularly chastises herself that she should.

The garden centre is built on a hill, and from where Penny is standing she can look down across the nursery and out over Dundarave Beach. Across the Burrard Inlet, she can see the two residence towers of the university. If she turns her gaze westward and looks hard enough, she can make out the faint shape of Vancouver Island.

Finding a bit of shade, she wills herself to pull it together. *Breathe deeply. Inhale. Exhale. Breathe. Where did I put my water? Did I bring it?*

Nope.

Penny. Penny. Penny.

She admonishes herself to stay on task and get the job done. She's not going home without a plant, regardless of her present state of mind. She inhales deeply the reassuring odour of the bark mulch beneath her feet and the raw scent of the ocean beyond.

She remembers as a young child helping her father spread the pungent pieces of chipped bark and dirt out between the bushes and plants in their front garden. She wasn't ample back then. All she remembers is being very small and very quiet.

"Beep! Beep!" a child's voice announces. She hears the metal garden trolley before she sees it. At first glimpse, Penny is not quite sure whether it is being piloted by a boy or a girl. The hair is shoulder length, obscuring the face, and the clothes appear neutral. T-shirt, shorts. A ten-year-old, perhaps.

"Beep! Beep!" A six-pack of pansies has fallen off the trolley and is lying on its side, forlorn in the middle of

4

the aisle. Penny thinks about venturing out from the foliage to rescue them, but the kid and trolley are careening carelessly around and around a low plank table of lavender and heather, so she remains pressed up against some cedar hedges. There seems to be no parent in sight.

"I'm a race-car driver!"

Not sure whether she should respond to this, she doesn't.

"Look how fast I can go!"

Penny is overcome by a sudden irritability as the child knocks more plants to the ground and continues to bash about.

"Look at this!"

She thinks it might be a boy.

"Look at me!"

She looks around for backup, but nobody is there. Just her and the devil child.

"Beep! Beep! Here I come!"

She's pretty certain it isn't a girl, though she has learned not to prejudge. A good friend of hers once gave Penny quite a sermon about raising children with equal gender opportunities. The fact that the woman's son loves front-end loaders and her daughter adores little pink dolls has still not deterred the woman from extolling the virtues of non-gender-specific parenting.

Penny always takes care to send very generic birthday cards. That and a good chunk of money. This way, she escapes both the mall and any judgment for having bought the wrong gift.

The child swerves dangerously close to her, and she mumbles something about slowing down.

"Beep! Beep!"

She sees the kid is laughing now, fully aware of having secured the attention of an audience of one.

She doesn't want to intervene. Penny never intervenes. She is adamant about never sticking her nose in other people's business if she can help it. She recycles and feels that is enough.

But the trolley is careening toward her. "Stop! Stop!" she calls out in panic. Miraculously, the cart comes to a halt directly in front of her. The young child scowls and stares up at Penny with defiance.

A face only a mother could love.

"You can't tell me what to do! You're not my mother! I don't have to listen to you! F' you! F' you!" And with these parting words, the child takes off, abandoning the trolley with one final rough push in her direction. Penny has to react quickly to avoid contact.

Today is Penny's eighteenth anniversary. She has come here to buy a plant. She has not come here to lock horns with some ill-behaved brat. She has no children, and on considering this rude young child swearing and glaring at her, she isn't too upset about that. She tells herself there is no guarantee she wouldn't end up with such a specimen of her own. She looks forward to buying a plant and getting home. Maybe she will make a visit to the liquor store after all.

"Ian!" A woman in her early thirties appears from behind the hanging-basket display. "Ian!"

Ha! I was right. It is a boy.

Impeccably clad in designer Pilates wear, the woman is perfectly tanned and is wearing lip liner. It is eleven o'clock in the morning, and Penny can't take her eyes off this woman's fuchsia lips.

"Ian, come here, darling." No Ian in sight. "Mommy is going to count. Do you hear me?" The woman has acknowledged Penny with a "Gosh, isn't motherhood hilarious?" sort of expression.

Penny just stands there unable to move, transfixed as if watching a performance.

This woman is going to count.

"One."

Hmm. Okay . . .

"Two." The woman sounds confident, and there is some movement behind the lavender bushes.

Right. She's on track, this one.

"Two and a half . . ." The woman is losing her rhythm in counting.

"F' you!"

Ouch. That's gotta hurt.

She turns and speaks directly now to Penny—at least she has *her* attention. The cedar bushes are prickly, but Penny stays put.

"We're teaching him not to swear. He's not allowed to say 'fuck,' but he can say 'F.' He has anger management issues and ADD." She turns back to the lavender bushes and says, "Ian, come here, honey. I know it's hot and you're tired. Come out and we'll pick up a Slurpee at the 7-Eleven."

Reluctantly, little Ian comes out.

"Ian, come here. Mommy needs to talk to you."

The kid shuts his eyes and covers his ears.

"Ian, you are behaving badly and have scared this lady. It is inappropriate behaviour to run around with these trolleys at such high speeds."

The woman is bending down in a rather awkward way to be at eye level with the boy, but as his eyes are closed it only looks bizarre. Her French-manicured hands are open and pleading. All this is lost on young Ian.

"Ian, I need you to acknowledge what I am saying." She waits for a few seconds. "Say something, Ian."

Ian sticks his tongue out. Triumphantly, the woman turns to Penny. "He's getting it. He's opening up to the situation."

Throughout all of this, Penny has said nothing. She hasn't needed to, as the woman seems capable of having a conversation all on her own.

"Ian, open your eyes." Ian does. Things are going well.

"Ian, please say you are sorry to this lady."

Penny, still with her back up against the cedar bushes, shifts nervously from one foot to the other. The kid is kicking at the bark mulch with brand-new but unlaced Nike high tops.

"Ian! Do you or don't you want a Slurpee?" The kid considers this for another long moment and then looks Penny squarely in the eyes.

"Ian! What do you have to say to this lady?"

Quickly, he sticks out his tongue again. Having seen this action once before, Penny thinks that maybe this future reform-school dropout might want to expand his repertoire. It has lost half the punch it had just a moment ago. Thankfully, Ian runs away. His mother, however, turns to Penny once more.

"In his own way, I think he sees how he has misbehaved. In sticking his tongue out, he was reaching out to you and affirming your presence. You know he's gifted—we've had him tested. He's very bright, but he's in this kind of phase, you see, and, well, it can be a challenge at times."

Penny is nodding aggressively. Anything to get this woman to stop talking.

"Well, I've got to get a move on if we're going to get that Slurpee in. I've just opened up a fabulous fitness studio. Right beside Starbucks on Marine. Do you know where I mean?"

More nodding.

"Anyhow, let me give you my card. Where is it? Yes, here you go. I'm Skye Mountain, owner and instructor of Tranquility Fitness. We have everything from ashtanga to hatha to Pilates to aerobics. Something for everyone. Here, have a complimentary class on me."

"Thanks." Penny has finally found her voice and she stuffs the coupon into her purse.

"Well, gotta run. Nice meeting you!" And with those words she competently strides up the path—"Ian! Ian! Where are you, darling?"—her voice obscured by the greenery and vegetation.

Alone again, Penny breathes deeply.

Did that just happen?

She is aware of the penetrating heat. Aware of the sweat trickling down her back, down between her breasts. She can't seem to move, so she just stands there concentrating on the scents. The roses, the wisteria, the honeysuckle, the clematis.

She remembers buying clematis two years ago, maybe three. Their fifteenth anniversary, she calculates. She'd planted it right next to the front porch, where it would be sure to receive the right amount of light. It had certainly grown that summer, but it never flowered like in the picture that had caught her attention that day. Turned out it also wasn't one of the fragrant ones. Anyhow, Penny had pruned it wrong, and by the following summer it staunchly refused to grow. All she had to show for her purchase was a big hole in the ground and a small picture tag that had been attached to the plant. The following year, if she remembers correctly, she bought a cactus.

It has become quite a well-known story, these late-July jaunts to the garden centre. Anyone who works in Jack's office no doubt knows about their anniversary tradition. About how one year, early on in their marriage, just after they had bought the house on Haywood, Jack had forgotten to buy a gift. Penny, on the other hand, had spent the afternoon out at the garden centre, choosing the perfect rose bush. Carefully, she'd brought it home. Meticulously, she'd chosen the perfect spot to plant it. And it had looked marvellous right up against the weather-worn trellis, its blossoms pink and hopeful. It had looked so good, in fact, that not two hours later, most of its two dozen roses had disappeared, only to reappear in Jack's hand. An apologetic offering.

"Pen, look what I brought you."

Scrutinizing her husband standing there in front of her with his shirtsleeves rolled up and a pocketknife sticking out of his pants, it dawned on Penny that though she may have lived side by side with this person for a number of years, there was a lot she didn't really know about him. For instance, did he always carry this knife to the office? Had it come in handy before? What fleshy and white forearms he had in comparison to his always-tanned face! Why would he cut off almost two dozen roses when she could scarcely remember him ever buying her any flowers at all? Why didn't he cut off just one?

"Happy anniversary, Penny." The scent of the freshly cut stems wafted loudly between them.

"What time is it?"

"Oh, uh . . ." This question jarred Jack. Clumsily, he shifted the flowers to his left hand to glance at his watch. "It's almost eight thirty. I was late because those clients needed to see that house this afternoon. I didn't have the key and the tenants wanted me to—"

"Good, there's still time."

"What?"

"Are you coming with me? You don't have to, you know. You can reheat the dinner if you're hungry, I made your favourite, or maybe you already ate." She was moving quickly, retrieving her purse, her keys.

"Where are you going?"

"Birks."

"Where? Who?" He was really trying to pay attention.

"You're going to have to roll down your sleeves and get rid of that knife if you are coming with me."

"But your flowers?"

"Look, Jack, those were your damn flowers! God. Why I even bother!" She was halfway to the car before Jack moved from his spot on the porch.

"Wait!" he called out after her. Suddenly he, too, was rushing. Rushing past the ravaged rose bush, into the passenger side of the car, fumbling with his seat belt, Penny like he'd never seen her before, hands gripping the steering wheel, down 15th to Marine Drive. *Click, click, click.* The anxious sound of the turn signal. The harried left turn. The incredibly lucky two green lights and the even more fantastic parking spot.

"Let's go, then."

"Wait up!" Jack was rolling down his sleeves. She was already ten paces ahead of him. "Hold on, Pen . . . I'm coming. I'm coming."

Birks Jewellers was one of those high-priced stores that never had a sale. No "blowout end of season" event here. Only top dollar for overpriced diamonds "brought directly to you" from the backbreaking hard work of underpaid labourers in Third World countries.

Penny bee-lined straight to the diamonds.

"How much are these?" she asked the saleslady. Jack was definitely going to pay top dollar.

The lady's name was Daphne, or so her gold-embossed name tag stated. Daphne was at least sixty, with jet-black hair in a tight chignon. Her outfit was elegant and no doubt expensive. She wore a deep caramel blouse and dark slacks that blended tastefully into the rich, carpeted surroundings.

Quickly and quietly, Daphne manoeuvred herself behind the glass counters.

"Are you interested in earrings?"

"Yes, diamond earrings. Those, the ones next to the small ones." The way Penny was feeling, there was no need to beat around the bush.

"These are our 'classic' cut diamond studs. Is that what you are looking for?"

"Oh, yes. Definitely classic, don't you agree, Jack?"

Her husband nodded ever so slightly, bracing himself, hands flat upon the glass counter. He looked like he was in a bar somewhere, not quite sure what he was going to order.

Daphne displayed the earrings beneath the warm incandescent lighting. They sparkled brilliantly on a bed of burgundy velvet.

"Would you like to try them on?"

"Oh, yes. I suppose I should, shouldn't I, Jack?"

"Mmm." He remained planted in the same position.

From under the counter, Daphne produced a mirror. "May I suggest you come alongside to this end of the counter? The light is better here."

Dutifully, Penny walked over to the brighter area, leaving behind her jumble of car keys and overstuffed handbag on the thick velvet display mat. When she looked in the mirror, she didn't really notice the diamonds. What she saw was a dishevelled and anxious woman. Wild curly brown hair obscuring a small and sad little face, her blouse too tight across her chest.

"What do you think, Jack? Do you like them?"

"Oh. Yes. Very nice. Are they what you want, Pen? Is this what you're after?"

"Can you see them, Jack? Can you see me from there? Come closer. Come and take a really good look."

Daphne discreetly retreated as Jack approached his wife. Perhaps she had seen this many times before and knew not to interfere in these private moments in a marriage.

"What do you think of me, Jack?"

"I think they're great. I think you should get them."

"But what about me? What do you think of *me*?"

"I think you're great and...I'm a shit. I'm sorry, I should have called, and I think you really should get them, okay?"

They were the only two customers left in the store. Daphne was off in a far corner, and another sales associate was fiddling with some kind of barred gate that would seal the store off from the mall. The echo of other shopkeepers could be heard doing the same thing. It was nine o'clock. Closing time.

"Okay, Jack."

"Happy anniversary, Penny."

"Why, thank you, Jack, and happy anniversary to you too."

Later, out in the parking lot, they walked silently to the car. The summer sky was fiery orange and pink and the air was soft and warm. All the anger had gone from Penny's body, all the tightness from Jack's.

"Shall I drive home?" he asked.

She handed the keys over. Back then she had a convertible VW that she had inherited from Jack because he had upgraded to a different kind of "image" car.

"Can you put the top down?" she said. It wasn't really a question.

The sun was just dipping behind Cypress Mountain as they headed west along Marine Drive. Penny always adored long summer days. In six months' time it would be dark at four thirty, but tonight the air was inviting, the possibilities endless.

"Let's go for a drive." The wind was blowing her hair back off her face. The diamonds visible. Sparkling.

And so they didn't take their turnoff. Instead they drove past all the small shops in Ambleside and Dundarave. On and on they drove, winding their way past quaint cottages and beautiful homes, some of which Jack would one day come to sell. Past the yacht club, past Horseshoe Bay, all the way to Sunset Marina, where Jack would finally pull over. He shut off the ignition and turned to his young wife.

"Ah, Pen," was all he could say. It looked like he was holding something invisible in his big open hands. Another awkward apology.

There in the waning light, she remembers, they embraced and kissed. And it was in that marina parking lot that they decided it would be best if Penny would simply pick out whatever it was that she wanted for their anniversary. She never returned to Birks for more jewellery but somehow fell into the habit of choosing something from the garden centre. Something beautiful that she would plant in a special spot. Something they could watch and admire together. Something that would grow.

"Hey, Penny! Over here. Hellooo!"

God, it's that woman . . . What's her name? "Oh, hi."

"Penny Stevens! Fancy meeting you here."

"Yes. It's nice to see you, too."

"Sure is hot. What brings you out here on a day like this?"

"Oh, it's our anniversary and . . . well, we, I mean I, always pick out something from here. I wouldn't know what to ask for, and Jack, my husband, well, he's just relieved to not have to go shopping for anything. You know how men are . . ." *Who is this woman? What is her name? Where do I know her from?*

"Oh, Jack, I can just see him at the mall. He's hilarious! God, he'd have those salesgirls all in a tizzy in no time, I'm sure. He just cracks us up. Where does he get that energy?"

"Viagra."

"What? God, *you're* hilarious!"

For the second time in less than five minutes, Penny is having a conversation in which she really doesn't need to speak. This mystery woman who probably works with her husband is in full swing recounting more "hilarious" stories from her adventures at the office. Penny notices that she has immense and unreasonably white teeth. *Has she bleached them, or has she had them lasered? What kind of toothpaste does she use? Can toothpaste alone really make any difference?*

This woman has many hilarious things to tell her. When she throws her head back with laughter, Penny can clearly see her epiglottis.

"So, what are you going to buy?"

"Oh, I don't know. Something will catch my attention. I really don't have my heart set on any one thing."

Mrs. Big Tooth considers this for a moment and taps her forehead with her finger. "Hydrangeas. I think they're fabulous!"

"Oh, well, thanks, I just might check that out." She is hoping this encounter is coming to an end. "Well, nice to see you."

"Yes, you too." Thankfully, the woman begins to head toward another aisle. Before she is out of sight, however, she yells out, "How many?"

Penny is taken aback. "Sorry? How many what?"

"Your anniversary. How many years?"

"Oh, eighteen." It's hard to believe when she says it.

"Eighteen! Right. Right. Of course, eighteen." Again, the woman is nodding and tapping her forehead like this statistic is one she ought to have remembered. Like she was one of the thirty or so guests who had gathered there on the dock the day of their wedding. Someone who perhaps would have witnessed Jack and Penny tie the knot on that windy afternoon. Penny had almost fallen into the ocean after Jack's overexuberant liplock. Penny was too young, too shy, and too stunned to do anything about it at the time. What could she have done? The rhythmic thump, thump of a boat against the dock had drowned out any chuckles or comments.

She had married a man twice her age. Literally. She had been twenty-two and he had just turned forty-four. Her mother was sixty-six at the time, her father eighty-eight. Numerologists could have a field day with those numbers.

Nowadays the only time a forty-four-year-old guy lands a twenty-two-year-old girl is if he is loaded. As for her parents' scenario, the only time a sixty-six-year-old man fathers a child is if he is a celebrity starting a "second

20

family," complete with nannies for his young bride and a personal trainer for his old body.

Neither of these statistics applied to either couple. Her father was a self-employed shoemaker with a grade-ten education. Her mother had worked for years in an office downtown. She had all but given up on ever finding a husband.

They had married because she had a slight limp that caused her left heel to wear a little bit quicker than the right one. Alice liked the fact that this cobbler never remarked on this circumstance. She would bring in the matching pair, and he would fix only the left one. When she would come to pick the shoes up, he would have polished both of them.

"Here you go, young lady. One pair of shoes as good as new." Compared to him she was young. She was forty-three that June.

It was somewhere around the tenth shoe repair that Wilfred had worked up the nerve to ask Alice out. He had always assumed that he would remain a bachelor, but he couldn't seem to put this woman out of his mind. Suddenly he was filled with an over-whelming urgency to find a wife. He surprised him-self, at age sixty-five, by falling deeply and truly in love.

The following summer they married in a beautiful outdoor ceremony. The bride wore a simple white dress and the groom wore his only suit, a dark blue. He had made her shoes.

Twenty-three years later, Penny married Jack because he couldn't take his eyes off her breasts. She was the new accountant in the office. Fresh-faced, a bit plump, but eager to please. At first she was a little intimidated by this loud and boisterous man who towered a full foot above her.

"Bring me another cup of coffee, sweetie."

She knew he dumped them down the sink. At six-foot-two, he could easily look down her blouse. He did and she knew it. At five-foot-two, she could have easily worn sweaters and turtlenecks. She didn't and he knew this too.

Within four months they were engaged and married. It happened so fast. She remembers the thrill and the frantic pace of that spring and early summer. How she and Jack, flushed and giddy and passionate, made their announcements and dove full steam ahead with their sudden plans. She was exhilarated and impulsive. It was quite a story.

"Penelope," her mother, the only person who called her by her full name, had asked in a quiet moment, "are you sure you know what you are doing?"

"Oh, Mother." Young Penny couldn't think of much more to say than that. In fact, she didn't think much at all.

"Penelope, don't rush this. Slow down, child. This all seems a little too fast, don't you agree?"

She did not. For the first time in her methodical, well-organized, and fiscally balanced life, Penny was carefree and spontaneous and rash. It felt good. Life was good then. Now, somehow, the narrative seemed to have skipped ahead. And here she finds herself, all these years later, not quite having a grasp on why she married her husband. Yes, he is charismatic and loud and winning whereas she is not. Sure, maybe the cliché is true: opposites attract. But an attraction has got to hold, and these days Penny is having a hard time feeling any connection to these memories. It seems so long ago. Perhaps her mother was right. She should have slowed down. She should have thought things through.

"Can I help you, ma'am?" A young university student who looks like he's having way too much fun manoeuvring a mini front-end loader filled with Japanese maples comes to a stop alongside Penny.

"Can I help you find something today?"

"Well, I need something for our garden . . ."

"You're in the right spot, then. Are you interested in some kind of tree?"

"No."

"What kind of plant, then?"

"I don't know, but not a tree."

"A shrub?"

"No, uhm, not really." Her headache is not going away, and every encounter with strangers is a tax on her nerves.

"If you tell me what you're looking for, I can direct you to the correct spot."

She takes a deep breath. *Jesus, is this kid pushy!* "I would like a flowering plant. Blue."

"Do you want it for a window box, for a border, for a hanging basket?"

Probably pre-law, the way he's cross-examining me. "Uhm, no."

"Did you want a perennial or just an annual? It's a little late in the season, you know."

"I just want a blue plant. A plant that is blue. I will stick it in the ground and I will water it and maybe it will live. More likely it will die."

"Hmm." He considers this for a moment, totally oblivious to her mental state. "How about a hydrangea?"

"Perfect."

Two

"I saw some woman from your office today." It's just before dinner, and Penny is fixing herself a gin and tonic.

"Who was that?" Jack asks as he pours a beer into his favourite mug.

"I don't know her name, but she knows you and thinks you're hilarious."

"Well, that could be any number of people then."

"I see."

"Do you think I'm hilarious?" Jack has taken a big sip and is pretending to be unaware of his beer moustache.

"Of course, honey." She has bought some pre-made chicken kebabs, and she hands them to Jack. "The barbeque should be hot enough now."

"Righty-o!" There seems to be some genetic pre-disposition in men toward barbequing. Jack dons his apron, takes the tongs out from below the stove, and strides eagerly out to the deck. If Penny had asked him to cook the same meat in a frying pan in the kitchen, he would have given her a bewildered look. Outside, in the fresh air, the male sex must feel virile and all-powerful. The raw meat and fresh air must conjure up prehistoric caveman yearnings. The smell of the hunt, the blood of the kill.

"Oh, damn!" Penny holds up a bag of pre-made salad to the light. "This is totally unacceptable," she says, more to herself than to Jack.

"I can't hear you, Pen."

"How long till you're ready out there?"

"Oh, maybe fifteen minutes, give or take. Why?"

"Second salad in a week that's gone bad on me. I'm just going to zip down to the grocery store."

"Can you return a salad?" he asks. "Is it that bad?" He has a stomach like a tank and thinks that people are too queasy and fearful of upset tummies and flu and food poisoning. "Here, let me take a closer look . . ."

"It's the principle of it, Jack. Look at the expiry date. It shouldn't expire until August third and it's already brown. I'll be back in no time."

She grabs her sunglasses and his keys, as her car is blocked by his SUV. It's a metallic silver, eight-cylinder Volvo with lush charcoal leather interior and all the bells and whistles. As she turns over the ignition, the vehicle hums to life. Automatically, the air conditioning kicks in, and in no time Penny is cool and comfortable.

She notices the hydrangea leaning sadly against the garage and reminds herself to plant it after dinner. *Happy anniversary to us!*

Looking around the Volvo's interior, she sees the requisite paraphernalia of her realtor husband. Various pages and file folders and realty guides are strewn about, and sticky notes are stuck everywhere. Though he has an office, this is really where her husband conducts most of his work. Penny feels like an interloper and is a little uncomfortable in her husband's vehicle. She shuts off the music so she can focus all of her attention on driving. Except for the brand name, there is no comparison between Jack's Volvo and her station wagon, circa 1982. Hers had been second-hand and already ten years old when she replaced the other car, but she instantly fell in love with it. Also, it has been faithful and reliable, and that means a lot to Penny. Here, in Jack's immense vehicle, she has to adjust to all the different controls and the power brakes and really focus on the handling.

Within minutes, she is carefully sliding the beast into a parking stall. Since she is at the supermarket, Penny figures she should stock up on bottled water. Their filtration system at home is not working, and the company is sending some repairman next week. The bottles are heavy and cumbersome, so she will need a buggy. She roots around in her change purse for a quarter. She has nickels and dimes and loonies and toonies. If she were at the competitor's chain, where you need a loonie for a shopping cart, she would most likely be in possession of quarters. It is an unwritten law. Never having the right change is closely related to the second law of thermodynamics, which says that "shit happens" and "change is constant in life." The problem being one never has the *right* change.

"Damn." Time is of the essence here. Penny considers going inside and getting a quarter from the cashier. Or, if she is lucky, maybe she can find a lone coin in the glove box or underneath a seat. Maybe, like his wife, Jack has a stash of change somewhere in his car.

The glove box comes up empty except for an assortment of napkins from the local Tim Hortons drive-thru and Starbucks coffee shops. Feeling blindly around under the seats only produces more of the same napkins, used and rolled into tight little balls.

Penny wonders what the guys at the dealership detail shop think of people when they come in with their vehicles for service and cleaning. Jack leases his Volvo and must bring it in at least twice a year for requisite oil changes and maintenance. They would definitely see him as a coffee-drinking professional. No toys, therefore no family. No fuzzy dice hanging from the rear-view mirror. Radio tuned to the oldies station. God knows what he's got on disc.

On the other hand, what would the guys think if she were to pull up in her old station wagon? When was the last time she even had it cleaned? She had to take it in a couple of years ago when the alternator blew. Had to have it towed from Park Royal one afternoon after a full day of shopping. They were having a one-day white sale at The Bay, and Penny had been thinking about finally replacing their old pillows and linens. She had read an article about dust mites and mould and bacteria that grow and thrive in bedding, especially pillows. It was also time to replace the old flannel sheets from the Reagan administration. When it comes to politics, Penny tends to define an era by what's happening south of the border. "The Mulroney Reign of Terror" didn't have the same ring to it. Maybe it's just that she's Canadian and realistic. Anyhow, the sheets were really old, and the sale, coupled with a rare 25 percent scratch-and-save coupon, was too much for Penny to resist.

So, in her old Volvo bursting with pillows and sheets, Penny set off for home. She was almost out of the parking lot when all the lights on her dashboard started to flash. Seconds later, the car simply shut off. It was like an out-of-body experience. To be happily going along only to realize that you have died.

To this day, she remembers her panic. How, thankfully, a man in a shining Jetta had come to her rescue and called the towing company. How in her frenzied state she couldn't even find the hazards. Penny recalls how, despite her ineptitude, the traffic adapted to her misfortune and how, like a clogged artery, the cars slowly crept by.

And of course she will never forget the tow-truck driver. R.J. Donovan. "The 'R' is for Richard, but don't call me Dick!" What a character he was. Bandana. Tattoos. The muscles on his arms bulging. And he certainly swore like a truck driver.

It was a bumpy ride to the dealership, what with all the "assholes" on the road that day, but R.J. turned out to be quite knowledgeable about investments and had made a small nest egg buying and reselling Harleys.

Penny remembers how she held on tightly to the dash that day as he spoke articulately about finances. How he distrusted mutual funds but believed in motor-cycles. He had five parked in his garage. They were going to be his retirement ticket.

Penny worked then and still works for the *Sentinel*, the local newspaper that publishes three times a week. She writes the Friday financial column and is always looking for something different to offer her readers. Fresh ideas are rare or too often risky in her field of work. How many times has she reminded people that it was RRSP time or warned of the tax deadline or discussed capital gains? When had she told people to buy a Harley and park it in their garage for ten years and then sell it? She couldn't help but like the guy and thinks that the column she wrote that week for "Money Makes Cents" has to rank as one of her most original articles.

She wonders what R.J. thinks of the financial scene today. If he has bought any more motorcycles.

At any rate, Penny can't remember if they cleaned and vacuumed her car when they fixed it at the dealer-ship, but she did recall that it was the alternator and that it cost almost six hundred dollars.

But here she is now, rooting through her husband's

luxury car. She still hasn't found the elusive quarter. The secret compartment in the armrest is filled with ballpoint pens and two different packets of chewing gum. The last place she looks is in the ashtray.

Here, she finds two lipsticks. Mulberry Wine is a deep maroon shade, and Playful Pink is, as its name implies, a bright, ridiculous colour.

Suddenly Penny doesn't feel like getting a buggy after all. They have enough water for tomorrow, anyway.

She takes the salad to the customer service desk, where she asks a pimply teenager to page the manager. Two minutes later a pimply assistant manager is turning the lettuce bag over and over in his hands.

"You say you bought this from our store?"

"Yes. Look, it's your brand."

"Do you have the bill, ma'am?"

"No." Penny can see where this is going.

"Our policy clearly states that a receipt is required to return merchandise."

This assistant manager is most probably just some kid who has worked here for twenty minutes and is now drunk with power. Penny watches him stand there behind his desk. If it were table-height and if he had a swivel chair, he would certainly have had his feet propped up on it. As it is, he is a rather short and scrawny kid, and the counter comes up to his chest. She can see only his bow tie and three buttons.

Then, out of nowhere, the tears just come. Big drops splash onto the customer service desk. She is sobbing and there is no stopping her. What other customers might think when they see her tears and her brown salad is not known. It is not a common sight in this tidy little supermarket. People just don't cry here. Not over salad or even over spilt milk, for that matter. In this wealthy community, people keep it together.

A number of employees come to the rescue.

"Here's a Kleenex."

"What's going on here, Ted?"

"Josh, go get another one of these Caesar salad thingies."

Soon Penny is holding a fresh bag.

"Here you go, ma'am." The assistant manager is talking to her like she is four years old and has just dropped her ice cream cone. And then, because she hasn't suffered enough, and because young Ted can't resist, he says in his assistant managerial voice, "Make sure next time you bring in your receipt."

When Penny gets home, Jack is waiting out on the deck.

"What took you so long?"

Her eyes are puffy and red. "Here's the salad."

She tells Jack that she's suddenly not feeling very well. That he should go on and eat without her.

"You're not hungry?" he asks, still clutching his tongs.

"Not at all." Does he notice her blotchy face? Has he noticed the bright pink lipstick she put on out in the car before coming in? What does he prefer? Playful pink or sultry maroon?

"What about tonight and everything? I mean, we were going to go up to the club."

"Listen." She brushes past him and pours herself a glass of red wine. This one has a picture of an owl on the label. "You can go on without me."

"But it's our anniversary." He says it like it is a question.

"Go ahead, if you like."

"You sure?"

From upstairs, she can hear her husband clunking around in the kitchen. He has eaten and is loading up the dishwasher. The smell of the leftover kebabs wafts up the staircase to the bedroom where she is sitting.

The last thing she hears after the front door closes behind him is his whistling and then the sound of his car disappearing down the road.

Three

It's not that Penny hates Jack or that he is an evil person, but he just can't seem to stop putting his dick into other women.

Looking in the mirror, she first reapplies the Playful Pink. Not surprisingly, she doesn't feel playful in the least. Mulberry Wine is more to her liking. She goes into the bedroom and gets her glass of Merlot, which is set precariously on a pile of paperbacks next to her bed. They are all mysteries, and they are all overdue.

The idea of a mystery novel appeals to Penny. Analysis. Deduction. Motives. Passion. A solution to a crime is found. She likes reading stories in which events are neatly presented. Where, from out of the fog, all is made clear. Recently, however, her concentration has been lacking. She has had to go back and reread sections. *Was it that guy? Is he a good guy? Who said that again?*

She's also gotten into the habit of watching game shows in the evenings. She gets a kick out of watching that Canuck, Trebek, force his contestants to phrase their answers in the form of questions.

"An eighteenth-century philosopher's famous quote, 'I think, therefore . . . this.' Yes, Jane?"

"I am."

"Ooooh, I'm sorry. You didn't phrase it in the form of a question. The answer is, 'What is "I am"?'"

Isn't that what all philosophers grapple with? she muses.

Overall, though, her favourite show is *Who Wants to Be a Millionaire?* She likes it because of the music and the lighting. Mostly though, she likes it because a player can have three lifelines. The world would be so perfect if people really did have lifelines.

Penny Stevens—even you can save your marriage and find true happiness.

Is it a? Drink more Merlot.

Is it b? Lose weight.

Is it c? Stick your head deeper into the sand.

Or is it d? Give that man his walking papers.

With tougher questions like this one, Penny could poll the viewers. She could throw up her hands and sit back in her seat while audience members electronically voted for what they believed to be the right answer.

Well, Penny, it looks like an overwhelming 86 percent chose b. You do know that TV makes all people look fatter, don't you? I'm serious! I'm serious!

If for some reason she didn't trust the audience, she could always call an expert. Maybe she would call Dr. Phil.

Penny would start out by saying what a great fan she is and thanking the doctor for taking her call. She would then read out the question and wait for Dr. Phil's reply.

You gotta ask yourself, Penny, How's that working for you? You know, what walks like a Penny and talks like a Penny usually is a Penny where I come from.

Although Penny does like mysteries, she has never been a fan of this kind of puzzled Rubik's cube kind of thinking.

Just give me the answer, damn it!

But this is real life. Penny has no lifelines to speak of. And anyway, the audience could be a pack of idiots, the "expert" could be wrong, and just because two incorrect responses are eliminated doesn't mean you won't still end up making a shitty choice.

Deep down, Penny knows she is depressed. She's just not ready to face up to it yet. Old Dr. Wilcox has gently broached the subject a few times. While she lay with her feet in the stirrups and the hot lamp shining where the sun doesn't and shouldn't ever shine, he had suggested to her that she might want to give herself a chemical lift in the right direction. Odd that they've never had a face-to-face chat on this topic. He's always offered her Prozac while tapping her back or Paxil while peering into her ears. Then again, he has seen her through adolescence and yeast infections and a miscarriage. It might be more for his sake than hers, but he has made the offer on more than one occasion.

Penny swigs the remainder of her wine. The lipstick is too purple for her complexion. Too dark. What kind of a woman, she wonders, can carry off a colour like this? She must be dark. And bold. Definitely assertive.

No! That's giving her too much credit. She is, after all, sneaking around with a married man. Albeit an undeniably irritatingly sexy, aggressive, and highly sexed man. Shit!

Penny makes a face into the mirror. She can see just a faint hint of crow's feet. It's the single saving grace of being plump—no wrinkles to speak of, really.

She throws the two lipsticks in the garbage.

Playful Pink. Mulberry Wine. Whose job is it to name these products? What kind of qualifications does one need to get a job like that? You would certainly need to be decisive, and given Penny's present state of mind, she would most likely be disqualified immediately. It took her two years just to decide on a colour for the master bedroom. She ended up going with Boston Fog. She had liked Perennial Putty and Twilight Serenade and Tuscan Sunset, but it was the fog that won out in the end.

"So you're going with the olive green?" Jack had handed her back the bookmark-sized sample after considering it for a full ten seconds. She recalls his relief when she finally decided upon the paint colour. She had always been thrusting assorted samples into his hands.

"It's Boston Fog, actually."

"Well, it looks green to me."

Maybe the fog in Boston really is green. Maybe the interior decorator with a minor in colour analysis did indeed go there. Who knows? At any rate, Penny has been waking up in a fog for the better part of the last two years.

She likes it, though, this muted colour. Just as in makeup choices, she tends to migrate to soft and subtle shades. Nothing too dramatic. Nothing too loud.

Oh, waiter! More Merlot, please.

A couple of glasses of wine and no dinner can be dangerous. She takes hold of the banister with her left hand and clutches her empty wineglass with the other.

Downstairs in the kitchen, Jack has made a superficial attempt at cleaning up the dishes. His plate and tongs are soaking in a few inches of cold water. All the condiments and seasonings are huddled together in the corner of the counter like a mismatched choir, taking up less space but still not put away in the right spot.

There are some kebabs that she could have, but Penny can't face up to meat right now. She pours herself another glass of wine. She could have a cheese sandwich. Maybe just some cheese and crackers. *So Parisian!*

In the pantry she finds a box of Wheat Thins. When she takes it off the shelf, she can feel that it is empty. One lone cracker has survived along with a pile of crumbs. Jack!

Maybe people feel guilty finishing off a box of crackers or a bag of chips. Maybe it's like taking the last piece of cake when everybody is sitting around looking at it.

Was it last year or the one before when she ate the last piece of Jack's birthday cake right in front of him and his colleagues at the office? It had white icing with blue cursive writing on it and a clown holding balloons. She had eaten the "ack" of "Jack." The "Happy" and "Birthday" had already been devoured by Jack and Brett and Mary, his secretary, and by Blythe, the new female realtor whom he was just starting to screw.

Penny had barely finished stuffing the last crumbs of her first piece of cake into her mouth when she loaded up her paper plate with the last piece. She rarely, if ever, came by Jack's office. The joviality and camaraderie of the people made her feel insecure and out of place. She wished she had just stayed home instead of systematically devouring the last piece of that unfulfilling cake.

"I just adore cake! Who says you can't have your cake and eat it too?" Blythe was very tall and very thin. She had one of those "artistic" haircuts where one side is cut short and the other side hangs down dramatically. She looked so off balance she made Penny nervous.

"I'm Blythe, by the way. Jack has told me so much about you. Nice to meet you finally."

Unconsciously, Penny had tilted her head to one side. It somehow seemed necessary when looking directly at this woman. She couldn't think of anything to say.

"I like your hair." Penny tried tilting her head the other way.

Blythe had stayed at the job for just over two months. She left because apparently she "couldn't deal with the office politics." Two months was a long time by Jack's standards, and somewhere around week six, having had his fill of Blythe, Jack had become enamoured of some other young apprentice. This had not gone down well with Blythe, who, before leaving for some restaurant management job up in Nelson, accosted Penny coming out of Whole Foods.

"Your husband is a pig." She had dyed her hair black and lopped off all the hair on the one long side so that she now had a traditional bowl cut. "You should leave him."

"Thanks. I like your hair." Penny almost didn't recognize her.

But Penny can't seem to be able to leave Jack. It's not like he has any sort of vise grip on her. She has all the freedom she could ask for. He never makes any demands on her. In fact, he doesn't ask her for anything at all. Financially, he supports her almost one hundred percent. Penny quit her accounting job shortly before she and Jack were married, and she makes less than two thousand dollars a month with her column. If she were to quit, he wouldn't blink an eye. It's just that Penny, over the years, has come to feel invisible to her husband.

When she found out about his first affair, around their fourth anniversary, she raged and threatened and cried for days. Jack was truly distraught at what he'd done, what he had inflicted upon his young wife. He solemnly promised to "never be such a prick again."

Makeup sex was great. They screwed on the kitchen floor. They humped in the downstairs powder room and even did it like dogs in the potting shed. It was the best two months of their marriage. Then, perhaps, the novelty wore off and he got bored again. Work got very busy and he started wearing his special cologne that made Penny sneeze. He was constantly showering.

He was having an affair with Grace, the Chinese lady from accounting. This tidbit Penny gleaned from a courteous, anonymous phone call from a previous fling, who was no doubt still fuming over having been cast so rudely aside. In her indignation, the woman had switched allegiances and was firmly rooting for Penny, sending her outraged support whether she welcomed it or not.

"But you said you'd stop, Jack!"

"I know. I know."

"What is it with you? Why are you doing this?"

"I don't know."

And he really didn't. He was truly totally in the dark when it came to his relationships with women. When Penny raged at Jack, he was as puzzled as she was furious.

"What makes you do this to me, Jack?"

"Christ! I don't know. I really don't know what to say."

After that encounter he swore off women again. In one of those futile attempts to save what little they had together, Penny decided that having a child would be a good and solidifying thing to do. She became obsessed with taking her temperature and following her cycle. She forbade Jack to wear tight, restricting pants.

"What the hell did you do with all my underwear?"

"Jack, you've got to get serious about this baby thing. You'll have to make some changes too." He'd shown his Jockeys to enough ladies, thank you very much! And Penny was on a mission here. They were going to be a regular monogamous couple. No more affairs. This was going to change him. This was going to change everything.

But it didn't.

Penny was two weeks shy of her twenty-seventh birthday when she called Jack at the office to tell him that she was pregnant.

"God, Penny! That's great! Whadda ya know! Me! A father!"

She loved going to the doctor. She got a little pamphlet in which there was space to write down any and all questions an expectant mother might have for each trimester, and that offered detailed information. How to deal with nausea. How much weight gain is expected per month. It outlined a healthy diet. It suggested which vitamins and supplements to take and which to avoid. In the last trimester, Penny and Jack would go to a special "birthing class." Later, they could even take a parenting class!

But they never got that far. Two months into her pregnancy, she awoke to severe cramps. In the early-morning light, Jack drove her to the Emergency at Lions Gate Hospital. There, on a small stretcher in a corner of an overcrowded ward, Penny lost her child.

Hours later, sedated but dressed, she would turn back and see the large, bright red stain on the whitest of white hospital sheets. Another patient would be waiting for that bed, and those sheets would soon be at the laundry.

And that was it. They never spoke of it again.

Penny went back to tending the house and writing her column, and Jack occupied himself with the business of selling real estate. He threw himself into his work and had a record year in sales. They stayed clear of one another, each safely ensconced in their own worlds.

She needed him but didn't know how to ask.

They could have easily tried to have another child. She was young. There was no reason to worry.

"Miscarriages happen all the time, Penny." Dr. Wilcox

had been so good. She had desperately wanted someone to hold her.

"Wait six months and let the body heal, and you'll be back in business. I promise you."

But Dr. Wilcox couldn't make Jack promise her what she needed. He didn't understand that Penny had not only lost the life inside of her, but was also losing her grip on a life she was desperate to cling to.

"Hi. How was your day, Pen?" Jack came home later and later. He'd often grab some fast food on the way. Penny wasn't much into cooking those days.

"Great."

"Well, that's good." He might have been looking at her, but Penny was certain he didn't see her.

Most evenings he would retreat up into his study and watch television while she curled up on the sofa and reread the same chapter of a book she would never finish. Nothing ever changed.

She had tried to have a baby and she couldn't do that. She had tried to keep her husband and couldn't do that either. Suddenly, she didn't want to try anything anymore. She didn't have any rage left, and in a way she was comfortable where she was. Living in this big old house and digging in that jungle of a yard gave her a kind of solace she couldn't find anywhere else. No amount of exercise classes or self-help groups could offer her anything. She liked to be in her house, crunching numbers. She liked to be in her garden, sifting through the dirt.

"You've got to get out more! The gang is going to catch an early show on Friday and then have a few drinks. You should join us, Penny. It'll be fun." Her colleagues at the *Sentinel* all seemed very sincere and genuine in their efforts to include Penny in their monthly girls' night out. She'd gone once and laughed her way through some innocuous romantic comedy, but after the miscarriage and the mounting failures between her and Jack and life at large, the last thing she wanted to do was go out and have a good time.

Even her mother agreed that she was becoming a prisoner in her own home. "Penelope, I'm worried that at my age I'm having more of a life than you. Go shopping, for Heaven's sake! Buy something ridiculous. Go somewhere you've never been before. Get out of that house."

But her home was a fortress, not a prison, to Penny. She felt protected and insulated from all the chaos and craziness of life. She liked the sameness and predictability of each day. She was grateful that she could work from home and never have to interact with anybody, save for the odd appointment or staff meeting. In comparison, other people's lives were so full and colourful.

It made her head spin, and she had difficulty listening with any conviction to their tales and troubles.

And, all these years later, she is still here, standing in the kitchen, slightly drunk and hungry.

Then she sees it. The blessed jar.

Nutella is a deep, dark-brown nut spread that Penny recently rediscovered at the local supermarket. She first tried it back in the early nineties when they went to Europe for a summer holiday. Jack had never been overseas, and Penny had been on a mission to instill some culture in him.

What is that? she'd wondered over breakfast at a small *pension*, looking at two little blond kids eating what appeared to be a dark paste smeared on thick slices of heavy brown bread. Breakfast had been straightforward in England and France. Coffee, toast, eggs, maybe a croissant with jam. The German breakfast, though, was another matter altogether. Thick, rich cheeses and all sorts of luncheon meats were laid out every morning. A basket of fresh-from-the-oven buns and hearty fibre-filled brown breads were offered by Annaliese, their host. If one wanted a cereal, it was a kind of "Flocken," a mix of oat or bran flakes that didn't really appeal to Penny.

"*Bitte schön*. Please. Take many." Annaliese's English was limited but forceful.

"*Oh, nein, danke*. Very full. Very full." Penny found it odd that when speaking English in a foreign country, her vocabulary shrank and her grammar and syntax went out the window.

"*Bitte schön.* You must eat. It is *gut, ja?*"

"*Oh ja, gut. Danke schön.*" Annaliese was too strong to be refused. She could have worked in one of those beer halls in Munich with the kind of arms she had. But the smell of the cheese and the sight of the meats was too much to bear. On the third morning of their stay, Penny asked for fruit.

"*Nein.*" Annaliese stood tall. Her hands on her hips. Apparently there would be no such option at this bed and breakfast. *Nein.*

The following morning, Penny closely observed the two young boys eating the mysterious spread that seemed to contain neither cheese nor meat. She simply could no longer contend with the stinky Limburger or the fatty frankfurters. She was hoping there wasn't an age limit to this item. The Germans had so many rules.

"Excuse me, please. Could I try some of that?"

She did, and it was divine. For the last three days at the *pension*, Annaliese had the Nutella jar waiting at their little table in the corner. Penny would tear apart a hot bun and spread the hazelnut and chocolate mixture so thickly that it would sometimes drip down onto her plate. Then, with her fingers, she would wipe her plate clean. It was too good to waste.

At the time, she thought it remarkable that such a sweet and delicious treat could even be considered a breakfast choice. Least of all in a country like Germany, where people took things seriously.

"What is the population of Vancouver?"

"How many metres tall is Grouse Mountain?"

"How many kilometres to Banff?"

She never forgot the Nutella, and when Penny saw a jar standing in between the honey and the peanut butter at her local store, she grabbed it without checking the price. It was worth every penny of the five dollars and forty-nine cents it cost.

She is leaning now with her elbows on the counter. Holding the jar at an angle, she is able to spoon out every last bit of chocolate. Soon the jar is empty. Dutifully, Penny takes it out into the garage and puts it in the recycling box. Back in the kitchen, she finishes off her wine and decides that she will clean up the dishes in the morning.

With difficulty, Penny climbs the stairs to the bedroom. As lubricated as she is, she will not go to bed without brushing her teeth. Her parents instilled this habit into her from a young age, and Penny likes her routines.

When she removes her watch, she notices it is earlier than she imagined, but the heat and the events of the day have taken their toll. She is tired and heavy, and undressing takes all of her effort.

Penny slowly opens the faucet and observes the water swirling down the drain. It is making a particularly loud sound, she thinks. She fumbles for her toothbrush and manages to squeeze out just enough paste. She will have to buy some tomorrow. Maybe she'll go to the other store, where you need a loonie for the cart. Maybe not.

When she finally looks at herself in the mirror, she sees that she has Nutella smeared all over her face. She looks like a kid after a birthday party.

Happy anniversary, darling.

Four

The first thing Penny sees when she opens her eyes every morning is the water stain on her ceiling. It looks like William Shakespeare's head: bald at the crown with hair flowing down the sides and back. She easily makes out the intelligent eyes, the mouth, and the nose. She thinks for the hundredth time that she really should paint the ceiling. She doesn't know, though, if she could do that without having to repaint the walls. Really, she should have done the ceiling in the first place.

She doesn't mind old Will, though. He doesn't seem to be looking down on her with any judgment. She's thankful it isn't any image of the Virgin Mary or Christ on the cross. Then she'd really have to get her butt in gear and dig out all those paintbrushes and drop sheets.

She once saw a television program where people made pilgrimages from far and wide to witness bizarre and questionable sightings of religious figures in odd places.

Somewhere down south, the face of Mary appeared on the screen of a movie theatre. It was visible only when the lights in the auditorium were on ever so dimly. People would be coming down the aisles, carrying their popcorn and drinks, looking about for a seat, then their mouths would drop open and, if they were so inclined, the rapture would take place.

At the time, the theatre was playing some Disney feature with an up-and-coming teen star who had just gotten out of rehab, and the public had come in droves. Penny is grateful that she doesn't have thousands of people wanting to see the famous bard on her bedroom ceiling. Her house is truly a mess, and she doesn't want to be in the limelight.

Her head is pounding. Her stomach is queasy. Her tongue is thicker than usual. She climbs out of bed to look in her medicine cabinet for some relief. She doesn't dare look in the mirror. She'll have to go downstairs and get some Tylenol, as the bathroom cabinet has come up bare. It's the only thing that will take the edge off last night, and she knows it will be a full twenty minutes before the effect kicks in. We all pay for our sins, she thinks.

As she passes by the den, she sees her husband's bare bum hanging out from under the plaid blanket. He is in the fetal position on the couch, rear end facing outwards. Who knows what time he got home. And it appears they've both had too much to drink. She can literally smell the booze wafting out into the hallway. This makes Penny even more determined to get first dibs at the pain relievers.

The kitchen is in the same state as it was last night. Apparently Jack did not feel the urge whenever he got home to finish up the dishes. She lets out the cold water standing in the sink and pours herself a fresh glass directly from the tap. She swallows the last two gel-cap Tylenols left in the bottle in the kitchen cupboard.

A fresh cup of coffee is the next order of business. She is on automatic pilot as she puts in the filter and the two scoops and the water. Soon the machine is burping and gurgling and producing the reassuring sounds of caffeine.

It is Tuesday morning. Penny glances briefly at the calendar and notices that her second yoga class will be starting in twenty-eight minutes. Under peer pressure from a colleague who writes a health and wellness column for the *Sentinel*, she reluctantly signed up for a two-month summer course.

The first class almost killed her. It was supposed to be an introductory level of gentle stretching and relaxation.

The teacher, a thirty-something *haute couture* hippie named Lamaraya, had started the class off by asking them to sit cross-legged and chant. This was fine with Penny. Kind of like being in the church choir—just mouthing the words while holding your hands in the prayer position.

They chanted for three minutes. Looking about the class, Penny had the familiar feeling that everyone knew what they were doing except her. The way they said "ohm" made her feel inadequate. Nobody else seemed shy. Nobody else was faking it like her. She could tell because she felt "ohms" coming at her from all sides.

"Now we are going to do Sun Salutations. How many of you have done these asanas before?"

What?

All but Penny and the lone man in the class raised their hands.

One particularly fantastic position turned out to be called "Downward Dog." In this stance, she found herself violently shaking with her feet and hands spread out on the mat, shoulder-width apart, and her bum as high up in the air as she could get it.

"Try and raise your hips a little bit higher, Penny, and lower your heels to the ground. That's it. And breathe. Inhale. Exhale. Good. Good."

Finally, she simply couldn't hold it any longer and let herself crumple up on her mat while everybody else was effortlessly holding the pose through endless, deep yogic breaths.

"Just go into Child's Pose, Penny."

Very quickly this became Penny's favourite move. Basically, she rolled herself into a ball and lay with her arms to her sides, her forehead to the mat. This I could perfect, she vowed.

The only other person who seemed to be struggling with the class was the man. His name was Bob, and he had never done yoga before. He was balding, about Penny's age, with a hint of a tire around his midsection.

Penny liked that Bob was in the class. He diverted attention away from her, allowing her more time to perfect the Slug Pose.

She wonders if Bob will be there again today. Then, looking at the clock, Penny wonders if *she* will be there today. Does she want to go? Should she go? The class will start in twenty-five minutes. It takes three minutes to drive down the hill.

She decides to go. She can't face cleaning up the kitchen, and she doesn't want to face Jack this morning either.

She grabs a breakfast bar and downs the rest of her coffee. Her yoga mat is still in the Volvo from last week, but she'll have to quickly change into her exercise pants and her Real Woman T-shirt.

She climbs the stairs two at a time and surprises herself with this burst of energy. Jack is still sound asleep, but he has since turned himself around on the little couch.

She notices his red face and open mouth. He must have had a lot to drink last night as he looks to be sweating. Then she sees the cord attached to the blanket. He has the electric blanket on full blast. He must have had it on all night. She can't imagine anyone needing a heated blanket at this time of year, and she is reminded, yet again, that she truly does not have a clue as to what goes on in her husband's head.

One is not supposed to sleep with it on either. She read the instructions and thought at the time that it was silly to assume people would remember to turn it off just before falling asleep. How many lawsuits had there been? What kind of damage would it do to a person? Had there been fires? Had people died?

Quickly she unplugs her husband. *There. Ungrateful bastard.*

She should really wake him up and have it out with him, but she doesn't have the energy for it. Not if she is going to face Lamaraya this morning.

In two minutes she is in her yoga garb. She has brushed her hair and twisted it into a careless updo. She doesn't have time to brush her teeth, so she takes a swig of blue mouthwash.

Luckily, Jack has parked out on the street and hasn't blocked Penny's car. It is a short drive down the hill, and exactly three minutes later she is patiently waiting for an elderly couple in an Oldsmobile to vacate their parking spot.

Situated in the heart of a picturesque shopping village, the yoga studio is flanked on one side by an upscale hair salon and on the other by an organic pet eatery, so the signs claim. The only advertisement for the studio appears on its green awning. One word in small, unassuming script: Breathe. From the outside, the studio appears rather small. Upon entry, however, there is a feeling of lightness and expanse. Gleaming hardwood floors, vaulted ceilings, and two skylights make it feel like a person has passed into another world. The pale green walls and assorted pillows in rich reds and purples feel light years away from the busy commerce and traffic just outside the studio's small wooden door.

Penny is surprised to find herself excited about the class and wishes that the seniors could hurry it up a bit.

The old man is helping his wife into her seat. On the roof of the car is what looks to be a brown paper bag of groceries. His entire torso disappears into the car. Perhaps he is buckling her seat belt. Another minute passes, and finally he has emerged and is shuffling back over to the driver's side.

As Penny watches this old couple, she is reminded of her parents. Of how her father would always pull out the chair for her mother. Of how he would stand when she entered a room. How he would open doors for her and offer his arm. Penny loved to watch them dance. Even at the end, when Wilfred was in a wheelchair, he would push himself up and forward out of his chair every time Alice came to the Manor House to visit him. He never lost his gentleman's touch, his manners and courtesies, his tenderness toward his wife.

Maybe this couple is just like her parents, thinks Penny. Her throat tightens with emotion, and she finds herself on the verge of tears. The sound of the Oldsmobile roaring to life brings her back into the present.

Their groceries! The old man is backing out of his parking spot with the brown paper bag sitting on the roof. Within seconds, Penny has freed herself from her car and has run up to the driver's-side window.

"Hello there!" She is tapping at the window and pointing to the roof of their car, but of course they have no idea who she is or what she wants.

"Your groceries, sir!"

But he is shaking his head.

"Your groceries are on the roof . . ."

Maybe he is deaf. He is shaking his head from side to side. His wife looks terrified, staring straight ahead. He gets his front end clear, and in the two seconds before he steps on the gas, Penny grabs the brown paper bag.

"Wait! Stop!" But, like a cliché, she is left holding the bag.

A few things have fallen out and she bends down to retrieve them.

Oh my God! She looks down at what she has in her hands. "Oh my God!"

She is not holding groceries.

She has only ever seen money like this in the movies, when a bad guy opens up a black suitcase and reveals tidy rows of bundled bills. But it's probably Monopoly money, prop money, because it is a movie, not the real thing. Penny is pretty sure she's not holding Monopoly money here. She thumbs through a pack and sees that they are all crisp, new, one-hundred-dollar bills.

Holy shit.

She looks in the brown paper bag and estimates there are another twenty or so packets like the two that have fallen out. *How much is one packet? Ten times one hundred is a thousand . . .*

She carefully calculates the width of the bundle. *One thousand times ten is . . . ten thousand. Dollars! Oh my God!* She drops the two packets into the bag and looks up into the sky.

Okay, twenty . . . no . . . no . . . more . . . twenty-two times ten thousand dollars is . . . Okay, twenty-two times one thousand is twenty-two thousand times . . . God, how many more zeros?

She's always been good with numbers, but in her excitement she thinks she is holding two million dollars. Finally she calculates it to be two hundred and twenty thousand dollars. Then to make sure, she checks the packets again, and there are indeed twenty-two in total.

She has forgotten about her car. It's still running, and the driver's-side door is ajar.

"Excuse me. You going to park there?" A Filipina nanny in a black Mercedes SUV with three kids seated in the back is waiting for the spot.

"Oh, sorry. Yes, I'm just . . . sorry." Penny feels like she should explain the whole thing to this young woman.

"You parking?"

"Yes. Yes. I'm parking." She gets herself and the two hundred and twenty thousand dollars parked. The black Mercedes purrs out of sight.

Okay, think, Penny. Think. Think.

It never crosses her mind to make off with the money. If anything, Penny is worried that she will somehow get into trouble merely by being in possession of it. She is also anxious for the old couple.

Okay. Okay, I have to go to the police. Where is the police station? What time is it?

The yoga class is starting in five minutes. For a moment, she actually considers going to her class and clearing her head.

Of course, it would be crazy to do that. It wouldn't look good to the cops, either, when they figure the "crime," or rather, the event, took place at 10:25 and the money wasn't turned in until noon. *I simply had to go to my yoga, Officer. I'm very dedicated to my practice. Namaste.*

No. That wouldn't fly.

It takes her another few minutes to get herself together and remember where the local police station is. She puts the brown bag on the passenger seat and then decides to put it down on the floor. There are no squeegee people in this neighbourhood, but it would just be her luck to have the money stolen before she can turn it in.

The police station parking lot is reserved for officers, so Penny has to go around the block and park on the street. Before she goes in, she finds a lipstick and quickly applies it. Why she does this she does not know. Also, she refixes her hair. She looks like a very presentable good Samaritan with pink lips. *Not playful pink. Just plain pink.* She feels her outfit is too tight, but there is nothing she can do about it at this point.

It is about half a block from her car to the front entrance of the station, and when Penny catches a glimpse of her reflection in the storefront windows, she realizes she is walking very upright and determinedly. She glances over her shoulder a few times. It is very unnerving carrying two hundred and twenty thousand dollars that don't belong to you. But it is also very exciting.

She remembers in grade three, when somebody stole the jar of donations for the Christmas hamper.

How terrible everyone felt. How disappointed their teacher was. How appalled Santa was going to be. Then, out of nowhere, the jar miraculously reappeared, all coins accounted for. And then how happy everyone was. How proud Mrs. Hammond was. They had a class party with candy canes and homemade shortbread cookies.

Penny feels like she is nine years old again and can't wait to hand over the cash.

Once inside, she goes directly to the information desk. A woman with a very bad perm is dealing with a teenager whose underwear is visible because his jeans are too low.

"Listen. Constable Jeffries will be more than happy to escort you to your own private cell if you can't remember your last name." She has some sort of form that presumably the kid is supposed to fill out.

"I didn't do nothing, lady!"

The receptionist presses a button and two officers appear.

"I got nothing to say."

Penny clutches her bag tightly to her chest.

"May I help you, ma'am?"

The teenager is now over in the corner talking with the two cops. Penny can see the glint of one officer's gun in his holster. They seem to be having a more relaxed conversation, and she can only wonder what the kid's crime is. *Can you get busted for a crime of fashion?*

"Can I help you with something?"

"Hi. Uhm, I was on my way to yoga class this morning and, well, I ran into this couple. Not like an accident or anything . . ."

The woman is nodding. Her perm is really, unbelievably bad.

"I was waiting for them to park. He was really old. She was too—"

"Is there something in the bag, ma'am?"

"Oh, yes. Yes. This was on top of their car." She puts the bag down on the counter and slides it over to the receptionist. "He was going to drive off with it on his roof. I thought they were groceries. I tried to stop them, but he couldn't hear me and they just drove off."

The woman is looking directly down into the bag now, and Penny can see she really needs her roots done, too.

"I think there is two hundred and twenty thousand dollars in there."

"I see." She presses a different button and another officer appears and whisks away the money. "I'm going to need you to come and talk with one of our officers. Can I get your name?"

"Oh. Penny Stevens."

"Come this way." The receptionist motions animatedly across the lobby to one of the policemen who are dealing with the youth. Penny falls in step behind her and is led down a long corridor to a small room with nothing more than a bare table and three metal chairs. "Can I get you a coffee?"

She declines the offer and glances up to see a clock on the wall. It doesn't look like there will be any cake or candy here. It is exactly eleven o'clock. She wonders if the old couple have realized their mistake yet.

And she thinks about Bob. Is he doing the Downward Dog?

Five

Two hours later, Penny is sandwiched between Mr. and Mrs. Jenkins. She is holding the brown paper bag, but the money has long since been removed to a "safer" space. Where that would be, she has no idea. They are, after all, in a police station. The bag is just for the photo op.

Dalton, the photographer for the *Sentinel*, has positioned them like this. No doubt there will be some catchy headline beneath the photo in tomorrow's issue. He is very happy that he was the first on the scene. Maybe he will be able to sell a photo to the *Vancouver Sun*. It is not every day that a sum this size is returned to its rightful owner. There is a lot of goodwill in the room. It is palpable, and everyone is smiling. The world needs more of this type of stuff. With the financial crisis and all the health-care and education cuts and home invasions and weapons of mass destruction still missing, everybody is eager to hear some good news. It's going to sell some papers, that's for sure.

Mitch is the next of her colleagues to show up. Penny has never been interviewed for anything before and is quite amazed at how quickly all these individuals appear. Clipboards and tape recorders. Pens and paper. It's all very exciting.

Poor Mr. and Mrs. Jenkins, however, look like they'd rather be somewhere else. He is doing most of the talking. She is holding on tight to her purse. Maybe she put the money in there. Maybe she's going to give him hell when they get home. Maybe she's told him a hundred times not to drive with their life savings on the roof.

The story that Mitch is able to extricate from the old couple is that they were sick and tired of all the monthly bank fees. They decided to close their account because the new bank manager wouldn't waive the fees despite the fact they have been clients for the past fifty-eight years.

"That's a lot of money to keep under your mattress, don't you think?" Mitch is leaning forward now, really getting to the heart of the story.

"Didn't say I was going to keep it under my mattress." Old Mr. Jenkins is proving to be a hard interview.

"Did you have someplace in mind?"

"Yup."

"Sounds like you're just fed up with bureaucracy and big corporations."

"Come again?"

"Do you not like banks?"

"Banks are fine. I just don't want to pay the fees."

"I see." Mitch is getting frustrated. This is a big story, and he can't seem to get anything interesting out of the old guy. "Did you ask to see the manager?"

"What for?"

"When you made the decision to pull out all your money, did you speak with somebody about it?"

"No. I told the teller to clean out my account. Plain and simple."

There's no way they would have handed over two hundred and twenty thousand dollars just like that. In a brown paper bag, no less. But Jenkins isn't talking. Mitch will have to go find the teller and the manager. Penny watches him make a note of it and smile at the couple.

"Well, thanks, Mr. and Mrs. Jenkins. I'm sure you're both very relieved and happy to have this incident end on a happy note."

"Yup." And with that, Mrs. Jenkins takes her husband's arm and guides him out of the station.

Mitch scribbles a few more notes to himself and joins Penny, who has finished up with Constable Wallace. He greets Wallace with a hearty handshake and a slap on the shoulder. They both have kids at the same school, and their boys play on the same elite AAA junior boys' hockey team. Both dads probably envision their sons playing in the NHL.

"Hey, Mitch. I hear your boy's gonna be cut for crying in the change room again. You shouldn't have raised him such a sissy."

"Yeah, right. You should talk." They feint each other as Mitch makes a fake move for Wallace's gun.

"Good to see ya, buddy." Wallace is smiling broadly, and Penny can see that one of his eyeteeth is chipped and slightly discoloured.

"Listen, Constable. Mind if I borrow Ms. Stevens here? I'm on the trail of a hot story." He winks at Penny.

Wallace turns to Penny, his voice hushed and serious. "I want you to let me know if this fella bothers you in any way. I wouldn't trust him if I were you."

Mitch rolls his eyes and Wallace gets Penny to sign something. "She's all yours."

Mitch must have been good-looking when he was

younger. Penny thinks he is still an attractive guy for his age, which is about fifty. He has kept in reasonable shape and dresses well without trying too hard. It's his skin that catches her attention. Deep crevices line his face. He must have spent a lot of time out in the sun.

"Looks like you're a hero now, ol' Penny!"

Mitch has always called her "old" Penny. Possibly because her name is old-fashioned. Mitch, on the other hand, will always be a little kid. *Wanna play a game of catch?* Or maybe he thinks of her as matronly. She can't compete with the svelte figures of the girls in advertising or classifieds. She's pretty sure, though, that he doesn't call Sylvia, the editor, anything else but Sylvia. Sylvia is in her late fifties, with prematurely grey hair, piercing blue eyes, and a very sharp mind.

"I guess so, Mitch." Penny is wondering how he will conduct the interview.

He is rifling about in his bag for something. "Did Dalton get your picture already?"

"Yes."

"Shit." He is phoning someone now.

"Why? What's the problem?"

He pulls out his phone and dials. "I'm calling Linda." There is a brief silence. "Hi, Linda. It's Mitch here. Time is . . ." He checks his watch. "Five minutes to one. Yeah, anyway, if you get this message, looks like Dalton beat you to the scene. He's already done the deed, but if you call him on his cell, maybe he'll agree to take a few more shots for you." Then he turns to Penny. "Did he take a shot of you with the Jenkinses?"

"Yes. I was holding the brown paper bag."

"He took a shot of Penny and the old couple with the money," he says into his cellphone. He looks at Penny as if she might want to add something. She shakes her head. "Okay. Bye."

Linda Campbell is the beauty consultant at the paper. Once a week she writes about a "new look," a "hot find," or the "latest trend." Lately she's got into doing makeovers. She proudly displays her before and after pictures on the bulletin board in the *Sentinel* coffee room. In the spring, she pitched an idea to the staff that combined her beauty column with Johnson's monthly home-renovation column. How she got Johnson to agree to this, nobody ever found out. He is a man of few words. Nobody even calls him by his first name. He is simply Johnson.

At any rate, maybe due to the popularity of home-renovation shows and beauty makeovers, Linda realized the potential to show her readers how beauty can transform not only your physical self, but also the space in which you live. The idea was given the go-ahead, and Linda has been off and running ever since. Calls it "Renovate Your Life," which Penny finds a bit silly.

"What's going on?"

"Oh, Linda wanted to catch you before Dalton got here."

"What for?" Penny can't imagine what the beauty consultant would want down at the cop shop.

Mitch shrugs and turns on his recorder. From his leather shoulder bag, he gets out his notepad and turns to a fresh page. He asks her all the requisite questions, his silver pen silently scrawling out her answers. Penny likes his tone of voice. He really is very professional, she thinks. She likes how he leans forward and looks her in the eyes. He is really listening to her. She tells him all there is to tell. Occasionally he checks his notes, adds a comment here and there. Ten fifteen. Parking spot. Oldsmobile. Brown paper bag. Yoga.

"What kind?" he asks.

"What kind of what?" she asks back.

"Of yoga."

"Hatha . . . I think. Why?"

"Oh, Maureen pulled something and she has to give running a break. She's looking for some other kind of exercise." He jots down "hatha." "Well, unless you've got anything else to add, I think I get the picture."

Penny can't think of anything else to offer him. "That's pretty much it."

"Wow." Mitch stares at Penny wistfully. "Over two hundred thousand bucks. Quite a tidy sum. Man, those people are damn lucky." He is shaking his head as he packs up his notepad and recorder, and Penny wonders if he would have done the same thing she did. Then she asks him if the story will appear in Friday's issue.

"I'm going to do all I can to get it in there for tomorrow. Friday for sure. This is a hot story, old Penny, and you are the star!"

"And I'm sure the story is in good hands. See you, old Mitch."

A flicker of something registers across his face, and he gives her a wink. Penny starts for the door, but just as she is about to leave, Mitch startles her as he lets out another "Damn! Two hundred thousand big ones!"

"Two hundred and twenty, actually." Penny likes to be accurate with her numbers.

"Damn. That's something. That's really great, Penny. Damn." She leaves him smiling and contemplating this new amount, and looks forward to reading the article herself. It *is* exciting.

Outside it is boiling. It is a quarter past one, and ol' Penny is starving. She wasn't offered anything to eat at the station. *So much for the star treatment.* They did offer her some stale coffee. She declined seconds. Maybe it's one of those myths that all cops thrive on doughnuts. Her stomach rumbles. She would kill for a bear claw right about now. If she were living on the other side of town, she could jump into her car and get a doughnut or two at the Tim Hortons drive-thru, but there are no such businesses in her neighbourhood. She weighs the pros and cons of driving over to North Vancouver to get her carbohydrate fix against walking a few blocks up the street to the French bakery. Their pastry is divine. Should she leave her car here? she wonders. Should she get into her car and drive across town? Should she even be eating doughnuts? In the last twenty-four hours, all she has consumed is Merlot and Nutella and half of a breakfast bar that tasted like cardboard. Now she is considering adding a cinnamon bun or a honey maple twist to her diet. *I'm not thinking clearly. I've got to eat something right now. Okay. What am I doing?*

"Penny! Hi there! Hold on. Hi. Glad I caught you."

It's Linda.

"Are you all done with the station? We got word at the *Sentinel,* and nobody can believe it. I mean, two hundred thousand dollars! Imagine. Wow, and you were there. I mean, it could easily have fallen into someone else's hands, and who knows what they would have done? I mean, anything could have happened."

Penny can only think about doughnuts. She is still unsure whether she will buy local or opt for the drive-thru. She looks at her Volvo and then she looks up the street. She can't remember if the bakery is on 16th or 18th Street. She seems to recall they might just offer more upscale kinds of pastries, and she really has her heart set on the basic garden variety. Cheap and filling. Maybe one glazed and one with sprinkles.

"It's really awesome. This is a big story, Penny."

Linda Campbell is always using words like "awesome," and Penny often wonders how old she is.

"I wanted to catch you before you go. I have this idea I want to pitch to you." Penny is still standing in the same spot. She hasn't decided where she will go for her doughnut.

"It's a pretty amazing idea. Do you want to go for a bite and we could talk about it? My project is on the back burner right now because of that legal issue. It's no biggie, but it puts me behind at least a month."

Two weeks ago there was an emergency staff meeting, and about thirty people crammed into Sylvia's conference room, which held ten at best. The air conditioning was on the fritz, and people were getting edgy. Sylvia had called the meeting to explain that there was a court case involving Linda and Johnson's monthly renovation. The homeowners, unbeknownst to *Sentinel* staff, had gone ahead and cut down a pair of Douglas firs that were blocking their view. Their neighbours produced information regarding property lines. Lawyers were hired, and Linda and Johnson were no longer transforming the sunroom, but the *Sentinel* had been named in the lawsuit.

Penny had been reminded how much she loved working at home. "I'm starving."

"Have you had lunch? I know this awesome café."

"How far is it? Do they have doughnuts?"

"No doughnuts, but I can drive. My car's just across the street." She is really animated now, probably never imagined it would be this easy to get Penny on board. "Oh, this'll be fun. Just us girls. We'll be there in two shakes."

"Two shakes" gives Linda's age away, thinks Penny, as her colleague leads her across Marine Drive. The sun is sitting directly overhead, and the day has turned sweltering.

For some reason Penny suddenly remembers the hydrangea she bought for her anniversary. She had left it leaning at the side of the garage. Normally she would get mad at herself for this kind of oversight. She hates killing plants, but she is good at it. Over the years, she has wasted many dollars buying healthy flowers and shrubs and trees only to have them wither under her care. She cried once over a hanging basket that got infected by aphids a week after she bought it. She could get emotional over the hydrangea, but she is too hungry.

"Where are you taking me, Linda?" But Linda doesn't hear the question because she is busy throwing magazines from the passenger side onto the back seat.

"Sorry about the mess."

"Where are you taking me?" she asks again, as she buckles herself in.

"Café du Moulin? Do you like French?"

"Oh, Linda, I'm not in the mood for that right now, to be honest." Penny has never been fond of French cuisine for lunch. The odd dinner, maybe, but definitely not lunch.

"No, don't worry. Uhm, what about Thai? You up for something spicy?"

"No. Sorry I'm being so difficult. Gosh, I haven't eaten and I'm sort of light-headed here." Then she adds, for extra emphasis, "I'm also hungover from last night."

"Big party?"

"Anniversary. Eighteenth. Had too much wine. What can I say?"

"And your husband? Hungover too, I take it?"

"Oh, you bet." She thinks about telling Linda that she drowned her sorrows all alone but decides against it. It's not any of her business, and it's not like they are bosom buddies either. Her head is throbbing.

"Wanna just grab a coffee then?"

"Love to!"

Linda starts the car, and soon the air conditioning is providing some relief. She drives one of those retro cars that have always reminded Penny of a hearse for midgets.

"It's very spacious in here," she says, somewhat surprised.

"It works for me. I can fit all my cosmetic trays and boxes in with room to spare. The back seats flip down if I'm ever bringing a wardrobe for a shoot, so that's a bonus too."

"That's great."

"So is Starbucks okay with you?"

"Linda, I am so sorry to be so hard to please, but could we just go somewhere and grab a doughnut? I really need a doughnut."

"How about Tim Hortons?" Linda looks hopeful.

"Perfect."

They are there within ten minutes.

"Do you want to go inside?"

Her answer is fast. "No! No, uhm, let's just eat in the car. If you don't mind. Do you mind?"

"Not at all."

Linda pulls up behind a carpet-cleaning van. They can hear the men ordering from the sign menu and the muffled voice of an employee coming through the speaker.

They are up next. Linda inches her car forward, rolls down the window, and leans on her elbow. She speaks slowly and loudly into the little metallic holes that indicate the microphone. "One low-fat medium latte and one cranberry-orange muffin and . . ." She looks over to Penny expectantly. It is her line now.

"Oh, just get me a large regular coffee, cream and double sugar . . ."

Linda turns back to the speaker and adds, "One large coffee with milk and . . ."

"Cream, please."

"Cancel the milk and make it cream, please. And double sugar."

"And order me a Long John—no, make it a Boston cream."

"One Boston cream, please."

"Actually, I'll take a Long John."

"Make that a Long John instead, please."

"No, uhm . . . I'll take both the Long John and the Boston cream, if that's okay?"

Linda smiles at Penny and waves off her comment. "Make that one Long John and one Boston cream, please."

A man's voice is discernible over the motorists' idling engines. He sounds entirely bored and unenthusiastic. "That's one low-fat medium latte and one cranberry-and-orange muffin and one large regular coffee with cream and sugar and one . . ."

"Double sugar, sorry." She has waited too long for this and wants to get it right. "Sorry, Linda."

Linda leans out and gesticulates with her fingers at the sign. "That's double sugar, please."

There is a pause. "One large regular coffee with cream, not milk, double sugar, and one Long John and one Boston cream doughnut. Will that be everything?"

Linda looks at Penny.

Penny looks at Linda.

What the hell. "Could you just throw in one of those honey-glazed ones too?"

Linda is playing it cool. God knows what she is thinking. Penny can't imagine Linda ever ordering herself three doughnuts. She was probably one of those kids who rationed out all their Halloween candy to last over the entire year. She probably had to throw out fifty-two chocolate bars in June because they had gone stale. *Does chocolate even go stale?* Penny never throws anything out. Except lettuce. And apples and oranges. Well, lots of fruit. She has thrown out lots of bananas. And tomatoes too. *Are they fruit?* And, of course, dead plants.

"We'll take another honey-glazed too, please." Penny loves that Linda used the pronoun "we." Who would have ever thought that the financial columnist and the beauty queen would be here, together?

"Is that everything?"

Linda looks hopefully at Penny.

She nods.

"Yes, thank you."

"Your total is six dollars and . . ." The exact amount could be anything. There is too much noise to make it out.

"My treat!" Penny has a ten-dollar bill ready in her hand.

"No, this is going to be on me." Linda gets two fives out and refuses to take Penny's money. Soon they are at the cashier window. Penny can see that the total comes to six dollars and fifty-five cents.

"Here, let me get rid of some change at least, Linda."
She has this annoying habit of trying to pay out the exact
change. Maybe it's because Jack has the annoying habit of
leaving little piles of quarters and dimes and nickels and
pennies all over the house.

One time Penny did a sweep of the house and col-
lected coins from virtually every room and closet and
shelf. She started out with a shoebox, but it proved to be
too flimsy for the job. She ended up using two ice cream
buckets and one similar-sized bucket that she had got
when she went to see the latest Harry Potter movie. She
hauled it all in to her local supermarket because there
was a machine that would swallow up and automatically
count your money for you. She was thrilled to discover
that her efforts had been worth exactly one hundred and
sixty-three dollars and ninety-nine cents, even after the
small fee for using the service.

The moral of the story is that all those pennies and
dimes do add up. It's true. She's been meaning to write
a column on that for some time.

"Don't worry about it, Penny. I got it." Linda hands
the woman at the window her two fives.

"Here." Penny can't leave well enough alone and hands
Linda one quarter and two dimes and one nickel and five
shiny pennies. "Perfect, now you get a toonie back."

"Thanks." Linda is, indeed, given a toonie in change. All is right in the universe.

The two coffees are passed in first, followed by a large bag with the doughnuts and muffin and napkins.

Penny feels embarrassed by her pushy behaviour with the money, but instead of letting it go she pushes on.

"You know, you'd be surprised at how much money you have at home. In coins, I mean. My husband, you know, well, I swear he doesn't think pennies and dimes are real currency. He just deals in paper and the odd loonie or toonie." She takes an enormous bite of the Long John first. "God, that man," she says with her mouth full.

"Do you want a napkin?" Linda has pulled over to the parking lot. She has tried to find some shade, but the trees are newly planted and offer only a little bit of cover from the blistering sun.

Penny grabs the napkin as she washes the last of her doughnut down with a slurp of coffee. She realizes that if Linda and she were on their first date, it would more than likely be their last.

"Sorry, I'm not normally this deranged." She shrugs and smiles at Linda and takes the Boston cream out of the bag.

"Here." Linda hands her another napkin. "Your shirt."

"Oh, geez. I'm a mess today!" Penny sees she has dribbled coffee on her T-shirt. She sticks the doughnut in her mouth so she can dab at the stain with both hands.

"Do you want me to hold that for you?"

Penny shakes her head and says something inaudible to Linda. A little bit of the filling from the Boston cream plops onto her lap. Penny regards it with a light heart. She waves Linda's concerns away with her free hand and takes the doughnut from her mouth with the other. "Don't worry about it. I'll just throw these straight in the wash. Lickety-split." She gulps some more of her coffee and starts in on the Long John. "Tim Hortons really does make the best coffee." The lid is not on properly, and more coffee spills on her Real Woman T-shirt.

"You're dripping!" Linda startles her with the intensity of her voice. Maybe she is worried about the interior of her car. Maybe she thinks Penny will smear chocolate and cream and honey glaze all over the tastefully beige cloth decor like an out-of-control toddler with an ice cream cone.

"Oh, it's okay. I mean, don't worry. I won't make a mess . . . I mean, I won't mess up your car. Just myself." With her index finger she deftly removes the blob of cream from her lap. She thinks about licking it up, but at the last minute she avails herself of yet another napkin and politely wipes her fingers clean. "There."

Linda hasn't even opened her latte. Her muffin is still in the bag.

"Penny, I wanted to talk to you about an idea I have for a feature."

"Oh? What do you have in mind?"

"Well, Mitch is going to run the story on the couple whose money you returned today—"

"The Jenkinses."

"Is that their name? Jenkins?"

"Yeah, those poor people. They're so embarrassed. I hope Mitch doesn't make them look stupid or anything."

"No. No, I'm sure he will handle it tactfully. He's going to run it in tomorrow's or Friday's paper." She carefully pries open her latte with her perfectly manicured nails. She does not spill a drop. "I was thinking of doing a feature on *you*, Penny."

"On me?"

"Yes."

"Oh, like some hero or something? No. No, I don't want to do that. I'm happy I returned the money, but it's really a short story. They screwed up and I helped out. Sorry if I sound unenthusiastic, Linda, but I can't see your readers being interested in a longer piece. I mean, look at me."

"Well, that's just it."

"What's just it?"

"I think people would be very interested to follow up on you, Penny."

"Follow up on what?"

"I'm thinking about a 'Renovate Your Life' feature."

"What? For whose life?" Penny has stopped eating.

"It's amazing to see a person consciously evaluate her life on physical, emotional, financial, and spiritual levels."

"Uh huh."

"I've been searching for just the right debut candidate, and I think you're it!"

"Me?!"

"What we do is present Penny Stevens as our community 'everywoman.' People might already know you from your column, but if they don't, everybody will know you after this week's feature. You *are* our local hero, but you are also just Penny Stevens and, like many other women, you face your own set of dilemmas and concerns and hopes and dreams." She pauses here for dramatic effect.

Penny is speechless, so she doesn't say anything.

"Our readers will connect with you because they will get to know you and watch you transform and basically renovate your life into something more meaningful." Linda sits back in her seat and sips her latte. Despite the fact that they are parked roughly twenty feet away from the grey concrete wall of a discount sports outlet store, the beauty consultant appears to be looking far off somewhere. "You will take our readers along with you on an amazing journey of self-realization and actualization."

Penny has all of a sudden lost interest in her uneaten honey-glazed doughnut. She realizes she has been subconsciously digging her nails into her paper coffee cup.

"What do you think? It could be totally awesome!"

"No, I think it would be very . . . uh, *un*awesome for me."

Linda doesn't hear her. "We'll formulate a game plan together, Heather can start you off with diet and exercise, and Johnson can take a look at your house. Depending on our budget and your needs, we can do anything from a mini-facelift to a major reno."

"Oh, I don't know about that. I'm not looking to do any renovations just now."

"We'll have to do an assessment and take it from there. Also, I've got Charlie on board, from the *Designer Chicks* show. That's 'Charlie' for 'Charlotte.' She's a clutter buster, and the show is on hiatus and she's looking to do some freelance. We'll get a landscape architect for your garden. And we can't forget your inner self. I've got a possible lead on an awesome spiritual adviser. You're probably financially sound, but we can get an outside wealth-management consultant to give you the once-over. It's very healthy to re-evaluate your situation from another point of view. That's my mantra, anyway. And, of course, I would be honoured to do your makeover. Skin, hair, wardrobe. You have a lot of natural features that I'd love to work with."

Penny has now crushed her empty coffee cup in her fist.

"Are you done with that?" Linda says. She holds open the bag for Penny's garbage.

"Aren't you going to eat your muffin?" is all Penny can think to say.

"Why? Do you want it? You can have it." Linda is bending over backward. She must really want her on board.

"No. No, thanks."

"So, what do you say, Penny?"

"No. No, thanks."

"I'm talking about the chance of a lifetime here. A total life transformation."

"I know, and I thank you very much, but I don't think I'm the person you're looking for."

"But you're perfect."

"Then why bother with the reno?"

"We could do so much for you . . ."

"*To* me, you mean."

Linda shifts in her seat and turns to look directly into Penny's eyes. She grabs Penny's elbows in what must be a very uncomfortable position for her. "Do you have any idea of the value of what I'm proposing to you? Do you know how much this would cost if you decided to do this on your own?"

"I couldn't imagine."

"And this will be totally free!"

"Again, thank you so much for thinking of me. You should have no trouble finding someone else." *This woman won't take no for an answer.*

"But I want you!" *Did she just shout at me?*

"But why me?" *Did I just shout at her?*

"Because you are Penny Stevens! Because you're so perfect for this, Penny . . . so perfect! And we would make you so much better!"

"I see."

"I have a vision here." Linda places her index fingers at her temples. "And these visions, well, they can be very strong. I can help you transform your life. I know change can be scary, but the journey begins one step at a time."

"Who said I want to change? Who said I wanted to go on any journey?"

"Listen to me and answer this question truthfully." Linda fixes her with a determined stare. "Can you honestly say you are happy with the life you lead? On all levels?"

"Can *you*, Linda?"

"Yes. Yes I can. I've been on my self-discovery journey for a long time, and it was only last year when I went away for a two-week intensive workshop to Saltspring, where I met and faced my demons in the communal sweat lodge. I had to re-evaluate my whole life and strip it down, and I've been building it up ever since."

"Well, listen, that's great and I'm happy for you, but—"

"I can help you."

"I'm not asking for your help. I think that's a key point here."

"But you need it! Take a look in the mirror and tell me you are a happy woman."

"I think 'happy' is overrated."

"See! There you go!"

"Look, if you are so happy, why are you yelling at me?"

"Because I'm . . . I'm . . . I'm passionate!"

If Penny could look in a mirror, she would not see her best self. With coffee stains down her front and crumbs in her lap, skin pale and unhealthy, hair frizzy and uncombed, and her intestines twisting with sugar and gas, she knows she is not putting up a good defence to Linda's attack. But she resents Linda's very generous offer. She's not asking to be pitied, and she's not asking for anyone's help. She's looked after herself for four decades and doesn't want to be anyone's project, regardless of their good intentions. She knows she looks a sight and that her life is indeed in shambles. But that is her doing. Very simply, she doesn't want to be renovated. Not by Linda. Not by Heather or Johnson or any chick named Charles.

"What do you say? Will you at least think about it, Penny? Here's my card with my home number. It could be awesome. What do you say?"

Penny's response comes from deep within her. From her bowels, to be exact. The combination of wine and breakfast bar and chocolate and doughnuts and this stressful encounter has produced a large ball of gas. Without any warning, Penny lets one go. It is a B flat, and there is no way in this small space and in this heat to ignore it.

"Excuse me. God, I'm sorry, Linda."

"No problem." She puts the car into gear and hits a switch to open the sunroof and all the windows.

"Oh, this is not my day. I'm so embarrassed."

"Don't be. We should get going anyways. I've got to get back to the office and finish up a few things."

"I haven't been eating properly these last few days. I'm under a lot of stress and my husband and I . . . we just, you know . . . ?"

"Sure."

"Well, it's not like I'm in crisis or anything. I just need to get some sleep. I haven't slept properly in days."

"I see."

"I mean, it's not like I can't sleep. I don't take sleeping pills or anything. At least I haven't for a while. I admit I used to, but that was a long time ago. Before the days of Paxil, praise the Lord!"

"Sure." Linda is a lot less talkative on the ride back, which seems to take twice as long, and Penny figures she has said enough.

"Shall I drive you to the *Sentinel* or leave you at the station?"

"Oh, my car is at the station. That would be awesome, Linda. Just awesome." Nothing feels wonderful to Penny right now, but she's trying to hold it together.

Linda pulls into the parking lot at the back and Penny is thankful Linda can't see her jalopy of a car.

"Thanks again, Linda. It was great going out for coffee. The next one's on me. And good luck with your renovations. I'm sorry . . . I just can't, you know . . . do the 'life reno' thing for you. It's just, you know."

"I understand completely. I hope I didn't offend you, Penny."

"Oh, not at all. Thanks for the offer."

"Okay, take care."

"You too!"

Penny watches as Linda's mini hearse pulls away and disappears into traffic. Slowly she walks up and around the corner to Marine Drive. Luckily she is on the shady side of the street and her car won't be super-unbearable, as she has no air conditioning and no sunroof and no automatic windows.

She spots her Volvo halfway up the block just as an officer is placing a ticket on her windshield.

"Oh, hello there! Hello! It's me! I mean, I'm here so you don't have to ticket my car. I'm leaving."

"Two-hour limit during business hours, ma'am."

"But I—"

"We all have to play by the rules. They are clearly

posted, and should you want to dispute this ticket, you have seventy-two hours to do so."

"I don't want to dispute anything!"

"Please don't shout, ma'am."

"My name is Penny Stevens and I just rescued two hundred and twenty thousand dollars from the Jenkinses!"

"Please calm down, ma'am."

"Don't tell me to calm down!"

"Ma'am, let's just take it easy." He reaches for his walkie-talkie at his hip and quietly moves away from Penny.

"Remove that ticket from my car immediately!"

The officer is speaking in police code. The conversation lasts all of ten seconds.

"Ma'am, help is on the way."

"What help? Why is everyone trying to help me? I don't want your help. Here, take this ticket." Her arms are too short to reach the ticket from the sidewalk, so she walks over to the driver's side and snatches it from beneath the wipers, one of which is broken.

Again, out of protocol and maybe out of fear for what a crazy woman might do, the officer takes another step back and raises his arm. People are starting to take notice and gawk at them.

"Please stay where you are." Then footsteps are heard from behind.

"Over here, Wallace."

"Why, if it isn't our local hero, Penny Stevens."

"Hello again!" Her voice comes out a few decibels louder than necessary, and even Wallace is taken aback. He and the other officer exchange knowing looks.

"Is there a problem here, Officer Hillcrest?"

Hillcrest puts his arms down and readjusts his shirt. "Traffic violation 17b. This vehicle has been parked here forty-five minutes over the posted time."

"I see." Wallace nods knowingly to Hillcrest and winks. Then he turns to Penny. "Is this true, Ms. Stevens?"

"It is, but I couldn't park out back, and I was forced to park in the street. I was in there for a long time with you guys . . ."

"But we concluded our business well over an hour ago. Is that not correct?"

"But I went for coffee!"

"I see." He speaks to Hillcrest now. "She went for coffee, you see."

Hillcrest is up against the wall here, but he has logic and rules on his side. "Still, it is a two-hour time limit. Clearly posted."

Wallace nods in agreement. "He's got a point there, Ms. Stevens."

"Fine. I'll pay the damn ticket then." She is shaking with rage, waving the ticket in the air. "You'll get your goddamn money! I'll pay! I'll pay!"

"I'm kidding! I'm just having some fun here. It's a joke—just a joke."

"Well, I'm glad I can provide fodder for your jokes. I don't think this is a laughing matter. I'll send the cheque in the mail!"

Despite the shade, the inside of the car is boiling.

"Ms. Stevens, please. You don't have to pay the ticket." Wallace is knocking on her passenger-side window.

"Oh I'll pay. I'll pay!" she yells through the glass. "You'll get the money all right, Constable Wallace!" Then, knowing she shouldn't say it, she adds, "Maybe you can take some of the money and get some decent coffee and doughnuts! You'll get your money! Ha!"

Soon she is lurching out into traffic. A small gaggle of onlookers watch helplessly as she almost collides with a Handy Dart bus. She thinks she can hear Hillcrest yelling out, "Your seat belt! Your seat belt!"

• • •

Five minutes later she is pulling into her driveway. The first thing she sees is the dying hydrangea leaning against the garage. Forgotten and untended. Now that she is no longer hungry, she can produce tears.

She sobs as she takes in her mess of a garden and her broken front-porch step and peeling paint and dirty windows. Inside she cries when she sees the dishes from the night before and the newspapers piled up in the corner and the dripping tap. When she catches sight of herself in the front-hall mirror she sees a short and fat and dirty and broken forty-year-old woman holding a parking ticket.

It takes her a full two minutes to find the cordless phone and another minute to find the fancy business card.

"Hello. It's Penny."

The voice on the other end is calm and reassuring.

"Linda. I need you to renovate my life!"

Six

Jack comes home at five thirty to find Penny still clutching the phone in one hand and Linda's phone number
in the other.

"Are you all right?"

"No." She's been sitting on the kitchen chair for a
couple of hours, unable to move.

"Are you phoning somebody?"

"No."

"What's going on?"

"I'm falling apart."

"Oh." His interrogation comes to a stop here. Like
most men, he prefers to fix things when he can or

ignore them entirely and hope they resolve themselves on their own.

The moment passes awkwardly, and Penny sees that her husband is either unable or unwilling to respond. She herself can think of nothing to say other than, "You're home early."

"Yes. Yes I am." He is often home late.

"There are kebabs left over in the fridge."

"Oh, great . . . great." He hates leftovers.

"Are you hungry? How many do you want?" She hasn't moved from her chair, and Jack hasn't moved from his spot.

"Moderately hungry. We could grab a bite at the club."

"No, I'm not up for going out. Give me a minute. I just need to pull myself together."

"Oh sure." No doubt relieved his wife is heading back to the safety of domesticity, he turns on his heel. "I'll just do a bit of work before dinner." For a sixty-two-year-old man he moves astonishingly fast. In less than five seconds Penny hears the door of his den click shut. He is safe in there.

And she is safe in her kitchen. Her fridge and her stove comfort her.

"I'm going to clean you," she says to her stove, "first thing tomorrow." Strangely, she feels buoyed by the concept of scouring her range. Cleaning her appliances has always lifted her spirits. It's just that she doesn't do it very often. Maybe that's why she's been so depressed lately. *Was it a full year ago when I last cleaned out the fridge?*

She takes the kebabs out and removes the Saran Wrap. On the top shelf of the refrigerator she spies a bowl of pasta from three nights ago that will do for a side dish. She knows she should not bother with cooking at a time like this. That she shouldn't be considering side dishes at a moment when she is having a nervous break- down. But chopping and cooking and heating things up and placing them on a plate and then eating them has always made her feel better. Whenever she has been at rock bottom, there has always been something good to eat. She knows, too, that this is typical self-sabotage. She took Psychology 101. She knows what's going on, but she reasons that sometimes these coping skills, however misdirected, can actually be of some tangible use. People need to eat dinner, and coping is usually a good thing. She knows she's going to have to start making some changes, and it's really this that is scaring her more than anything else.

"Dinner!"

"Coming!"

She hears Jack venture down the stairs much more

slowly than normal. Penny enters the dining room from the kitchen carrying the platter of kebabs.

"What'll you have to drink?" she asks.

"Oh, I'll just get myself a beer."

"Will you need a glass?"

He grabs a Stella Artois from the fridge. "No, bottle's fine."

They sit down together at one corner of the large oak table. The polish has worn off where they sit day in and day out. The rest of the surface is like new. Unscathed.

"Are you feeling any better?"

"No."

"Are you sick?"

"No."

"Did something happen today?"

"Yes." She does not provide further details. Jack nods and takes a sip of his beer.

"Do you want to tell me what happened?"

"I found two hundred and twenty thousand dollars. Then I went for coffee and doughnuts, and then I got a parking ticket."

Jack puts his fork and knife down and sits back in his chair.

Penny has lived long enough with this man to know that he will likely proceed cautiously here.

"I see. Where did you find the money?"

"On the top of an old couple's car."

"Who did you go to coffee with?"

"Linda, the beauty-column writer from the paper."

"And the parking ticket . . . ?"

"Constable Wallace. No, wait. It was Officer Hillcrest who gave me the ticket. But it's Wallace who's going to get it."

Jack nods and Penny thinks he looks like he's playing Clue. *Colonel Mustard did it with the rope in the library.*

He needs more information. "What did you do with the money?"

"I took it to the police station."

"And this . . . this Officer Walton gave you a ticket?"

"Wallace? No."

"Who gave you the ticket?"

"Hillcrest. But that was after coffee and doughnuts."

"First he gave you coffee and doughnuts?"

"I was there almost two hours and they only offered me one dead cup of lukewarm coffee!"

"So who gave you doughnuts?"

"Tim Horton." Penny is gnawing on the last piece of chicken on her skewer. For leftovers, they are really quite good.

Jack takes this all in and thankfully doesn't push

further. Too many questions can produce tears, and tears lead to blaming. "Well, it was good of you to return that money." Then he can't help but ask, "Were they able to find the owners?"

"Yes. Their name is Jenkins." She stands up and starts to clear away the dishes. "I'm tired. I'm going to hit the sack early. It's been a long day."

"Do you think you will get a reward?"

"I doubt it. So far all I got was a parking violation, but you can read all about it in Friday's *Sentinel*."

"By golly, Pen! You're a star." When he speaks like this Penny is reminded that she has married an older man. Normally, she can't match his stamina or imagine him qualifying for his seniors' card in three short years.

"Oh, speaking of being famous and all that . . . I have agreed to renovate my life."

"What do you mean?" For the first time in this exchange he looks concerned.

"Well, I guess that since I'm such a sad and pathetic case, people want to help me. Change me into someone better."

"Who does?"

"Linda and some other people at the paper. She wants to do a feature on me. Don't worry, Jack, I'll probably be a hopeless case, but I might get a new haircut and maybe lose a few pounds."

"I see." The concept of change has always unhinged Jack. She can almost see his unspoken thoughts float up from where he is sitting.

"I can't talk anymore. I'm dead tired." She goes into the kitchen and quickly hides what she can in the dishwasher and sink. Jack is still sitting at the table, unconsciously tearing at the label on his beer bottle.

"Goodnight, Jack." It's not even seven o'clock, but it's been a full day.

"Goodnight, Pen."

She climbs the stairs slowly. The second stair from the top creaks. It always has. *Will they renovate that?* She walks down the hall to her bedroom. The bed is still unmade from this morning. Her pyjamas are in a heap at the side of the dresser, her terry-towel robe crumpled by the closet. *If they're going to help me, do I have to clean the house first?*

Penny peels off her T-shirt and yoga pants and almost drops them on the floor. Then she remembers her laundry basket and feels a sense of triumph as she divides the shirt and pants between lights and darks. Next she adds her socks to the darks and her bra to the lights. She takes off her panties and is about to throw them in the basket of lights when she notices they are torn and beyond repair. So, after a small hesitation, she throws them in the garbage.

In the shower, she closes her eyes and stands under the hot stream of water. Even though it was a blistering day, more than thirty degrees in the shade, she loves having scalding showers. She takes a dollop of shampoo and massages her scalp.

After rinsing the conditioner through her hair, she spies her legs. *Damn, girl.*

She hasn't changed the blade in her razor for months. If there are refills, they'll be under the sink. She has to be careful not to slip as she tiptoes and drips all over the faded linoleum. She is in luck. Just behind the tampons and maxi pads is an unopened pack of cartridges. She removes one and quickly gets back into the shower. It takes ten minutes to shave her legs and underarms, and the water is getting slightly cooler.

Penny emerges from the shower and dries herself off. Somewhere she has a fancy body lotion that she got for Christmas. She would never buy this kind of stuff for herself but is always happy when someone else does. She roots through the cabinet and drawers and can't find it, but then notices a rectangular packet of a free sample she received in the mail. It is called *Revive!* and promises to make her skin 72 percent more supple in two weeks and to decrease her wrinkles by 65 percent after four weeks.

She doesn't have that kind of time but empties the contents out over her face and neck anyway.

It isn't quite seven thirty when Penny is in bed. It will be light out for almost another two hours, but she can't keep her eyes open any longer. Within five minutes, she has fallen into a deep and bottomless sleep.

Around six thirty in the morning, Penny wakes up screaming. Her body is bathed in sweat and her heart is pounding.

She dreamed that she was ambushed in one of those extreme makeovers. Linda and her renovation team jumped out from behind a parked car and filmed her as she was loading groceries into her beat-up Volvo. Of course, she was naked.

Her heart slows down as she realizes that she is fully clothed in the middle of her king-sized bed. Then her heart speeds up again as she realizes that Linda is indeed coming over today. She remembers she has agreed to allow essentially total strangers to come into her life and assess the damage, so to speak.

What were you thinking, woman!

She's going to need another shower, but she decides she will drag out the vacuum first and then clean up her room and her closet. Of course she'll have to do the kitchen too. Also, the recycling needs to be done. She calculates that if she does this in two hours, then she can have a shower and be ready for Linda at nine thirty.

It's going to be another hot day, and Penny is moving fast. She slams closet doors shut and she opens windows wide. As she passes by the den, she sees her husband asleep on the couch. He is dead to the world while his wife flies around the house in her pyjamas.

Downstairs she makes a pot of coffee and gets the newspaper from the front porch. There is a headline about some Republican White House aide having written a kiss-and-tell tome about George Bush. She wonders if George will pick up a copy and check it out. He'll certainly have the time.

Penny likes following politics. Especially at election times, and this round is particularly interesting. And hopeful. Barack Obama and Hillary Clinton. It's going to be a first for America either way. These are exciting times and so entertaining because it's real. Penny likes to keep abreast of what's going on south of the border as well as Canadian affairs. That is the only time her high school French comes in handy. She's nowhere near fluent, but when she listens to the French-language debates, by the time the fifth candidate has spoken, she really gets it since they all end up saying the same things by that point anyway. She likes the fact that Canadians will elect a person only if he or she has taken and passed a French fluency test. Maybe the Americans should have instituted a sort of competency test as well. Like basic geography. That might have eliminated a candidate here and there. Might have saved some stress. Some embarrassment. A few thousand lives.

Flipping to world news, she reads that Osama bin Laden is still in hiding. He's probably got a lot of time to read. And Penny wonders what's on his bedside table. Light fiction. Inspirational verses. Self-help, perhaps. Maybe he'll read that biography.

Then, on the bottom of page eight, Penny catches a glimpse of an article about the Canadian prime minister. Behaving very nicely and quietly. Just like a Canadian.

She takes a second to glance at the entertainment section. Joan Rivers is on the front. *Holy plastic surgery!* Then Penny recalls that Saddam Hussein had something like twelve look-a-likes but poor George Bush, on the other hand, had only one—his father.

As tempting as it is for Penny to linger over the news, she throws today's paper into the recycling. If she's going to get anything done today, she can't get caught up in international politics and celebrity gossip.

While the coffee is brewing, she gets the Hoover out of the closet. They've had this sucker for almost twenty years, a big, heavy beast that refuses to die. A few of the attachments have gone missing, but the lungs of the machine are as strong as ever.

Penny quickly runs around the house and gathers up all her area rugs and runners. These she takes out onto the porch and hits with a broom handle before she shakes them vigorously. She is sweating profusely, and it isn't even seven o'clock.

Inside, the coffee is ready. She loves fresh coffee and pours herself a cup with half-and-half cream. Even though she knows cream has more fat content than milk, she reasons that since she rarely ever finishes a cup, she is actually consuming fewer calories than if she were to drink a full cup of coffee with milk. What the people from the diet and wellness program might think about this, Penny doesn't want to know.

She drinks half her cup of coffee and then walks with determination into the living room, where the vacuum is lying in wait. It is a beautiful morning with sunlight streaming into the room. She sees that the room is incredibly dusty. One more thing to add to her growing list.

Outside, birds are no doubt chirping, but Penny can't hear them as the Hoover comes to life. She is focused on her work, as her body jerks forward and backward into one corner and under the couch and over behind this table and around that stool. The Hoover is incredibly heavy and cumbersome, and she wonders why some enterprising housewife doesn't design some battery-powered backpack vacuum that people could just strap onto their shoulders. Kind of like those leaf blowers that have replaced the need for rakes. Perhaps more men would be enticed to do the housework if they looked a little more like superheroes. The only time Jack ever gets excited about cleaning anything is when he can borrow the neighbour's pressure washer. He's cleaned the shed, the garage floor, the stone walkway, and the wooden steps off the back deck.

He almost killed himself once, too. He was up on a ladder trying to clean the trellis, and he misjudged how powerful the machine was and blew himself backward onto the lawn. It was quite a sight to see one's husband fly through the air like that. He landed with a giant thud, splayed flat out on the grass, like a kid making a snow angel except he was clutching a giant hose in one hand and his heart in the other. The neighbours and Penny and the newspaper kid quickly surrounded him.

Is he okay? Did you hurt yourself, buddy? Geez, that was quite something!

Hank, the owner of the washer, had to pry it from Jack's hand. Jack lay there stunned and speechless. *Buddy! Can you tell me your name?*

A minute later Jack was back on his feet, and the newspaper kid was on his way again. Penny only shook her head as Jack and Hank finished off the afternoon on the porch with a bottle of Crown Royal, laughing and retelling the story a hundred times.

To this day it is still revered like a glorious battle. As if the guys had been comrades in war. The trellis was the trench where Jack was badly injured, where Hank came and saved the day.

All it takes is for Hank to mention that the trellis is looking a little dirty, and the men howl and slap each other on the back.

"Christ Almighty!"

"What?" Penny yells over the noise of the Hoover and bends down to turn it off.

"What's this?" Jack's full head of white hair is standing on end. He is slipperless, wearing striped pyjama pants with a light green Homelife T-shirt that says "Number One Closer." Penny catches her breath.

"I'm vacuuming." She is huffing and puffing.

"I can see that. What in the world is going on?"

"I told you."

"Told me what?"

"I told you last night that I'm going to renovate my life."

"What's got into you? What are you talking about?"

"People are coming over at nine thirty and this place is a mess. I can't talk right now, okay? Look, I have to get things cleaned up before they get here."

"People are coming here? Who? When?"

"From the paper, Jack. I told you." She always feels like she is repeating herself and explaining things over and over to her husband. If he would just listen to her the first time, they could avoid these encounters altogether.

"Help me understand one thing, Penelope." He is using his condescending voice and her full name now, and she knows from his tone that he thinks this whole thing is some kind of joke. "Tell me why it is you are running around like an idiot and cleaning up the place when I presume it is these 'people' who are supposed to help you! What in Heaven's name are you doing?"

"Just leave me alone!"

"This is just like the time your mother got you that maid service!"

"I don't want to talk about that, and don't bring up my mother!"

"Every single goddamn time you had the maids coming, you spent the entire day before cleaning up the house!"

"Look, this is none of your business."

"Well, it's my house too, and maybe I don't want my house renovated!"

They were descending now into the familiar and cyclic dance of the "married couple."

"I am going to renovate myself, and there is nothing you can do to stop me!"

"Penelope. I want you to calm down."

"Jack. I don't want to calm down."

"Christ."

He stands there with his arms dangling at his sides, she with the hose limp in her hand. There is so much to say here, but neither person can find the energy to get the words out. They stand there in silence for quite a while. Jack is breathing heavily now; she is sighing quietly. Outside, a crow is screaming.

Jack is the first to make a move. "Those goddamn birds!" He opens the French doors to the balcony. "Shut up! All of you! Shut up!"

She is still in the middle of the living room, shaking her head slowly from side to side. "Wow. That's telling them."

"I'm not in the mood. It's too early for this."

"What? For birds to be out?" She wants to irritate him. Badly.

"I said I'm not in the mood."

"Are you tired? Did you go out again last night?"

"No, I did not."

"You know, you're getting older, Jack. People your age need their sleep. You need to get to bed on time, don't you think?"

"I think I've had enough of this conversation." He strides past her and heads up the stairs.

"There's coffee for you, honey. Brewed fresh just for you."

But he has disappeared, and soon the sound of the shower tells her that he has no intention of hanging around here this morning. In fifteen minutes he will be dressed and shaved. He will have applied some cologne and gone on his way.

The Hoover roars back to life and she throws herself into her housework with a passion. She grips the hose so tightly that she gets a cramp in her hand. Her teeth are clenched; her stomach is growling.

Checking the clock, she realizes there is no way she is going to be able to get done what she set out to do. She wheels the vacuum back to its closet and decides that her time would be most wisely spent tidying the kitchen, getting a piece of toast into her, and having a shower.

It takes a good half an hour to do the dishes and get rid of some newspapers and eat a slice of bread. The time is nearing nine o'clock, so she decides that she had better get upstairs and into the shower before Linda arrives.

Jack's towel is hanging over the shower rod. She can smell that he used some other kind of shampoo and she can see he has opened a new bottle of cologne. It is called Hummer.

Just like with those paint samples that she struggled with years ago, she wonders who is in charge of giving names to perfumes and the like. She's seen a few Hummers around West Vancouver, but she's not putting an order in any time soon.

Her hot shower is cut short by the dishwasher and the fact that Jack already used up a lot of water. It's less than twelve hours since she's last showered, but she wants to look especially good this morning, so she quickly shampoos and rinses her hair again. It takes another few minutes to find something to wear. She ends up choosing a cotton skirt and a pale pink short-sleeved top. She combs her hair and applies a pale pink lipstick and assesses herself in the mirror. *Very clean. Very nice. Very boring.*

It is almost nine thirty and already over twenty-eight degrees. Her hair has sprung into unruly curls and she is beginning to perspire. She can feel the telltale circles appearing under her arms. She looks up at the kitchen clock.

Nine thirty-two. *Do I have time to change? Maybe that sleeveless thingy Mother got me to buy on sale . . .*

She is not two steps up the stairs when the doorbell rings. *Damn it.* "Coming! Coming!"

As she reaches for the doorknob with one hand, she futilely adjusts her hair with the other hand and fixes her face into position, hoping to elicit a relaxed yet "pleased to see you" kind of expression. She wants Linda to like her. She wants to like Linda. She wants to be better, better than she is, or rather she wants to look like she can handle this. Whatever this is.

"Hello!" Her voice is perky. She is half laughing as she opens the door.

"Hi."

Her composed face falls away. "Oh. Hello." It is a tall and handsome young man. "Can I help you?"

"Actually, I am here to help *you*. Hopefully." He doesn't move from his spot.

"Sorry?" Her voice is flat, no longer cheerful.

"Sorry. I'm Aaron Taylor."

"Sorry?"

"Linda sent me. From the *Sentinel*?"

"Oh." She is still standing with one hand holding the door. Her other hand has moved up to her forehead. "Sorry, I . . ."

"It looks like I've taken you somewhat by surprise. I'm sorry. I thought Linda said nine thirty. I should have called."

"Oh, no, don't worry. I'm sorry, I just . . ." By now they both had said enough "I'm sorry's" to star in a Hugh Grant movie. "Please, I'm sorry . . . come in. Please."

"Actually, why don't you join me outside? I've taken the liberty of walking around your garden just briefly. I don't want to tramp all this dirt through your house, and it's going to be a scorcher."

"You walked around my garden?" Penny thought perhaps she sounded like she was going to accuse him of trespassing or something. She just couldn't for the moment fathom what it was this man was up to. "I mean, you're certainly free to explore."

"Well, lets take a stroll together, shall we?"

"Right now?"

"No time like the present."

"I'll just get my clogs." With her mind racing, she roots about the front closet for her clunky shoes. *Who is this guy?*

"All set!" Penny has found her happy voice again, but she isn't as confident-sounding as before.

"Great."

For a brief moment they stand there on the porch and survey each other. No doubt he is thinking he has got himself into some kind of weird situation with a confused lady perspiring in front of him. She is wearing bright red clogs.

"What do you say if we just start along this side and make our way around the house?"

"Sure." She feels silly standing here with this man discussing how they are going to navigate around her house.

The young man looks to be in his late twenties, or maybe he is thirty. Penny has never been any good at telling people's ages. Maybe that's why she married Jack. She takes a second good look at the man as they slowly meander along through her garden, and discerns that he is quite simply gorgeous. Yes indeed.

"Lots of cedar trees and juniper bushes. I see that that laurel hedge is getting rather high." He is wearing a plain white T-shirt tucked into a pair of Levi's. She's always liked the simplicity of this look.

"What are you planning to do with this?" They have come round to a large pile of soil in a corner of the back yard.

"Oh, that . . ." Her voice trails off. She'd thought at one point about digging out some lawn and building up a flowerbed, or maybe putting in a bit of a vegetable garden. It was last summer when she had this load delivered, and of course she's done nothing. She had such plans. Now the pile is beginning to grow on its own. An assortment of weeds and airborne seeds have found their way to this mound of earth, but no amount of greenery can hide the neglect. Looking at this little corner of her garden, untended, forgotten, Penny feels terribly sad. She loves her flowerbeds, and this just won't do. She vows to deal with this yardwork first thing.

"I'm sorry. It's really quite a mess." How did she forget about this for so long? She senses tears coming and bends down to remove something invisible that isn't in her clog.

"Well, that's why you hire a gardener." He takes a

few steps away from her to inspect a bush more closely. His arms are long and lean and tanned.

"You're a gardener!" Penny exclaims.

"Yes. Yes, I am."

"Oh, yes, of course!" It is all slowly coming into focus. "You'll have to excuse me. I haven't been myself these last few days. So much has been going on and here you come and I think, 'Where's Linda?' and of course, you're the gardener!"

"Who did you think I was?"

"Well, of course you're a gardener, but now I get that you are the guy, 'the gardener,' for the reno thing."

"That's me. Aaron Taylor at your service." He is standing with his hands on his hips in the middle of the garden. His smile is wide and easy.

"Well, Mr. Taylor, looks like you've got your work cut out for you."

"Call me Aaron."

All at once she feels tongue-tied and embarrassed and shy. There is a pause, and then, "Call me Penny."

"Is that short for Penelope? I love that name."

"Yes, Penelope." She likes the way her name rolls off his lips. Maybe it won't be that bad after all, thinks Penny. At least not this part.

"Ohm" my goodness! Woman skips yoga class and recovers hundreds of thousands of dollars!

Wednesday, July 30
Mitch Williams

At approximately 10:30 a.m. Tuesday morning, Penny Stevens had her mind set on yoga. Ms. Stevens, the North Shore's very own financial columnist, admitted she was not keen on the early class and almost didn't make it. Thankfully, for Mr. Samuel Jenkins and his wife, Ruth, a retired couple living out in Horseshoe Bay, she did.

With minutes to spare before the introductory yoga would begin, Ms. Stevens eyed the maroon-coloured Oldsmobile pulling out of a choice parking spot. Having just concluded business at their bank, Mr. and Mrs. Jenkins were almost on their way when Ms. Stevens appeared at the driver's-side window.

She was motioning for them to stop. However, with both poor vision and impaired hearing, neither of the senior citizens could decipher what, exactly, Ms. Stevens wanted.

They drove off leaving Penny Stevens holding over $200,000 in a brown paper bag that they'd left on the roof of their car.

"At first I didn't realize what it was," Ms. Stevens remarked. "When it sunk in, I headed over to the police station as fast as I could. It was quite daunting, actually."

Two hours later, Mr. and Mrs. Jenkins were happily reunited with the money they had withdrawn from the bank.

When asked if this method of wealth management is advised, Penny Stevens was quick to reply, "Well, no. I don't think it's the safest way."

This good citizen was also happy to learn that she will not have to pay her parking violation, which she incurred during the time she spent at the police station. Good news for this Good Samaritan!

Read Penny Stevens's column Money Makes Cents every Friday in the business section of The Sentinel.

Seven

Half an hour later, Aaron and Penny are sitting in the shade on the front porch. The air is heavy and the humidity hangs like a wet towel. Nothing seems to be moving. The birds are silent and the bees and insects are quiet too. Even the odd car that passes the house seems to be crawling slowly by.

"Penny." Aaron's voice seems loud. "Why do you go by that rather than Penelope?" He has finished jotting down a few notes to himself and slides his pen and notebook into a nylon carrying case.

"Everybody calls me Penny. Though I like Penelope. It makes me feel taller somehow. I guess it's a bit of an old-fashioned name, but I had older parents. My mother was in her forties and, well, my father was sixty-six when I was born. If my mother hadn't dissuaded him, my name would have been Myrtle."

"Yikes. You dodged a bullet there, for sure."

"Yeah, kids can be mean. Still, if I had a penny for every time someone told me the sky was falling or offered a penny for my thoughts, I'd be a rich woman."

"For real?" He is shaking his head and smiling.

"For real."

"Did it bug you?"

"Sure it did. Weren't you called anything, or were you able to escape the schoolyard experience?"

"Well, they didn't call me 'Aaron the Baron' or anything like that."

"Lucky you." He probably was considered too good-looking to taunt. Some people have an unmistakable aura of confidence. She has met a few people like that, who seem to just sail through life.

"I do, however, remember being called a few choice names on more than one occasion."

"Kids can be so terrible. Honestly!" She can't imagine anyone calling Aaron anything but gorgeous. Must have all been jealous of him, she reasons.

"Can I get you something to drink?"

"Sure. It's too early for a beer, but I've gotten into

the habit of drinking tea when it's hot. I figure if they drink it in South Africa they must be on to something."

She disappears inside to the kitchen, which has a window that looks out onto the porch. While she waits for the water to boil, she watches the young man, who is now standing at the top of the steps. His hands are on his hips as he looks to be surveying her front yard one more time. He runs a hand through his dark brown hair. It is a bit long, and on anybody else it would look like they were in need of a haircut, but somehow on him it looks perfect.

She wonders what it would be like to be him. To be a beautiful person. And not just on the outside. Talking with him has been, well, weird for Penny, but he hasn't seemed to mind. She doesn't think she's ever met anyone so drop-dead handsome in her life. Can't even think of a movie star as compelling as the gardener on her very own front porch! She hopes she's not embarrassing herself and figures he must be used to females being a bit flustered in his presence. As the water comes to a boil, Penny thinks she'll have to invite her girlfriend Susan over for a visit the next time Aaron Taylor is in her garden.

She quickly puts together a tray with milk and sugar and a few biscuits. Taking a big breath and willing her nerves in order, she strides outside.

"Here we are." She wonders if she should get another chair as there is only the lone, rickety rocker. She decides against it and joins him somewhat clumsily on the steps.

"Milk and sugar?"

"Great. Thanks, Penelope."

It startles her to be called by her full name, and for a few minutes they busy themselves with serving the tea and measuring the sugar. Aaron tells her he has a few clients in this neighbourhood and is looking forward to being involved in this "reno" project for the *Sentinel*.

"Do you watch any of those improvement shows?" he asks.

"Well, no, but I think I might take a look. I'm not sure what I want. I mean, she just sprang this idea on me yesterday and I haven't even really had time to give it a thought."

"Well, all I am saying is you might want to get some guidelines on what you want—or don't want, you know?"

"Okay." She is getting a bit nervous at the thought of just how big this renovation might get. "What about your thoughts for my garden?" It certainly needs some work.

"I don't know exactly what my budget would be, but I was thinking of something along a mermaid theme."

"A mermaid theme?"

"Yes, themes are very big. I see fountains and lots of water and fish and fantasy right here in your front yard."

"In my front yard?"

"Yeah. Something in the style of that one over in Stanley Park." He drains the last few drops from his cup and stands up. "I'll have to get my hands on a really big rock too. I'll want the mermaid to be life-size, so the rock'll need to be at least four or five feet." He is gesticulating wildly with his arms.

"Oh, I don't know about that. The neighbours might not be in favour of that." *No freakin' way!*

"You think they'd mind?"

"Well, possibly. Yes." *Most definitely yes!*

"Is it the topless issue you think they'd have a problem with?"

She can't imagine what her neighbours would say if they were to come home and find a mermaid perched in the centre of her yard. Would they think she'd gone bonkers? Would there be letters to City Hall, to the mayor, to the *Sentinel*?

"No. No, it's not the nudity. It's just not, you know . . ." *This simply can't happen.*

"But you do like mermaids, don't you, Penny?"

"In parks, yes." *In children's books, fine. Cher, in that movie. All good.*

"Perhaps in your back yard?"

"No, not in my front yard and not in my back yard." It is dawning on Penny that this guy might not be the right gardener for this project. "It's just that it's a bit too bold for what I'd want."

"But don't you want to be bold? Don't you like fantasy? Taking a space and transforming it?"

The tea seems to have worked, because despite the mounting heat, Penny has stopped sweating. Her mind, however, is racing.

"I think I have more of a traditional garden in mind. Some perennials, some annuals, and some overall tidying and maintenance."

"But I have a vision! Can't you picture it?"

"I'm afraid I can." Penny's stomach has dropped and she is wondering how she can possibly extricate herself from this pending nightmare.

"How about I trim the laurel bush, fix and paint the back fence, reseed the lawn, fix up the pathway to the porch, and put in new plants that will flower year-round?" A large smile creeps across his face.

Penny stares at him a moment, then feels an overwhelming sense of relief. "That's exactly what I want! Were you pulling my leg?"

"I hate kitsch! I hate gnomes! I hate people who prune their bushes into the shape of animals!"

"Aaron Taylor! You're awful!"

"And Penelope Stevens, you're so sweet. You should have seen your face!"

"You should be an actor. You really had me going there."

"Well, the sad part is that I have actually had jobs where the client *has* wanted that kind of thing, and I've had to maintain my composure and nod, and then, when it's all said and done, they paid me handsomely for it. There's no accounting for taste."

"Oh my." Penny is relieved but wonders if this young man plays this prank on other customers too.

"I was teasing you, Penelope, but I meant what I said. You have to be clear and strong with these people. Myself included. You need to be able to draw the line and say no when somebody is trying to force something on you. You're so nice. I can see that. But people can be aggressive on projects like these. I want you to speak up when you don't like something, okay?"

Penny's sense of dread rears its head again. "I'm starting to think that getting my life 'renovated' is going to be a bigger thing than I imagined. You know, when

Linda first asked me, I said no. And she really used the word 'vision,' too! I should have listened to my gut."

"It will be fine as long as you stay focused on what you want. It'll be great. Really."

"I guess. Just don't do that again, okay?" Aaron bows penitently before her and Penny can feel herself blushing. She turns to gather the tray and busy herself so she can hide her face. Aaron helps her with the cups and follows her inside. The air is thick in the kitchen. She is blushing now at the thought of having such a hunk in her house, and then she blushes again at the thought of blushing. *For God's sake, get a hold of yourself, Penny!* Thankfully Aaron gives no indication that he has noticed Penny's awkwardness.

"Okay, so . . . when will you be coming back and starting the work?"

"I'll get in touch with Linda. The place has got to be photographed first, and we'll have to finalize our plans."

"Sure. Sure."

"Well, thanks for the tea. It hit the spot, but I've got to run. I'm due out in Caulfield in a half-hour."

They head outside and soon they are standing by his truck. Aaron tosses his notes through the open window onto the passenger seat.

"Are you sure I can't convince you about the mermaid? Could be very cool."

"Unequivocally no. How's that?"

"Perfect."

Before he can climb into his truck, a car horn honks three times.

"Hellooooo!"

It's Linda.

"Well, speak of the devil." Aaron gives Penny a wink.

"Good morning, you two! Oh, is it still morning?" Linda looks a bit frazzled for once. She explains that she had intended to come earlier but had gotten entangled in rescheduling some contractors.

Aaron checks his watch. Penny can see it is eleven forty-five. "You still have fifteen minutes."

"Oh, if I could just wake up every morning to you!" Linda grabs Aaron's face in both her hands and gives him a kiss on the lips. "You look more handsome every day! It's not fair!" She slaps him playfully.

"And you look simply marvellous, Linda." He takes a step back from her and considers her more closely. "New colour? I like it."

"You don't think it has too much red in it?" Linda gives her locks a toss.

"Not at all. Very sexy."

Penny wonders if they kiss and talk like this all the

time. Linda can't seem to keep her hands off him, but he doesn't seem to mind.

"Now, Penny, didn't I score you a beefcake hunk of a gardener!" Linda turns to Penny with one arm draped over Aaron's shoulder. Again Penny can feel redness coming into her face. Even her ears feel hot, and she doesn't know what to say.

Aaron shrugs like he's heard this a few times before. "Well, ladies, I leave you to talk about whatever it is you ladies like to talk about."

"As a matter of fact, we have very important business to discuss concerning a very new beauty product that us gals simply can't go without." Linda is digging in her handbag and pulls out a tube of lipstick. "Voila! Non-surgical collagen organic handmade lipstick!"

"Okay, I'm outta here." He starts his truck and Linda has to yell over the engine.

"Let me try it on you!"

"No thanks. It's not my colour."

"It guarantees to puff up your lips and make you a better kisser in minutes."

"Bye-bye, ladies."

Linda and Penny stand in silence at the end of her driveway and watch his arm wave goodbye until he turns the corner and is out of sight. The opened but unused lipstick is sweating in the sunlight.

"God. It should be a crime to be that good-looking, don't you think?" Linda muses.

"Definitely," Penny agrees. It's approaching thirty-five degrees. "Let's get out of this heat. I can offer you some lemonade." She's still thirsty after the tea.

"That would be great."

Inside the house, Penny feels Linda's critical eye checking out every nook and cranny.

"I guess I'll have to give you a tour."

"We can do that later. I'll be coming by in a few days with a camera crew because, of course, we have to photograph everything before we start anything. People really love to see the before-and-afters. Johnson will be there. He'll be able to give you some ideas of what he could do to make the space work better for you. The interior decorator, Charlie, will also be there. She's awesome—really nice person. And of course Aaron will be back. Heather, your personal trainer, might be there too. And me, of course!"

"Gosh, that's an awful lot of people for just one person."

"Nonsense."

"I'm sorry I'm being so nervous, Linda. It's just that I feel like I'm going to be exposed, you know. I'm not used to being the centre of attention, and now everybody's going to be privy to what's in my house and my garden, what I eat, what I shouldn't eat, and what colour I dye my hair."

"Oh, Penny, you watch too much TV!"

It's settled. Penny makes a mental note that tonight she is going to sit herself down in front of the TV and watch as many improvement shows as she can. She is going to take the gardener's advice and make sure she is up for the challenge.

Again, Linda is digging around in her handbag. She pulls out the tiniest cellphone and without dialling, begins to bark at it.

"*Sentinel*," she says in a commanding tone. Nothing is happening with the phone as far as Penny can tell, and Linda sighs and repeats her line. "*Sentinel*."

Penny motions to Linda that her lemonade is ready. She has already drunk half her glass and tops it up while watching the woman in her kitchen struggle with her phone.

"Damn phone!" Linda takes a sip of her lemonade and again repeats, "*Sentinel*." There is a brief pause, and

Penny can hear an automated voice say something back to Linda.

"Shut up!" Linda yells at her phone and snaps it closed as if to stop it from yelling back at her. "I hate these phones! God!"

Penny's phone is in clear view, but somehow she senses Linda's commitment to triumph over this technological glitch. After a few more aborted attempts, she can stand it no longer.

"Do you want to use my phone?" It is a beige model from the 1980s that still has a cord on it. Penny's mother always refuses to use the cordless one when she visits. She's certain they give you cancer.

"Jesus! You'd think that if you spent a couple hundred dollars on a phone and pay fifty bucks a month in fees that the stupid thing would work! Is that too much to ask?"

Penny doesn't say anything but nods sympathetically.

Linda gives it one more try. "*Sentinel.*" The two ladies stare at each other until the voice comes on again, prompting Linda to speak very loudly and deliberately: "SEN-TI-NEL!"

Penny feels her stomach tightening into knots. Of course, the voice comes on again.

All of this reminds her that technology and common sense don't always go hand in hand. Just last week she spent the better part of a day on the phone with an Internet support techie trying to figure out how to "de-porn" and "de-spam" her e-mail account. She's heard enough about Viagra and penile erectile dysfunction to last a lifetime. Being designated the office Luddite was awkward, but sometimes it's just easier to keep life simple. *Just dial the bloody number!*

"I have the number for the *Sentinel*." She avoids Linda's gaze, as she does not want to see her expression when she realizes that Penny still has a rotary phone. It's a good thing, too, because the cordless is always getting lost. She dials the number and hands the receiver to Linda. "Here, it's ringing."

Linda takes hold of the receiver as if she doesn't know what to make of such a foreign yet quaint object. "Hi there, it's Linda calling . . . Yes? . . . No, I won't be able to make that, but tell them I can do it for Monday or Tuesday . . ."

Penny toys with the lipstick Linda has handed over. It is a nice enough colour, so she disappears into the bathroom to apply it. Immediately she feels a tingling sensation and remembers Linda claiming it would puff up her lips. *So far so good, but will it make me a better kisser?*

One of the bathroom light-fixture bulbs is out, so it is a bit dim as she takes in her reflection in the mirror. Despite all the excitement of the morning and the fact that her hair is springing every which way, Penny feels energized and a little bit hopeful. She can hear that Linda is no longer on the phone.

"So, what do you think? Is it me?" Penny poses in the entranceway to the kitchen and gives her best pouty model look.

"Not bad. They've got only a few colours, but it really does something to your lips. Can you feel anything?"

"It's tingling, that's for sure. When does it stop? The tingling, I mean."

"Oh, it'll stop soon. Do you like the colour?" Linda's face is right up to her lips, inspecting closely.

"I feel like I've been to the dentist, except it's only my lips. Am I drooling?" The sensation is growing stronger and more intense. Penny feels like her lips are going to explode. "What's this stuff made of, anyway?"

"Oh, fruit and cinnamon, peppermint, some sort of organic mineral. And that one's strawberry flavour. It's all handmade locally, and the stars from Hollywood are all banging the doors down to get a hold of this product. What do you think?"

"I think I need some ice!" Penny goes to the freezer and grabs a tray of frozen cubes. "My lips are on fire!"

"Wow. I've never seen it do that to anybody." Linda is impressed.

Without thinking, Penny has taken out two ice cubes and put one on her top and one on her bottom lip. For a split second there is relief. A split second after the first second, she realizes that her lips are frozen to the ice.

"You should have rinsed the ice cubes first," Linda says, prompting Penny to want to throttle her.

She ducks her head under the kitchen faucet and rinses her lips under lukewarm water. Forty-five seconds later, she is still aware of the pain in her lips, but at least the ice cubes are gone.

"Are you okay?" asks Linda.

She nods.

"Can I see your lips?"

Penny has covered up her mouth with both hands. "It hurts," she muffles through her palms. Slowly she takes her hands away.

"Wow! Your lips really do look bigger, though." Linda is an optimist.

"Well, they're bloody well killing me!" Penny is a pessimist.

Linda tells her not to worry and that it's all part of the journey.

"What journey? The one where my lips fall off?"

"I can see you're anxious, but I want you to embrace these new experiences. I want you to enjoy the process."

"Well, this little process was not enjoyable. I can tell you that." Penny licks at her swollen lips and marvels at the audacity that she should welcome this pain into her life.

Linda furrows her brow and nods sympathetically. "Come here," she motions with outstretched arms, and for a fleeting second Penny thinks she is going to give her a hug. Instead, Linda takes hold of Penny's shoulders and marches her into the small bathroom. "Look at yourself, Penny Stevens. Really take a long, hard look at the person you see. Now love that person. Tell her she is beautiful and wonderful."

Penny nods at her reflection in the mirror, but Linda doesn't loosen her grip. Penny absolutely does not want to articulate these affirmations here in this cramped little room with the beauty consultant. She wants to cool her lips.

As there is no proclamation forthcoming, Linda gives one final squeeze and releases Penny from her clutches.

"I have to get going, but I'll be back in a few days with the camera crew. This is all going to be so exciting." Linda takes a moment to reapply some of her own lipstick and fluff her hair. Satisfied with her efforts, she turns to Penny. "In the meantime, I want you to spend some time visualizing your goals."

"Like bigger lips?"

"Remember, it's *your* journey." Linda turns on her heel and swirls out of the small room.

"But I don't know where I'm going." Penny follows her across the foyer to the front door.

"It'll be fine. And Penny?" Linda turns at the bottom of the porch steps and flashes a wide smile.

"Yes?"

"Your lips look awesome!"

Project Penny—a life under renovation!
Sunday, August 3
Mitch Williams

Staff at the Sentinel are thrilled to be a part of Project Penny. Wednesday's paper ran the story of Good Samaritan Penny Stevens, who retrieved $220,000 from atop an Oldsmobile owned by Mr. and Mrs. Samuel Jenkins.

Ms. Stevens did not hesitate to do what many of us hope we would do given the same situation. In a world where crimes are committed every day, it is refreshing to be able to report such a kind act. And the staff at the Sentinel wanted to give something back to Penny Stevens, their co-worker, a 40-year-old financial columnist with whom they have worked over the past years.

The project, headed by Linda Campbell, will follow Ms. Stevens as she embarks on a total life overhaul.

Initially, readers can expect to see weekly columns as Ms. Stevens embarks on her lifestyle journey. Further along, as the project evolves, Dalton Horne, staff photographer, will provide before and after photos of all facets of Project Penny.

"We are going to transform Penny from the inside out!" exclaims the beauty contributor. As some of you may recall, Ms. Campbell recently spearheaded the launch of Make Me Better!, a service she calls "a pick-me-up for companies large and small." She recently did a staff makeover for the employees of the now defunct Beach Hut. "When you look good, you feel better. And when you feel better, well, everything's better. Those gals looked just fabulous that day!" Ms. Campbell did hair and makeup for over a dozen workers at the longtime West Vancouver eatery, which unfortunately had to close earlier this month. Many customers complained upon hearing the news that the lease was not being renewed.

"It was pretty sad to see the Beach Hut close," concurred Ms. Campbell, "but they'll always have that memory of looking great, and now they have the skills to do it themselves. It's awesome, it's life-changing!"

Heather McCann, fitness coach and personal trainer, who recently completed the Vancouver marathon with a personal best of 3 hours, 34 minutes, will collaborate with the beauty consultant.

Also joining the team will be a landscape architect and a home-renovation specialist.

Look for Project Penny updates in our Home and Life section to keep abreast of Penny's progress.

We wish her the best of luck.

Eight

Living in a wealthy, conservative neighbourhood has its advantages. Professional middle-class people tend to be quiet and keep to themselves. As a rule, people go to work, raise their families, and take vacations in the summer. Wild parties rarely occur, and if they do they are immediately dealt with and fines are imposed. There are restrictions on how messy one's yard can be and even bylaws for the amount of smelly odours a restaurant may produce. With all these rules, however, nothing extraordinary tends to happen.

All in all, it is a beautiful place to live. Rich, clean, tasteful, and predictable.

Penny has lived here her entire life. For the first twenty-two years, she lived with her parents three blocks up and five streets over, at Kings and 19th. For the past eighteen years, she has lived here at Haywood and 14th with her husband. She likes the fact that whoever designed the neighbourhood was logical, that the avenues progress in alphabetical order from the waterfront to the mountaintop, and that the streets continue numerically from right to left. This has always made Penny feel secure. Grounded. Yes, life has been predictable, but that is how she has wanted it to be.

These last few weeks, however, have been entirely hectic and chaotic.

Over a dozen times she has submitted herself to Heather, not including the initial goal-setting meeting. On that first day she had to do the requisite weigh-in, and Heather also measured her height. In addition to these basic details, more in-depth specifics were required. Her chest was measured, as was her waist. Each individual thigh was charted to within a millimetre. Her left was smaller than her right.

"How many inches do you think you're going to lose, Penny?" Heather was busy filling in her chart with all these numbers and statistics.

"I'm only five-foot-two. I've got nothing to lose!" Penny remembers saying.

Of course she has since learned that one of her goals is to lose about twelve inches from various parts of her anatomy. Another goal is to reduce her body mass index, which seemingly was calculated by squeezing excess folds of her flesh between digital metal tongs. Good fun it was.

And if that wasn't enjoyable enough, the exercise has been the equivalent of condoned torture. She's waiting for the so-called endorphins to kick in, but so far that hasn't happened.

And then there has been Linda. Every single day.

"Hiya! How's my shiny new Penny today?" Right from the start Linda was gung-ho.

"Sore."

"Are you visualizing, Penny? You know that you're not going to get there if you don't see it. If you don't believe it."

And Penny was trying. Hard. But she also reasoned that having people like Linda and Heather on board more than made up for her lack of enthusiasm and inability to perceive a thinner, tauter, and totally pumped shell of her former self. At this point it was still only a mirage to Penny. To her handlers, however, it was a reality, and Penny was pretty sure that even if she didn't "believe" it quite the way Linda and Heather did, she was going to get there—whether she wanted to or not.

"Here. Check these out." Linda had brought over half a dozen large binders with material and wallpaper and coordinating paint samples. "Start conceptualizing your new space."

More visualizing for Penny. She didn't tell them how long it had taken her to choose the colour for her bedroom. And all the free makeup samples that Linda dropped off every day—creams and concealers and foundations. If she followed the instructions by the rules, she would be hidden under three layers of products. And that's not even including the eyeliner, which she has yet to apply in a smooth line, or the expensive eyeshadows that are supposed to be used all four shades at the same time on each eye.

"Explore and play with them all. Get a feel for each product and fantasize your new look."

Visualize again.

Every night before bed, Penny does just that. She slathers on the foundation and sets it with puffs of powder. She pencils in her brows and lines her lips. She uses every colour of the rainbow for her eyes, and when it looks odd she adds some more. When there is nothing more to apply, she hits the dimmer switch and steps back from the mirror.

Visualize.

Try as she might, Penny simply can't conjure up anything other than a clown. The thought of any- body seeing her like this is impossible, and she washes her face, scrubs away all the traces and pigments of her painting. She doesn't have a knack for decorating her- self. That is apparent.

And yet she keeps on trying. There is something possible about this impossible situation that Penny Stevens, Good Samaritan, has found herself in. She just isn't sure what it is yet.

And if the intrusion of Team Penny wasn't shock enough, the doorbell and the phone haven't stopped ringing.

"Hi, I'm So-and-So, and I'd like to make an appoint- ment to discuss this and that about your house, your garden, your wardrobe, your being . . ."

"Hi, hope I'm not calling too late (too early) . . . I just read about you in the *Sentinel*. We should get together for coffee . . ."

Every time Penny opens the door or picks up the receiver, she has to brace herself. Suddenly people are interested in her. They want to know "how she is doing."

They want to know "what is going on." The once quiet and unassuming little Penny has been thrust into the limelight. She's an instant celebrity. People want to know about her, and most are more fascinated with Penny's renovation than she is herself. Nobody's ever been fascinated with her life before, and somehow this public preoccupation with it seems ridiculous to her.

"This one lady wanted to know if I'm on a lactose-restricted diet." Today Penny is on high alert. Johnson and the woman from that designer show are scheduled to come and assess the damage, so to speak. And Penny is feeling particularly nervous.

"Are you?" Jack doesn't look at his wife, as he seems to be deeply involved in an article about violence in hockey and salary caps for players.

"Lucy in publicity wants to know if I'm going to try hot yoga. I haven't spoken more than two words to her since last year's Christmas party." The coffee machine beeps to signal that it is ready.

"I see." He is not a fan of hockey, but he keeps his head down.

"The other day at the checkout, the cashier gave me the latest *People* magazine and told me to look on page 101. She even dog-eared it for me. Told me to check out the haircut on Renée Zellweger." Penny has to bend down because the half-and-half is on the back bottom shelf, obscured by a box of soy pudding that Heather, diet and drill sergeant extraordinaire, dropped off the other day. When she opened it up, Penny gagged. Regardless of how healthy the stuff might be, there was no way she was going to get any of this slop down her gullet.

"You should have seen the cashier's hair! It was twisted up with one of those claw clamps that say to the world, 'Hey, I'm too busy to even attempt to style my hair, so I'll just attach this plastic contraption and hope no one notices . . .' Meanwhile, she's an expert on celebrity hair! God, people have a nerve!"

"They do indeed." Jack folds up the paper and checks his watch.

"Yesterday Susan called me up and asked if I'd heard of colonic cleansing. A friend of hers did it. Said it was apparently 'amazing.' Told me I should try it. Do I look like someone who should cleanse their colon?" Penny's vocal cords are constricting, and her voice is notching up a register.

"Gosh, look at the time, Pen." It is eight thirty-five. He rarely leaves for the office before eleven o'clock.

"Are you off this early?"

"Yes. Yes, I am. Things to do and papers to sign."

"Well, I think that contractor guy is coming by later. Maybe you should be here when we start making plans. I really have no idea about this stuff, Jack."

"Sorry, but I've got to meet with someone."

"Call them and tell them you'll be in a bit later." She never meddles with his schedule, but things are heating up and she feels overwhelmed and outnumbered by these people. "Who is it?"

"Who is what?"

"The person you're meeting with."

"Oh, Joe. That's who I'm meeting."

Her husband was never a clever liar. His brilliance lies in speaking the truth and going about his business utterly unaware of the effects on those around him. He'd be the kind of guy who gets caught holding a smoking gun only to reply, "Geez, you got me. Well, I'm hungry. What are we having for lunch?"

"Phone him and tell him the situation."

"Who?"

"Joe! For Heaven's sake, Jack! Have you heard anything I've said?" She stares at the man in front of her. He is physically here but mentally already out the door.

"I'm late already, Penny. You do what you think best. Just no weird stuff. No homo colours. No flowers in my den. That's all I can really think of."

She wagers he hasn't really heard a word she said.

Penny watches Jack climb into his SUV and disappear. A few minutes after he has driven off, she is still standing in the same spot in her kitchen, looking out the window across the front lawn. She can't find her agenda book and begins to question what's on today's program. She wrote it down. She's pretty sure it is the interior contractor guy, or did he reschedule? Didn't Linda say something about a later date? That she'd have more time to do some "envisioning." Will it be Johnson with his tape measure? Will it be Heather with her calorie counter and her stopwatch? She doesn't think Aaron is due to arrive today, but maybe Linda will pop in with another "must-have" lipstick or eyeshadow or pair of capris. Was it Saturday that the one called Charlie came by with the Ikea catalogue? She was big into storage and seemed excited about throwing things out. The second half of Penny's coffee has gotten cold, so she dumps it out. Charlie would be so proud.

The phone rings. It's Heather. Turns out she's the one who should be coming over today, but there is a change of plans.

"How about I meet you at the gym?" asks the perky voice. It is more of a statement than a question.

Heather is "petite," but everything about her seems big. Her enthusiasm is great and her muscles are huge. Her perpetual smile is wide and even her teeth look large. She is always pumped and ready to "go for it!" If you look at her closely, you might even say that her head is too big for her petite body, but maybe it's just all that curly dark hair that cascades down her tanned and sculpted shoulders. She is Penny's personal coach, and she is here to kick her ass.

"We're going to the gym again?" The only parts on Penny's body that are not sore are her earlobes and the tip of her nose.

"We have to step up the schedule here because our readers will want to see results! We can't let them down!" After the last article quite a few people wrote in with questions and comments. Heather had a number of new clients sign up, and she is eager that Project Penny be a triumph. "There's a cardio class starting in one hour, and then I want to do some weight training with you."

"I can barely walk."

"Step up to the plate, Penny." She is always talking like this. Telling her not to "drop the ball" or to "get into the zone" or to "make the connection."

"But I can't drive. I don't feel safe using the pedals."

She can hear herself whining and feels like she is five years old, not wanting to let go of her mother's hand.

"Face the music, Penny! You have to make the commitment and then the results will follow."

Penny wonders how Heather's other victims are faring with all the pep talk and pressure. She's mentioned quite a few success stories, likely wanting to spur Penny on. Is Heather this intense with all of them? Does she harass the others the same way? Or is Penny just special?

"I'm really sore and incredibly tired, Heather. Could we do this tomorrow maybe?"

"Tomorrow is always a day away, my friend. There is no time like the present. I'll pick you up in fifteen." Click.

Penny has always been in awe of people like Heather. Pushy yet focused. Some might say she was bossy, but Heather would answer that she was "results oriented." Penny may think she is irritating, but Heather would maintain that she is "motivational."

When she bends her aching body into the passenger seat of Heather's bright red convertible Mustang blaring techno-pop music, Penny decides that she quite simply hates this woman.

"I hate you." The hot August air is madly blowing her frizzy hair and Heather's luscious locks every which way.

"What's that?"

"Nothing," says Penny, but inside she is happy she said it. She feels lighter.

The fitness club is a massive property that is forever undergoing renovations. There are three separate gyms, and yoga and Pilates studios and saunas and whirlpools and a regular-sized kidney-shaped pool that offers aqua-fit classes.

The first visit, Penny managed to run—or, rather, stumble quickly—on the treadmill for twelve-and-a-half long minutes. It was supposed to be a twenty-minute jog, but the lungs and legs and soul gave out on poor Penny.

"We can work with that. No problem. Good effort, Penny. Good effort." Heather had been kind that first day, jotting down her time and achievement in her file and smiling encouragingly. On subsequent visits, however, it became apparent that Penny ought to be overcoming these limitations, and when she approached the ten-minute mark, Heather would move in to coax her on.

"Come on, Penny. You can do it! Go, girl. Go! Go! Go!"

Penny kept looking straight ahead, holding tightly onto the bars, willing Heather to stop with all the cheer-leading and pushing and goading.

"I . . ." Penny momentarily lost the ability to speak.

"Yes! Yes! Go! Go!" Heather, on the other hand, was never at a loss for words.

Maybe this is the norm for a personal coach. Penny doesn't know. It certainly is turning out to be a weird partnership. It isn't like any relationship she's ever had before. At least not willingly. When she was bullied back in school, that was different. She's agreed to all of this.

After the fifth attempt, when she broke through the fifteen-minute level, Heather let out a scream and Penny almost fell off the treadmill.

"Yes! Yes!"

Penny held on that day, clinging to the machine with equal parts shock and determination, and managed to remain upstanding until the machine blinked and congratulated her: *WORKOUT COMPLETE. WELL DONE!*

Heather was beaming and Penny was delirious.

Since receiving that gold star, Penny has hit all the machines in the circuit. She's climbed and lunged and run and skied. The elliptical trainer might have been her favourite, as she felt like she was literally bouncing along. Next week Heather wants to take her to a new studio, where she will attempt non-gravitational yoga.

Presently Penny is toiling on a stair climber set on level "beginner." When she progresses and gets really proficient at this exercise, Heather tells her, she can set it at "random" or "cross-train." When she is really advanced, she can program it to "challenge." She doubts that she'll get that far. She can't tell what levels other people are at because they tend to drape their towels over the computer screens. Others hide this information with their books or magazines, which really amazes Penny—that anybody could even focus on reading anything while grappling with these climbing contraptions. It's all she can do to stay upright and conscious.

Penny was supposed to have gone into an aerobic step class, but unfortunately the instructor was a no-show, so Heather has opted for this workout instead. A few people say hello to Heather, as she is also a trainer here. Others nod at Penny because they have noticed the articles in the paper and consider her public property.

"You're Penny Stevens!" a lady exclaimed fifteen minutes ago in the change room.

Penny is amazed that people are amazed that she is who she is. It's not really that exciting. She has always been who she is, but now it seems that who she's always been isn't enough anymore. Despite the fact that humans are creatures of habit, everybody is screaming for change. For "new and improved."

Just yesterday Linda asked her what colour she was thinking of for her "new look."

At first she didn't know if she was talking about clothes or the colour for her walls or, God forbid, another lipstick.

"Your hair, silly!" Linda was forever changing her own hair. Right now it was a deep reddish brown. Last month it was strawberry blonde. Last year's Christmas party she straightened her hair and dyed it jet black. If somebody held a gun to Penny's head, she couldn't truthfully say what colour it naturally is. Maybe even Linda has forgotten.

"Do I have to dye my hair? I mean, I don't have any grey hairs, do I?" She was fortunate. At forty, she still had no stray greys anywhere. Just light brown. The colour she was born with.

"Colour is the number-one thing that can really change your look."

It was apparent that change was coming.

"But then once I become a blonde I'll always have to deal with my brown roots, right?"

"So? You'll be a blonde."

"But then I'll always have that problem. Right now I don't have roots, so why should I change my hair?"

"Look, just tell me what sort of colour you want to

be, and I'll pick out a great one," Linda said, as if Penny were a child. "You don't want to stay that mousy brown."

Penny had to think only a second. "I want to be nondescript brown."

Linda had to think only two seconds. "Okay, we'll go for highlights."

So it was decided that next week she, Linda, and somebody else whose name she has forgotten will go into the big city somewhere "for her hair." Dalton has even booked a photo session. Why they can't find a salon on the North Shore is not for Penny to question. Anybody who is anybody goes over the bridge to see their "stylist." Penny, of course, goes to where there is no lineup.

Thankfully, the stair climber beeps and tells her that she has travelled 4.2 kilometres, that she has burned 190 calories.

"Good job, Penny! Good. Good. Good. Here, hydrate!" Heather is in action with positive accolades and H_2O in a bottle that reads BELIEVE.

"I can't believe I did that." She is panting so hard she can barely speak.

"Well, you did, girl. Drink some water." Heather fills in another column on her chart.

The idea of swallowing anything but oxygen is not appealing to Penny in any way. She is standing on the ground now but still holding onto the stair-climber handles with both hands. She feels her heart beating out of the side of her neck. Sweat is pouring down her forehead, making it difficult to see. Also, she doesn't like being called "girl."

"I think I'm going to throw up."

"Let's call it a day, Penny."

"Let's." Penny offers up a silent prayer of thanks that Heather seems to have forgotten all about the weights she had planned for today. And no mention of stretching either. *This is my lucky day!*

Then she sees a young man sporting an ungodly tan and a six-pack coming over to talk to her personal coach. He looks like he could be another trainer, or perhaps a friend of Heather's. She smiles to herself as she makes her retreat. She used to think a guy with a six-pack had a beer belly.

There are stairs leading down to the showers and lockers, and Penny's legs can barely navigate the steps. It's almost more treacherous doing this than the workout, and she takes care to hold onto the banister as she descends. She doesn't trust her balance.

Her key is tied onto her shoelace, but she is scared to bend over and remove it for the time being. Instead, she sits for ten minutes on a bench and sips at her water and contemplates the many different shapes and sizes and colours of individuals that come into and leave the change room.

Not everybody is perfectly thin. Not everybody is young and energetic and perky. A couple of middle-aged ladies maybe ten years older than Penny emerge from the steam room. They speak in some Eastern European accent and, except for the damp towels in their hands, are totally naked.

Penny instinctively wants to avert her eyes. First, because in North America it is rude to stare at naked people. Second, because there is a lot of flesh here. She regards her own fleshy knees and big bosom and wonders if she'd ever have the nerve to prance around naked in a public change room.

The ladies get fresh towels and disappear into the showers. Shortly after, they reappear smelling of apple shampoo and fresh soap. Penny can't understand what they are talking about as they produce huge white reinforced bras from their gym bags. Leaning forward, they manoeuvre their breasts into the bras. They sit down and take a breath before they hoist their specialty-sized underwear over their hips. It is a relief when they are finally clothed.

After they leave, she forces herself to get up and into the shower. She moves slowly and deliberately because she is severely fatigued. Her heart has calmed down and the red blotches have disappeared from her face, but she feels like she has just run a gauntlet, and she can only think about getting home and crawling into bed.

Penny doesn't bother drying her hair or applying any moisturizer to her face. When she finally drags herself back upstairs, she finds Heather chatting with a few other aerobics instructors and personal trainers, as well as the buff Adonis.

"Penny! There you are!"

"Can we go now?"

"Let's just do a quick weigh-in." There is a digital scale right by the entrance, where presumably really keen or really depressed clients can weigh themselves as they leave.

"Not today, Heather." Penny is moving toward the doors.

"Seize the day!" Perhaps Heather is not used to her clients saying no, or maybe she wants to impress her co-workers. At any rate, she blocks Penny's exit and stands with her hands upon her hips. Penny thinks she looks like a female Yul Brynner.

"No."

"What?" Heather is taken aback.

"I'm tired. I just want to go home."

"It'll only take a sec. Big article next week, and you've really been working hard. Here, give me your bag."

"Please, Heather, I'm not into it." She senses that the other instructors are looking a little uncomfortable.

"Come on, Penny! Get with the program and you'll see results!"

"No." Because she is so tired, Penny remains quite calm.

"Penny! Don't say no, embrace yes!"

"No."

Heather appears incapable of reading the situation.

"Why don't you stand on the scale, Heather, and add one hundred pounds. I'll wait for you in the car."

As Penny steps around Heather, still frozen in place with her mouth open, she glimpses a photo of two obese, smiling women with their arms around each other, and Penny recognizes the ladies from the change room. The caption reads, "Congratulations, Elena and Katja! One hundred pounds and counting!"

Heather doesn't play any music on the way back, but she still puts the roof down for the short ten-minute drive. The hot breeze blows Penny's hair dry in no time. It must be nearing thirty degrees, but it feels wonderful to stretch her hands up overhead, to feel the warm winds kiss her arms and face.

She thinks about Elena and Katja and wonders about their story. *Who are they? Where are they from? Will I see them again?* Then she thinks about herself and her story. Why she feels so reluctant to fully participate and buy into her own "life renovation."

She thinks of the plans she had all those years ago. For her and Jack. For their life together. When they bought the house, she had big dreams. It was going to be wonderful. Everything was going to be great. And then she stopped dreaming. All the hopes for the old house were shelved, put away. And it wasn't because it couldn't be done. She could have paid somebody to do it—they had the money.

And all the ambitions she had had for herself slipped away too. She likes writing for the paper, but it isn't exactly what she set out to do. She had wanted to go back to university. Get a Commerce degree. Penny liked going to school, and she was bright. She could have done it, but she didn't.

Instead, she chose to remain in her big house and change nothing. Now, with all this recent goal-setting and targets to aim for, Penny is coming to realize just how adamantly she has been committed to never altering a single iota of her unhappy life. It even feels like an inconvenience to have to admit that, yes, she has been remiss, letting the world slip by her. It's been easier to blame it on "life." On Jack. On her parents, for giving her inferior genes. This way Penny doesn't have to take any responsibility. She doesn't have to own up to her part in all of this.

And the two ladies at the gym—Elena and Katja. They could have given up, resigned themselves. But they didn't. They even seemed joyful.

All these thoughts are swirling around Penny's head as Heather's car speeds her homeward. Penny's glad she didn't give up on the treadmill last week. She's tired, but the sun is shining and crazy Heather is here, guiding Penny onwards. Maybe the endorphins are finally making an appearance. Coming out of the gym and into the sunlight has triggered something in Penny. She watches Heather drain the last of her fruit smoothie and hopes she hasn't let her down. She reminds herself that she *is* lucky as she gives Heather a smile.

Soon Penny will be in her kitchen. Maybe the carpenter will be there. Perhaps the gardener. She still doesn't know what colour her living room will be, but things are happening.

One day at a time. One day at a time. Maybe I can do this.

Heather asks if she wants her to put some music on.

"Sure." Some energetic band begins to sing about falling in love and letting go. "Turn it up." Penny is feeling much better.

"Okay." The music is belting out a steady rhythmic beat. Heather shakes her head and smiles.

"I love you!"

"What's that?" says Heather over the music.

"Nothing." But Penny is glad she said it. She feels lighter now.

Go, Penny, go!
Wednesday, August 13
Mitch Williams

"Back in the '80s it was Cardio! Cardio! Cardio! Now we have choice, and that is what I am offering to Penny. She is so sweet but often timid to try new things. If a person just does the exercise bike, then only those muscles are being worked. Why not try the elliptical trainer? Or the stair climber? Or the treadmill? And, of course, never forget the weight machines. It's a well-designed all-round circuit that is both cardio and strength. In addition, it's also nice to wind down with some Pilates to stretch those muscles out," says Heather McCann, fitness coach and personal trainer.

It's been over two weeks since Penny Stevens, our favourite Good Samaritan, embarked on her life renovation.

"I'm tired," Ms. Stevens admitted when I caught up with her on the Stanley Park seawall. She was doing a 10-k walk-run-jog-crawl while her ever-present trainer, Heather, biked alongside, motivating her to keep up the speed and visualize the goal.

"It's very important to have someone helping you along the journey. That's why all top athletes have coaches, and Penny is no exception. She needs to hear that she can do it. To help her aim high. Strive higher. And never give up."

Heather McCann has spent a total of about 15 hours with her new protégé. McCann says she can hardly wait for the upcoming photo shoot. "She is going to look and feel fabulous!"

If you happen to see Ms. Stevens at the local gym, park, or grocery store, make sure you give her your support. Likely she needs it.

Keep up the good work, Penny!

Nine

Penny no sooner says goodbye to Heather than she sees Charlotte come around from the back garden. "Oh, hello."

"Hi." Charlotte is wearing blue jeans and a white T-shirt and, despite the heat, heavy black ankle boots. Her dark brown hair is covered by a red bandana.

"I've just got back from the gym. I didn't realize you were coming today. Sorry. Have you been here long?"

Charlotte apparently doesn't feel the need for small talk and walks past Penny holding her bulging sports bag. "No."

"Is there something you need me to do? Do you want to come in?"

Charlotte shakes her head and continues on in the direction of her truck.

As if on cue, the front door opens. "Hellooooo!"

Penny spins around and sees Linda appear on the porch, one arm linked around Jack and the other waving a set of spare keys. "Look who the cat dragged in."

Jack is clearly not amused, and his smile looks painful.

"Heather snatched you up before I got a chance to swing by, so I thought to myself, where can that husband of hers be?" She is showing no sign of letting go of Jack. "So then I remembered . . . of course, Homelife! Then I had to do a little bit of sleuthing."

Jack just nods.

"He's a hard guy to pin down. I called everywhere. Finally that last gal said you were probably headed for lunch. And she was right! I had him paged at the country club."

None of this is news to Penny. He's never without his phone, but will blatantly ignore her calls. When she complains to him, he'll lie and tell her that he needed to charge the phone.

"Oh, honey," Penny offers up a concerned sympathy, "didn't you have your cell?"

"Batteries."

"Well, there it is." Penny turns to Linda.

"Anyhoo, had to twist this big fella's arm, but I got a second set of keys. Might come in handy in these next few days and weeks."

Jack is a security freak, and Penny thinks if he hadn't gone into real estate, he could have made a fine career in home protection. When they were first married, they lived for a couple of months in a monstrous pink apartment block right by the seawall. If she took the garbage down to the chute at the end of the hallway, she'd often traverse the thirty or so feet and return to find the door locked. Jack would insist it was all in the interest of safety. He was constantly backing up his computer files and doubling up on firewalls and Internet security. He didn't want pets, and at first Penny thought he might be allergic to them, but he confessed his greatest concern would be that the dog or cat might be stolen. He never left his car unlocked and never left a quarter visible in the change compartment. Thieves, he said, were everywhere.

"You gave Linda the spare keys?" Penny finds this incredible.

"Seems I had no choice in the matter."

Linda is glowing again with a kind of inner smirk that Penny has come to recognize as determined stubbornness hidden beneath a veil of unselfishness and kind-heartedness.

"I'll have you know, Linda, that Jack would never normally do this. I'm amazed I got my own pair." Penny looks at Jack, still trapped by Linda.

"Well, I have my ways," she teases and gives him one final squeeze before releasing him at last.

Jack shrugs and gives his most alluring grin, finally sensing an opportunity to extricate himself from the situation. "Ladies, I have to run. I now am really late." He jogs down the porch steps and crosses the lawn, barely avoiding a collision with Charlotte, who is carrying flattened cardboard boxes toward the house. Once in his SUV, he blows them kisses and speeds off.

"My goodness, Penny, that husband of yours is quite the charmer."

"So I'm told." She's heard that before, but she's never seen Jack so manipulated against his will. That Linda managed to bamboozle those keys is in some ways reassuring. Penny isn't the only one feeling out of sorts.

"Good day, Penelope." Aaron is pulling a huge blue tarp loaded with branches and leaves and wood across the yard.

"Aaron, hello!" *Is the entire gang here? God, I must look a sight!*

"Hot out today, hey?"

"Uh huh." Penny watches him take the garden hose and wet his hair. As the water trickles down, his T-shirt clings to his torso, leaving nothing to the imagination.

"Did you go to the gym?"

"Uh huh."

"Good. Want to come see what I've been up to?"

Penny detects a knowing smile flash over Linda's face.

"Sure. Coming." She leaves her gym bag on the porch and follows Aaron around back.

"I hope you don't mind, but I reorganized that pile of dirt. I'll put it all back if you don't like it."

Before Penny sees what he has done, she almost walks head-on into a bright orange, six-foot metal wall.

"Whoa!"

"Heads up, Penelope! Sorry about that. We should have mentioned this to you. It's not every day that a giant bin of this size appears in a person's back yard."

"What is . . . ?"

"Courtesy of Charlie." Aaron indicates Charlotte, who is presumably beyond the open door to the basement.

At the mention of her name, Charlotte sticks her head out. "Cheers."

"But this is really big. Are we going to fill this all up? Do I have this much junk?" Penny cannot fathom the necessity of a dumpster. She thought the renovation was about tidying up and sorting through a few things—not chucking half her life away.

"Come look at your new flowerbeds." Aaron leads her to an area where there used to be huge juniper bushes. "I transplanted one of them over there." He indicates a shady corner.

"This looks great." And it really does. There are some annuals and shrubs and what look to be perennials, but Penny can't concentrate with Charlotte rooting around in the rec room.

"You okay, Penelope?"

"Yeah. I mean, I thought I was." She gestures to the bin and the basement and the sounds emanating from within.

"Sounds like you need to talk to Charlie." Aaron probably is trying to reassure her, but the thought of having any sort of conversation with the woman is daunting. Charlotte doesn't even really speak. She must save up her words for that television show.

"Uh huh."

Linda appears with her purse and key ring, no doubt the spare set of keys already attached. "Gotta run, gang. Bye, Charlie. Talk to you tomorrow, Penny. Aaron, come give me a kiss, you're delicious!"

Aaron, T-shirt still damp, takes Linda into his strong arms, dips her, and plants one firmly on her perfectly frosted lips.

"Swoon." Linda sighs and leaves Penny staring, speechless.

Fifteen minutes later, Penny is feeling much better. Aaron was right. She needed to talk to Charlotte. And Penny was right, too. Charlie didn't have much to say. But she did listen.

"Uhm, Charlotte, can I have a word with you?"

"Charlie."

"Right. Charlie, I need to . . . I mean, all of this . . ." Penny indicated the little piles and boxes spread around the basement.

"Too fast?" Perhaps the clutter buster was picking up on Penny's reluctance.

"Yes. I think I need some time to sort through some of this stuff. I mean, I haven't gone through this in years. This is a big task . . . I'm feeling worried . . . I need time to . . ."

Charlie nodded.

"I think I need . . ."

Charlie nodded some more and Aaron looked on hopefully.

"I know it's a mess and a lot of it is junk and I need help and there is so much stuff here that I don't know where to start—"

"I'll stop."

"You will?" Penny was caught off guard. "Oh, that's great! Thank you. I appreciate your efforts, really. But I'm not . . . I'm not—"

"Not ready."

"No." Penny was quick to concur.

"Not yet." Charlie was quick to jump in.

"Yes, right."

At any rate, Penny had spoken up and put her foot down. And Aaron had watched her do it. Before he left, he complimented her.

"You asserted yourself, Penelope. Well done."

She loved that he didn't call her Penny. She did feel taller every time he said it, and when he was bidding her farewell, she secretly wished he'd take her into his arms and dip and kiss her too. Unfortunately, she wasn't assertive enough to demand his affections like Linda did.

One day at a time . . .

. . .

There are five messages blinking on her machine when Penny finally gets inside her house. One is from Johnson, who wants to come by in a day or two and asks if she has come to any decision yet regarding the living room and the built-in bookcase idea that he proposed yesterday. Another is from the office, reminding her of her deadline for this week's column. She hasn't even begun, so she instinctively reaches forward and erases the message. Two calls are from Susan, her high school friend who lives out in the valley with four kids. She desperately needs to go for lunch. Every once in a while she gets to the point where she phones Penny up and arranges a minimum three-hour therapy session at a local restaurant. The last time they went to Milestones at one o'clock. They ate lunch, and Penny listened to Susan complain about Doug, who is balding and a bit overweight, for what seemed like an eternity. He doesn't earn enough money. Their house is too small. They never go on vacations, and the kids are driving her crazy.

Five o'clock rolled around, and they were given dinner menus. By that time Susan had had three glasses of wine and had gone to the bathroom four times. Penny couldn't believe it when Susan ordered herself a Bellini and a chef's salad. Penny didn't order from the dinner menu. Instead she just had another coffee refill and glares of incredulity from her waitress. Well, she certainly got her money's worth on that day. She went to the bathroom seven times, as she recalls.

Penny'll have to call Susan back.

The last message is from a woman at her husband's office.

"Hi, Jack, this is, uhm, Jo. I waited for you at our, uhm, meeting today. I tried you a billion times on your cell, but you're not picking up. Could you call me?"

Penny thinks about erasing that message too, but at the last second she can't bring herself to do it. She plays it again. Of course, she's heard it all before. *Jo. Jolene. Didn't Jack mention something about a new secretary? Is she playful in pink?* Then Penny sees Jack's phone on the kitchen counter, plugged into an outlet. The batteries really were dead.

In the distance, a lawnmower is going. Penny looks at the clock, which reads 12:05. It is lunchtime, and suddenly she is hungry. Famished.

In the fridge there is some low-carb bread and a pre-made salad from a catering company that Heather has employed. She makes herself a sandwich and takes out the bowl of greens and low-fat dressing. A neighbour brought over a bunch of strawberries, so she decides to wash a few and slice them onto her salad. She had some strawberries this morning in her cereal and will have to finish this bunch up herself because Jack is highly allergic to them. They are ripe and delicious.

By 12:49, Penny has washed and dried the breakfast and lunch dishes. As tired as she was a few hours ago, she feels strangely invigorated after her salad and sandwich. Her mind is lucid.

She decides her time would be best spent writing her column. If she is focused and manages to get it finished before four o'clock, she can e-mail it to the office and get a quick visit in with her mother before dinner.

Upstairs, she retrieves the file folder titled "Summer." Last month she wrote about the pros and cons of paying down one's mortgage versus investing in mutual funds or maxing out RRSPs. In September, she plans to write about budgeting for the family vacation on a monthly basis, because a lot of people consider autumn the real start of the year. But this is August, and she doesn't have any set idea for her piece as of yet.

She keeps a file on previous topics she has written about as well as columns she has come across from other papers and magazines. Her readership is not very large or demanding. In a given year, she will grind out fifty-two very basic themes designed to cater to any level of investor or individual trying to make safe and straightforward choices about money management.

She decides she will write about saving for a rainy day. When she thinks about it, it hasn't rained in over thirty days. Forest fires are raging inland, and water levels are dangerously low. Normally, at the height of summer, Penny can water her lawn on even days. However, this year there is a total ban on watering of any kind. Of course, some people ignore these bylaws altogether. The Shermans across the street have a luscious green lawn and overflowing flowerbeds. And Aaron had to water the new plants and bushes. On the other extreme, there are people who follow these rules to a tee. The McBrides, a few houses down, have the brownest patch of grass on the block.

She decides to go ahead with the article and laughs to herself. Anyone who has lived through the four seasons in Vancouver would never believe there'd ever be any water shortage. One can always count on the rain in this neck of the woods. Yet water shortages are a threat, and any danger always makes good headlines. And there will always be people who claim that the sky is falling. She knows because people have been telling her this all her life. It's a good thing, too, because they tend to be the ones you can count on when it all does come crashing down.

Surprisingly, she writes the article in just under an

hour. It feels good when she presses the Send button. It is now a quarter to two, and Penny feels energized and uncharacteristically spontaneous.

Now where is that cordless phone? Penny couldn't part with her rotary, so Charlie moved it upstairs and installed a new phone with a built-in message machine for simplicity. She looks about the kitchen, on the table, on the chairs, on the shelf, and on the windowsill. Finally she finds the receiver on the telephone itself. On the same day that Johnson came by to measure for the shelves, Charlie came by and started in on her "clutter busting" and "clarifying" of Penny's "space." There is evidence of her handiwork all over the house, and Penny has to continuously ask herself, if something has gone missing, now, where would Charlie put that? It usually makes sense, but it feels like it is someone else's house.

She decides that she will give Susan a call.

"Hello?" Susan picks up before Penny can hear it ring.

"Hi, it's me, Penny. Wow, you were quick on the draw."

"What?" A child is crying in the background.

"You picked up fast."

"Who is this?"

"It's me, Penny."

Susan doesn't say anything.

"I'm returning your call."

"Wow, that was fast."

"What?" says Penny.

"I just called you."

"Yes, I know. And now I am calling you back." *Are all conversations with mothers this stupid?*

"So, what's up?"

"Well, you called me and you said something about going for lunch." She feels like she is on the defensive for having called. Maybe she has called at a bad time. Maybe she should have waited till tomorrow.

"Lunch? It's almost two." Susan sounds really wound up.

"I know. I just wanted to call and maybe set up a date some time this week if you can escape."

"If I don't escape I'm going to run away." The receiver drops onto something and Penny can hear Susan trying to reason with one of her kids. Finally she hears her scream, "Because I said so!" Then something inaudible from the child and then the sound of a door being slammed and then footsteps coming back to the phone. "Sorry about that."

She doesn't know what to say. "Oh, no problem."

"So, do you want to go for lunch?" Susan's voice and demeanour are suddenly impeccable, like she is booking for a business lunch.

"Yes. Definitely." Penny tries to lighten up the mood and adds, "Let's do lunch!"

"Two thirty?"

"What?" Penny is confused.

"Is two thirty too late?"

"For what?" She is still confused but doesn't want to upset an already upset person.

"For lunch."

"Lunch?"

"Do you or don't you want to go for lunch?"

Penny feels like she is in the witness stand and her friend is the prosecuting lawyer. "Sure I do." She recalls having had a lunch just over an hour ago, but this doesn't feel like the right time to mention that to Susan.

"Well, then, are we going to go, or are we just going to talk about it?"

"No. No. I mean, yes. Definitely, let's go."

"Where?" Susan would make a great attorney.

"Sorry. What?"

"Where do you want to go for lunch?" Susan sounds like she is going to blow.

"Uhm . . . just so that I'm getting things right here, are you wanting to go for lunch *today*, Susan? I mean, is that what you are saying?"

"What does it sound like I am saying? Could I be any clearer? Any more desperate? Are you or are you not going to have lunch with me?"

"You tell me where, Susan, and I will be there as fast as I can."

She can hear her friend beginning to cry and again the phone is put down, while Susan invariably rummages for tissue and blows her nose.

"Doug is coming home any minute. I called him and told him I was going to leave the kids if he didn't get his sorry ass home." She is crying fully now. "I love my kids, Penny."

"I know, Susan." She can hear the anguish in her friend's voice.

They decide to meet at the place that used to be called the Avalon. It has gone through about three resurrections and renovations and owners, but everybody still refers to it as "the place that used to be called the Avalon."

"Whoever gets there first orders a round of drinks." Susan has calmed down a bit. Her voice is steady now. "And Penny?"

"Yes?"

"Thanks."

Penny calculates that it will take Susan a full hour to drive in from Maple Ridge. It's weird that every time they meet for lunch Susan insists on coming over to North or West Vancouver. Penny would happily drive out her way, but Susan never wants to dine closer to her place. Perhaps it's because Susan still thinks of the North Shore as her turf. In the ten years she has lived out in the valley, she has never made the transition to actually calling it "home."

Still feeling full of energy, Penny quickly changes into a skirt and a rose-coloured linen blouse. She applies a bit of sunblock and foundation makeup to her face and adds a quick coat of mascara. She is about to put on a bit of lipstick when she realizes that she is holding the "killer" collagen tube in her hand. Her lips begin to hurt just thinking about it.

Without actually consciously formulating any plan, Penny looks at the clock on her bedside table. She looks at the lipstick in her hand. She has more than enough time to drop by the Homelife office.

• • •

Jack's office is located in the heart of Ambleside, where more than thirty realtors have been able to eke out an average income in the low six figures selling prime real estate to wealthy buyers. In recent months, however, house prices have been dropping and sales have declined dramatically. Jack has weathered the ups and downs of the market in the past and isn't too worried. Penny, however, thinks things are going to get worse before they get better. She's loath to take on any unnecessary debt, whereas Jack will urge clients to buy homes they can't really afford. It happened on a large scale south of the border, and if the American dream comes crashing down, the Canadian reality isn't too far behind.

A beautiful young receptionist asks Penny if she can be of any assistance.

"Is Jack Stevens in?"

"Can I ask your name?"

She squares her shoulders and sucks in her stomach. "Penelope Stevens."

"Oh. Oh, sure. Just give me a minute. I think he might be out with a client." Penny smiles and patiently waits while the girl pages Jack. Of course he doesn't have his cell, but she tracks the address and number of the residence Jack has listed. Turns out he is, indeed, showing a house, out in Tiddley Cove.

"Oh, okay. Can I leave something with his assistant?" Before the girl can answer, Penny is striding down the corridor to Jack's office. She hasn't been here in almost a year and hopes he is still in the same area. They are forever changing cubicles and offices and assistants.

Thankfully, because Jack is one of the firm's longest-serving and oldest employees, they tend, perhaps out of respect, to leave him in one place. She can tell her husband is still occupying the same office before she even enters. On the door is his trademark cartoon. It's a picture of Buckingham Palace with Jack superimposed in the forefront. He is shown proudly putting a Sold sticker on the For Sale sign. For some reason he keeps this picture wherever he goes. He had it when the company was first based in lower Lonsdale and before the renovations of this office took place. At that time he shared a cubicle with another realtor, who went on to make millions in the mid-1990s dot-com craze. It's a funny enough cartoon, she thinks, but the real reason he probably likes it so much is that he looks a lot younger in the photo.

She walks into his office and takes a cursory glance over his desk and over the bulletin board. This morning's newspaper is in the trash, and a half-empty cup of cold coffee has left a mark on some papers. A red dot is blinking on his phone machine. Penny thinks about playing the message, but before she has the nerve to press the button a girl comes out of nowhere.

"Can I help you?"

"Oh, hello." She sees that the girl can't be a day over twenty. She feels the need to provide details. "I'm Penelope."

"Penelope . . ." She's not making the connection, or perhaps Jack hasn't connected the dots for her.

"I'm Penny Stevens."

"Do you have an appointment?"

All the energy that she had seeps out of her in this one instant. The girl is young and perky and assertive, which only magnifies Penny's fatigue and sense of futility. "I'm Jack's wife."

"Oh."

It is the usual reaction to this bit of news. The two women stare at each other then out the window and then at their watches.

"You must be Jolene." This startles the girl and makes her fiddle with her ill-fitting blouse that is just a tad too small. Her pants look as though they are painted on, and Penny wonders how the girl can breathe. Luckily she is as skinny as a beanpole, so this ensemble just looks uncomfortable. At least there is no excess flesh bulging out anywhere. On Jolene it all looks a bit gaudy and out of place for the office, but Jack has never cared how his assistants dress. He's more the type to be concerned about how they undress.

Jack, you're sixty-two, what are you thinking? Are you thinking?

"Nice to meet you." Jolene reaches out a hand with incredibly long fingernails. Considering the amount of typing she has to do, it's amazing she can function with such talons.

Confronted with these thoughts, Penny does what she came here to do. *I've already used some of your makeup. It's only fair, really.* "Nice nails."

Jolene's face lights up. "They're fake." She smiles.

Really?

"Well, they look great. Where do you get them done?" Penny once got a manicure and spent the next week worrying about chipping and peeling and splitting her nails. She invested so much time trying to figure out how to go about her daily life without hurting her nails that when the colour finally wore off, she vowed to never be a slave to her nails again.

"I go to the Academy."

"The Academy?"

"The Academy of Nails."

"I'll have to check them out. Nice colour, too."

Penny pauses, and then says, "You know, Jolene,

you look like somebody who really knows how to put it all together."

"Oh, thanks." The nine bracelets she wears on one wrist jingle as she runs her hand through her bleached-blonde hair.

"I've got this fabulous new lipstick that I can't wear. It's not my colour, you know? Not me. Anyway, it's brand-new and I think it would look just terrific on someone like you." Penny pulls the lipstick out of her purse and hands it to Jack's assistant.

Jolene inspects the tube closely. "I've never seen this brand before."

"Oh, it's totally new. I got it from my stylist. Makes your lips all puffy. All the stars are wearing it."

"Wow." Jolene is licking her chops.

"Anyhow, it's yours if you want it." Penny is making for the door. Her work here is done.

"Wow. Thanks."

"Nice to meet you, Jo."

"You too. And thanks again for this." She is happily waving the lipstick as Penny turns and walks away.

"Just tell him I dropped by, would you?"

"Sure. Any message?"

"No. Just give him a big kiss for me."

. . .

Outside the air is sticky. A few high clouds are forming in the horizon. Penny checks her watch. It is two twenty. A few blocks up the hill is the Manor, where her mother now lives. It hasn't changed much in the twenty years since her father lived there. In fact, two aides still recall her father being a patient there as well. If things continue on as they do, Penny figures she'll be checking into the Manor somewhere around 2044.

There is no way that Susan will get to the old Avalon any time soon, so she pulls up outside a convenience store and buys an African violet and goes to visit her mother.

Alice is sitting in a semicircle with four other ladies and one confused man when Penny finally finds her in the activity room.

"Hi, Mom." She gives her mother a kiss and nods to the others in the group.

"Get me out of here." Alice takes the violet from Penny's hands and undoes the brake on her wheelchair.

"Mom . . ." She feels embarrassed when Alice talks like this. She was always so quiet and proper when Penny was growing up that at moments like these she feels like a complete stranger.

"Who in the world dreams up this crap?" Alice takes a half-finished paper plate decorated with bows and fake flowers from her lap. "I wouldn't be caught dead wearing this."

"Oh, it's a summer hat." It is truly hideous, but Penny doesn't want to get her mother all fired up. One time she agreed with Alice that the Easter candles in the shape of a cross with a dripping Jesus were really awful. Her mother had become quite incensed on that day, and a nurse had to step in and placate her. The candles were removed and subsequent Easters featured only bunnies. Even the painted eggs proved too challenging for the staff and patients. Penny recalls one Easter when somebody forgot to boil the eggs before they decorated them. There was so much egg white and yolk all over the tables and floor and chairs that a visitor fell and broke his hip, and one resident impaled another with one of her knitting needles. At times, the Manor is more like a kindergarten than a nursing home.

On the whole, however, life has been good for Alice at the Manor. She's made friends easily and keeps busy, barely having enough time to watch her favourite television shows because she signs up for daily activities. "Adventures," she calls them.

And she's never been one to brood or lament the past. She walked with a cane for the last two decades, but the toll of her years added up. When her eyesight began to fail it affected her balance, and since she turned eighty, she has been using the wheelchair full-time. So, when it came time to make the move to the Manor, Alice did it without fanfare, full steam ahead, looking forward, not back.

"Scoot up alongside that garbage can, Penelope."

She glides her mother to the container, where Alice promptly unloads her creation.

"Godawful what they have us doing. No wonder people go stark raving mad in here. I wouldn't wish this crap on anybody!"

"Mom."

"How's your garden, Penelope? God, I'd love to get my hands on some dirt. Why don't they have us garden?"

They have arrived at Alice's room. It is quite tasteful, with soft furnishings and a small sitting area by a pair of French doors that lead out to a patio. She is one of a handful of patients who have a private room.

"Actually, you'll have to come by for a visit and see the place soon. I've got a gardener now, and the lawn is really starting to look good."

"What do you need a gardener for? You've got Jack. How is he? Why don't you have any kids yet?" Alice is relentless in her quest for grandchildren.

"Oh, Mom."

"Marta Vanderhoerst just had her eleventh and twelfth great-grandchildren. Twins! For Heaven's sake! Do you know it costs thousands to get fertilized if you can't have kids? Some people can't have enough and others can't get anything. You and Jack better get started or you'll have to get fertilized. Also, be careful of the fertilizer you use on the lawn."

Penny wonders if her mother talks like this always or if she just saves up her thoughts until her daughter comes for her visits.

"So, how's Jack?"

"Good. He's fine."

"How old is he now?"

"He'd be sixty-two." Penny knows what's coming next.

"How old am I?" Alice is leaning forward, counting invisible years on her fingers.

"You're eighty-four, Mom."

"How did that happen, Penelope?" It's hit or miss here that Alice might begin to cry. Today, thankfully, she shrugs it off. "Jack's older too. Tell him I told him to knock you up before it's too late."

"Mom."

"Put that violet on the shelf there so that I know where it is. Get some water for my spider plant and that ugly one from Mrs. Jeffries. It just won't die, but I'm not going to kill it."

Penny parks the wheelchair by her mother's bed and goes into the bathroom to fill up a cup with water.

"I'm meeting Susan for lunch."

"Lunch? It's too late for lunch! I ate hours ago."

"Yeah, I know, it's sort of a lunch-dinner thing. Susan's really stressed out with the kids, you know."

"How many kids does she have?"

"Four."

"What kind of a person has four kids these days? We should be like China. Set limits on things. You better have a baby soon, Penelope."

"Anyway, she kind of called and needs to get out of the house for a bit."

"You're a good friend to her."

"Oh, thanks, I guess."

"Especially when she was such a little witch to you all those years."

"Mom!"

"It's true."

Penny and Susan met in kindergarten and went

through elementary and high school together. They were close friends until grade eight, when it became apparent to Susan that Penny wasn't exactly the "coolest" kid on the block. Suddenly Penny didn't get any phone calls or birthday invitations.

"She was a right cow to you."

"Okay, Mom, come on." At times Alice can become quite unhinged.

"Remember that time she said she'd be your partner for that class trip, and then she unloaded you only to be unloaded herself, and then she had the nerve to ask you to change your partner so she could be your partner again?" It was uncanny how Alice was able to recall the smallest, pettiest details but couldn't remember how old she was.

"Yeah, that was a long time ago, Mom."

"Is she still fat?"

"I don't know, Mom. She looks all right to me."

"That's the problem with you, Penelope. You've always been too nice."

Oh, I have my moments.

"Look, Mom, I've got to go. I'm meeting her in ten minutes."

"She was the one who got you to wear that belly-dancing outfit for that costume party. Remember that?

All those kids laughing at you! Nobody else dressed up and she knew it. Serves her right to be fat with four bratty kids and a lame duck husband. And you know something?" She didn't stop here for Penny to answer; she was in full swing now. "I never liked her mother. Stuck-up, self-righteous snob. Ha! Serves them all right!"

"Okay, Mom, you're starting to scream. Just calm down." She helps her mother transfer to the bed and takes her shoes off and places them side by side next to her night table. "Mom, I'm sorry it's such a short visit, but I have to get going."

They kiss and Alice gives Penny a squeeze and holds on just a few seconds to let her daughter know that she really loves her.

"Oh, you're a good egg, Penelope."

"Bye, Mom. See you soon."

"Bye, sweetie. And dear?"

"Yes?"

"Have fun and give that Susan my love."

Reining it all in
Friday, August 15
Penny Stevens

With all the beautiful weather we are having, it's hard to think about saving for a rainy

197

day. We, out on the West Coast, get our fair share of rain, that's for sure. Nevertheless, we should all have access to extra funds in times of unexpected expenses.

I am not talking about putting money aside for a vacation that you are hoping to take. That's something you expect to save and plan for, something specific that you can calculate. I am talking about saving for a rainy day. Yes, even in Vancouver! You might need a new roof, and you don't want to be caught in the rain when that happens!

A good formula that works well is the 10 percent solution. After taxes, an individual should set aside this amount from their net monthly salary. Where should this money go? Mutual funds are a good bet for the long haul. GICs offer another answer. RRSPs should be reserved for their intended use and not be tampered with, as a working person will pay dearly if the funds are withdrawn early. A high-interest savings account, if you can find one, is better than nothing.

Getting into this habit early, before you have overextended your budget and lifestyle, will help you commit to the plan. There will be growing pains when commencing a budget, such as this one, if you haven't adhered to a savings plan in the past. We tend to "need" all of our money. In fact, many of us need more than we have, which, of course, leads to overextension and credit card debt, and even bankruptcy.

Kind of like me, at the moment. I have consumed many more calories than I have needed for quite a while now. The scales do not lie, I am sad to report. I have overextended my belt size by a few notches, and these habits are going to be hard to break. I am struggling to make diet—a different kind of budget—and exercise—a different kind of habit—become a daily part of my life.

And guess what? It's hard!

Ten

Penny walks by the Please Wait to Be Seated sign and sits in a booth in a corner where the lighting is dark and the sounds of the kitchen are far away. Aside from a few employees huddled over at the bar and a couple over by the window, the place appears to be empty.

The booth is covered in red leather. A tin or aluminum lamp hangs down very low over the centre of the table. She has to hold the drinks menu directly under it if she wants to read anything. It's the kind of upper-midlevel eatery for young urban professionals that offers drink specials based upon the days of the week. On Mondays, it's margaritas. On Tuesdays, it's Tangerine Madness. Wednesday is Wacky Piña Colada Day. The list goes on to reveal nothing that Penny would want or recognize. A waiter in black pants, a white shirt, and a vest that has the same kind of pattern as the carpet approaches the table.

"Are you waiting for somebody?" He looks like he's either finishing a shift or starting one. Penny feels like her presence here is bothering him.

"Yes, my friend is joining me for a late lunch. Really late, I guess. I hope it's not too late." She does one of her little hiccup laughs.

"Will you want menus?" His tone is unenthusiastic, and she wonders how long he has worked here and if he hates his vest.

"Yes. That would be great. Thanks."

Like a ballerina, he turns on the spot and glides away to the secret place where menus are kept. He returns carrying two large books that look like the ledgers Alastair Sim uses in that Christmas movie. The name of the restaurant is embossed on the front but Penny disregards it. Like everybody else she knows, she will always refer to it as "the place that used to be the Avalon." End of story.

There are pages and pages of appetizers, starters, carb-free meals, poultry, seafood, steak, pasta, vegetarian, and items for the "little ones." Probably because they feel compelled not to ignore the odd elderly person who might inadvertently darken their door, there are even seniors' choices. Funny cartoons are in the margins and prices are all in pennies, so that if you buy the chicken teriyaki entrée it tells you it will cost you nine hundred and ninety-five cents. It's a good deal, under ten bucks, thinks Penny, and she decides that she will order it. With rice. Or maybe just a salad. Heather would approve. She wishes she had brought her coins from home. Strangely, she has an appetite.

Susan arrives at exactly three o'clock. She is wearing a gorgeous pale beige blazer and matching pants with a cream blouse and a string of pearls. She looks fantastic, and Penny can hardly believe this is the same person she spoke to an hour ago.

"Hi. God, you look great. Good to see you, Susan."

"Five months!" Susan has a tendency to forgo huge chunks of conversation and just jump in wherever her mind takes her.

"Sorry? Five months?"

"I bought this outfit for my niece Gillian's wedding when I was five months pregnant with Ben."

"Oh. Well, it's lovely."

"I'm so fat I'm wearing a maternity suit!"

"But you look really good."

"I look fabulous! Damn it. Have you ordered?"

"No, not yet."

"What are you drinking?" Susan takes off her blazer and hangs it on a hook at the edge of the booth.

"I was thinking wine, maybe?"

"No. Highballs." Susan arranges herself on her side of the booth. She is wearing bright red lipstick and smells of lavender. She tends to spray on huge amounts when she applies perfume. "What's on special?"

The waiter returns with two glasses of ice water. Susan interrogates him for a bit and then promptly orders two gin and tonics. "Make them doubles."

"Have you had a chance to look at the menu, ladies?"

"No." Susan is doing all the talking. "What are you having, Penny?"

"Oh, I was thinking of ordering the teriyaki chicken." She wants to speak up and change her drink order. The last time she had a gin and tonic was at an Oscars theme party, where the hosts rolled out a red carpet to make their guests feel like celebrities. They had arrived on empty stomachs, and the last thing Penny remembers was Rob Lowe singing with Snow White in some bizarre dance number. Jack was so embarrassed by her. All week long he berated her for not being able to hold her liquor.

"I'll have that too." Susan manages to pick up both of the monstrous menus without knocking anything over.

The gin and tonics arrive and are placed on two round coasters advertising local breweries. Penny sips at her drink and listens to Susan talk about "life on the farm." Unconsciously, Penny is making indentations on her coaster with the tips of her nails.

"So I told Doug to get up the nerve and at least ask." She is going on about some promotion or other about which Doug doesn't apparently feel that motivated.

"You know what I mean?" Susan leans forward and looks intensely at her.

Penny's mind has been wandering while Susan's lips have been flapping. As her friend has ranted on topics as varied as daycare, dental hygiene, the Atkins diet, potty training, spam, Doug's weight, her weight—among other things—Penny has nodded her head and agreed in monosyllables. She hasn't yet really had to come out with a full sentence because the conversation has been rolling along quite nicely until just now.

"Sorry?"

"Are you even listening to me?"

"Yes, of course." She feels like she is in history class and has been caught daydreaming.

"What are you doing with that?" Susan's tone is stringent and a little scary.

"Oh." Penny looks down at her bent and frayed

coaster. A crescent-shaped nail pattern runs along the edge. She has gone almost completely around it. "Kind of pretty, don't you think?"

"I'm in a crisis here, and you haven't heard a word I've said!" Suddenly Susan snatches the coaster away from her. For a split second Penny thinks she is going to throw it Frisbee-style across the room. Instead, Susan sticks it in her purse. Penny's mouth is momentarily frozen open. Then, as if to finalize this transaction, Susan snaps the buckle on her bag shut.

"What are you doing?" She looks around the restaurant and is thankful they aren't surrounded by other diners.

"I am removing this distraction so we can have a conversation." Susan has crossed her arms.

"We're not having a conversation, Susan. I'm just sitting here listening to you."

"Obviously not very well."

"What do you want me to do? Take notes?"

"I want you to bloody well listen to me!" Susan's forehead is shiny, and discernable beads of sweat have appeared over her upper lip.

"Well, it's not like I haven't heard it before."

The waiter appears with two plates loaded with teri-yaki chicken.

"Here you go, ladies. Is everything okay?"

"Super." Susan doesn't take her eyes off Penny.

"Fine." Penny looks at the spot where her coaster used to be and feels her face becoming extremely hot.

As the waiter glides out of view, Penny exhales a heavy sigh. "Look, I'm sorry. That wasn't called for. I'm just a little overwhelmed myself."

"I see."

"I've been under a lot of pressure lately."

"From what?" Susan continues to stare at her friend.

"From a lot of things."

"A lot of things? Like what?"

"Like from everybody." They are talking in short sentences now, with bad grammar.

"Like everybody who?"

"Johnson."

"Johnson?"

"Yeah, and Linda."

"Linda? Who is Linda?"

"Linda the beauty person."

"Beauty person?"

"Oh, and Heather and Charlie. They're brutal." Penny is on a roll now. "Aaron, but he's gorgeous. You'll have to come over and see what I mean."

"Who are all these people you are talking about? Are you on something?"

"I've been at the gym four times already this week. My legs are killing me. And everybody is watching me."

"Who is watching you do what?"

"Well, work out and lose weight and decorate my house and redo my garden. Also, I have to get a new haircut."

"Why? Are you going on a cruise or something?"

"I wish."

"Well, what's this all about?" Susan has picked up her utensils and is starting to shovel food into her mouth.

"I'm getting renovated."

"What?"

"I am renovating my life."

"What do you mean, you are renovating your life?"

She doesn't think Susan has ever asked her so many questions in all the time they grew up together or that they have known each other as adults. For the first time ever, Penny has the floor and it is her friend who is listening.

• • •

When Penny finishes spelling it all out, she releases a huge sigh, takes a big swig of her drink, and leans back into the red leather.

"Two hundred and twenty thousand dollars?"

Penny nods.

"In a brown paper bag?"

"Yeah. Crazy, heh? Like they saw it in some movie or something."

Susan is leaning forward and making slurping sounds with her straw, trying to get every last drop out of her glass. She has moved on from gin and tonic to some kind of tropical drink with crushed ice and an umbrella. Penny is still reclining back on her side of the booth. She has had three gins and can feel her toes pulsating and a warmth emanating from her heart outward. The deep muscles in her calves and thighs feel tender as she rubs them absentmindedly.

On the table are about seventeen coasters that Toby, their waiter, has brought them. Susan and Penny have divided them into three categories: those they feel are well designed and marketed, those they feel are uninteresting, and those whose product they wouldn't drink because the coasters are too masculine and sexist.

"Toby! Can we have some water, please?" Susan has always been able to make quick connections with people. When she talks about Janet, she could be talking about a close friend or the salesgirl who helped her this morning. When she talks about Lisa, it could mean her sister-in-law from hell or a bank teller.

"Here you are, ladies." Toby places the two ice waters on coasters from the discarded pile.

In the few hours they have been in this establishment, they have learned that Toby is indeed a dancer. That he attended a national ballet school back east and that, no, he is not gay. He has come out here to be with his girlfriend, who teaches at the Goh Ballet. He hates waiting on tables, but jobs are hard to come by and the competition is stiff. His next confirmed gig isn't until Christmas, when he will dance the role of the Nutcracker. Two or three times a month he has auditions. He hates his agent but loves to dance. Last year he earned twenty thousand dollars dancing in a peanut-butter commercial.

"Toby, what do you think of this?" Susan is holding up a coaster advertising a big-busted woman holding two steins of beer. The tagline reads, "They're for you!"

"Well . . . I don't really drink beer."

"Well, if you had to drink beer, Toby, would this be a brand that you would consider, based on this ad?" Susan is not letting him off lightly.

"No."

"Why not."

"Because I don't really go for that kind of . . . look."

"Really?" Unconsciously, Susan has adjusted her blouse. After nursing four babies she knows her breasts are not her best feature.

"And you're a dancer." Penny normally doesn't strike up intimate conversations with strangers, but there is something inviting about this young man. Like he could be the long-lost son she never had. "Ballet is beauty with discipline, isn't it? I mean, this is too voluptuous, too much excess. You wouldn't say she was beautiful, would you?"

"I think all women are beautiful, regardless of size."

"Hmm." Both ladies sigh.

"But I couldn't lift and pirouette somebody with knockers that size."

Penny and Susan hoot at this.

"Yeah. And also my girlfriend would probably not find this ad that enticing."

"So you take your girlfriend's tastes into account when making decisions about what to buy?" Penny simply adores this young man.

"Of course, isn't that what every man should learn to do?"

"You're a smart man, Toby. A very smart man indeed," Susan and Penny concur as they watch him spin away from their table back to the kitchen. A few more customers are starting to come in now, and soon the place will be in full swing.

"How old do you think he is?" Penny can't tell if he is just out of high school or in his late twenties.

"Twenty-two. Twenty-three."

"So young and so confident. Why wasn't I ever that way?" Penny is descending into an alcohol-induced state of wallowing in self-pity.

"Jack and I don't have sex anymore." The words come out so quickly she doesn't have time to edit herself.

"Oh, Penny. I'm . . . sorry."

"I don't think any kind of personal trainer or life coach could renovate our marriage." As if on cue from some ever-ready and deep reservoir, tears spring to Penny's eyes. She's always hated her ability to cry at the drop of a hat. Of course, this comment has been more like the dropping of a bomb.

"Damn it. Now my mascara is going to run."

"Oh, Penny." Susan dips her napkin into her glass of water and without saying anything hands it across the table. Penny dutifully dabs at her eyes.

"I can't take it anymore."

"How long has this been going on?"

"For years." She watches Susan take this in.

"Years? Have you thought about going to see a counsellor?"

Penny just waves off the thought.

"Does Jack maybe need to see his doctor?"

At this, Penny throws her head back and laughs.

"Seriously, Penny. There are all kinds of medications out there. I mean, if he is having trouble performing, there is no reason to be shy about it. He is over sixty, isn't he?"

"I didn't say 'he' hasn't had sex in years, I said 'we' haven't done it in years. Jack is very active, my friend. Just not with me, I'm afraid."

"Oh, Penny. I'm so sorry."

"So am I, Susan. So am I."

"How long has the affair been going on?"

"This particular one I couldn't say exactly, as I have been distracted with all these people in my life right now. You should have come by the house today. It's a zoo."

"You mean there has been more than one affair?"

"More than one and fewer than fifty. That's a pretty safe ballpark, I guess."

"Oh, Penny, I don't know what to say. I just—I don't know how to respond."

"Well, what can one say? I mean, look at me. I haven't said anything. I've been a complete mute on the matter."

"Are you certain of these affairs? Could you be mistaken? Are you absolutely positive?"

"He is without a doubt most certainly diddling about. He doesn't even take care to cover his tracks anymore." The downpour of tears is starting to come effortlessly now, as Penny is no longer trying to hold them back. The constriction in her throat loosens and she feels a release of all the tension she has been bottling up. It feels good to say the words, and she doesn't care that she is out in public. Toby swings by with more napkins and she feels loved.

"Jack Stevens is a sixty-two-year-old dick who sticks his prick into anything that moves. If we raised sheep, they wouldn't be safe."

"Who are these women?"

Penny can't really say whether Susan likes or dislikes Jack. It is Doug who can't stand him, who has always said that Jack is a snob who has an elevated sense of himself. "They are all different, 'these women.' Some have been lonely. Some have been married. Most are young and impressed with his money, I guess. Some are middle-aged, and one was even older than he was, come to think of it. I don't know, he's got that undeniable . . . what is it . . ."

"He's charming, you mean? He's always had that twinkle in his eye . . . kind of thing," Susan offers like she's putting together pieces of a puzzle.

"Maybe some just wanted to have a bit of fun themselves and didn't mind doing it with a Casanova wannabe. But he is so bloody . . . charming . . . and bloody relentless, do you know what I'm saying?" Penny is surprised to hear herself talking like this. All these feelings have been buried for so long, she is taken aback by her ability to articulate the situation this well.

Susan just nods.

Jack does have that kind of flirty playfulness about him. Like that soap-opera star with the thick head of white hair and perpetually tanned face. Always holding a martini in one hand. Ever ready to pull out your chair, to open the door, to offer to light your cigarette. When Penny considers Doug, well, he's the complete polar opposite. Yes, he is a bit overweight, but he is a good father and a steady partner.

"I don't know what I'd do if Doug ever did that to me," says Susan, as if reading her friend's mind.

"Doug, as my mother would say, is 'a good egg.' He

will never do this to you. Plus you'd never stand for it in the first place."

"I guess you're right. How have you managed to keep it together all these years?"

"Well, in the beginning we fought. I made him promise never to stray again, and we were once even pregnant."

"When was that?"

"God, I was so young. In my twenties. Then I lost the baby, and I often wonder if things would have turned out different if I hadn't miscarried."

"Why didn't you tell me?"

Penny doesn't answer. She remembers feeling like a failure, and at the time, the thought of confessing her husband's infidelity was too much to bear.

"You never got pregnant again?"

"We never really tried, and then the idea just fell away. Now, of course, we don't have sex and I'm forty and, well, that's it, I guess."

"So he's having an affair with someone again?"

"This one is pathetically young. She made a fatal error and left a message at the house today, so I swung by his office. Decided to take a look for myself. The company is providing job placement for kids fresh out of college, trying to save money by paying minimum wage. This girl could be my daughter."

"Why do young women do this?" Susan is now starting to dent her own coaster.

Penny knows Jack is committed in his quest to become the next Don Juan of Homelife. She's seen him at work. He'll approach anybody. Most of the time, when she has been at a party with him or in the same room, the ladies have laughed off his comments, assuming he wasn't serious. But even if he has a 99 percent refusal rate, if he encounters one thousand women in a given year, at least ten will be up for a bit of a game, she calculates. *You've got to hand it to him—he's a great salesman and won't take no for an answer.*

Penny has stopped crying now, and Susan has motioned for Toby to bring them some coffee. A busboy has cleared off their table, but the coasters remain spread out before them. Susan reaches into her purse and takes out the one she took from her friend.

"God, I can be so bossy sometimes." She looks Penny in the eye and places the coaster in the palm of her hand.

"I wouldn't have you any other way." And Penny means it. She's always admired her confident and occasionally pushy friend. If it weren't for people like this in her life, she would never go out for lunch. She'd never go shopping across the border for shoes. She's become too good at being alone, reclusive, retreating into her thoughts.

"I'd say this has been fun and we should get together again soon, but I'd be lying if I didn't feel just awful for you. Penny, I want you to call me whenever you need to talk."

"I will." The coffee feels good going down her throat.

"I mean it."

"I know you do."

The two friends sit quietly and sip at their coffees. The restaurant is busy now and they can see Toby carrying a large tray over to a booth by the window. When the bill comes, it reveals they owe six thousand, three hundred, and eighty-nine cents. Susan pays the bill, and Penny leaves a twenty-dollar tip. They split the coasters between them.

Outside in the soft evening air, they embrace and say short sentences and pat each other on the back.

"My car is two blocks away. I'll go slowly and walk off those drinks. Thank God for that coffee," Susan says.

"Are you sure you're okay to drive?" Penny is parked below in the parkade and knows she is in absolutely no state to drive. In fact, she might call a taxi and come and pick up her car tomorrow.

"While you barely touched your cup of coffee, I had three and I never even finished that last drink. This whole conversation has sobered me up. I'll be fine."

"You sure?"

"Completely. Thanks for asking."

Penny watches as Susan walks down the sidewalk toward her minivan. As her friend's figure gets smaller and smaller, she feels a lump swelling in her throat. She often has this reaction when saying goodbye to people. Sometimes she feels this way when she visits her mother and then has to leave. When the carpet cleaners came the other day, she watched them load their hoses and tanks into their truck and thought that she'd likely never see those two young Iranian men again. They were in university, and this was just their summer job. The moment was gone. It would never be the same again.

Then again, she is drunk right now, so there is the alcohol factor playing into her emotional state, of course.

Bye bye, Susan. Let's do lunch soon.

The evening is still young, and since Penny knows that Jack is unlikely to be coming home any time soon and that she herself is in no mood to face him or her house or any messages that might be on her machine, she decides to venture into the giant bookstore that is right next to the restaurant that used to be called the Avalon.

Bookstores have become immense these days, and this one looks to be the size of a small apartment building.

"Excuse me, where is the washroom?"

"Upstairs behind the travel section." A young girl is busy moving armloads of hardcover books onto a shelf with a sign that reads "New Releases." This seems to be a taxing job, as the poor girl looks like she weighs about the same as maybe five of these hefty tomes.

"There isn't one on this level?"

"Sorry."

Penny sighs and begins to walk slowly toward the escalator. All around her are books and paperbacks and posters advertising books or announcing upcoming releases. There are all sorts of gadgets and candles and gifts too. In one corner, there is a coffee house with large overstuffed armchairs and tables made of solid wood. In another corner, there is a music section selling CDs and soundtracks and another section selling DVDs. There seems to be no limit to what one can purchase in this world of books and music and lattes and all variety of things. So many things amidst the voice of that sexy long-haired Italian guy crooning about *amoré* over the store stereo system. Penny tries to recall the singer's name but instead remembers that she is quite drunk and that her bladder is beckoning.

She feels graceful gliding onto the escalator, looking down upon all the rows of books and people stopping and inching through the aisles. Everything is so organized here. Alphabetical. Balanced. That's why people like to get lost in places like this. Everything makes sense here.

As Penny steps off the escalator, she stumbles and almost loses her balance.

"Christ," she mumbles, hoping that no one saw that. No one did, it appears. Or perhaps the sight of a tipsy woman all alone in a gigantic bookstore is not of particular interest. Perhaps countless women before her have come in here, not knowing what they are looking for while their husbands are boinking their respective Jolenes. What does one read while one's partner is doing the nasty with a woman who wears fake nails the length of animal claws? Whose nails are painted the shade of Afternoon Tryst?

And then there's Susan. Now her best friend knows everything. No more hiding behind the pretence that all is well. Penny has spilled the beans and there is no going back. She can't decide if she feels lighter for having unloaded that burden or horrified at having revealed the naked truth. Either way, it wasn't very pretty. Whether she hid behind the façade of her life or exposed it for what it is, she's definitely on shaky ground now. And she has to pee.

"Where is that damn washroom?"

"Hi! Can I help you?" She is accosted by a young man in a blue smock with a happy-face name tag that says "Hi, I'm Trevor."

"Trevor. Where is the travel section?"

"Oh, here. Let me show you . . . Come this way." His long, skinny legs stride confidently through a maze of swirling titles and images. Penny has trouble keeping up with the young man as her gait is unsteady.

"Are we off to somewhere exotic?" he asks.

Around the corner she sees maps and atlases and a standing cutout of that guy from the TV travel show. *Hallelujah!*

"No. We are off to pee." She disappears down the fluorescent corridor into the second door on the right. Once inside, she immediately goes into the last stall. If she can, she always chooses an end stall. Just like when she goes to the movies, she wants the aisle seat.

She is alone now in this perfectly tiled haven. The music is playing louder in here, but the sound of her urine momentarily drowns out the sound of the vocals. She can't believe how much liquid was inside her. Finally, she has emptied her bladder.

Two full rolls of industrial-sized toilet paper hang to her left, and in front of her, hanging on the door, is an ad from a local cellphone company. Apparently, Penny can purchase up to four phones for just one easy sign-up fee. She and her family could have up to one thousand minutes of free talk time, excluding weekends. It's one of those retro ads, like the opening credits to *The Brady Bunch*. A forty-something generic-looking mom and dad and two offspring, one boy and one girl, with perfect teeth.

Is a thousand minutes over the course of a week a good deal? Who are these people, and who are they talking to?

Penny is disturbed by this family. For the first time in her life, she feels a compelling urge to deface an ad, to commit vandalism. She is shocked to find that from somewhere deep within her, she feels what can only qualify as hatred for this family. Especially the mother. She is certain the woman is laughing at her, mocking her. Penny has to look away.

She should get up and walk around, maybe go outside and suck in some fresh air. But the toilet seat is so comfortable. She could stay here forever, if only that irritating family wasn't egging her on with their shiny phones in assorted colours.

A beautiful song is playing on the sound system. An old song. Of course, a song about love. She should get up right now and march over to the music counter and ask who the artist is. It's a lady singing now. With a rich, silky voice. But she doesn't get up. Her legs feel heavy and her head is throbbing. Sitting here without the distraction of her friend and conversation, Penny feels even more drunk than when she left the restaurant. She'll have to just sit here and breathe, she decides. It's been a long time since she's been this intoxicated, and she curses herself for letting Susan order those gins.

Penny shuts her eyes and breathes deeply in and out. This causes the room to spin around her. She opens her eyes and tries to breathe just like her yoga instructor taught her, but she forgets the exact way she is supposed to do that alternate nostril-breathing move. She gets confused inhaling and exhaling. She has her thumb and one finger on her nostrils, so she breathes out of her mouth. For the life of her, she can't recall how she is supposed to breathe, but she is certain that plugging her nose was part of the equation for taking spiritual yogic breaths.

Mrs. Brady continues to stare condescendingly at her from the perch of her faultless world. This impeccable mother of two knows how to do just about everything. She knows how to iron a tailor-made shirt, bowl a flawless game, host a perfect party. She goes to church every Sunday and sits in the front row. She runs marathons and mends socks. She works and she volunteers. She has sex three times a week and always achieves an orgasm. Needless to say, she knows what *her* husband is doing every minute of the day, and she most certainly knows how to do alternate nostril-breathing.

Inside her purse, Penny finds an old lipstick, and without thinking she effortlessly defiles the smiles of Mom, Dad, Junior, and Sissy. *There.*

An hour later, Penny is still sitting folded up on the toilet seat. She has listened to an entire CD of the mystery lady and is now three songs into a country-style band. People have come and gone while she has been doing her deep breathing down in her end stall, but nobody seems to have noticed her. Thankfully, she has been left alone. Perhaps the odd person made note of the slightly worn pumps at the far end of the room. Maybe the giggling teenagers remarked that somebody was taking a real long time. They would know because they were in there primping and squealing and confiding and comparing for an eternity. When they finally left, Penny let out a sigh of relief. *Peace at last.*

Three songs later, she is ready to leave. She has spent the better part of quite a lovely evening here in her stall.

She has listened to some great music; she's done some yoga and worked on her core muscles. She's even done a bit of art therapy, she realizes, as she looks at her Brady Bunch. Quite a full day, really.

Before she gets up, she takes out her compact and hesitantly checks herself out. It's bad. She looks like hell. Her hair is a mess, but she remembers getting one of those fold-up travel combs as a gift for buying too much makeup at her favourite department store. She finds it among the dozen beer coasters and runs it through her hair a few times. A little lipstick couldn't hurt either. Unfortunately, she has to resort to the same colour as her family of four, as her good lipstick is in the Volvo.

She is very stiff and very sore and it is with great difficulty that she holds her compact with one hand and her fire-engine-red lipstick with the other. She's never been good at applying her makeup, and today is no exception. She remembers when she was back in kindergarten learning to colour with Mrs. Miklins screaming at her to "stay in the lines, child! Stay in the lines!"

She glances in her mirror and sees that she'll have to wipe it off at the sink. *I look like a clown.*

She moves to stand. "Shit!" The sound of her own voice echoing throughout the washroom startles her almost as much as the searing pain coursing down her legs. A moment passes and she slowly and carefully tries again to get up onto her feet. "Wha?" A few futile attempts with different foot placements and varying arm positions only cause more pain and deep panic. *Shit! I can't get up.*

Nobody ever thinks about not being able to get up from a public toilet seat. People think about the fear of public speaking. The fear of death. Having toilet paper stuck to the bottom of their shoe. People dream of being naked in public places. But nobody, Penny is certain, has ever declared their fear of paralysis on public toilets. You would think that if you had the steam to walk into one of those stalls, you would have the same gumption to get yourself out again. The time frame for paralysis, barring any freak accident, is too short.

Oh my God!

Time slows down. Penny can hear the ticking of an invisible clock. Someone comes into the washroom. She tries to move again and cannot believe the intensity of the pain. She is close to tears, but the panic is holding them back for the moment. Her mind is racing. *Oh my God! Oh my God!*

A pair of high heels clicks next to her stall. A moment later a toilet flushes. Penny realizes that she is going to have to ask for help. She listens to the sink and soap dispenser being used. The heels click again. The person has left. A few minutes later, what sounds like a toddler and a mother come in just to wash their hands. She cannot bring herself to speak and is left alone once more.

Two whole annoying songs with far too much banjo for Penny's present mood play before another person comes in to use the facilities. She lets them pee and wash up because she doesn't want to interrupt the natural process. She has had enough time to muster up her courage, and she waits for them to finish wiping their hands before she speaks.

"Excuse me, I'm down in the stall at the end here." There is no reply and she unconsciously hiccups out of nervousness. "Hello?"

Still no reply.

"I was wondering if you could give me a hand? I seem to be stuck here and I . . . I can't seem to get up."

There is no answer. Only footsteps. Retreating.

The effect of the muscle spasms and pain and disbelief have totally sobered Penny up. She is filled with a humiliation she didn't know was possible and a fury she didn't know she possessed. *Oh no! This can't be happening. Oh, no, no, no.*

She looks directly up into the eyes of Mrs. Brady. The woman is most certainly taunting her. So smug and self-satisfied. *Hey, lady, take your damn phone and shove it. Ha!*

Did Mrs. Brady just whisper something to her dolt of a husband?

Then take your husband's and shove it up his derriere too! And don't call me! I'll call you! Ha, ha, ha . . .

The lipstick has found its way into her hand again. Before she knows what she is doing, she is leaning forward and vigorously smearing the tube all over the four smiling faces and all over the walls of her cubicle.

It is utter abandon that Penny is feeling now, and it is exhilarating. She presses so hard that clumps of lipstick form on the stall door and fall down onto the tiled floor. She is putting her heart and soul into it. Her eyes well up with tears and she begins to shake with a laughter so strong and unstoppable that her whole body is vibrating. She can't remember the last time she felt this good. *Screw all of you and your phony phones and fake smiles!*

She has begun to howl hysterically, so loudly now that she does not hear the voices on the other side of the door.

"Excuse me, can we help you? Are you okay?"

Penny continues to wail and keen and sob and laugh.

"Are you okay in there?"

"Fuck you, Brady!"

"Pardon?"

"—and visualize this! Ha! You think you're so superior. Ha!"

"Uhm, Katie, go and get Trevor to come in here."

"But, Tanya, this is a girls' washroom!"

"This is like a fucking emergency! Go! Now!"

Penny, still oblivious to what is happening beyond her stall door, has shut her eyes and begun to rock herself like a baby. Back and forth. Back and forth. Ever so slowly, the laughter is subsiding. An odd burst breaks through now and again. She is luxuriating in the aftermath of this outburst like a lover after multiple orgasms. She is wearing a very wide smile. She hasn't smiled like this in a very long time. *Aaaaaahhh.*

"Ma'am, my name is Trevor. I am the assistant manager here. Do you need some assistance?"

Quickly Penny opens her eyes and beholds three pairs of feet on the other side of her cubicle.

"Ma'am, are you okay in there? Could you open the door?" He is wearing a pair of enormous brown brogues that shift nervously on the tiles.

The two girls launch into a flurry of half-finished sentences and snippets.

". . . this girl came out and said someone was in here and like . . . couldn't get up or something . . ."

". . . so we came in here . . ."

". . . and she was screaming and laughing and like . . . swearing too . . ."

". . . totally swearing and . . ."

". . . so then I went and got you, and Tanya stayed here in case, like . . ."

Penny can see their shoes moving this way and that. The girls are wearing two very similar kinds of sporty slingback sandals. Their feet look tiny compared to Trevor's. She wonders, if she'd had a son, would he have feet this big? How big were Toby's?

"Ma'am, just open the door. Can you do that? Can you reach the handle?"

There is silence as she considers her options. At one point she hears the door to the washroom swing open and then someone quickly saying "sorry" and retreating.

"Ma'am, we need you to open this door now."

Penny manages a barely audible whisper. "I can't."

"Pardon me, ma'am?"

"I can't seem to stand up."

"Are you hurt? Are you in pain?"

"I can't . . . my legs are . . . I'm having trouble." The indignity of Penny's predicament is simply too much.

Her cheeks are burning and her heart is pounding. She cannot fathom how to face Trevor and those girls.

"Ma'am, can you open the door? Do you want me to call an ambulance? How can we help you? What can we do for you?"

How can she possibly open up this door? How can she handle them seeing her like this? How does a person even get into a pickle like this?

"Ma'am?"

A couple of coasters roll out from her purse. A big-bosomed brunette lands squarely between Trevor's brogues, and suddenly Penny is reminded of a fishing trip her father took her on when she was eleven or twelve years old. They'd been out on the lake for hours, and no fish had dared to venture in their direction.

"Dad, stop whistling, you're scaring all the fish away."

They waited a long time that morning until, miraculously, some misguided trout took the bait, its mouth gaping wide, eyes bulging in astonishment.

"Where's the thingy, Dad?"

"What's that?" asked her father.

"The stick! The killing thing. You gotta kill it, Dad."

But Wilfred had forgotten it, perhaps never imagining they'd come this far. The fish was flopping around the wooden floor of the boat as Penny and her father stared helplessly at it.

"Hit it, Dad! Kill it or something!" But there was nothing that they could really bludgeon it with. The oars were attached in loops to the sides of the boat, and a person couldn't just strangle a fish with their bare hands.

Then Penny remembers grabbing the Canada Dry bottle. It was rolling to and fro between Wilfred's big rubber boots. Penny took matters into her own hands that day, and seventeen blows later that fish was dead.

Sitting on the toilet now she can hear Heather's voice saying, "Sometimes you just gotta step up to the plate and get done what needs doing."

"Trevor?"

"Yes, ma'am?"

"Go next door and get Toby. He's a waiter at the restaurant that used to be called the Avalon."

Eleven

Left alone again in her porcelain sanctuary, Penny imagines the conversation between Trevor and Toby.

"Hi. I'm from the bookstore." His name tag and bright smock probably give him away.

"Hi there."

"Yeah, I'm the assistant manager and we've got a situation happening right now."

"I see." Toby, of course, would be polite but cautious.

"We've got a lady over there and she's asking for you."

"For me?"

"Yup. She's wanting you to come over there."

"To the bookstore?"

"Uhm, yeah, if you could."

"Who is this lady, may I ask?"

"She says her name is Penny. She says she had lunch here today and you were her waiter."

"Okay . . . ?"

"She said you'd remember her because of the coasters and—"

"I got it. What's up?"

"She's stuck and can't move."

"She's stuck in the bookstore?"

Penny wonders how this poor assistant manager is going about conveying the severity of the situation. He should be in university. Dealing with the public can be very demanding and mostly unrewarding.

"Actually, she's stuck on the toilet."

"I see."

What kind of mental picture might that evoke?

"So, how can I help you?"

"Well, she's asking for you by name."

"I see."

Inside the washroom cubicle, Penny has fiercely struggled to pull up her panties. She's managed to get them only past her knees, but the skirt covers the essentials and it's as good as it's going to get. In doing this, the pain nearly caused her to pass out, and she figures the only threat left to her survival might be facing Toby and the bookstore gang. She is acutely aware that she may very well die of humiliation.

It is Trevor who is the first to speak. "Hello? It's me again. The assistant manager. I've brought Toby with me, as you asked."

Penny mumbles something.

"Penny, it's me, Toby."

"Hi Toby."

"What's up? What can I do for you?"

"You're not going to believe this."

"Try me."

"Well, Toby, first of all, thanks for coming. I couldn't think of anybody else to ask. I mean, I know we've just met, but I get a sense you are a very caring and sensitive young man, and, well, you're also close by and, well, I don't know, I didn't want to call anybody who'd have to come from far away and, well, here you are." She is rolling her eyes as the words tumble from her mouth.

"Okay, well, here I am."

"Yes. Uhm, I think I need someone to come in here and help me out of the store and call a taxi for me."

Trevor, perhaps in an attempt to assert his role of

authority in charge, is quick to jump in. "I can call a taxi for you, ma'am."

"Could I ask you to leave us in private to sort this out?" Penny wishes that the manager and whoever else is in here would just leave.

"Fine! Whatever." Trevor's size-thirteen brogues march past Toby. "I'll give you five minutes and then I'll have to call the police or something." The sound of his footsteps makes distinct echoes until he is out past the heavy door.

Without a word, Tanya, who has been standing guard while Trevor went to get Toby, retreats as well, leaving the two alone at last.

"Is everybody gone?" Penny wants to make sure before she unlatches the door.

"Just me."

"Oh, Toby." She sees that he is wearing a stylish pair of black and white loafers that resemble bowling shoes. They're a good size, not massive like Trevor's.

"You okay in there? I see you've lost a few coasters."

"I've lost more than that, I'm afraid."

"Well, let's sort this out. What do you want me to do?"

He really is a lovely young man, thinks Penny again. She takes a deep breath and speaks slowly and deliberately. "Okay, Toby. I want you to come in here and just get me out of here as fast as possible."

"Okay."

"And don't be alarmed as I've had a bit of a . . . a sort of . . . breakdown."

"Okay."

"I'm dressed, so don't worry about that."

"All right."

"It's just that I'm a bit rough and it's a bit of a mess in here and I don't want those other people seeing it just now, you know what I mean?"

"Yeah, okay."

"Okay, Toby . . . just . . . I'm so sorry . . . God, this is just awful."

"I don't mean to rush you, Penny, but that guy did say that he'd just give us five minutes, so maybe we should go for it."

"Sure. Right. Okay, let's . . . go for it."

She releases the latch and lets the door gently fall open. She doesn't dare look Toby in the eye.

"Hey there." She is grateful that Toby is somehow able to disguise any look of shock or horror both on his face and in his voice. As if he's rescued a dozen other such damsels in distress, he is polite and calm, and, being a dancer, he is wonderfully graceful.

"First, just pass me your purse." He does not comment on the state of the walls or the clumps of lipstick all over the floor.

"Next, I'm going to lift you up by your right arm and together we are going to walk out of here, okay?"

"Okay." She feels like she is a four-year-old kid again who has peed her pants at recess, and now the kind school nurse is guiding her into a dry pair of underwear.

"On three. Okay?"

She just nods as she is mentally preparing for the pain now and has no energy to waste on small talk.

"One, two, three!" Toby lifts her up and twirls her out of the stall and into the centre of the washroom. His choreography is a success. Small beads of perspiration, however, are forming on her forehead. She adjusts her clothing as he averts his eyes.

"Do you want to wash your face?"

"Is it bad?"

There is a time for honesty, and there is a time for expediency in all relationships. Considering what Penny has already gone through, she is glad he opts for the latter.

"No. You look fine."

The pain, as expected, is bad. Her legs feel locked up, the muscles seized tightly. She pretty much leans all of her weight onto Toby, but somehow he handles it without complaint. Perhaps all the years at the barre fine-tuning his body have prepared him for this moment. This ridiculous, impossible moment.

Tanya is there to open the heavy door as they limp out into the corridor that leads back into the store. Trevor and a few employees gawk as Toby guides Penny past the travel section, through the religion aisle, around the children's corner, finally passing through the self-help zone. The irony of this last area does not escape her.

Careful not to lose their balance, Toby and Penny cling to one another as they descend on the escalator. To the untrained observer, the young man and the older lady could simply be passionate lovers needing to touch and embrace and connect, regardless of the public around them. Only on closer inspection would people see the wild look in her eyes, the stunned look in his. The careless smears of bright red lipstick across her lips and the scarlet smear of shame slashed across her cheeks.

"How are you holding up?"

"Fine. Thank you." They are so polite.

Penny can only imagine what is transpiring back upstairs in the aftermath of her little "moment." That poor Trevor. Maybe he can still submit a late application to a college. Vandalized toilets are no place for the likes of tall and skinny and eager assistant managers.

The sun has set, and outside the pavement is still warm.

Penny inhales deeply. After two hours under the fluorescent lights in that washroom, she is grateful for the evening air.

"Not that you haven't done enough for me, Toby, but could you call me a cab now?" If Trevor ordered one, it is long since gone.

"Where is your car?"

"Look, I'm not in any shape to drive." She is leaning against a concrete post and doesn't know how long she will be able to stand.

"Let me just swing you home. I'll take a cab back. You don't want to risk leaving the car overnight."

Having just vandalized a public facility herself, she reasons it would be only fair if her old car was tampered with. Toby, however, seems to have dug his feet in on this issue and won't hear of her taking a cab. In the few minutes that they banter this scenario about, the pain in Penny's legs causes her to give in.

"In the parkade. Are you sure this is okay?"

"It's a done deal."

With great difficulty, Toby essentially piggybacks her down the narrow staircase to her car below. At age forty, Penny can now truthfully say she has been saved by a dashing young man. Literally carried off her feet.

"Have you been experiencing any pain in your legs lately?" This question is posed as he is heaving her into the passenger side of her Volvo.

Penny makes a long story short, telling Toby about the ramifications of being a Good Samaritan. How her life has now been turned upside down. About her house and garden. Her gruelling workouts.

"Your legs probably have too much lactic acid built up, and that's why they were in spasm."

"Yes, well, this has never happened before."

"You can't overdo it. You have to build your work-out slowly."

"I have a personal trainer."

"Well, you should sue them. This shouldn't happen." Toby stretches his legs and rubs his neck muscles, no doubt wanting to prevent injury himself. "I'm serious. You should sue the person who did this to you."

"I think I might." Penny wonders if you can sue somebody when you're getting a service for free. She doubts it, but the idea of holding somebody else accountable for her behaviour tonight is very appealing.

Turns out Toby is nowhere near as graceful a driver as he is a dancer. He has never driven a gearshift but promises Penny he is a fast learner. After a few sorrys, shits, and other assorted expletives, Toby manages to exit the parkade.

"Sorry. Oh shit. Oh sorry I said that. Shit!" The car stalls as they are about to turn into traffic.

"You had it in second." She wonders if maybe this wasn't such a good idea.

"Sorry." He starts the car again and they turn onto Marine Drive.

By the time they are crossing the underpass from North Vancouver into West Vancouver, Toby's driving has vastly improved, but he is still gripping the steering wheel as if the amount of pressure he applies is in some way related to keeping the car moving.

"You're doing a very good job." She hopes they don't stall again. "Really."

"Thanks." He still has his hands clenched at ten and two o'clock, but he gives her a quick smile.

They fly by Park Royal shopping centre. A soccer game is underway on Ambleside field. She tells him to turn up 13th.

"I suggest eating bananas for the potassium, which will help with the acid build-up, and having an Epsom-salt soak as soon as possible."

"I bet you've had your share of sore muscles." She

wonders how long he has been dancing. Did other boys make fun of him?

When they turn west onto Haywood Avenue, Penny catches sight of Jack's Volvo careening toward them at great speed from the opposite direction. For a second she thinks he must be heading off somewhere. Then suddenly he swerves into their driveway.

"Oh!" The word escapes from her before she realizes what is happening.

Toby has slowed down and notices the large white-haired man stumbling out from his SUV. He looks to be clutching at something near his crotch.

"You know that guy?"

"Yes, I do." She doesn't know if she should make Toby drive past and pull up in front of some other house or if she should just play it cool.

"You think he's okay?"

"Probably not."

Toby has come to a full stop. Neither of them can take their eyes off of Jack, who is now crawling up the front porch steps.

"Who is he?"

"Oh." There is a beautiful pause during which she is struck by the absurdity of her life. Why did she marry Jack? How come they live in that house? Why don't they have any children? Who exactly is Jack Stevens, and is he really grabbing at his own balls for all the world to see? As much as she would like to avoid her life, she cannot. "That's my husband."

"Your husband?"

"That's Jack. That man is my husband. Sadly."

"This is your house?"

"Indeed it is."

Toby looks over at Penny and back again to Jack, who is now sort of writhing about, trying to get his key in the door. They can't make out what he is saying, but it doesn't sound good.

"Should we go help him?"

"Yes, I guess so."

Toby pulls Penny's car up behind Jack's. Just before he puts it in park, it coughs and sputters to a standstill.

"Okay, Penny, take my arm." He is by the passenger-side door now, helping steady her onto her feet. "Can you make it?"

"I'm just fine, thank you." Of course she isn't. The pain is still travelling down her legs, but Penny wants to muster up as much poise as possible. For once, she wants her husband to be the one to feel humiliated.

As they approach Jack, who is just now becoming aware of their presence, she calls out casually, "Hi there, darling."

He is too wrapped up in his extreme pain to notice small details such as his wife's limping and her smeared face. "Jesus Christ!"

"This is Toby. He was nice enough to drive me home."

"Can I help you?" Toby looks from Penny to Jack.

Jack stops mumbling just long enough to squint and look up at the young man who seems to be familiar with his wife. "Wha . . . ?" The pain in his pants takes his breath away.

"Do you think he's having a heart attack?" Toby addresses Penny, perhaps hoping she has some insight into the matter. She recalls vaguely that the warning signs of heart attack involve a painful arm. Though she can't remember whether it is the left or right one, she is pretty sure the symptoms never have anything to do with grabbing one's groin. She is pretty certain her husband is not having a coronary, but before she can allay Toby's fears, Jack interrupts them.

"I bloody well wish it was a goddamn heart attack! Christ!"

Toby looks at Penny, who merely shrugs and doesn't seem too worried about what her husband is going through. She leans closer in toward Toby's ear.

"It's his thingy."

"What?" Toby isn't sure he heard correctly.

"He's not having a heart attack. He's very fit. Very sprightly." She turns to Jack now. "Is it your thingy that's causing you so much pain, darling?" She never calls him "darling," and now in the space of one minute she has used the word twice.

"It's on fucking fire!"

Like a seasoned doctor, Penny turns back to Toby. "Yes. Just as I suspected. It's his penis."

Toby nods. What else can a guy do?

She watches thoughts flicker across the young man's face. If he's horrified, he's hiding it nicely. Maybe he thinks he has fallen prey to some "candid camera" prank. Maybe he thinks he's getting punk'd. It could happen, even in West Vancouver.

"Don't be alarmed, Toby. It will subside if it is what I think it is."

Toby nods again. He probably wants to help the man in front of him, but Penny reasons he might be a touch hesitant in this situation. What little information he has is not good.

Jack is now in a sort of fetal position with eyes tightly shut. He continues to clutch at himself and mumble and groan quietly.

Penny has produced the house keys from her handbag and steps over Jack, who is partially blocking the entrance.

"Did you stick your penis somewhere you shouldn't have, Jack?" She doesn't look at her husband because she is concentrating on getting the door open and remaining calm. The muscle spasms have passed, but her body is still tightly wound and not yet ready to release itself from her ordeal. "There." The door opens and she beckons Toby inside.

"Do you want me to help him inside?"

"Oh." She regards her husband for a moment and quickly realizes that it might be a good idea to get him off the porch.

"Do you think we should call an ambulance? He doesn't look so good."

"No. We don't need to call any ambulance, but I will call a taxi for you. If you could just put him in the living room, I'd appreciate it greatly." She talks about Jack as if he were some cumbersome package, too heavy and bulky for her to move on her own.

Once again, poor Toby leans into the task at hand. The two men don't talk, and it is a straight line from the door to the living room. When Jack is installed on the couch, next to fabric and paint samples, the older man mumbles a reluctant thank-you. Toby nods and quickly comes back into the kitchen.

"Jack messes about with other women, you see. And he's paying the price for it right now. I would advise you to save yourself the pain and embarrassment and stay loyal to your girlfriend. I doubt this will be a deterrent to Jack, but you, on the other hand, may see it through other eyes."

"Yup." Toby is standing outside the kitchen now and listens as she orders him a taxi. Occasionally he glances over in the direction of the man curled up on the couch.

Penny goes into the living room and bends over her husband. "Do you have any money on you?"

Jack opens his eyes and glares at his wife.

"Here, let me check your wallet." She reaches into his back pocket and pulls out a grey leather billfold. He does not protest and lets her rummage through it until she finds a hundred-dollar bill. "Voila!"

Penny never has more than twenty-five dollars in paper money on her person at any given time. She prefers to use her bank card for just about everything. Jack, on the other extreme, always travels with at least a couple hundred dollars. He is the kind of person who likes to be able to reach in and pull out a few crisp twenty-dollar bills. She prefers to have her unused money sit untouched in her bank account. Again, Penny is struck by the fact that she and her husband have always been opposites.

"I insist." She offers the money to Toby, who is standing in the foyer, wide-eyed, taking it all in like he doesn't want to forget any part of this adventure.

"No. It's fine." He has clasped his hands behind his back, showing no intention of taking any money from this lady.

"Toby, now listen to me. You spared me the embarrassment of having to call 911. You drove me home and probably lost considerable tip money. Now you have to take a taxi back. I am not letting you out of here without taking this money."

"Look, don't worry about it." The lights of the taxi appear through the kitchen window and he reaches for the doorknob.

"Take it. Please."

He looks at Penny, her face still red and desperate. Then he glances past her down the hallway to the living room. He nods and accepts the money. "Look after yourself, okay?"

"I will." She opens up the door and sends the young man out into the soft warm night air. "And Toby?" He is down the first few steps of the front porch, and she can no longer see his face.

"Yeah?"

"Thanks again."

She hears the sound of the car door opening and then closing as Toby gets in the taxi. When the car backs up and turns onto the street, the headlights illuminate her front lawn. In the next moment he is gone.

The faint aroma from the honeysuckle wafts up the front steps to where Penny is standing. A few bugs are drawn to the light from the foyer, so she decides to close the door behind her and sit out in the dark.

Crickets are chirping, and in the distance, if she concentrates, she can hear the purr of cars on the road. The air is so soft and the quiet nighttime sounds are so gentle that she wants to inhale deeply all of the darkness around her. She likes it that she can't see anything. That nobody is talking to her. Talking at her. Aside from the time spent alone in the washroom, this is the first moment of this long day where Penny finds stillness, calmness.

"Penny!"

She inhales deeply.

"Pen! Are you there?"

As her eyes adjust to the darkness, she sees that there is another mound of earth that must have been

dropped off today and that there are a bunch of inter-
locking bricks lying in piles next to the side of the garage.

"Penny! I think I need help. I need something.
Christ! Are you there?"

Yes, she sees that there is so much that needs to be
done. So much work ahead of her. So much that while
she was at the gym today and out having way too many
gin and tonics and telling Susan everything, the gorgeous gardener came back. While she was stuck on the
toilet, the clutter-buster woman came and cleaned out
her telephone table. She knows this because when she
phoned for the taxi, she was taken aback by the sole current Yellow Pages book in the drawer. Usually she has
four or five old dog-eared copies covered in doodles and
scrawled with obscure numbers. She inhales deeply.

"Pen-neee!"

In fact, the more she considers her porch, her yard,
her kitchen, she sees she's really let things go for too
long. Everything is in disarray, but she's been so good at
closing her eyes that she hasn't really seen it until now.
She hasn't wanted to. She inhales a deep breath again.

"For the love of God, woman!"

"I'm coming!" she yells. She gets up too fast and her
legs remind her to move more carefully. "Shit!" Next door
a light goes on and the neighbour's yappy Bichon Frise

starts to bark. Penny has disrupted the idyllic tranquility of the evening and quickly retreats inside her house. Her chest is constricting, and her breaths are again shallow.

She marches as best she can into the living room to find her husband clutching a swatch of checkered upholstery.

"I need help, Pen."

"I can see that." She stands erect with her arms crossed.

"I think I'm having some kind of allergic reaction or something. I'm in a lot of pain."

"Jack, listen to me." He groans. "Listen to me, Jack."

He stops moaning and looks attentively at his wife.

"By any chance, Jack, did your young secretary happen to get any of her lipstick on your penis?"

"Ah, Penny, now come on."

"If I am going to help you, I will need to know the details. So, you can lie there in pain or you can tell me. It's your choice."

"Look, I don't want to get into an argument here." He has closed his eyes again and is rocking back and forth.

"I don't want to get into any argument either. We should have argued years ago. It's too late for that now." Penny sits down in an armchair that is covered in paint samples. "Did you kiss that girl at your office?"

"Jesus Christ!"

"Did she kiss your penis?"

He has opened his eyes and is staring straight up at the ceiling. The pain must be overwhelming because she notices he has been crying. From the corner of one of his eyes a constant stream of tears flows down across his cheek and onto the couch.

"Jack. Look at me."

"What?"

"Did she?"

He turns his head slowly and looks at his wife, who is fanning herself with the paint cards. "Maybe."

She neatly folds all the paint cards into a single pile and rises from her chair.

"I'm going to cut up some cucumber for you. I bought some the other day, so you're in luck. While I do that, get your dick out of your pants and just lie there."

"What are you going to do?"

"I'm going to make a cold compress for you that will hopefully take the sting away."

Penny imagines her husband listening to her open and close the fridge door. Hearing the tap running. Hearing her chop something as if she were tossing a few ingredients together for a last-minute meal.

By the time she reappears with a dishtowel filled

253

with the cucumber and tied at the corners, he has unzipped his pants and pulled his underwear down to his thighs. A square piece of checkered material is strategically placed over his genitals.

"Okay. Put this on it." She hands him the lumpy towel and watches Jack place it on his penis. She only used half the cucumber, so she sits down at the end of the couch holding the other six inches in one hand and the salt shaker in the other. Jack sighs as he places the compress onto his tender skin. She notices him wince every time she seasons and chomps on her snack.

"How's that feeling?"

"Oh, it feels really good. Much better."

"Good. I'm glad to hear it." She swallows the last of her cucumber and takes another upholstery square to wipe the sweat away from Jack's forehead. She runs her fingers through his thick white hair.

"What do you think of this for the couch?" She is holding a flower-patterned square up so that Jack can clearly consider the sample.

"I don't know about that stuff, Penny."

"I don't mind this one, really. I just wonder about the matching window coverings and it being too busy, you know?"

She reaches for a binder filled with all sorts of design patterns and colours and options for complementary wallpaper and curtains.

"I don't know if I want to go full tilt with all this stuff. I mean, if I recover the couch and do the walls and the windows all in the same pattern, I think I might feel kind of claustrophobic. I could never buy another couch as long as we lived here. I mean . . . nothing would match, you know what I'm saying?"

"Yes. That's a good point." Jack is able to breathe a little easier now.

"What about this one?" She holds up the entire binder, which is quite heavy. She has opened it up to a beige quite similar to the material that is on the couch right now. "Do you like this one?"

"Very nice."

"I know it's plain, but I like this colour. Do you? Do you like this colour, or are you just pretending to like it? Be honest with me."

"I like it very much."

"Because if you don't like it, I want you to tell me. Maybe you would prefer something more colourful. More dramatic. How about maroon? Look, there's a lot of choices in here. I want you to pick one out. Tell me what your favourite is."

"I don't think I have any favourite."

"Well, why don't you look through it and tell me."

"Sure." Jack props himself up on one elbow while Penny moves in closer with the sample book. He is able to turn over the pages only with difficulty but does not complain.

"This one's nice." He stops to consider a subtly striped taupe material.

"Hmm. Yes. Not bad." Penny has to stretch her neck to see it.

They continue like this until they have looked through the whole binder, like any couple mulling over delicate decisions. Occasionally Jack comments on a material, and most of the time Penny nods in agreement. They resolve to avoid wallpaper at all costs and, if the upholstery is too busy, they will not opt for matching curtains.

"I'm glad we had this chat, Jack."

"Me too."

"We haven't talked like this for a long time."

"I know."

They are quiet for some time.

"Pen?"

"Yeah?"

"What happened to your face?"

"Oh, I got carried away while I was vandalizing a bathroom stall at the bookstore."

"I see." Jack has repositioned himself back onto the couch, sort of halfway between a sitting position and lying down. Penny has put the book on the floor.

"Can I see it?"

"What?"

"Can I see your thingy?" Penny has slid closer on the couch and motions at Jack to remove the dishtowel.

"No, don't! Just leave it."

"I want to see it, Jack."

"It's much better. Just leave it."

"I want to see it!" She grabs at his hands covering his groin.

"Ah, for Christ sake!" He pulls the compress away to reveal a very large and angry red penis.

"It's so red." She is shocked to see it such a bright shade.

"Yes, it appears so."

"And it's so big. Why are you still erect? Why is it so big?"

"I don't know, Penny. I don't know." He replaces the cloth over his skin and groans.

"Did you take one of those sex pills? Is that why you're still so big?"

"Maybe." He has closed his eyes again.

"Does it hurt, though? I mean, being that hard for so long. Does it cause you discomfort?"

When Jack doesn't answer, Penny stretches and stands up. "I think I'm going to head off to bed. Are you okay here?"

"Just fine."

She leans over and kisses Jack full on the lips. "Make sure you tell what's-her-face to find a different lipstick. That you're highly allergic to strawberry."

"How can you be so sure that it's from some lipstick, Penny?"

"Because I gave it to her."

Twelve

Lucky Penny adds colour to her life!
Friday, August 15
Mitch Williams

"It is such an honour being a part of Penny Stevens's transformative journey. And it was so exciting taking Penny to Rocco's salon. It was a fabulous afternoon, and the results are simply awesome." Ms. Linda Campbell, a long-standing client, knew she had to make it happen. Rocco Rodriguez, formerly with Belle Vision Atelier, was thrilled when informed he could offer his talents up to the cause.

"A good haircut can alter one's look, and Penny was definitely due for a change.

Maybe next time she'll go for a bolder shade. I wanted her to really experiment with colour, but she opted for highlights in the end. Rocco is a whiz with colouring. I myself simply can't resist the allure of a new shade and how that impacts your appearance. Penny is certainly less adventurous than most and was adamant that Rocco only cut off a few inches. The result, however, is a vast improvement. The split ends of her once frizzy hair are long gone. Rocco deep-conditioned her locks and gave her a trim to the jaw line, framing her face and accentuating her natural beauty. A hint of blonde adds a streak of sunshine to our Penny." Linda Campbell was very pleased with the day's events.

Next week, Ms. Campbell will complement Rocco's handiwork with her own personal makeup method and beauty regimen for Penny.

And remember, if you're still able to recognize Ms. Stevens, tell her she looks great because, as Linda Campbell has been known to say, "When you tell someone they look great, they feel great. And when they believe it, well, that's when they truly change inside. We all have the capacity to effect positive change in the world. Remember that and life will be awesome!"

Good advice, indeed. 'Nuff said.

All around Penny, Vancouverites are enjoying the gentle breezes of a West Coast summer. The heat wave has broken, barbeques are fired up, and the sun is shining.

The regular hectic pace of life has slowed a bit, and people are more relaxed and easygoing. Everybody, that is, except for Penny. Her life has gone into overdrive, and even though Linda is constantly telling her that "everything is working out just awesome," Penny is finding the opposite to be true. She has become anxious and prone to outbursts.

And today is no exception. It is three against one, but Penny is determined to stand her ground. "But this is where I watch TV."

They are standing in Penny's living room. The carpet has been ripped up and furniture has been pushed back, pictures removed from the walls. It looks like a war zone.

"But it would work much better upstairs." Linda does most of the talking while Johnson stands in the background waiting it out. Occasionally, Charlie will nod vigorously or speak in one-word statements. "Definitely," or "beautiful," or "brilliant." Linda, however, will never give up and natters on incessantly. "You should watch TV upstairs."

"But I don't want to watch TV upstairs."

"But that way you would allow this 'space' to be used for 'living.'" Linda is indicating quotation marks with her index and middle fingers. She does this a lot, and Penny wonders if Linda thinks she sounds better when she talks like this. Mostly Penny finds it irritating.

"But this 'space' is my 'living room,' and in this 'room' I like to 'live,' and in the evening when I 'choose' to watch a program, I like to watch it 'here' on this couch in this 'space.'" *The woman simply doesn't listen.*

"Penny, have you even been watching that design show I told you about?" Linda is always talking about some hit program where people come in and rip up a person's house and rebuild it from the ground up.

"Yes, Linda. I watched it. Right here, in fact." Fingers going at it again. "Right here in my 'living room.'" She doesn't have the heart to tell Linda she hated the show and thought that they overdesigned the house. She couldn't bear that group of wannabe models-turned-actors with tool belts and hammers. She couldn't stand all the women in tight, clingy, V-necked T-shirts and that overbearing host in love with himself who was always yelling about something or other. Clearly, Linda is envisioning a similar kind of scenario here. She has nowhere near the resources of that show, but she is no doubt trying to achieve the same kind of results on a smaller scale, aiming for "Renovate Your Life" to become a regular feature at the paper and to parlay her success into a private business on the side.

Linda has told Penny she recently paid upwards of two thousand dollars for an online course that will teach her how to become a personal coach. For two months she will undergo intense therapy and come to understand what specific obstacles she has subconsciously placed in the way of her own success. In November, just before the American Thanksgiving, she will fly down to Colorado and live communally for one week in a log house with other aspiring coaches. Then, if she survives, she will be qualified to help other people sort out their lives. Penny hopes Linda's teachers will tell her to stop talking in quotation marks.

"Didn't you notice, Penny, that nobody, absolutely nobody, had a television as part of their living-room decor?"

"Sure. But that was a television show, and this is 'Renovate Your Life,' and last time I checked it was 'my' life we are renovating. Not some family of eight who live in two rooms and share one bathroom."

Two nights ago, she started watching that very show but flipped to another channel when they turned one of the kids' rooms into a submarine and the rec room into a home theatre like the deck of *Star Trek*, complete with captain's chair and a wide-screen projection television. She flipped back and caught the last ten minutes of the show when the family arrived home to view the renovation for the first time. There was a lot of screaming and jumping and tears. The mother almost fainted, and Penny couldn't take it any longer. She's pretty sure she would have screamed and fainted too.

"I want your living room to be a place of relaxation."

"I relax by watching TV."

Linda turns to look at Charlie, who is fiddling with the tape measure. Johnson has his eyes fixed on the ceiling and clearly wants no part of this conversation.

"Armoire?" Charlie addresses Linda as if Penny isn't in the room.

"I don't know if we have that in our budget." Linda doesn't even bother to ask Penny if this would be okay with her. Penny watches Linda pace about the room and sigh and flip her red hair this way and that. She hopes it will be really cold in Colorado and that Linda will have roommates as frustratingly pushy as she is.

"Or maybe we could work it into the built-in shelves?" Charlie is looking hopeful.

Linda shrugs and turns questioningly to Johnson. "Well?"

He nods, and they in turn look hopefully at Penny. "Well?"

"Fine. But I don't want any doors on it."

"You'll regret it," says Charlie, who likes everything out of sight.

"No. I don't think I will."

Relieved, Penny sits down in one of the lawn chairs that are in her living room while the couch is being recovered in a blue and yellow striped fabric. The three renovators huddle to discuss their new design plans, and Penny looks about the room. The green shag carpet has been ripped up and thrown off the balcony into the orange dumpster below. The walls have been painted a creamy yellow, and there are a few empty boxes in the corner, courtesy of Charlie.

Penny is supposed to decide which of the knick-knacks, bric-a-brac, whatnots, and thingamajigs she simply can't part with. The rest will be boxed or, as

Charlie has often implied to be the simplest solution, tossed. The clutter buster has already relegated a coffee table from Penny's university days to the basement. With the TV in the bookshelf, there will be a lot more space, and Penny can see that. Even the heavy curtains that are rarely drawn have been taken down and recycled to Goodwill. They haven't picked out any new ones yet, but Linda tells her they will head out to Ikea in a couple of days for a very inexpensive pre-made pattern that will offset the French doors beautifully.

Penny wonders how many people from those TV shows secretly hated their makeovers and couldn't wait to rip down the fishing-pole towel racks and unplug the serenity waterfalls. The more she watches these shows, the more she's coming to realize that these remodelled houses are kind of like a fashion show where one designer is always trying to outdo the other designer. Nobody actually intends to live like that.

Penny, on the other hand, has got to be vigilant. She lives here. This is her house and, like Aaron warned her, things could easily get out of hand. She touches her newly chopped and highlighted hair, happy that she stayed firm, keeping Rocco's scissors at bay and not walking out strawberry blonde or jet black.

A photo shoot for this week's installment is going to take place later today at Lamaraya's studio. Penny, Linda, Charlie, and Johnson will meet up with the rest of the gang at Breathe, where Dalton will photograph not only Penny, but also her entire entourage.

Penny has chosen a light pink lipstick and black capri pants with a soft orange Lycra halter top. She's lost a little bit of weight, but mostly she just feels better. It comes as no great surprise to realize that eating well and exercising can make any person feel and look good. It's bloody hard work, though, and Penny wonders how she's going to keep it up after all of this is over. *Will it ever be over?*

"Oh, you are NOT serious. Tell me this isn't true," Linda screams at Johnson, who is now looking at the floor.

"It'll work." He is holding a moulding about a foot long, comparing it against the existing baseboard.

"No! No! No!" Apparently something is dreadfully wrong.

Penny should probably go and see what all the fuss is about, but she has learned that Linda tends to over-dramatize. Instead, Penny gets up awkwardly out of the lawn chair and goes to investigate one of the boxes Charlie has provided. She notices they are already labelled: Keep, Store, Give Away, and Discard. Penny sighs and picks up a couple of candleholders she made at the do-it-yourself ceramic studio. She makes a move to place them into the "Keep" box, but Charlie has materialized behind her.

"Think about it, Penny."

"Oh, I made these myself," she offers, as if that will explain why she would put such things in the first box.

"Special memories?"

"Well, no, not really. I . . . I thought people keep this kind of stuff. Things that they made. Personally." She rambles on, hoping to clarify her choice.

"Not necessarily."

"Maybe I'll store it?" Penny makes a move to place it in the second container.

"Tell me, why would you want to keep these?" Charlie takes them from Penny's grasp and holds them prominently, one in each hand.

"Oh, well . . . I sometimes, you know, use candles and . . ."

"When was the last time you used these?" Charlie blows off the dust that has settled uniformly over the two creations.

"Okay, it's been a while." Penny slowly removes the two holders from Charlie's hands and places them into the "Discard" box. Charlie smiles.

Linda takes out her cellphone and belts out the name of a local hardware store that she has on speed dial. Luckily, today her technology isn't letting her down, and soon she is talking to some employee about tracking down discontinued items.

"We have GOT to get our hands on about twenty feet." Linda has taken the strip of moulding from Johnson and is now using it as a baton, waving it absent-mindedly as if conducting a symphony in her own head. Presumably the person on the other end of the line has gone off in search of said item as Linda continues to orchestrate, talking to herself, pacing back and forth. Johnson hasn't moved, and Charlie is leaning against the wall, arms crossed, watching, waiting.

Penny, meanwhile, has boxed up all of her paper-backs. "Look. I read these years ago. Like you said, I don't need to have these all out. Right? I mean, they're a bit tattered and dog-eared, right? And so many of them!"

Charlie comes closer as if to inspect the titles. She shakes her head when she sees which box the paper-backs are in. "Nobody stores books."

"Oh." Penny was hoping that Charlie would be proud of her. That she would get some sort of encour-agement for finally filling up a whole box without the painstakingly slow and arduous process of having to defend and clutch and finally release the objects to the basement or the dumpster. "Am I supposed to throw them out?" It feels sacrilegious to discard books.

"No."

"Oh." Penny feels like she is back in primary school, in the "slow" group of her peers, as she tentatively begins to move the books over into the "Give Away" box. Before she has grabbed a second handful, Charlie steps in and simply changes the labels.

"Right. Thanks." What is it about Charlotte Ames that reduces Penny to a bumbling idiot?

A shriek erupts from Linda. "I adore you! You have saved us! Thank God!" she gushes into her phone. "What store are they in?" Linda gives the thumbs-up sign to the other three people as if they couldn't possibly guess that she has gotten good news.

"Richmond? Shit. What time is it?" She switches the receiver into her other hand and checks her watch. It's two o'clock. "Damn. It's gonna be tight. We're doing a photo shoot—yes, no kidding, and . . ." She rattles on to the likely uninterested party about spearheading the project. "Yup, total makeover. We've been at it nonstop for weeks . . ."

At the mention of this, Linda cradles the phone between her chin and shoulder and makes the universal tapping-on-wristwatch move, signalling to her troops that time is up.

"Gosh, I'd love to keep chatting, but I gotta run. Thanks again, you're a life-saver!" She snaps her phone shut and claps her manicured hands. "Awesome, let's go."

At this command, it takes less than a minute for Penny, Charlie, and Johnson to exit the front door, where they wait another five minutes for Linda to collect her immense handbag and keys, scribble a note to herself, and use the washroom to apply more makeup and fluff her hair. She has one foot out the door when she has to return for her sunglasses, which, in the end, she discovers are in her purse.

"Let's motor," says Linda, and Penny thinks she notices Charlie giving Johnson a look.

They decide to take Johnson's Prius, as Charlie arrived on her motorcycle, and Linda's hearse is chock full of bags and crates and makeup trays and magazines.

"Shotgun!" Linda has the enthusiasm of a teenager, and Penny wonders where she gets all of her energy. She never sees her eat anything.

Charlie and Penny fold themselves into the back seat and the car silently begins to roll forward. It is jarring, somehow, not to hear the rumble of the engine, almost unreal. The car is as quiet as the driver.

"So, how many pounds?" Linda catches Penny's reflection in the rear-view mirror.

"About five or so."

"Really?" At this, Linda turns her head to look directly at Penny. Maybe she is wanting a different answer. A bigger number.

"Pretty much."

"Hmm." Linda faces front and smoothes her lap. "We can work with that," she says, as if a lower number would have put the project into jeopardy.

The first week Penny didn't lose a single ounce, and Heather was devastated. She had to submit her column for the project, and Heather wanted results. She glossed over what the scale was reading and focused on all that Penny had done. Just reading the article made Penny tired. Linda, however, reminded everyone to keep the faith, and the next week Penny lost three pounds. Thank God.

Heather's update that week was a celebration. Vindication! The fact that Penny almost threw up at the gym and didn't have the strength to get up off a public toilet didn't matter. Yippee! She was getting skinnier.

And off they finally come!

Sunday, August 17

Heather McCann

Yes you can!

It was hard work that paid off this week for Penny Stevens. She embraced a very active lifestyle with three gym workouts, two walk/cycle circuits of Stanley Park and a visit to a climbing wall. I also took Penny to the supermarket and taught her how to buy healthy choices from the periphery. Avoid the aisles at all cost!

I've included a few of the recipes below. My favourite is the tofu smoothie!

Penny has been a bit sore but is working through her discomfort and trying new things. She tells me she's never eaten so much watermelon in her whole life. She even tried a grapple!

And the result you've all been waiting for? THREE POUNDS and FOUR INCHES, Ladies and Gentlemen!

Sometimes the body holds onto its fat and doesn't want to let go. Don't despair if this happens to you. Stay committed like Penny, and focus on the adventure of all your activities. Enjoy how your body is responding to all the challenges.

Stay tuned, readers. Next week we will be kayaking out in Deep Cove, doing the Grouse Grind and inline skating out in Kitsilano. Of course, we'll also be at the gym. Don't be shy and say hi if you see us!

Penny realized she was more happy for Heather than for herself when she read the article. Her trainer seems to have more riding on it than she does. Even though it was Penny that was under the microscope, Heather was determined that Penny would not fail.

Johnson slides his hybrid into a one-hour parking spot around the corner from the yoga studio.

"Did you bring your tool belt?" Linda is carrying a portable cosmetic case. Charlie will be posing with a garbage bag, and Johnson is supposed to wear his leather belt and hammer. Mitch will have a pen and clipboard, Heather will likely have a stopwatch and a whistle, and Aaron will arrive with a rake or a shovel. Penny will simply be coiffed and gorgeous—perfect.

Johnson produces his prop from the hatch of the car, and Penny and her cast of characters walk into Breathe.

They find Lamaraya meditating on an authentic yogi ball that she brought back as carry-on from her latest trip to India, where her guru teaches. Master So-and-So.

For a moment everyone is still. Silent. Penny doesn't dare disrupt the tranquility, but Lamaraya must be aware they are here. She's been expecting everyone. The moment stretches uncomfortably until the group's attention is turned to Heather, who arrives with a burst, carrying barbells and sporting the most intensely striking lime-green leggings and matching tank top.

"Hi all," she says, looking at the team and taking in Lamaraya on the cushion.

"Well, this is different."

The yoga instructor brings her hands together into the prayer position, leans a bit forward, and inhales and exhales deeply. Slowly she opens her eyes and acknowledges the people in her midst. "Welcome." Lamaraya rises with ease.

Penny makes quick introductions, and people step forward and smile and shake hands. Within minutes, Dalton and Mitch arrive and the studio is abuzz with movement. Linda takes the lead and directs the team and Penny, all the while complimenting Lamaraya on the feng shui of her space and thanking her for the use of the studio.

"I adore this room. It has an amazing aura. Love the colour scheme. Penny, wipe that lipstick off, tissues in my case. Heather, do you by any chance have another outfit handy? You're going to clash with these walls. Charlie, find something to fill up your garbage bag with. Oh, I feel so peaceful here! Hurry up, everyone. I'm on a tight schedule."

Heather has remained uncharacteristically subdued and quiet. She's made no secret that she is put off by Lamaraya, since she envisioned herself the sole "remodeller" of Penny's physical body. When Linda called a meeting involving all parties working on the Penny Project to compare notes, everyone arrived on time carrying their respective scribblers and folders and timelines and goals. Mitch and Dalton were there too, because, of course, one would be writing all the articles and the other would photograph the process as it developed. Even the boss, Sylvia, was there, overseeing each department and even going so far as to compliment Linda for the initiative. Everyone was hoping readers would respond to the story. That they'd get more than the normal amount of letters and positive feedback on the feature.

And quite a few people have written in. A few in particular have commented on the yoga, how beneficial it was.

I am so happy to hear that Penny Stevens is also adding yoga to her exercise regimen. When I had to stop running due to bad knees, I tried all the aerobics and circuit workouts and found them to be spiritually lacking. After a long run, I was much more relaxed and de-stressed. Workouts are good for burning calories, but a person needs to stretch their muscles and release the tension. And Penny Stevens is just starting out. I think the element of yoga will keep her committed to the project.

Good luck,
Chris Adams

For 15 years I have been dieting and trying to lose weight. I did everything. And I stuck with nothing. I'm not an exercise person. Never have been. Then a year ago a friend and I joined the rec centre's intro to yoga. It is the only thing that I have ever stayed with. Some people aren't made for the gym. I'm so glad I discovered yoga because I was about to give up! I love hearing about Penny Stevens. I can totally

relate to her. I also like reading about her
house and garden.

Thanks again,
Anonymous

Those articles struck a chord with Penny. It was touching how people were reacting to the column, wishing
her well—complete strangers. And Sylvia was very
pleased. So delighted, in fact, that she invited Lamaraya
to take part in Project Penny.

This still does not sit well with Heather, who is
pumping her weights while Linda and Dalton discuss
where the best lighting is. It doesn't look like Heather
has any other clothes, either. But Linda deftly solves that
crisis too. "No worries. We'll just put you in the back."

Heather pumps a little harder and Penny looks
away, hoping her exercise coach is able to do a few vis-
ualizations and positive affirmations. It looks like she
needs them right about now.

"Boo!"

"Aaron!"

"What's up, gorgeous?"

"Photo shoot. I'm a celebrity, you know." She is glad
she looks good this day. She needs every shred of confidence she's got.

"Every woman's a celebrity. Everyone's a star. It's just that most of them don't know it."

"Sure. Right. I keep forgetting that. Must write it down."

"Let me look at you."

"Oh."

"You know, Penelope, you really are looking good today."

"Oh, thanks. Linda picked this out for me . . . I don't really know anything about clothes." She waves off his comments, blushing at the same time.

"You don't know how to take a compliment, do you?"

"Oh, well, thanks. I must have lost about five—"

"I don't care about that."

"Well, everybody else seems to be really interested in that."

"That's because they're all idiots."

"Oh?" Penny wills herself to say more than "oh." She'll have to mention her assertiveness with the TV. Aaron will be impressed.

"The most important thing is how you feel." He hunches down, trying to make level eye contact with her. "How do you feel?"

"Oh, good." She is definitely not comfortable with this man staring so intensely at her. Pretty soon she's going to break into a sweat under his scrutinizing gaze, and she doesn't want to have to reapply her foundation. It was Linda who told her to wear some makeup in the first place, and she feels ridiculous sporting mascara and blush and concealer for a workout picture, but she's merely following directions. Seems like everybody has lists of instructions for her these days.

"Well, that's great then. Just remember that, Penelope. After all this is over, it's how you feel that's important."

"You're right. I'll try not to forget that."

"Have fun. Just relax and remember everybody's crazy. This whole thing: Linda, Johnson, Heather, and me and my rake here, we're all nuts. Remember that. And when Dalton gets going with his Nikon, pretend it's just a joke between you and the camera. You'll be amazed at how much fun you'll have."

"Sounds like you've done this before."

"After I got kicked out of my parents' house with nothing but the clothes on my back, I spent a year or so doing runway and some magazine spreads. Crazy times, but it put me through college and I got the down payment for my condo, so I shouldn't complain."

"Wow." Here this guy offers up a big, juicy insight into his life and again her ability to talk in sentences with him is impaired. Of course it makes sense that he was a model. This would be a really good opportunity to perhaps ask him some questions, but her brain is apparently fried. Maybe because Penny has been hanging around Johnson, who rarely speaks, and Charlie, who's just a tad ahead of him in the speech department, she has now caught the same monosyllabic virus that is plaguing members of the reno crew. *If only Linda would get it.*

"Yeah, I've got some stories to tell, that's for sure."

"Gosh, I bet." *Gosh? Did I just say "gosh"?*

The photo shoot *does* turn out to be fun. Maybe more *funny* than *fun*. Cameras and cables everywhere. Mitch fiddling with some handheld electronic device. Dalton playing with some other sort of digital toy, measuring the distance between his camera and the designated spot where Penny will ultimately be placed.

It is quite something watching Linda interact with Lamaraya too. Like a human sponge, she seems to be sucking up all the essence and aura that Lamaraya exudes. Having one of those chameleon personalities, Linda has always gravitated toward anything new. Over the years at the *Sentinel*, Linda has been telling Penny that she has just found some new thing that has "totally changed my life!" She recalls Linda doing Reiki and tantric dance and hatha yoga and hot yoga. A few years back, after Linda's divorce, she went to church and briefly became "born again." That was the worst for Penny, because Linda was forever after her salvation, like she was going to get extra Air Miles if she brought another heathen into the flock.

"Come to our discussion group. You never know, it might totally change your life." Like clockwork, Linda asked Penny every week.

"Oh, that's fine. Thanks, Linda. I don't really go in for organized religion."

"Oh, but it's not really religious at all."

"Really?" *Just how disorganized could it be?*

"Yeah. Just a group of people getting together and talking and stuff like that."

"So what do you talk about?" Penny shouldn't have asked.

"Just life and stuff."

"So, like, do you share recipes and talk about movies?"

"Well, we watched a movie once."

"Oh?" Penny had already seen Charlton Heston lugging all those commandments up the mountain. She politely told Linda that it wasn't going to work for her.

"Suit yourself."

Penny recalls Linda giving her the cold shoulder for a few weeks until she got involved in some kind of primal scream therapy. She would walk around quite red-faced and occasionally have to go into her office and quickly close the door and put her face into a pillow. Yes, Linda's been into a lot of stuff through the years, but the pillow was definitely preferable to the proselytizing. Overall, though, Penny admires her for continuing along her endless quest for whatever she is searching for. She sure is trying.

Today, she certainly is chatting up Lamaraya, and Penny would not be surprised to learn that Linda is now heavily immersed in a yogic and spiritual journey that is going to, yet again, change her life. Why not?

"Oooo! This looks great. How much is it?" Linda is holding a pamphlet that she found on a table by the corner.

"It's *dana*," says Lamaraya.

"Pardon me?"

"You pay what you feel you should pay."

"Really?" Linda has spent a fortune for her self-help over the years. "What's the normal amount?"

"Some pay nothing and others leave a considerable sum."

"Like it can be free? That's awesome. I mean, I'd love to come. I used to do meditation, but I've gotten so swamped. I miss it."

"Yes, we are all so busy." Lamaraya explains how she hosts monthly weekend retreats at her acreage up in Pemberton. They practise yoga, meditate, and listen to dharma talks, spiritual readings, and lessons on life. All the money raised goes to an ashram in India. "We often do cleanses, as well."

"I love cleansing!" As if that seals the deal, Linda stuffs the leaflet into her purse.

Penny observes the sunlight streaming into the studio. The gleaming hardwood floors are warm beneath her.

"So, how is our Good Samaritan?" Mitch pulls up another yogi cushion and, with difficulty, joins Penny, who is on her yoga mat in a pool of light, clasping her knees, rocking back and forth.

"Very well, thank you." She continues rolling.

"Aren't you the nimble one."

"I love this move. It's called The Ball. One of my favourites after Corpse Pose. Does wonders for the spine." She stops rolling and comes to a sitting position.

"So, may I have a moment of your time, Ms.

Stevens?" Mitch produces his recorder and asks if he may turn it on.

"Of course." Penny makes a dramatic sigh. "I don't normally talk to the press. You're lucky I like you, Mr. Williams."

"That's what all the ladies say." He smiles and presses the button to record.

"So," he asks.

"So," she answers.

"Being difficult, are we?"

"Aren't all divas supposed to be?"

"So you're a diva now?"

"Of course." She gives him a wink. "Right. Let's get down to brass tacks. I've lost five pounds. Make sure you get that in there."

"Five pounds, as noted."

"Heather would kill me if we left that out."

"So, you feel threatened by your trainer?"

"She tries to do me in every day!" It was a constant battle for Penny to find the right amount of balance with a personal coach who was almost killing her.

"How do you think she'll do it?"

"Murder me, you mean?"

"Any inklings?"

"Well, barbells will likely be involved."

"I see."

They both glance over to where Heather is now lunging with alternate weights in each hand.

"Seriously, Heather is a good trainer. Perhaps the best because she is working with *me*. I'm no picnic, my friend." Penny is forever admonishing herself for not being grateful enough.

"You dislike picnics?"

"Let me clarify. I adore picnics if I get to choose the food. Heather has me on a low-cal diet and I am eating strange things."

"How strange?"

"Let's see, no wheat, no dairy, very little red meat . . ."

"What does that leave?"

"Not much."

Penny has brought along the file folder that Heather provides each week. In it Penny has written down everything she has eaten, as well as all the activities and exercises she has managed to survive.

"I'm supposed to record how I feel and check in emotionally, but I've been too tired, if you get my drift."

"So? What do you think of your life reno so far?"

"Seriously? I'm a bit overwhelmed. I mean, look at

us all." Penny waves her arm to gesture at all the individuals here at Breathe.

"So, you are overwhelmed? Are you conceding defeat, Penny Stevens?"

"Okay, okay. There are times when it's fun. I liked the water aerobics and always enjoy walking around the seawall." She doesn't dare admit to anyone that she has thought about quitting. Only briefly, after which she's felt guilty. She's given herself lots of pep talks these days and only ever rants out loud at home. With Jack.

"And the house reno?"

"Really good. Aside from having to face up to the fact I've become a bit of a hoarder and that Charlotte Ames can be brutal, the place is looking great. Johnson has made my living room elegant."

"What about the garden?"

"Fabulous. Have you seen it recently? So much better. Tidy. I'm very thankful. It's really coming together."

"All in all, then, Penny, how would you rate this experience overall?"

She shuts her eyes and draws her knees in tighter and thinks before she answers. Penny has to admit that all the problems lie with her. Reluctance to exercise. Fear of change—even when it's positive. The entire project is about improvement, and things are getting better. The house and garden are coming along faster than Penny, but just the other day she did forty minutes on the treadmill. She reminds herself to remember that.

"I guess I would have to say that despite my initial doubts and misgivings—okay, maybe 'aversion' would be a more accurate way to put it—I think the team would support me in saying that, well, I think I may be slowly coming around."

"You're getting into it?"

"Sort of, yeah. Some of it. Yeah."

"Great. This is good, then, isn't it?"

Of the hundred or so photos that are taken that afternoon, Penny hopes she can get her hands on the one of Lamaraya upside down. It's the oddest pose and looks impossible. Unadvisable, really. Like no human should ever attempt it. And the fact that the woman is smiling makes it all the more amazing.

Penny wants to enlarge it and hang in up somewhere prominent so that every time she feels inundated by insecurity and lack of confidence, she can look at Lamaraya and smile too. Life upside down can work. Maybe.

Thirteen

Billy, the neighbourhood "fat kid," is slowly pulling an old Radio Flyer wagon with a hundred or so copies of the *Sentinel* precariously balanced on it. The paper is delivered on Wednesdays, Fridays, and Sundays, but Billy has been known to be a day late once or twice a month. Penny is anxiously awaiting today's paper because she knows she is on the front page of the Home and Life section.

This afternoon, Billy's mother, whose name Penny can't recall, is helping him with his deliveries. Penny has seen her do this before. In fact, she often sees this petite, energetic woman and her large son walking past her house. She's been helping him with the paper route for as long as Penny can remember. *Poor kid. High school is not going to be easy for him.*

Penny comes out onto the porch as Billy begins his laborious way along the path up to her front door. A steady stream of sweat pours down his freckled face. He is panting audibly, one arm shielding his eyes and the other offering the paper up to Penny at the top of the steps.

"Thanks, Billy."

"Welcome."

When he turns away, she watches his backside slowly retreat down towards the street. She catches sight of Billy's mother, who gives a quick wave to say hello. Penny watches Billy bend over and pick up the handle of his wagon. Slowly, he starts off down the block. His mother is already off, delivering copies to the other side of the street.

This afternoon, Penny takes the *Sentinel* directly to the dining-room table. For once the house is quiet. No contractors or consultants or chatter on this day. Jack left hours ago, and Penny is happy to have the house to herself. Normally she reads the news curled up on the sofa or, if nature calls, on the throne. She pretty much reads the paper from front to back, usually discarding the flyers directly into the recycling. It's a good community paper, and Penny likes to keep abreast of what her colleagues are writing.

Today, however, she takes extra care with each segment, laying them out carefully across the clean and polished wood of the table. Gently, she glides the Home and Life section out of the folds.

Staring up at Penny is her very own face. She knows it is her face because she remembers posing like that, and she knows it is not some other person because the caption under the five-by-seven colour photo reads "The new Penny Stevens!" Nevertheless, it is somewhat unnerving to be staring at yourself and wondering if indeed this is who you are.

Look at her! The woman in the photo is sitting cross-legged on her yoga mat, staring directly up into the camera. Her hair, which Penny remembers arranging herself that morning, bears no resemblance to the tousled yet stylish coiffure gazing back at her. Linda had rearranged and fluffed and applied an endless stream of hairspray. On the bottom left of the page is the smaller, old, cropped black and white photo of Penny standing with the brown paper bag holding the Jenkinses' money. She was wearing pink lipstick that day too. *Look! That's me!*

The other photo at the end of the article is the group picture. In the back row, from left to right, are Heather,

Aaron, Mitch, and Johnson. Linda is in the middle row with Charlotte to her left and Lamaraya to her right. Front and centre is Penny. It is quite a good shot, with everyone holding their respective gear, smiling. It could have come across as cheesy, but somehow Dalton has captured his subjects in a very natural, real moment. Maybe it was the studio. Even Heather looks calm.

It is really something seeing this last month of her life laid out in front of her. All these people and all this advice and activity. Penny gets up and goes into the kitchen for a glass of water. She wants to be in a perfect state of mind when she reads the article.

"I am learning to embrace my new lifestyle. Changing is harder on the inside, but the results are seen on the outside and I am liking this new me very much."

"Did I say that?" Penny leans forward and places both hands flat upon the newspaper in front of her, like she is wrestling with the words and wants to hold them down, stop them from jumping up off the page. *I don't think I said that.* She leans back and looks up at the ceiling, presumably to summon the strength to go on.

"She was ready," says Linda Campbell, the beauty and lifestyle consultant here at the Sentinel. Linda is known to have an eye for transforming both the "physical and the spiritual" in a person's world, and Penny Stevens is no exception here.

Penny has a queasy feeling in her gut and takes a moment to check out the picture again. Satisfied that it is indeed her, she reads on.

"At 40 years of age Penny was out of shape and out of the times. Slowly, we are working with her and teaching her to take time for herself and to make that a priority." Heather McCann, Penny's fitness coach, is also very pleased with the progress Penny is making. "She is learning to embrace 'yes!' and has a positive outlook to her workouts. We are climbing that mountain one step at a time."

"I'm pumped!" says Penny Stevens, who is a new woman these days . . .

"I am?" Penny is standing up now, backing away from the dining-room table. She needs to breathe and can't seem to do it sitting that close to the article.

After she finally does sit down and finish the column, she refolds the Home and Life section back into its place and immediately recycles the entire paper.

For a moment she thinks of phoning up Mitch. Where did he get this tale from? Hadn't she bared her soul to him? This is a different woman presented here. She thinks about calling up Linda. Maybe she could threaten Linda to retract the story. But what good would that do? "Renovate Your Life!" is about change. Losing weight and looking better. What would the point be in telling the truth? That Penny Stevens is not sure she can ever be what other people want? That she is worried she will gain all the pounds back once Project Penny wraps up?

The article is simply giving readers what they want—telling them that it is possible to change their lives. If Penny fails, then what message would that send?

And threaten Linda? What could Penny do? Run out into West Vancouver wearing shoulder pads from the 1980s and cheap lipstick from Wal-Mart? She could phone up Heather and tell her that she has eaten a bag of Timbits and can't make it to that step class because she has a reservation at the Golden Arches later this afternoon.

Probably, though, nobody would care. People like to read this stuff. They buy into it and don't really care whether it's true or not. People like Cinderella stories. They can't help it. The feminists have tried to debunk them, and they succeeded for a millisecond, but they seem to be back bigger and better than ever before. Cinderella gets a new dress, goes to the ball, and snags the handsome prince. While they are on honeymoon in Cancun, the castle is redone in designer colours, and when they come home they find they have all-new, shiny stainless-steel appliances. They live happily ever after and, as Martha Stewart would say, "It's a good thing."

There's definitely something to be said for having support and seeing results, but Penny wonders what some readers, the ones like Penny who are struggling, will really think when they see this article. The photos look great, but they don't tell the whole story. She remembers chatting with Mitch, who reassured her that she need not worry. Now, having read the article, she regrets not worrying. She should have been frantic. She should have insisted on being hysterical!

Anybody who knows Penny would not believe she is "thrilled and pumped! Every morning I jump out of bed. I can't wait to get to the gym."

Just the other day, Jack, who has been cautiously observing this woman who was formerly "Penny, his wife," argue, fight, and disagree with these people, finally became exasperated himself.

"Why don't you just phone up Sylvia and tell her you want out?"

"Because I can't!"

"And why not?"

"Because!"

"Ah. I see." But he wouldn't understand that Penny had made a commitment to these people. That she couldn't just walk out on the process and leave them high and dry. Her colleagues. And the readers. And Susan. Even her mother, who couldn't wait to show off her daughter to all her friends at the Manor.

Then again, it shouldn't come as any surprise that her husband wouldn't understand. He never did appreciate what a commitment was.

"Hey, beautiful!"

Penny spins around and sees Aaron's head at her open kitchen window.

"Sorry." He laughs, seeing her face. "I should have called. I'm here to finally take out those old cedars." He is wearing a sleeveless maroon T-shirt, and the sight of his muscles makes her once again wonder if maybe he has an unsightly birthmark somewhere. She desperately wants to imagine some imperfection on this man.

"So? Shall I come round?"

"What?" Penny does not grasp what he is saying. She is still reeling from the article.

"Can I come in?"

"Sorry. Of course."

Aaron comes up the front steps and starts to remove his shoes. Normally he and Penny stay out on the porch to talk, but today it appears the gardener has other plans.

"Can I see it?"

"Sorry? What?"

"Can I see the inside? The reno?" He has one shoe on and one shoe off.

"Oh! Of course. Of course." Maybe he's read the article too and wants to see what all the fuss is about. At least she can't complain that her house is a mess. It has never looked this good. This tidy.

"Well, my lady, lead the way." Standing this close to him, Penny smells his aftershave. It is a citrus blend and is very compelling.

"Okay." Since they are in the foyer, which is right next to the kitchen, she figures this would be the place to start. "May I present the kitchen?" She makes a grand sweeping gesture with her hand, and Aaron bows slightly and steps into the room.

The kitchen is the room that most benefited from Charlie's rigorous distaste for excessive junk. Every magazine and dish that wasn't needed or in its rightful place was either thrown away or put out of sight. Every stitch of paper or out-of-date coupon was removed from the bulletin board. All magnets disappeared from the fridge. The hand-knitted oven mitts that Alice made two years ago were thrown out. They were truly hideous.

Johnson pulled off the unsightly rubber baseboards and replaced them with six-inch mouldings. The walls were painted a sage green, and new handles were put on the cupboards.

"It really was a sight. I have to admit." Penny watches Aaron take it all in.

"Sometimes a room just needs a tune-up. I redid the bedroom two years ago when I got sick of the cranberry thing, and afterward I realized how dark the place had been. How I never saw it before, I can't imagine." He runs his large square hands along the countertops.

"I guess I never realized what a pigsty I was living in either."

"Don't beat yourself up over it, Penelope. All of us

have a hard time seeing ourselves as we truly are, don't you think?"

"I suppose so."

"No, seriously. Think about it. Half the time people are pretending they are something they are not, and the rest of the time other people have a hard time accepting us for who we are."

"Well, I'm having a hard time pretending to embrace the 'new and improved me.' I don't feel 'new' and I certainly haven't 'improved' very much. I'm getting the distinct feeling that people can't really see me being anything other than 'new' and 'shiny' and 'skinny.'"

"My father just couldn't see me being anything other than a lawyer."

"Is that why you left home?"

"Among other things." He winks at her. "Are those Denby mugs?" Charlie chose Penny's best dishes and displayed them prominently behind the glass cabinets. The mugs she hung on little hooks. Of the eight, only five weren't chipped.

She watches him hold a cup tenderly in his hand and then replace it on the hook. She wonders why she has never truly appreciated her mugs. She makes a mental note to adore all things Denby but then remembers that she has never been a trademark or brand defender. When somebody asks her what kind of car she drives, Penny will say "yellow." If pressed for more information, she will add that it is a station wagon.

In the living room, Penny explains about the couch, how it used to be a plain beige. Aaron says it looks "spectacular—kind of retro French Provincial." Penny, of course, agrees with him and thinks she wouldn't mind seeing what his living room looks like.

"My favourite thing is the bookshelf," she says. It is painted white and contrasts nicely with the pale yellow walls, which is exactly what Aaron says. Only quality hardcover books and the odd ceramic bowl adorn these shelves. And, of course, the controversial TV.

"But you like the TV in this room, right?" He is looking at her closely.

"Yes, I do."

"Well then, it's good." Aaron goes over to an old black and white photo of Penny and her parents. "Your folks?"

"Yes."

Next to that picture is a nicely framed photo of her and Jack on their wedding day.

"So, what does he think of all of this?"

"Jack? He likes it, I guess." She doesn't know what else to add because she and Jack haven't really talked about anything much recently. He is quietly going about his business while she continues on her public quest for home- and self-improvement.

Aaron runs his index finger over the top of the frame as though he's checking for dust. "Did they do anything to the upstairs?"

"Mostly just Charlie doing her thing up there—you know, throwing away stuff." They filled four bags with clean used clothing that Linda took for recycling. Another two bags went directly into the orange bin. Charlie would have gotten rid of more—Penny is sure of that.

Aaron doesn't make a move toward the stairs and instead props himself on the back end of the couch. Likewise, Penny leans uncomfortably against an end table, hoping it can take her weight.

"The inside looks great, Penelope. Love the curtains. And Jimmy should be here soon. It'll be a huge improvement getting rid of those trees."

Penny awkwardly regains her balance and walks with him to the front door. "I don't think I've seen your partner before."

"No. I don't call on him unless I really need help on a job. This is going to be a bit tricky." Out on the porch the air feels sticky.

"Does he mostly work on other yards? Does he have his own clients?"

"Jimmy? God, no! Gardening never really was his thing."

As if on cue, a blue Jeep pulls into the driveway. Aaron waves and Penny finds herself smiling and waving at the young man getting out of the vehicle.

"How long has he been helping you out?" She is feeling a new wave of confidence growing inside of her, as she has been holding a somewhat normal conversation for at least a minute now.

"God, let's see. We've been together since just after I started my own company, so that makes it eight years, I'd say."

"Well it's good to have some help when you need it."

As Jimmy comes closer, she sees that he looks like a cross between Denzel Washington and Tiger Woods.

Jimmy takes hold of her hand, and as he lifts it ever so lightly, Penny finds herself curtseying. "Pleased to make your acquaintance, Ms. Stevens. Jimmy Prentiss at your service. I hope Aaron is behaving himself in your company." There is a slight accent to his speech.

"He has been a perfect gentleman."

"A perfect gentleman, you say? Then he's got you fooled." Jimmy throws his head back and laughs, and

Penny thinks she has never seen such a beautiful smile. *Not one, but two gorgeous guys. Am I lucky or what!*

Aaron motions for Jimmy to come up onto the porch. "You must be dying of thirst." As there are no chairs, Jimmy sits on the top step. "Let me get you something to drink before we tackle the cedars."

Before she can say anything, Aaron has disappeared into the kitchen, and she is sitting down next to Jimmy.

"Don't worry. He's like that all the time. He's always taking over other people's houses. Today it might be just your garden—tomorrow it will be your life." Jimmy's voice is hypnotic, and she feels like she's met him somewhere before.

He rubs his temples and lets out a painful sigh.

"Hard day?" Penny notices his fingers are clean and his shirt doesn't have a stain or a mark on it, which she'd expect from a landscaper.

"It's been a great day. Saw my favourite clients today out in White Rock. It's the traffic that gets to me."

"Oh, you have clients in White Rock?"

"Yes. A lovely old couple. He's eighty-nine and she is eighty-three."

"I imagine anyone that age would need help in their garden. Look at me. This place was a mess, and I'm half their age."

Aaron comes out onto the porch with three glasses of water with lemon wedges. He offers the first glass to Penny, careful not to drop the other two. The second glass he presses up against the back of Jimmy's neck.

"Oh, man!" Jimmy's hands fly out before him and she notices their immense size.

"Here, Aaron, give me that." He takes it and before drinking he presses the cool glass up to his forehead. "Actually, it feels good." He takes a long drink. "And it hits the spot too."

Penny drinks her water and remarks to herself how much better it tastes with just a hint of citrus.

Aaron empties his glass and puts his arm around her. Again she thinks she smells his cologne, or perhaps it is the taste in her mouth.

"I didn't even know I had a lemon. Thank you."

"For you, anything."

Jimmy rolls his eyes and Aaron stands up.

"Okay, bud. I'm not paying you by the hour, and we gotta get this job done or Penelope here will have us fired."

Jimmy slowly comes to his feet. "Okay, boss."

Aaron tells Jimmy to get the saw and rope and a few other things from his truck. Slowly Jimmy saunters over to Aaron's truck, rolling his eyes and shaking his head as he leaves.

"So you guys have people as far out as White Rock?"

"Oh, no. Those are Jimmy's clients. He's a social worker."

"Oh, a social worker."

"Yeah, he's also going to university part-time and getting his masters'. So he helps me when he can." Aaron disappears into the house with the glasses.

"Oh, I see." That helps explain why his shirt is so clean, Penny thinks. A moment later he is back outside. "He has an accent." She says this fact more like a question.

"Yes, he hails from Dominica, not to be confused with the Dominican Republic. Don't get him started unless you want to hear about poverty and bananas and the nuns at the Catholic school and his grandmother. God, he loves that woman! Just take a tip from me, and don't ask." He is smiling and rolling his eyes too. Then he adds, "It is a nice accent, though, don't you think?"

"Yes. Very nice."

Penny goes inside but keeps her eyes on Aaron and Jimmy and the three soon-to-be-gone cedar trees. They have a ladder up against one, and Jimmy, now shirtless and on the second highest rung, is using a large handsaw and removing branches. His abdomen is a perfect six-pack.

Soon the tree looks very odd. Aaron is yelling something at her, but she can't make it out so she comes out onto the porch.

"You sure you don't want some bush sculptures? Maybe Mickey Mouse ears?"

Now it is Penny who is rolling her eyes. "No, I'm sure, but thank you."

It takes them about fifteen minutes per tree, making a lot of noise and mess. After two-thirds of a tree has had its branches removed, Aaron has Jimmy tie a rope around the top of the cedar. Then a cut is made at the base of the tree and Aaron gently guides the tree to fall away from the garage and the newly planted flowerbeds.

From what she can tell, the guys are having fun despite the heat and all the chaos they are creating. When the final tree comes crashing down, they let out a cheer and Penny applauds from her spot on the porch.

Then something happens. For a moment Penny thinks that Jimmy is hurt. Aaron is holding onto him in what looks to be an embrace. *Is he bleeding? Is he okay?* She stands up and shields the sun from her eyes. *Do they need bandages? Did Jimmy cut his lip? His face?*

She is two steps from the bottom of the stairs when the creature appears. Its head is eye-level with her, and she recoils in disbelief. It is grey and scraggly, and Penny can't process what it might be or from where it may have come. She falters, still holding the glass in her hand when she miscalculates her footing and falls, tumbling off the porch.

"Penelope? Penny?"

In the distance, she hears voices. Like they are on a ship. There is a lot of fog and confusion, and though she wants to open her eyes, she can't. It feels like one of those CBC heritage commercials about early Canadian culture or something.

"Penny! Are you all right?"

Who are these people? Where am I?

"Jimmy has gone inside to get some paper towels and water. You've hit your head. Just a bit of blood, here."

Who the hell is Jimmy?

She hears footsteps returning.

"Is she okay?"

"I don't know. Maybe we should call an ambulance." There are mumbles that Penny can't make out, then she feels someone wiping her forehead and down alongside her ear. She also feels very hot breath close at the other side of her head. "Haggis! Fuck off!"

"Ouch!"

"Penelope?"

"Yes."

"Are you there?"

"I guess."

"Are you in pain?"

"Yes."

"Can you open your eyes?"

"I don't know."

She hears footsteps retreating.

"Jimmy's calling you an ambulance. You've fallen and hit your head."

"I see." *Jimmy who?*

More footsteps. "Okay, they're coming. Jesus, she hit pretty hard." This voice is musical, but Penny can't put a face to it. In the distance, she hears sirens and rightly assumes they are coming for her. As the sounds get louder and closer, she forces herself to open her eyes.

Through dilated and bleary pupils she makes out three faces staring down at her. Two beautiful men— one white, one black—and a wolf beast.

She was wrong. It's not a CBC spot. Whatever this is, it's in black and white, but it's not very clear. She must be dreaming.

· · ·

The nurse attending Penny has an upside-down happy-face button on her lapel. She is fast, efficient, and in a bad mood.

"Name?"

"Penny Stevens."

"Age?"

"Forty."

"How many fingers am I holding up?"

Penny answers her rapid-fire interrogation as quickly as she can. She tries to match the nurse's speed with as much alertness and clarity as she can muster. Her head is throbbing.

"Would it be possible for me to get a shot of something to numb the pain? My head really hurts." She is hopeful.

"The doctor will have to see you first. You've got quite a gash there."

"How about just a Tylenol?"

"The doctor will be here when he gets here."

Penny thinks of asking for a double cappuccino with chocolate sprinkles on the side but doesn't have the guts to do it.

In the bed next to her a woman is moaning. She can't see her through the curtain but spots two pairs of pedestrian, non-medical shoes hovering at the bedside.

Across the aisle an elderly man is staring patiently at the ceiling. He is covered in blood, presumably from a cut to his head. Maybe, thinks Penny, this is the ward for head wounds. The once-white bandage wrapped around his forehead needs to be changed. Penny touches at the tightly wound gauze at her head and wonders how long she will have to wait, if they are going to admit her, or if they will simply let a clumsy forty-year-old woman go home.

Luckily, due to the copious amount of blood leaking from her head, she jumped the line and didn't need to spend any time in the waiting room. Screaming children, broken bones, and heart-attack victims also get preferential treatment.

Penny wonders what time it is and if anyone has called Jack. Then she remembers Aaron and that other guy. They were so kind.

"Ms. Stevens? I'm Dr. MacDonald. How are you doing?" He looks to be in his mid-fifties and has a very kind face and gentle voice. He doesn't rush her as she recounts her story to him, what she can recall.

"Something startled you and you lost your footing, hey? Happens to us all." He is examining her forehead and concludes that she will need a few stitches.

"How many?"

"I don't know. Five or ten? I'm a pretty good seam-stress, and where your hairline is, I think you'll find you won't even notice." He smiles at Penny, who can only blink mutely back. "Nurse Wilkins? Can you bring the kit?"

For some silly reason, Penny feels like she wants to cry. She would like her mother. She's never had stitches and is pretty sure she doesn't want them.

"Is it going to hurt?"

Nurse Wilkins arrives with a loud, rolling trolley with all the prerequisite needles and thread and band-ages. She begins to lay out these supplies in a meticulous manner while the doctor makes a few notes on Penny's chart and puts on another pair of rubber gloves.

"Are we going to do it here?" Penny can hear her voice getting small and tinny.

"What's that?" Dr. MacDonald stops what he is doing and looks at her. His gloves are raised in mid-air as if he has been caught red-handed.

"Are you going to sew me up right here?"

"Yes, are you okay?"

"Well, I'm wondering if maybe I should call my hus-band. Before we get started, you know?" She wants to keep on talking and delay the stitching. She talks to the doctor but also keeps her eye on the nurse. The metic-ulous order of the bandages and gauze and thread lie waiting silently. The needle, laid out so perfectly, glints in anticipation.

"There are two gentlemen in the waiting room asking after you," says Nurse Wilkins as she picks up some antiseptic liquid. Like any nurse in any hospital in any underfunded province in the country, she's no doubt under the gun to get the process going. Even free medicare has its costs.

"Oh, yes, my gardener. He was there when I fell." Penny has the feeling that Nurse Wilkins is sneaking closer and closer and might possibly snuff her out with ammonia.

Dr. MacDonald must know when a patient is anxious. "Nurse, could you find us a mirror, please?"

"A mirror?" Wilkins looks from her operating trolley back to the doctor. There is no such thing on her meticulously organized table of instruments.

"Yes, a mirror. Just a small one, if you could. I want to show Ms. Stevens what it is I'm going to do."

Wilkins is not amused. Clearly this does not fall under what an attending nurse is required to do. For a moment it looks as though she may refuse. Penny looks from the nurse to the doctor. The doctor looks at the nurse. The nurse again looks at the tray and back at the doctor, back to the tray and then finally shrugs.

"Whatever." Briskly she turns away, her white shoes squeaking as she goes in search of the mirror.

By way of explanation, or maybe wanting to set his patient more at ease, Dr. MacDonald says, "Nurse Wilkins is one of the best emergency-room nurses here at Lions Gate."

All Penny can think of to say is "Okay." She doesn't wonder if all the other nurses are even more miserable than Wilkins or if they also wear their smiles upside down. She doesn't want to hear how it's going to be great. She doesn't want to look at her gash in a mirror.

She's always found it ridiculous when she's gone through the drive-through oil change and the mechanic asks her to step out of her car and come and look at what the problem is. She goes there because she needs the oil changed. Or the filter changed. She's never gone in there intending to disagree with the young man in the McQuik overalls who holds up her oil gauge and assesses that she's down a quart or two. No, Penny has always felt it best to leave the general upkeep and main-tenance of cars and houses to the professionals. And today, even though it is Penny herself who is in need of repair, she does not wish to look under the hood. She does not want a mirror despite the good intentions of the professional in front of her.

Dr. MacDonald is smiling benevolently at his patient. He is wearing a lovely royal blue shirt and tie beneath his white coat. Penny has always loved men in a shirt and tie. Then again, she also loves a guy in jeans and a T-shirt. *What the hell am I thinking? My head is throbbing! I need a shot of something here! I should ask him where he got that shirt . . .*

Penny takes a quick glance at her forehead when Nurse Wilkins returns with a small compact makeup mirror. The good doctor carefully explains the procedure.

"We'll stitch this little bit right up. See here?"

"Fine." Penny doesn't dare inspect too closely. Wilkins takes the compact from her and snaps it shut, sliding it quickly into the pocket of her smock, and Penny wonders if it is the nurse's own mirror.

Penny lies down rigidly and keeps her eyes closed for the tailoring of her head, but when she dares to take the odd peek, she sees that Wilkins has moved up around to the top of her head so that the happy-face button is just a few inches from her face. It is also right side up now, which makes it easier for Penny to think happy thoughts.

She can't feel any discomfort from Dr. MacDonald's handiwork, but she can hear the sound of thread being pulled through her skin. It makes her stomach do little flips and rolls, and she worries she might vomit.

"You are doing very well." The doctor mumbles this more to himself than to the patient. "Just a few more and we'll have you on your way."

She closes her eyes tighter.

"Who is driving you home, Ms. Stevens?"

"I don't know." She remembers she came in the ambulance. At the moment, she has no further plans beyond surviving this ordeal.

"There." Dr. MacDonald straightens up and begins removing his gloves.

"Is it over?"

"It is indeed." He doesn't rush off to his next patient as Penny expects but stays to tell her that she'll have to take care to clean the wound and reassures her again that the scarring will be minimal. He gives her the usual drill. That she'll need to have someone wake her every so often to ask her simple questions. Name. Address. Concussions are no laughing matter. She must take care. *Oh, won't this be fun, Jack?*

Perhaps he stays to save her the trouble of having this conversation with Nurse Wilkins. Whatever the reason may be, she is filled with gratitude and relief.

Then, the doctor is summoned away to another

patient, and there is a brief moment where no one is touching or prodding her. She closes her eyes and lets herself drift.

"Penelope, sweetheart. You have to get up. Are you awake? We should get you home." Aaron gently caresses her arm to wake her.

After a long minute, she mumbles something and tries to open her eyes.

"What time is it?" Her eyes are still closed, but she feels as though she's slowly approaching the surface. She feels like she has been swimming underwater for a long time. She shuts her eyes tighter and tries to block out her feelings of complete foolishness and utter embarrassment.

How could she have entertained any romantic notions about this guy? Could she honestly imagine that any man like this, even under different circumstances, would ever reciprocate her feelings? She berates herself for lying alone in bed at night with her hand between her legs. Entertaining thoughts of physicality and pleasure. She never went so far in her fantasy to include actual lovemaking. Instead, she role-played little scenes where Aaron would come toward her, accidentally touch her, brush up against her. She always could smell him and felt herself get warm, get hot. She wonders if everyone else on the project knew about Aaron, that they automatically assumed she knew too, or if Linda and Mitch and Heather were all secretly taking delight in pulling the wool over unsuspecting Penny's eyes. She wonders if anybody will ever again look at her with love and desire.

"Is your partner still here?" *Boyfriend.* She wanted to say it. To get it out of the way.

"Yeah. He's looking for a wheelchair, or are you okay to walk?"

"I think I am." Careful not to disturb the bandage on her head, Penny moves slowly off the bed and places her feet on the cool linoleum. Aaron retrieves her sandals and helps her into them.

"Here, take my arm."

She takes his left arm, and with his other hand he grabs her purse. Jimmy had the idea that she would need her health card and had gone in to retrieve it just as the ambulance had pulled up.

"What a sight we are." They must make an odd pair.

"No worries. One foot in front of the other, Penelope."

From behind a nursing station, she catches sight of Nurse Wilkins watching them, which in turn makes Penny stand a little taller and walk a little faster.

Jimmy is just rounding the corner with a wheelchair

and almost runs right into them. "Hello! Your chariot, madame."

Penny takes one last look at Wilkins. "I think I'll walk."

"That's the spirit!" Jimmy abandons the chair on the spot and comes to takes her free arm. Just before exiting the double swing doors leading out to the waiting room, he makes a big show of waving goodbye to Wilkins.

Oh my God! Just keep moving. Don't look back.

The two men lead a giggling Penny past an array of people out into the warm evening air.

"I haven't got the car yet. Stay here and give me two minutes."

Jimmy disappears into a parkade, leaving Penny holding tightly onto Aaron.

"He's wonderful. You're lucky to have each other."

"Thank you. I think so too."

When the Jeep pulls up, Jimmy jumps out and comes round to the curb and opens up the passenger door. As it is only a two-door, he folds the front seat down and beckons Aaron inside. Penny can hear him talking to himself, cursing his messy car and adjusting things to make space for Aaron's long legs and her short ones. It is only when he helps her up into the front seat that she realizes to whom, or rather to what, he has been talking.

"Haggis, meet Penny Stevens. The woman you almost scared to death."

Haggis, it turns out, is an immense Irish wolfhound with beautiful hazel eyes and a very apologetic personality. Before Penny can even buckle her seat belt, he has climbed over Aaron so that he is directly behind her, and has placed his large head upon her shoulder.

"Oh my goodness." The dog sniffs at her hair and blood.

"Don't worry. He's harmless."

"Okay." Penny isn't entirely at ease. As she makes a move to pet him, he licks her hand.

"Oh." Inside this confined space, the dog gives off considerable heat.

"He is very sorry." Jimmy is vigorously petting Haggis. "Aren't you sorry? Yes, you are. You big furry four-legged beast."

"Your dog?" Penny can't get over the size of him and thinks maybe he's part horse.

"My dog. My baby. And by association, also Aaron's dog." Jimmy looks back at Aaron and smiles.

"Our dog," says Aaron, "but he takes after Jimmy, that's for sure."

"My goodness, is he ever big."

"Yes," Jimmy says, "he's a big boy with a heart of gold, and I am so sorry he scared you like that. And we're going to make it up to you by cooking you a dinner. Tonight. At your place."

"Oh, you don't have to." It's getting late and all Penny can think about is a big glass of red wine, a Tylenol or three, and some potato chips. Definitely not part of Heather's "lifestyle" plan, but head wounds allow for drastic measures in Penny's book.

"I know we don't have to, but we want to."

She looks over her shoulder at Aaron, who just shrugs. Haggis licks her face and she wonders how sanitary that is.

"Will your husband be dining with us?" Jimmy is insistent.

She hasn't given Jack a thought. What is he going to think now? In the space of a couple of weeks, she has gotten drunk in the afternoon, vandalized a toilet, been escorted home by a ballet-dancing waiter, remodelled most of their house and yard, pushed her body to the limit, and twisted it into all sorts of positions. She has fantasized about her gay gardener, has severely hit her head, and has a dog the size of a small pony asking her for forgiveness. Now "Jimmy" wants to cook for her.

"What's in your fridge? I might need to go shopping if you don't have anything."

"I honestly don't know."

Aaron pulls Haggis away from Penelope's shoulder. "I think I saw some chicken breasts when I grabbed that lemon."

That cool drink on the porch feels like a lifetime ago. "Oh, yes. Maybe."

"Do you have any fresh veggies? Any cheese?" Jimmy is envisioning something, but Penny dreams only of all-dressed Ruffles and Merlot.

"Heather has stocked me up on an endless supply of greens, but I think she took all my regular Cheddar and left me only low-fat cheeses and some kind of log of goat cheese."

"Goat cheese! Hurray!" Jimmy is ecstatic.

"There's no stopping him. You've really done it now," announces Aaron proudly. Haggis comes forward again and gives Penny a hundred-watt smile, showing her every one of his teeth.

"Good boy, Haggis. Daddy's going to make dinner."

Exactly one hour later, Penny, Aaron, and Jimmy are sitting down to a lovely meal of goat cheese and sun-dried tomato chicken with a generous helping of assorted vegetables on the side. Haggis has passed out in the living room after having eaten a healthy portion of chicken and potatoes and gravy.

Penny is feeling marvellous because she has already consumed two glasses of Pinot Grigio, and her head is no longer throbbing.

"This is delicious!" She is speaking louder than normal and her hands aren't quite working as well as she would like. "Oops!" She has almost knocked over Aaron's wineglass.

"Got it!" Aaron's quick to make the save and Penny feels like a klutz. Embarrassed again. Penny forever.

"Look on the bright side, Penny," says Jimmy as he gets up to retrieve something from the kitchen. "You've had a bit of wine, but you've forgone the painkillers. Alcohol's better than Aspirin any day of the week." He reappears with a damp cloth. "Before we leave, I'll make you my hangover cocktail. Never failed me yet." Jimmy mops up a bit of sundried tomato that she has pushed off her plate onto the placemats she rarely uses.

Sitting here at her dining table, Penny never imagined that she would entertain two such remarkable young men. She never would have believed that someone would prepare such a wonderful meal for her in her very own kitchen.

It was indeed a sight to watch Jimmy work his magic among all her pots and pans and spices that she never knew she had. And him hammering those chicken breasts and then stuffing them and rolling them up was quite a performance too.

"This is absolutely delicious! I have to say it again. I didn't think I had any appetite, but this is wonderful." She finds her wineglass empty, but Aaron is quick with the refill.

It is Aaron who gets up and begins to put together a dessert for them. Penny hears him washing and cutting and opening drawers and rooting about in cupboards. When he comes back into the dining room, he displays a beautifully arranged assortment of apples and grapes and oranges on a tray she forgot she had.

"My goodness! When can you move in?"

They are all laughing and don't hear the door opening. It is Haggis who jumps awake, barking, and lurches toward the door.

"Christ!" Jack falters and clutches his heart as the dog is going at it like he's willing to die to protect Penny and her new family.

"Jack!" The sight of her husband cowering in the corner of the foyer strikes her as amusing. She can't stop giggling. He has never liked dogs ever since he was bitten by a toy poodle when he was seven years old.

"Call that fucking thing off!"

Haggis has all four paws firmly planted on the wooden floor and won't take his eyes off the white-haired intruder. He is producing a low and steady growl that is undeniably menacing.

"Haggis! Come here! Haggis!" Jimmy comes forward and takes the dog by the collar back into the hallway.

"Christ!" Jack hasn't moved from his spot. That poodle certainly left an impression. He still has the two faint canine bite scars visible on his right ankle.

"Do you know Aaron, Jack? He's our gardener." Penny comes forward to retrieve the house keys from her husband's grasp.

"Christ Almighty!" His blustering and machismo cannot hide his fear.

Aaron comes forward and extends his hand. "Aaron Taylor. I think we've seen each other once or twice."

"Uhm, hello." He extends his hand. "Jack Stevens," still keeping an eye on Haggis as they shake.

"And I'm Jim Prentiss." Jimmy doesn't let go of the dog, as Haggis is still uncertain of this trespasser. "Can I get you some dinner? Lots left."

Jack declines. He looks from the remnants of the dinner table to the canine still growling and back to the two men and his wife. "What happened to you?"

"I fell today and got ten stitches."

"Christ Almighty."

Penny knows her husband doesn't like coming home these days to an endless parade of odd people going in and out of his house. And now this. "I'm fine, really."

"Right." His eyes follow Jimmy as he leads the dog into his kitchen. "Well, that's good then."

"Are you sure you won't have any chicken? It's delicious. Aaron made it with goat cheese . . . No! It was Jimmy! Oh, how can I forget that. Ooops." Penny realizes she is quite drunk.

"Or how about some dessert?" Aaron calls from the dining room.

Jimmy materializes from the kitchen. "May I offer you some fruit?"

Jack still hasn't moved from his spot.

She's down but not out
Wednesday, August 27
Mitch Williams

Tuesday afternoon, Penny Stevens, our very own Good Samaritan, was rushed to Lions Gate Hospital after suffering a head wound that she sustained at her residence.

She required 10 stitches but is recuperating at the moment.

"I had wanted to do another makeover for this week's update, but Penny will need her stitches out before I will proceed with any makeup applications. It's quite the gash," Linda Campbell announced upon sneaking a glance under Penny's bandage.

Ms. Stevens likely experienced a slight concussion and, therefore, is taking a time-out from her rigorous exercise schedule.

"Thank God," Penny exclaimed when told she had to take a break from her personal trainer, Heather McCann.

"Well, of course I'm very committed to the program. It's just very intense. I've never exercised so much in my entire life. Well, that's the point, I guess. Hopefully, I can get back into it real soon. I just don't want to rush it."

Look for Penny's next stunning makeover in an upcoming issue and make sure to check out Renovate Your Life on Tuesday, September 2, on the Home and Garden channel, 29, at 8:00 p.m. See for yourself the transformation of our Good Samaritan's residence.

And get better soon, Penny. We're all rooting for you.

Fourteen

"Seriously?" Penny is sitting on the top step of her porch chatting with Jimmy. Haggis is right next to her, pressing his weight against her shoulder. It is late in the afternoon and the first grey day in over two months, and everybody is a little relieved at the drop in temperature.

"He feels absolutely awful." Jimmy, of course, is speaking for Haggis, who does look a bit ashamed.

"Well, all is forgiven. Just a bump on the forehead." She wants to put the matter to rest. Jimmy's been calling nonstop. He even sent a gorgeous bouquet of flowers that apparently Haggis picked out personally.

The dog turns to her and bares his teeth in what appears to be a smile.

"See? He's happy you said that."

Aaron can be heard working along the side of the house, putting the final touches on his part of the garden transformation. Occasionally he walks by with a rake or heads to the truck to retrieve a shovel or a trowel. He waves at Penny and Jimmy every time he passes by, and it gives her pleasure to see a man so happy in his profession. She can't imagine him a lawyer or an accountant or whatever it was his father wanted him to be. She doesn't feel guilty sitting here watching him work because she can see he is content. He is whistling, pleased with the end result. Tomorrow the photographers and the film crew are coming, and the place, both inside and out, has to look perfect.

"Are you sure you don't want any trolls?" Aaron calls out from behind a rhododendron.

The dog's squarish grey head is very close to hers, panting lightly.

Penny considers him closely. "Haggis. That's an interesting name. How did you decide on that one?"

Jimmy smiles and the dog looks over at his master with the same sort of curiosity, as if to say, "Yeah. What gives?"

"Well, that's a long story." Jimmy bounds up the stairs in two steps and sits on the other side of Haggis.

Penny imagines they look like a family photo of Mom and Dad and a large unruly kid in the middle.

"Back in '96, I was living in London. I was living with Terry. My first 'relationship.' I moved in in November, and by Christmas we had bought new dishes and had painted the flat and had parties and had become the 'new couple' on the block."

Penny nods and smiles, thinking back to her and Jack starting out.

"Fast. Yeah, I know. But I was ready, you know? I was hungry for it. I never really had a chance to be myself, you know, back home. Living in London, so far away from home, was scary but also wonderful."

Haggis throws his head back and does an extended yawn as if to say he's heard this story a few times already.

"So, we met and one thing led to another and then one day Terry comes home with this adorable puppy." Jimmy takes Haggis's head in his hands and ruffles his fur and puts his own head up against the dog's head.

"It was love at first sight." Jimmy says this with his eyes closed.

"With the dog, you mean . . ."

"Absolutely. Of course, I loved Terry. He was the kind of person you'll never forget. Larger than life. Very impulsive. Just getting the dog was such a typical Terry thing to do. Sometimes I think he didn't know what he was going to do until he'd gone and done it. That was life with Terry. Exciting, improbable, spontaneous."

"So how did you decide on the name Haggis?"

"Terry named him. I tried to suggest other names, but Terry was fixated on Haggis."

"Haggis is a Scottish cuisine, isn't it?" Penny recalls a decade earlier being offered some on Robbie Burns Day. She politely declined.

"'Cuisine' is going a bit far, but it is indeed Scottish."

"And the dog is . . ."

"An Irish wolfhound! Precisely!" Jimmy is excited that she is making the connection.

Aaron rounds the corner, this time carrying a bright yellow bucket. "Is this man bothering you, miss?"

"Not in the least." Penny is laughing and then, in an instant, it crosses her mind that soon the project will be complete and she may very well never see either Jimmy or Aaron again.

"Anyway, we broke up because he met Alex." Jimmy says this matter-of-factly.

"I see."

"I didn't see that one coming." Jimmy is shaking his head.

331

"Of course not." She imagines it must have hit him hard. First partner and living so far away from home.

"He's married now and has three kids."

"Married?"

"Ring, white dress, chapel. The whole shebang."

"Oh my. Who wore the dress?"

"Alex."

"Actually wore a dress?" She doesn't want to sound too shocked. Maybe one day Jimmy or Aaron will wear one if they decide to make it legal. This is Canada, after all.

"Looked very lovely, I was told."

"They adopted . . . ?"

"No."

"Alex had children previously . . ." Penny is filling in the pieces, showing she is paying attention.

"No. Alex is not a man. Never was. Never will be."

"But . . . I thought . . ." All the pieces of the puzzle need to be rearranged. "I thought Terry was gay."

"Apparently we all did, including Terry. Turns out he was a bit mistaken declaring his sexuality as well. A bit too impulsive."

"So, he's not . . ."

"Not anymore. And I understand he's a great father and really happy."

"Wow."

"Yeah, that pretty much sums it up." Jimmy reaches out to pet Haggis. "But the way I see it, I ended up with this great friend here, and I learned a lot about life and such. You know, figuring out who you are and where you're going and all that stuff on the talk shows." Jimmy throws his head back and laughs. "I can tell you there's no better teacher than a lousy relationship."

Penny only nods to this. Normally, at this point in the conversation, a woman would jump in with some similar anecdote and try to further the bond by sharing her own past hurts and troubles. Penny thinks she must be missing a gene, as she's never been capable of doing this sort of thing. It's taken her more than a decade to finally open up to Susan, and that, of course, was after a few too many highballs.

"So the name has stuck?" She looks at Haggis, who is now arching his neck to give Jimmy better access to scratch him.

"Well, it was kind of appropriate this Irish hound was given a Scottish name by a heterosexual guy who once thought he was gay. I figured it was meant to be."

"I can see you guys are really close."

"Yes. Yes, we are. And he helped me tremendously through the Terry thing and all."

Penny was never allowed to have animals because

Alice was allergic to cats, and a dog would have been too much of a challenge for her parents. And Jack was so distressed by dogs. She's never had any connection to any animal. Looking at Jimmy and Haggis now, she wonders if she missed out on something special. Come to think of it, she doesn't feel particularly attached to any human being either.

A sudden sharp pang of sorrow, or perhaps regret, stabs her in the heart. She doesn't think of herself as depressed—she stopped taking Paxil years ago—but lately she has experienced mood swings that sneak up on her out of nowhere. Suddenly she will feel utterly hopeless and heartbroken. These feelings always surprise her, too, because logically a person should be aware of their own existence in the world, and if things are difficult one would suppose that person to be actively involved in sorting out their affairs. It always shocks Penny when the light bulb above her head reveals to her, Oh my God! I'm sad! I'm in despair! Why didn't somebody tell me?

"We walked and talked for hours, this dog and me. He saw me through some rough times." Jimmy is giving Haggis a back rub from the base of his head down to his tailbone. "And overall, I think walk therapy beats conventional talk therapy by about a mile."

"You think so?"

"I do indeed. You should try it sometime."

"You think I need therapy?" She actually did go once, but it wasn't to her liking.

"No. No. I'm just saying if you ever want to take the dog out, you know, you're welcome. You have our number, right?"

"I do."

"Good. Don't be shy."

But Penny always has been shy. She was born that way and doesn't anticipate changing any time soon.

As if on cue, Aaron appears and announces, "It's a wrap."

The outside reno is finished, and Penny loves it because it doesn't look like some overdesigned landscape masterpiece. It just looks good. Clean. Colourful and tidy and cared for. Kind of how she envisions her best self.

"We're good to go." The skin on Aaron's arms is shimmering. He's been sweating just enough to look like he's been working out at the gym, which reminds her that she has to call Heather this afternoon.

Jimmy dismisses Aaron with a wave of his hand. "Okay, you can go. Bye."

"Don't you have some real job to go to?" Aaron asks.

"Ha ha. Very funny." Jimmy waves Aaron off and turns to Penny. "I never work Wednesdays."

"Here I am working my ass off, and there you are sitting on yours all day long, talking Penelope's ear off, no doubt."

"I can't think of any other thing I'd rather do than listen to this young man talk." She has enjoyed the time she has spent out on the porch, procrastinating writing her column. It always amazes her how the time rolls around each week. Sneaks up on her.

"Yeah. I've been telling her my life story."

"God. Not that again." Aaron turns to her in mock seriousness. "He hasn't hit you up for money or anything, has he?"

"Oh, no, no."

"Good. Watch out for him, okay? He's been known to do it. He has no shame." Aaron wipes his hand on his pants. "May I be so bold as to ask to use the facilities?"

"Sure, go ahead."

"I'll be careful not to mess anything up 'cause your house is so freakin' perfect." He takes off his shoes and tiptoes into the house.

The bathroom downstairs is essentially the same as it was—just a lot less clutter and a new towel rack. Linda calculated the costs of the total renovation coming in just under three thousand dollars. Of course, the labour has all been free.

"Speaking of life stories, you haven't really told me anything about yours." Jimmy is looking at her with the deepest and kindest brown eyes she has ever seen.

"Well, you can read about me in the paper, if you care to." She looks out over to the neighbours', avoiding his gaze. She just doesn't want to look at Jimmy. She certainly doesn't want to discuss her life.

"Yeah, but that's just window dressing. That's not you—you."

"Well, that's what people want, it seems."

"Not everybody, Penny. Not everybody."

She swallows. A lump has formed in her throat, and her voice comes out a bit painfully. The words tumble out before she can edit herself. "I'm all alone. I'm married to a man who doesn't love me. Maybe never did. This is my pretty house, my garden. I hate my body. I have one friend who gets drunk with me once a month. I don't know how to be like other people. I'm sorry."

Inside the house the toilet flushes, and Aaron reappears at the front door. Jimmy has put his index finger to his lips and nobody is saying anything. Aaron discreetly retreats back inside. The silence of the moment is frozen. Even Haggis's tail is not moving.

"Don't be sorry, Penny." Jimmy says at last.

"I just can't seem to get it right." The tears she has

been suppressing are running freely down her cheeks. *These bloody tears! Here we go again.*

"Don't worry about getting it right."

"I just have so many people around me telling me what to do and I want to be grateful and I know they have good intentions and I'm trying."

"I know you are."

"But I don't know what I'm doing with my life, you know? I'm forty and I feel old, like it's all over." Because the tears are flowing so rapidly, Penny lies back onto the porch floor. She feels the salty liquid run into her hairline and into her ears.

Jimmy lies back too. The outside porchlight contains a large number of dead bugs.

"My mother was forty-four when she had me. My dad was sixty-six." She's not sure why she says this.

Jimmy looks over at Penny and touches her temple in time to brush a falling tear. "My grandmother in Dominica looked after me. She was the one who taught me everything. My mom had to work. Nana's eighty-four this November. She's my mother, as far as I'm concerned."

It dawns on Penny that Alice will be eighty-five in October. *Where does the time go? It's all rushing by too fast.*

"I want to go back to Dominica for Nana's eighty-fifth." She considers this for a moment. "You should."

"I will." He smiles.

Haggis has stood up and is now towering over Penny's face. Slowly, he bends down and begins to lick the tear-stained cheeks of this lady he's only known for a short time.

"I can tell you unequivocally, Penny, that this dog loves you." Jimmy has rolled over to his side and gently touches her on the arm.

"Well, it's good somebody does." She isn't holding back the tears, and it feels good.

"And I love you too." He has sat up now, but Penny can't see him because she has brought her hands to her face.

"But you don't even know me. You just feel sorry for me," she muffles.

"No. I love you."

"No you don't."

"Yes I do."

"No, you do not."

"Yes, I do too."

"No."

"Yes."

"No."

"Yes."

"Fine. You're delusional." She has taken her hands

away from her face. "Maybe you're crossing over just like your friend Terry!"

"Get up!" He takes hold of her hands and helps her to a sitting position. "No. You haven't turned me to the dark side, my dear. I find that I simply love you."

Penny stares at the beautiful man in front of her. "It's the heat—you're not well."

Haggis yips.

"Now listen to me, you stupid woman! I love you. I know we don't know each other, but that doesn't mean we don't or can't love each other. I mean, you gotta start somewhere. Maybe I'm just faster at love than you are."

She has to laugh. "I don't want to be some fly-by-night friend. Some one-night stand. I'll have you know I'm just a little vulnerable here. I'm not at the top of my game, so to speak. So don't set me up only to drop me tomorrow."

Haggis is sort of jumping around like he expects somebody is going to throw him a ball or something. "Woof! Woof!"

"Done. So, I hereby officially declare my love for you in a bond of deep and everlasting friendship, as God is my witness."

"Woof woof!"

"Put a cork in it, Haggis!" Jimmy squeezes her in a bear hug, and Penny can't tell if the dog is jealous that he's embracing her or that she's embracing him. The hug is fierce as she clings to him tightly.

"I'm not good at letting people in."

"Well, I'm in. And, if you love me, you gotta love my dog. He's part of the package. Haggis is the closest thing to a kid I'll ever get."

Upon hearing his name, the dog elbows his way into the embrace.

Aaron reappears at the front door, holding a tray with a teapot and three mugs.

"Okay, I quietly leave both of you crying out here, then I come back in two minutes and you're hugging and laughing. Can somebody please tell me what's going on here?"

"We've decided to become friends." Jimmy is looking deeply into Penny's eyes. "Isn't that right?"

"Yes." Her voice is small but solid.

"Okay . . ." Aaron puts down the tray.

"In fact, I think we are going to become best friends." Jimmy is sounding cocky now, and Penny keeps on nodding.

"I see."

Haggis has extricated himself from the huddle and is surreptitiously licking off the sugar from the biscuits.

"Well." Aaron is making like he is getting jealous.

"Where does that leave me? I mean, I would like to point out that *I* met her first."

"Whatever. You were too busy with your hose and your bushes to really be there for her, and, well I was. So there."

The banter goes like this for a bit, and Penny marvels at all the twists and turns her life has taken in these recent weeks. Meanwhile, all the digestive cookies have been divested of any trace of coating.

Aaron pours the tea, and they all sip in companionable silence. The faintest breeze rustles the leaves of the large oak. There is the slightest hint of autumn in the air. "So, big day tomorrow," Aaron says as he surveys the yard.

"Yes, I suppose there'll be a bit of excitement about the place. Linda is arriving with Johnson and Charlie and the camera crew at nine thirty in the morning. What time are you coming, Aaron?"

"'Bout then, I think."

"Well, Penny, I'll call you tomorrow, okay? And you can tell me how it all went." Jimmy gives her another long hug.

"Thanks."

Aaron slowly gets out of the lawn chair and stretches his back. "Okay, I'll see you tomorrow. And Penny?"

"Yes?"

"I was hoping that you and I could be friends too."

Penny finds herself smiling and waving as Haggis and his two dads leave.

It is getting close to six o'clock and time to think about putting something together for dinner.

Inside, she notices the red blinking light of the answering machine.

The disembodied recorded voice—Penny can't decide if it's male or female—announces in what she later believes to be a somewhat accusatory tone that she *has* . . . *n-i-n-e messages* . . . What with the accident, she hasn't checked the machine since yesterday, and she feels like a teenager who has missed school and needs a note from her mother to explain her absences.

Beep.

"Hi, Penny. Listen, I was wondering if we could change our weight training to cardio instead. Some big-shot actor and his personal trainer are using the circuit this afternoon. Who do they think they are? In fact, I'm going to complain to management that they shouldn't just roll over when these so-called stars roll into town. Anyhoo, see you there at two as planned, but meet me in the cardio room instead." Penny's chest is tightening. She simply forgot to tell Heather about the fall, the stitches. No excuse, she's pretty sure, but she dreads making the call. Before the machine advances to the second message, Heather can't resist one last comment.

"Breathe!"

Beep.

"God! It's me again. You probably didn't get my first message and you're most likely freaking out like I am except you're stoked for weights and I am mentally changing over to cardio. We have to adapt, Penny. Change happens. Be ready for it." There is a pause. "Actually, you're not going to get this message because you're here . . . duh! Of course! . . . I'm coming for you, Penny! Hold on!" There is another pause before she adds, "Breathe!"

Penny sighs and begins to prepare a vegetable patty for dinner. She wants to pour herself a glass of Merlot.

Beep.

"Okay, like, where are you? I wish you'd join the twentieth century and get a cellphone!" It dawns on Penny that it is the twenty-first century. *My! How time flies!* She does have a cellphone, but it is either turned off or the battery needs charging.

Beep.

"It's three o'clock, Penny. Where the heck are you? When you finally get in from wherever you are, call me on my cell." There is a long pause and Penny braces herself for more respiratory advice, but this time she only hears Heather sigh.

Beep.

"I forgot to give you my cell number—604-913-1651. Okay, whatever."

Beep.

"Penny? It's Jack. Tell me you were not with that dog today. Glenn drove by the house and said he saw you with something that looked like a small horse. Christ, Pen! You know I hate dogs."

Beep.

"Okay, Penny. I'm outta here. I take it you're not coming, you haven't called, maybe you're just not that interested. I don't know . . . but I question your commitment to this project." Penny can hear voices in the background and thinks she hears water running, perhaps a toilet flushing. Then, before she hangs up, Heather lobs her threat.

"Oh, by the way, I'm phoning Linda."

"Ha!" Penny throws her head back and laughs until tears come to her eyes.

Beep.

"Hi, this is Janet from Dr. Bernstein's. It's that time of year again." Penny has always marvelled at the never-ending, excited manner of speech that the dental staff seem to possess. "Time to shine those pearly whites! Call us, we've got a spot waiting just for you! And don't forget to smile!"

Penny can't help but "smile" and "breathe" as she crosses over to the wine rack and chooses an Australian Merlot.

Beep.

"Hi. Linda here. Listen, Heather just called me. As you can imagine, she's quite stressed about missing yesterday's training. Look, I know she's a bit . . . intense. Right now, the best thing is for you to give her some space. She's dealing with a lot of issues right now, and your absence has triggered something from her childhood. I spent half an hour with her on the phone and we're working on it, so that's good. I'm just listening right now. I think she just really needs to vent, and I want you to know that I'll support you in this . . . I was thinking that maybe tomorrow, after the reno crew leaves, we could have a non-violent intervention. Just you and Heather really connecting, and I could guide us toward a win-win resolution that really honours both you and Heather in your unique and core true selves. Okay, well, hope whatever you've been up to has boosted your spirits and has left you energized and passionate about life!"

"Cheers!" Penny pops the cork and pours herself a very large glass.

End of messages.

She looks around her kitchen. At the neat telephone desk and the uncluttered counters. On the table she sees the lone plate with a few crumbs left over from her toast this morning. *Yes, big day tomorrow.*

She raises her glass to the shiny new cupboard knobs and the white baseboards and crown mouldings. She toasts Charlie and Johnson. She considers her new clothes and aching body and lifts her glass to Linda and Heather. She thinks of Haggis and Aaron and her new best friend, Jimmy.

"Cheers."

Fifteen

It is a gorgeous morning when Penny rolls over and opens her eyes. The birds are chirping joyfully, and yesterday's cloud cover has disappeared. She rises slowly and stumbles to the washroom. At the sink, she splashes a bit of cold water on her face, careful to not disturb the stitches.

When her eyes focus and her brain registers the position of the hands on her clock, Penny gasps at the time. It's nine a.m.

Oh no! Oh no! What time did they say they were coming? Why did I sleep so late? Why does this always happen to me? Nine o'clock . . . Nine o'clock . . . okay, get clothes . . . get dressed . . . get it together!

She grabs some beige capris and a sleeveless white cotton blouse. A pair of brown slingbacks complete the outfit. Her hair is as unruly as ever, so she opts for a black hairband. When she considers herself in the mirror, she has to admit that she doesn't look that bad. Except for the huge bandage. She peels off a corner and takes a quick peek. Already the bruise has turned from an ugly purple to a muted brown and orange.

Penny quickly re-tapes the gauze and reconsiders the hairband. She takes it off and lets her hair fall over to one side, thinking maybe this will make the bandage less visible.

Does this look better?

She parts her hair on the other side.

What about this way?

Nope. It is even worse. For once, Penny wishes her beauty consultant were here, telling her what to do.

Last week Linda took her out shopping and had Penny buy about ten items, all basic everyday clothes in solid colours. She has strict rules to avoid front pleats and to not go overboard with flowery designs. Linda said her dresses with tulips and daisies and her skirts with matching blouses of roses and sunflowers "aged her," made her look matronly, or else resembled wallpaper.

Linda would likely know how to dress up a wound. In the meantime, however, Penny opts to let her hair hang forward. That's as good as it's going to get.

Downstairs, Jack has left a note for her on the kitchen counter. "Home late. Early meeting. I'll have dinner at the club." It surprises her that he even bothered to write it. He's been coming and going at all hours, avoiding Penny and her moods and crises whenever he can. And she's glad that she doesn't have to deal with him scowling at her. Or ranting about the reno. Or commenting about the dog. After the guys left last night, Jack kept nattering on about "that damn dog this . . ." and "that damn dog that . . ." He can't believe "how fucking big it is," and "It must eat like a horse," and "Could you imagine the size of its shit, Penny? Think about it!" She's glad he's not here today. It's just too much stress. She's supposed to be de-stressing and improving her life, not the other way around. She also doesn't want Jack commenting on her stitched-up forehead. He went on about it enough last night. There have been so many scars in this marriage that at this point it's best left alone.

While the coffee is brewing, Penny goes to the porch and retrieves the morning paper. For a time now, she has been considering getting the *Globe and Mail* but can't bring herself to cancel the *Sun*. She hates returning things or changing doctors or ending long-standing financial agreements with newspapers. One time, the *Province* phoned her up and tried to coerce her to change allegiance to their paper.

"No. I can't possibly do that. I have been a loyal customer for twenty years!"

She's always been a fan of loyalty. She remembers receiving the *Province* free for a two-week trial period. She read both papers front to back and felt that she had made the right decision to stay with the *Vancouver Sun*. When the *Province* phoned exactly fourteen days later to see if she would consider buying a subscription, Penny was armed with an organized section-by-section critique of the paper. After all, she was a columnist herself, so she took the job seriously and turned down the offer.

Recently, however, she has been toying with the idea of branching out and trying a national paper, broadening her horizons. Whenever she finds herself in a waiting room or some public space, she looks to see if there is a *Globe* lying around. Something about it is just better. She can't put her finger on it, but she can't cancel her *Sun*. And she doesn't want to have to recycle two newspapers and the three-times-weekly *Sentinel* as well. Penny wonders where all this loyalty has gotten her.

Today's front page warns about a recall of bad food. People are getting quite sick. Of course, the cows are mad and fish don't belong on farms, and now the pigs have the flu. Maybe they got it from the birds. There is also an article about recalling another politician, who himself cannot recall ever having said or done anything. *Well, at least somebody's being honest.*

Turning to the West Coast section, Penny reads about men and women in the local news. Some businessman has made another billion and looks quite happy. Some single mothers are camping outside the mayor's office to protest the closure of another shelter. They don't look happy at all. Then she reads about very angelic-looking women living in some bucolic town. Turns out polygamy is alive and well in Canada.

Faces of beautiful blond, blue-eyed children stare out at Penny, who in turn stares at the anonymous faces of young mothers pushing strollers alongside the country roads. She thinks she recognizes one of her cast-off dresses on a particularly young mother of twins.

She wonders if the world has always been this crazy. Perhaps it's the reno. Could it be her? Maybe it's different in the *Globe and Mail*?

Then, precisely at nine thirty, the crew arrives in full force. There are more cameras and cables than there were at the studio. More people too. A large white van carrying Mitch, Dalton, Heather, and some of the film crew arrives first. Linda's hearse and Aaron's truck pull up alongside the curb. Johnson arrives next in his Prius and parks directly behind Penny's yellow station wagon. Charlie is the last to arrive, pulling her Harley in behind Johnson.

Two hours later, various lights and umbrellas are set up throughout the house, and everything is ready. Charlie has finished staging the rooms, and Wang and Dieter, two international film students from the local college, have done some preliminary filming, scanning the spaces and getting their master shots for each take.

Linda and Heather seem to be having an intense, private discussion on the newly recovered sofa. Penny absentmindedly touches her bruise. She doesn't mind giving Heather a wide berth given yesterday's mix-up. And Linda looks extra intense, if that is possible. Earlier this morning the two of them made it explicitly clear that Penny was "off camera" today. For one thing, her bandage, and for another, as Heather so often reminds her, "We haven't hit our target yet." Though she has assured Penny they are "on track," she still hasn't defined what the actual goal is. Penny thinks people should know what they are aiming for. She's gone into the supermarket a few times without a grocery list and the results have not been pretty.

"We'll just edit you in."

It's been over a week since the photo shoot at Breathe, and Penny is absolutely fine with staying in the background today.

So imperfect Penny will watch while Linda steps in. Kind of like at a cocktail party, the viewer is led throughout the perfect home. Along the way the audience happens to meet the builder, the landscape architect, and the clutter buster, the personal trainer "weighs in," and, of course, Linda herself is at the helm.

The storyboard starts from Penny's porch and leads into her kitchen. From there, they take the viewer to the living room, followed by the downstairs bathroom. Upstairs they will show only the master bedroom. Finally, the filming will wrap up outside in the beautiful garden.

It is almost a month to the day that Penny found the Jenkinses' money in that brown paper bag, and she is reminded again of how the readership has taken a keen interest in this story. People keep writing in and responding to this happy tale. When an article tells about a person jumping into icy waters to save a puppy, it represents the best of humanity. When we so often read and hear about only the worst, these stories are a beacon. A momentary relief from all the politicians committing fraud, the bait cars, the shady real estate deals, and the dark underbelly of every man for himself.

And these stories are just so ... perfect. Project Penny is turning out to be a big success. The follow-up article from the photo shoot has elicited even more readership response. People continue to root for Penny. In a relatively short period of time, she has had the opportunity to make some big changes. Very rapidly, maybe too fast for her liking, but good nonetheless. And with everyone behind her, she really doesn't want to let anyone down. So Penny plays her part.

As usual, she is flustered with all the activity of the day. She keeps out of the way but manages to always have a full pot of coffee and cookies for the crew. A jug of fresh-squeezed low-cal lemonade sits on a side table as well. Everybody is so busy, focused. She smiles and occasionally directs one of the guys to the washroom. For the most part, however, she feels like an extra in her own home. Like she really doesn't need to do much more than open the door and remind the last person to lock up after the whole shebang is over.

Just as they start filming, she catches sight of herself in the front mirror. Still overweight, hair just a tad less frizzy than a few weeks ago. Suddenly she doesn't feel attractive in the least. Again, she touches at her bandage. *Maybe I don't belong in this spotless house.*

Penny watches from the sidelines as the camera travels from room to room. She watches and listens as all the members of Project Penny explain how it all happened. She watches as the camera goes outside and listens to her gardener describe the process. Even Charlie and Johnson manage to put a few sentences together.

Before she knows it, she hears Linda exclaim from the far side of the room, "Awesome!" She must really be pleased. "This has been totally awesome!"

And later, with the last of the trucks being loaded up, she finds she is both happy that the ordeal is over and sad at the same time. It feels like she just hosted a successful party and everyone had an awesome time and she is left alone. Again.

"Woof!"

"Haggis!" *Thank God.*

It's odd to walk the back alleys after living in West Vancouver her entire life, because Penny has never seen this side of her neighbourhood before. Sure, she has had to take her garbage out back every week, but she has never walked the length of her block or stopped to consider that Marjorie McBride certainly must be into single-malt Scotch.

When Jimmy picked up Aaron, he left Haggis with her. He insisted she take the dog for a good, long walk while they ran some errands. Said Haggis needed it and that any good friend would do this for him.

At first Penny didn't know what to say. She has never taken a dog for a walk. What if it ran off? Could she control it? What about other dogs? And if it pooped? What size excrement would she be dealing with? She is a practical person, after all.

Jimmy, however, refused to take no for an answer. He told her she would feel better, and he was right. She's feeling better. With every step.

Haggis, true to form, is taking his time, ambling along at a much slower pace than Penny would have imagined possible for a dog with such long limbs. He has stopped often to smell the markings of other dogs, each time leaving his own scent as well. So far she hasn't had to use the plastic bags that Jimmy stuffed into her pant pocket.

She looks over fences and sometimes, through open back doors, catches a glimpse of families sitting around kitchen tables. A garden birthday party for a dozen or so girls is in full swing. A little Chinese girl screams when she sees her and Haggis walk by, which only makes all the other little girls come running over to get a closer look at the woman with the "monster dog."

"Does he bite?"

"What's his name?"

"How old is he?"

"What happened to your head?"

Penny smiles, all the time holding on tightly to the leash. "Hi. He's harmless, but I don't know if they should pet him." She addresses the mother, who has come forward tentatively.

"He's not your dog?"

"Friends'." It's the first time she's spoken of Aaron and Jimmy as friends.

"Can we give him some cake?" A little redhead is jumping up and down. Soon other girls are chanting, "Cake! Cake!"

"I don't really know if he eats cake." Penny thinks she heard that dogs should never eat dessert or something like that. Then she recalls the digestive cookies the dog got into yesterday on the porch.

"It's Barney cake!"

Haggis jumps and barks, and the girls scream and squeal and jump too.

"Well, I suppose he could have a little piece."

The birthday girl herself comes forward, brandishing a rather large knife.

"Does he want a corner or a balloon?"

"What do you think, Haggis? A corner or a balloon?" The dog senses that food is coming and just smiles and wags his tail. "He'll take a balloon."

"Does he want a red one or a blue one?"

"Woof!"

"He said blue, I believe."

The blue balloon is almost in the centre of the half-eaten cake, and the little girl begins the arduous task of carving out the perfect piece for her newest guest.

"Here you go, dog."

Without even woofing out a thank-you, Haggis swallows the piece of cake in two bites.

"Okay, well, thank you very much, and Happy Birthday too."

She has taken three steps when a little girl comes running up and hugs Haggis. "You got a cool dog, lady."

• • •

Two hours later, Penny finds herself coming up the back path to her house. In her left hand she carries two tightly wound plastic bags containing precisely four turds. Aaron and Jimmy are sitting in lawn chairs, eating not-yet-ripe blackberries, surrounded by groceries.

"We were wondering when you two were going to show up." Jimmy looks particularly satisfied with himself.

"Lost track of time." Penny is trying not to smile. "So, what's in your bags?" The guys presumably had something important to buy.

"Oh, just some dog food. What's in yours?"

"Poop."

Penny watches Haggis clamber awkwardly up into the back seat of the Jeep. The guys wave and hoot the horn and are gone. She inhales deeply. Just a few hours ago, she was feeling positively blue, and then the sight of Jimmy and this dog flipped a switch in her. Clear-headed and energized now, she passes through the kitchen and heads directly for her computer.

This week she has chosen to write about finding the right financial planner. It takes her half an hour to cover the basics of matching an individual to an investment plan.

It dawns on her that the same could be said for finding the right marital partner. Why didn't she invest more time in learning about the biggest venture, called marriage? Why didn't she date more? Interview more prospective partners? Check out Jack's background and history and customer satisfaction?

She is about to wrap up her article when she simply can't resist adding a few last paragraphs.

> Today, out walking my best friend's dog, a rather large Irish wolfhound, I found myself exploring the backyards and alleyways of our neighbourhood.
>
> In life, we tend only to see the very polished and perfect-looking front doors and foyers of our friends and neighbours and businesses. When was the last time you dined at your favourite restaurant and came in through the back door? When have you ever gone through the garbage bins behind the family living next door?
>
> I am certainly not suggesting you do this. However, when entrusting someone with your financial security and future, I do think it wise to invest a little time looking at

their background and not just at the glossy brochures and promises.

Penny presses the Send button before she loses her nerve. She's not used to adding personal touches like this and figures Sylvia will probably edit out this last section anyway.

Sixteen

"Stop it, Jack. He can't eat when you are yelling like that."

"Christ!"

"Keep your voice down!"

"You've become like some kind of magnet for whackos, Pen! Christ Almighty!" Jack's chest is starting to heave, and his cheeks are beginning to get those reddish blotches that Penny recognizes when her husband is either drunk or furious.

"You are irritating him."

"That horse wouldn't know irritation if it climbed up its ass!"

"Out! Get out right this minute!"

"Why the hell should I be the one who has to go out onto the porch? That's a goddamn dog, Penny! Send it out to the porch!" Jack makes a big show of slamming cupboards and pouring the last bit of coffee into his travel mug, which he takes out front.

He's got a point, but she finds it amusing that a grown man is pouting and arguing about who has to go for the timeout. He serves coffee silently, sulking, staring straight out at the street. When she comes outside with the dog on the leash and asks him if he wants the last of the coffee, he looks away from them. She feels Jack's eyes on her back as they descend the steps. When she turns to see him stand up, he huffs and stomps back inside. Just before he slams the door shut, he can't resist one last parting shot. "Christ, Pen!"

But she is smiling. She can't help it. She is so glad she phoned up Jimmy and asked straight out if she could have Haggis for the day. Take him on a long walk again. She would make him a special dinner or would go buy the best organic dog food money could buy. He would be in good hands, she promised. Of course, one thing led to another, and the play date turned into a sleepover.

And this morning, Penny feels an overwhelming bubble of joy and excitement simmering just beneath her skin. Her entire body feels alive and invigorated and relaxed and happy.

Over an hour has passed, and Penny is not aware of where they have explored. Rather, she is keenly alert to the freshness of the air, the constant beating of her heart, the gentle ache in her lower calves. Haggis, too, seems to stop and smell the roses every so often. He'll resist the pull of the leash ever so slightly and put his nose high into the air. He'll tilt his head and sniff and audibly sigh, as if to say, "Stop, listen, ah." And Penny will stop and walk over to the dog and put her arm around him or ruffle his ears or run her hands along his back. And she will look at whatever Haggis is looking at or she will smell a flower or a bush, and she, too, will say, "Ah."

"God, it's so beautiful." She blurts this out before she can help it. Nobody is there to hear it but the dog, and of course he concurs. He's known it all along.

"Oh, Haggis!" A lump of sorrow mixed in with love swells up from somewhere deep within her. Then the voices of two boys are heard up ahead, and Penny sees two bikes turning down the lane. The boys are roughly twelve years old.

"Come on!"

"I'm comin'."

And they fly past her and Haggis, their young legs pumping the pedals. Eyes wide open. Spirits alive. Speed and light and motion. Haggis and Penny stay close to the ditch to let them pass and watch them as they recede down the alley. Their voices and bodies become smaller and smaller.

"Gosh, weren't they alive?"

Haggis looks down the lane and up at Penny and nods. There is something so wonderful about youthful energy.

"Yes. I agree." She laughs and pats Haggis on the head. Other emotions flood her now. She feels a renewed optimism and sense of awe. She is constantly taking deep breaths, like she hasn't been outside for ages, like she just can't get enough air into her lungs.

"I used to have a bike. It had a banana seat . . . but that was a long time before you were born. It was purple and had sparkles. I loved it. I loved that bike." Her hand flies up to her heart to stop it from popping right out of her chest. "What happened to my bike? Where did it go?"

Haggis brushes up against Penny, who falters and almost topples right over him. She regains her balance but then leans over and lets her torso fall forward until her head and arms hang down. Lamaraya told her students to do this when "life starts to overwhelm you."

As she hangs upside down, things look different again. The gravel is ten varying shades of grey, and the trees are the sky, and the ground is an endless, weightless blue.

Haggis comes closer and sniffs her ear.

"Oh!" It tickles, and she leaps upright and takes another deep breath. She is dizzy not just from her yoga pose but also from the manic swings of her moods and ever-changing emotions. She almost feels like she is drunk.

"I'm hungry. Are you hungry?" It's mid-afternoon and she hasn't really eaten anything today. Jack was in a foul mood all morning. It was the first Sunday in months that he didn't have an open house. He continued to rant and complain that there was nothing decent to eat. It was so rare for him to even be home for lunch. He wouldn't go out, either. He was pacing, following her around all morning. Glaring at the dog. Scowling at the world. All this upheaval and change was getting to him.

"I liked that goddamn chair, Penny."

"It is the same chair, Jack, just recovered."

"But it feels different."

"It's just cleaner."

"But it's not the same."

"It isn't ugly anymore."

"And I don't like where they put it. I can't see the TV."

"Then move it after they've gone."

"This is my goddamn house too, Penny."

"Well, then be here when the designer is here. You can share your 'vision' with her, and if it fits in with the 'overall concept' then you will be at 'peace' with the 'result.'" Penny was speaking with her fingers, quotations marks flying left, right, and centre. It felt good just to see Jack's mouth hanging open.

"And my goddamn beer is in the garage!"

"That's because my health and wellness coach does not 'envision' beer in the fridge."

"Christ Almighty!"

Poor Jack. Penny is having her own troubles adapting to all the changes and intrusions. She knew she would, but she never anticipated him being so off balance. Lately he's been hanging around, but not really there. Like he was checking up on her, on the place, not liking what he found, and then storming off again. He should go on walks, thinks Penny. He needs to get some fresh air.

Inhale. Exhale. Look at the sky. Look at the heavens. I'm hungry.

As they emerge from the lane, Penny reads the street sign. "24th and Gordon. Shit."

Haggis just looks at her.

"Sorry." She doesn't like swearing.

They are miles from the house and she doesn't have a cent on her. The only things in her pants are the keys to the house and four rumpled-up plastic bags.

"I don't have any money."

Haggis sits on his haunches.

"What are we going to do?"

He cocks his head to one side like he's considering their options.

"Should we walk to the corner store and steal something?" Penny has never stolen anything in her life, except the time she had a hankering for a turkey cranberry pita-bread sandwich from the grocery-store deli. She got so caught up watching the man build her sandwich—"Yes, mustard" . . . "No onions"—that when he handed it to her she simply took it and walked right outside and ate it.

"Should we, Haggis? Should we go and steal something?"

Haggis just regards her without blinking his eyes.

"I'm just kidding, God." She feels a tinge of disappointment that Haggis isn't a little bit game for an adventure. She feels young and spontaneous and up for just about anything. She wonders if this is what it feels like when mothers drive off, leaving their families behind them.

She could really sink her teeth into a turkey pita right about now, but the Safeway is nine blocks away. Her mother, however, is only two.

"Let's go see Alice!"

At the sound of this, Haggis perks up.

"You'll like my mother, I think. She's quite fun, though she might be a bit . . . shocked by you. Your size, I mean, though she won't be able to really see you." She picks up the leash, and they turn back in the direction they came from.

"She's old but not 'old' old, you know?" Penny herself can't believe her mother is old. She can see her digging up the potatoes in the back garden like it was yesterday. Never letting her limp stop her from doing anything.

"She lives at the Manor. She'll like you, but don't go and lick her or anything like that. And don't lick anybody else. And don't bark. There's lots of old people, and we don't want to get thrown out." Penny has never noticed any other dogs—or cats, for that matter—at the residence, but figures they stand a good chance of getting something to eat as long as nobody freaks out, mistaking Haggis for a wolf or a zoo monster.

"Good boy, Haggis. Good boy."

Three minutes of focused walking brings them to the lobby of the Manor.

"Stay here, Haggis. Sit." Penny unbuckles his leash, twists it around a pole, and then reattaches it. "I'll just be a minute." She wants to ascertain exactly where Alice is and devise the best and quickest route for her and the dog to meet up with her mother.

"Okay, just . . . sit." But Haggis doesn't, and Penny feels like she has asked him politely and that he should not embarrass her by just standing there with every-body looking on.

"Okay . . ." A few residents sitting on benches out-side are watching her. One gentleman with a walker is making a retreat into the refuge of the building. The others stay put and stare.

"Fine. Stand there, whatever. Just . . . be good."

Inside, she asks a male nurse where Alice would be. She knows she has embroidery on Mondays and choir on Tuesdays and bridge on Wednesdays. On Thursdays she does chair aerobics, and Fridays are either excursions or guest speakers. The weekends are wide open so there's no accounting for where Alice might be.

"She's out back."

"Out back? Out back where?"

Philip is a short, overly tanned young man with bulging muscles on his forearms. "Through this room, past the double doors, take the hallway on your right, and it's the first door on the left."

Penny retains the gist of what he said and thinks she will be able to find her.

"What's going on?"

"Oh, she's just with Mr. Miller. That's where they usually hang out, I think."

Penny stares blankly at Philip. *Where they usually hang out?*

Outside, she is surprised to see that Haggis is still standing and that a few of the people watching the dog have crept nearer, daring to take a closer look, if so able.

"Haggis! I'm back. Come on . . . Let's go see Alice, and remember, no barking."

She unbuckles him from the pole and leads him off along the west side of the building while the residents continue to gawk in equal parts confusion and fascination.

Before she finds Alice, she stumbles upon various groups and couples and clusters of people chatting and sleeping and daydreaming the afternoon away. Then, tucked behind a large lavender bush, she discovers her mother holding hands with a very happy and wrinkly old man.

"Mother!"

The old man cries out, clutching her mother's hand even tighter. Then from a pair of sliding doors emerge two housekeeping girls, who also recoil at the sight of the dog.

"It's okay. It's okay . . . This is Haggis." But nobody seems to really take in what Penny is saying because they are too busy wrapping their minds around this very big dog.

"Mom, I just . . . We just stopped by." Alice is blinking and peering from her daughter to the animal. Even in daylight her eyesight is poor.

"How are you, Mom?"

"How am I? You just about gave me and Ernest here a heart attack!"

"Sorry. This is Haggis."

"What?" Alice is speaking loudly.

"His name is Haggis."

"What is it?" She is really straining now.

"A dog."

"A dog?"

"Yes, this is Haggis, and he's really quite wonderful. We've been going on walks."

"My." Alice has settled somewhat and sits back in her chair.

There is a bit of an awkward pause as Penny looks over at Mr. Miller. He's nodding his head as if he's agreeing to something.

When he speaks, he screams even louder than Alice. "Very large dog!"

"Sit, Haggis." She is thankful that this time the dog complies.

"This is Mr. Miller, darling."

"Hello, Mr. Miller." She can't recall the last time her mother referred to her as "darling."

"Hello." Mr. Miller bows in his chair. "You can call me Ernest."

Penny slides another patio chair over and sits down. "I haven't seen you here before. Are you new?"

"What's that?"

"I haven't noticed you before. Have you been a resident long?"

"Sorry?" This Ernest yells loudly again.

"Are you new?" Now Penny is raising her voice to match his.

This seems to register, and he turns to Alice and asks, "When did I come here?"

"Oh . . ." She closes her eyes and considers this for a bit. "Just over a month, isn't it?"

"Is it?" asks Ernest, and Penny doesn't know whether he thinks the time has flown by or if he feels he has been here for ages.

"Betty died in June, and the kids moved you in here

in July," calculates Alice. "At first you only talked to Mildred, remember?"

"What's that?"

"Remember Mildred?"

"What?"

"Never mind." Alice grabs hold of his nearest hand, and he relaxes and smiles and nods again.

"I'm so sorry your wife died." Penny is eyeing their clasped hands.

"What's that?"

"Must have been a terrible blow for you."

"Yes . . . Betty, yes." He continues to nod and smile.

"You must be very sad . . ."

And now Alice grabs hold of Penny's nearest hand. "Never mind, dear. Never mind."

Penny has noticed over the years that any able-bodied senior male is quite a hot property. Even a deaf one like Ernest would be considered a catch at the Manor. Alice has recounted a few tales about other residents, but Penny always assumed that her mother wasn't into "fishing." Now, looking at her and Ernest together, she feels a bittersweet sadness. She remembers her own father and how he would stroke the back of Alice's bare neck and kiss her forehead. Haggis stirs beside her, and she instinctively reaches out to caress him. Maybe it's just the sense of touch and connection that people need. Haggis leans into her and nuzzles her arm. She can't remember the last time Jack touched her.

"Mom?" Penny decides to change the topic. "Can I get something to eat?" She feels like she's nine years old again, coming into the kitchen after school with a friend. "Can the dog get something too?"

"Oh, we've already taken lunch. Shall I have Ernest fetch you something from the snack lounge?"

"Oh, that would be great. Where are the snacks? I can go myself."

"Oh, it's not a bother. Ernest? Will you go fetch some snacks? For Penelope and the dog." She releases his hand and repeats her request a second time a bit louder.

"Yes. Yes. Can do. Can do." He is up and out of his chair in no time, seemingly glad to be of some use. Glad to have an objective and a destination in mind.

"Isn't he just the cat's meow?" Alice is beaming. "And he's young, too. Eighty-four. Just like me. We're the same age. Can you imagine that?"

Penny wonders what it must have been like for her mother to grow old alongside her father. Alice only knew Wilfred as an older man. He was sixty-five when Alice married him. Jack, on the other hand, was forty-four and was always young at heart. That, and stupid and horny.

"Where'd he come from?" Alice is indicating the dog, who is now lying with his head on his front paws.

"He belongs to Jimmy. My gardener's partner."

"What kind is he?"

"Oh, he's an Irish wolfhound."

"Is he part wolf, then?"

"Can't say for sure. I'll ask." Penny brushes the hair aside on her forehead. "He scared me too. Missed a step and had to have stitches."

Alice can't see but fumbles for her daughter's hands and holds tightly, squeezing. "Oh, do be careful, dear! How terrible!"

"Oh, it's fine. A lot of excitement, and the poor dog felt so bad."

Within no time, Ernest has returned with a large plate of digestive cookies, crackers, grapes, and dried prunes. He is very spry for his age and looks quite pleased with himself.

Penny and Haggis dig into the bounty before them.

"My heavens, girl! You're starved!"

"Didn't really eat breakfast, and then Haggis and I have been out walking and kind of lost track of the time. I'm starving. Can I get a bowl somewhere for water?" She is stuffing crackers and biscuits and grapes into her mouth like she hasn't eaten for days. Haggis, too, is wolfing down crackers and biscuits, but then again, he is a dog and will eat whenever the opportunity presents.

"My! You've made short order of that. We'll have to fetch some more." Alice marvels at the dog and her famished daughter.

"No, it's okay. We'll eat when we get home. It's just taken the edge off. My personal trainer would be so proud to hear me say that. She's always telling me to stop eating before I'm full." Since Ernest didn't bring any liquid refreshments, she's finishing off her meal popping grapes into her mouth. They are very succulent and tasty. "But Haggis needs some water. Where can I get a bowl?"

Before Alice can answer, Ernest springs into action, apparently having heard this last request.

"Water? No need for a bowl." Again he is up and over behind the lavender planter. They hear some grunts and can see his bony rear end sticking up as he fumbles with something out of view. "Ah ha!" Then there is a rushing sound, and Ernest appears with a garden hose. "Ta da!"

Water is spurting forth at very high pressure. Haggis gets up on all fours and then balances onto his two hind feet and begins to gulp at the water spraying in his direction. In this position he is more than six feet tall. Quickly he becomes drenched, enjoying every minute of this unexpected shower.

Everything happens so fast, and Penny can't make out what the other residents are saying because everyone is screaming and exclaiming God knows what. Some are covering their faces, some cry out for help. One guy, who never talks but is known to play the piano in the main lounge in the middle of the night, claps his hands together like it's a vaudeville act. "Go! Go! Go!"

Alice is yelling at Ernest, "Stop it! Stop it!"

"What's that?" But he is too focused on the dog to pay any attention to Alice. "Hey, boy! Hey hey!"

"Ernest! Stop it right now!"

In all the excitement, Penny is unable to get a hold of the leash, and Haggis is running loose in large circles.

The pandemonium lasts seemingly forever and then comes to an abrupt stop when Philip shuts the tap off and puts an end to all the fun.

There is just stunned silence and the sound of dripping, trickling water mixed in with Haggis's slurping at newly formed mini puddles. For a long time nobody speaks. Then all of a sudden various employees appear through any and all doors leading into the courtyard patio.

Haggis is soaked and chooses his moment well to shake the water a good twenty feet.

"Ahh!" somebody in a wheelchair exclaims.

"Nurse! Nurse!" A lady is gesticulating wildly.

"Ew!" says another.

Only the piano player is laughing and clapping and smiling like a kid. Ernest is just now registering the severity of the situation.

"Mr. Miller! Put the hose down!" Philip comes forward like a bouncer, muscles bulging, clearly not amused.

The residents all look at him, and for a second there is a glint of defiance in old Ernest. For a second you'd think he was wielding a gun, not a garden hose.

"Mr. Miller, put . . . it . . . down." Philip steps forward and removes the limp hose from Ernest's hands. Eighty-four years old but he must still have quite the grip, because Philip has to exert a bit of effort before he finally wrenches it free. Penny looks on and wonders how much trouble she's in.

Ernest glances from Philip and over to Penny and does a small bow. Then he turns to Alice, shrugs, and shyly smiles and salutes.

The piano player is the only one applauding. "Ha! Ha! Ha!"

There is some commotion as chairs and tables are wiped down and residents are wheeled away. Alice remains seated while Ernest is led off like a naughty child.

"I'm so sorry, Mom." Penny has picked up the end of the leash and is ready to make a retreat before the nurse returns, with reinforcements, no doubt. "I hope you don't get in trouble."

"Oh fooey! At my age, who gives a hoot! It'll give us all something to talk about."

"Sorry about Mr. Miller."

"Ernest is all grown-up. He can look after himself, I would hope."

"Well, I didn't mean to cause such a ruckus."

"Penelope, any excitement around here is welcome. Come and give your mother a kiss." Alice leans forward and holds her arms out in the space before her. Penny moves into the embrace.

"I love you, Mom." They kiss, and she can smell the distinctive scent of her soap. "Haggis must have been quite the surprise."

"Indeed, he was," Alice says, "but I'll tell you, if you truly want to surprise me . . ." She fumbles for her daughter's hands. "If you truly want to surprise me, come and tell me you're pregnant."

Penny takes a deep breath and tries to quell the anger that comes so quickly it catches her off guard. She reasons she shouldn't be angry with her mother and realizes what she is feeling is not merely anger, but rage.

She thinks she has been feeling this for a long time but has become very good at burying this emotion.

In her heart, she knows she is not upset with Alice, but she knows she must leave at once. She cannot talk to her. She cannot ask her old mother to give up hope for a grandchild. She cannot explain to an eighty-four-year-old woman that her daughter is alone, abandoned, discarded. She must leave before the tears come.

"Bye, Mom. See you in a week." She gives Alice one more quick peck on the cheek and yanks the leash, leaving with Haggis in tow. She is fuelled by excess fury and walks for ten minutes without noticing anything except the sound of her feet stomping along and the occasional word that flies unexpectedly from her own mouth.

"Pregnant!"

"Please!"

"Damn it!"

She has rerouted herself and the dog back onto the lanes and is getting within three blocks of home when she turns off a lane and up a street to a small park, where she sits on a bench.

"I can't go home just yet, Haggis. Let's sit." The bench is in the shade, and though the heat of the day is giving way to a gentle breeze, Penny is hot and deeply fatigued. They have been walking steadily, minus their stopover chez Alice, for almost three hours, and even the dog seems happy to take a break.

"So?"

Haggis is panting.

"What do you think?"

Haggis continues panting and looks like he is nodding.

"Yeah." Penny sighs. "Yeah. It's pretty bad."

Yeah.

"Yup. I just can't . . . just can't. I just, I don't know."

All the water from Mr. Miller's hose presses on Haggis's bladder. The dog stands up and walks as far as the length of the leash permits and begins to piss.

"Yeah, Haggis. Piss on it."

When he is done, he comes back and resumes his position next to her. She is not finished stewing.

"You know, I never thought I would be forty years old and so unhappy."

Maybe because animals can sense the intensity in humans, Haggis leans a slight bit into her knees. She reaches out and pets his great head.

"You know, I really am unbelievably unhappy. I can't stand Heather going on about how everything's great. How it's going to be fantastic when I lose the weight. And Linda! I mean, they're from another world!"

The words spew out. "I am so bloody angry and pissed off at all these people and myself and Jack. I bet you've met a few bitches in your lifetime, hey, Haggis? Oh, I shouldn't have said that. You're such a good dog. You really are a very good boy. Oh, Haggis."

For a long time, Penny is lost in her thoughts, but she keeps touching and stroking the dog.

"I shouldn't talk like that. I'm being unappreciative."

Haggis looks at her like he's truly seeing her. Really deeply interested in what she has got to say. He's not looking off past her. He's not sneaking glances at his watch. He stares deeply at her. Waiting. Listening. Understanding.

"We tried to have a baby. We did. Once."

Haggis cocks his head to one side. He doesn't interrupt, and she is glad, because she needs to talk. To get it out.

"I lost it." Penny bites her lip. "I lost it and then we never tried again."

A slight wind ruffles the tops of the trees.

"We should have tried. But I didn't think he loved me enough, you know? I think if you're going to bring a baby into this world, you have to do it with love. I don't think he loved me then, and I don't think he loves me now— God, that's for sure!"

Another lady, with a Weimaraner, comes into the park. Her dog checks out Haggis.

"Good boy, Haggis. Stay."

The lady gives a nod and smile while her dog pees all around the other nearby benches and bushes. Haggis and Penny watch them until they disappear in the direction they came from.

"Have you ever been in love, Haggis? I don't think I ever have. Real love. And I deserve that. I do. God, what's the matter with me? I mean, look at me, Haggis. Why doesn't anyone out there want to have puppies with me? Why not my husband? Isn't that sad? I should have never let this happen. I should have walked away a long time ago, but I was foolish. I thought things would change."

Haggis just waits.

"But nothing changed, and I didn't make anything happen."

She wonders what her life would have been like.

"So here I am, forty and fat and furious."

She wonders if she would be happy living out in the valley.

"It's not a pretty picture."

When she looks at the dog, she could swear he is sad. Maybe she's bringing up unresolved issues for him too.

Perhaps every time he sees another canine in one of those lampshades, freshly neutered, he, too, feels regret. He would have made a great dad.

"You're a kind and loving dog, Haggis. Yes you are."

It's time to get moving. "Let's go." Penny struggles to her feet and lets Haggis lead the way home. She is walking at quite a clip, stimulated by passion and irritation and her never-ending internal monologue. Haggis, however, is slowing down, possibly because he is not as incited as she is and also because Irish wolfhounds are not the most energetic dogs on the planet. By the time they turn up the alley, she is far ahead of him.

"Come on, Haggis. We're almost home."

Penny is thinking about calling up Jimmy and Aaron to see if her four-legged friend can spend the night. They come into the garden by the back gate.

"Ah, home sweet home. Just look at it, Haggis. Bloody gorgeous, isn't it?"

And it is a lovely yard. So lovely that Haggis just plunks himself down onto the grass.

"Oh, my! You're tired, poor boy." Penny gets right down onto the lawn and lies on her back next to him. "I'm exhausted too, but I feel buzzed somehow. Like I drank too much Coke or something. I never drink Coke. Only at the movies. With a popcorn. Usually I buy the combo. It's cheapest, but it's supposed to be for two. I never finish it. That's the only time I drink Coke, anyway. Kind of cuts through it all."

Haggis yawns and stretches his great body.

"You know, I can't recall the last time I went to the theatre. I just go by myself. Susan came with me a few times, but she's a movie talker, and I can't stand it. So I never tell her. I just go. I don't tell Jack either."

Penny waves away a fly that circles in for a closer look at the dog, who is too tuckered out to bother.

"I wish you and I could go see a movie." Once she sat across the aisle from a man and an assistance dog. The whole time the dog just sat there and didn't make a sound. And the man got to enjoy a film and didn't have to go alone.

"I don't know why, all of a sudden I am feeling so . . . I mean, it's always been this way. And you know what? I haven't really minded. I just went and did what I wanted when I wanted. And it was fine by me. Now . . . I don't know. I just can't bear the thought of being all alone."

The dog has now rested his great head upon the deep green grass.

"I'm so glad you're here."

His hazel eyes look heavy.

"I mean it."

She has rolled over onto her side, one arm petting the great animal. For a long time she says nothing but continues to caress the dog.

"Oh, Haggis . . . ," she whispers. "What am I going to do?"

Penny hears the phone ring and wonders if that is one of Haggis's two dads calling for him.

Jack appears on the back balcony with the cordless. "It's for you."

"You're home?" She swings her head around. He has surprised her.

"Yes. I live here."

"You wouldn't know it." She gets up and walks over to where he can easily throw the phone down to her.

"Hello?" It is Jimmy. "Hi. Yeah, we've had quite an adventure today. Walked and walked and walked. I think he's more pooped than I am." She talks and stops and listens to Jimmy and laughs and walk back over to Haggis.

Jack, observing her conversation, interrupts loudly, "I don't want that dog staying here again!" Absolutely no more sleepovers, he had told Penny. He didn't share the bed with her anymore, but there was a limit to things. "No way that horse is gonna sleep in my bed, damn it!"

Penny looks up from her conversation with Jimmy. When it registers what Jack has said, she says a few words into the phone and then covers the receiver with one hand.

"Excuse me?" Though she is dead tired, she is ready to do battle.

"You heard me. I'm not having that goddamn dog in my house!"

"Your house! This is half my house, and he's staying!"

"Oh no, he isn't!"

"Oh yes, he is!"

"I don't want him here, and that's final."

"What you want and don't want long ago stopped being my concern. Shall I make a list for you of all my wants? Shall I? Where should we start?"

Jack stares down incredulously at this new woman. "Ahh!" He throws his hands up in the air and goes inside.

"Just as I thought! Ha!"

Jimmy has heard all the screaming despite Penny's attempts to muffle the sound. "Are you okay?"

"I haven't felt better!"

"What's going on?"

"Nothing. Jack and I were just sorting out the details for Haggis's sleepover. If that's okay with you."

"Is Haggis going to be all right? Jack doesn't sound too pleased."

"Haggis is going to be fine. Can I feed him steak?"

"He'd love it."

"Then it's settled."

"Are you sure?"

"Absolutely."

"Well, okay. But tell Jack, if anything happens to our dog, then he'll have two angry fags on his ass."

The evening passes pleasantly enough with Jack brooding in the background and Penny and Haggis cooking up a gourmet meal in the kitchen, talking, laughing. She takes out two steaks, one for herself and one for the dog. Because it's well after six and past his mealtime and a good twenty minutes until the dinner will be ready, she takes out a can of wet dog food. She empties it out into a bowl and mashes it and then warms it up in the microwave.

When she takes it out of the microwave, she realizes it is too hot and leaves it to cool on the counter. Haggis sits patiently and watches her fly about. She really is in fine form.

Neither of them takes any notice when Jack stomps into the kitchen and grabs a beer, a box of crackers, and the bowl from the counter.

Penny is preoccupied with peeling and slicing and dicing the vegetables. She takes care to time everything just right. Lastly, she puts the steaks on and opens up a bottle of Okanagan Merlot. This one has a picture of an emu on the label.

The aroma of the wine makes her sigh. The smell of the steaks makes Haggis drool.

"Oh, poor boy!" The beast must be starving. "Here, let me give you a little bit of your appetizer." But when she looks on the counter and in the microwave, his food is nowhere to be found.

"Now what did I do with your food?"

Editorial
Wednesday, August 27

I am enjoying reading all the articles about Penny Stevens because I can totally relate to her. I am 38 and after two kids my body isn't what it used to be. I am trying to exercise every other day and I just can't seem to do it. I want to, but then I don't. It's frustrating. My husband bought me three sessions with a coach and that was a different experience for me. I thought I would really love it, but it's weird to exercise under the glare of professionals. I still have to book my final session and I am dreading it and, at the same time, I know it will be good for me. So it is refreshing to read about Penny Stevens and not have to hear about how easy it is for her. I like seeing the house and garden reno too.

Thanks again,
Sally Finlayson

Seventeen

Haggis couldn't keep his eyes open past midnight. Penny, however, is still awake well past three. So many thoughts are whirling about in her mind, coming at all angles and at breakneck speeds. She couldn't suppress these outbursts if she tried.

"I've always liked this room and the way the windows let the breeze in."

"I hate it when people say 'multitasking.' It's bullshit. Sorry."

"I despise 24/7!"

"I am going to read *Hamlet*. It's a classic and I should read it." This she says while looking at the stain on her ceiling, secretly pleased the reno team let old Shakespeare live on.

"There are so many things I should do before I die. I mean, I'm forty, so life's half over, right?"

"I've never gone on a road trip. I should."

"I have never really explored religion. I should. I suppose I should."

"I am so self-absorbed. That's the curse of us humans. I should volunteer somewhere."

"I have never gone for a total body massage. I should. One of those Swedish ones where they really pummel you. Or a Thai one where they walk all over you."

"I don't floss enough because I hate it, so I end up lying to my mother. I'm forty and I am still a child."

"I have no idea how I ended up forty!"

"How old are you, Haggis?" Penny recalls Jimmy saying he will be nine.

"You're a wise old man, Haggis, unlike me. I'm worried that I will never learn anything of value. That the next forty years will pretty much be like the last forty and that nothing is going to change and that I'm just going to get older and wrinklier and end up at the Manor holding Mr. Miller's hand!"

"Jack's an asshole." Penny, who has been lying on her back, suddenly kicks the covers off and sits up. "If

I sic you on him, would you attack him, draw blood? Have you ever killed anything with intent before?"

"I should read the Bible. But the New Testament, not the old. Too much so-and-so begat so-and-so. On and on and on. No, maybe I'll start with Jesus entering the scene. Or maybe just Coles Notes. God bless those people for doing all the work. Saved my bacon a few times, let me tell you."

"Or maybe Buddhism. I don't really like organized religion. It's too . . . organized."

"I don't think I'm ever going to lose the weight."

"Are you closer to Jimmy? Is he like your dad? Do you love him? Do animals ever worry about how they look? About their weight?"

"Do you think I look fat?"

When Penny sees that Haggis has closed his eyes and hears his gentle, even breathing, she is silent for a while, staring up at the ceiling.

"I love this house and I don't want to leave it. And not just now that it is tidy and pretty and perfect-looking. I loved it the second I saw it. It feels like yesterday. It's sixty-odd years old, maybe as old as Jack. I wonder how many people have lived here? How many people were born here? How many babies were begat here? In this room?"

"I haven't had sex in years."

She finally falls asleep and dreams of an endless stream of rosy-cheeked babies in strollers. She waves and the babies smile back and then the mothers, whose faces she can't see, wheel the children away.

She is in a deep sleep when the phone rings.

"Hello?" Her eyes are stuck shut.

"Good morning." The voice on the other end assumes it need not identify itself. Penny hates it when friends and neighbours phone up and simply say hi without further comment, like she has instant voice recognition. That, or call display. For this reason alone, she almost prefers telephone marketers. At least you can tell them apart from everybody else.

"What time is it?" She is groggy and it might be somebody calling from a different time zone.

"It's after nine," the voice states. "Did I wake you?"

"No . . . well, yes. I guess." The person is playing their cards close to the chest, forcing Penny to grope further along. "So . . . ?"

"How are you?"

"Fine. And you?"

"Fine, thank you." Still they are not offering up any clues.

"Great."

"Listen, I am really liking your last couple of pieces."

My pieces?

"You're personalizing it, and it's working. I liked that you brought in the dog and your thoughts, your diet. I'm hoping we can see more of that from you. We are getting a good response from this series. The readers like it. I like it."

Sylvia!

"And Mitch tells me that everything went well the other day. I just wanted to thank you, Penny. You really have been kind to let us all get a piece of you. I just wanted to touch base with you and thank you for a job well done."

She is happy to hear that Sylvia is pleased. Sylvia is the kind of person people like to please—want to please. Penny is happy to get off the phone. Before hanging up, she agrees to put more of her personal life into next week's column. What else could she say?

Haggis raises his great body and gets out of bed and does an excellent Downward Dog stretch. Penny watches him and thinks Lamaraya and all those yogis must be on to something. She rolls off the bed and onto all fours and does her best imitation of the canine pose. It feels good, and she promises to do it every morning.

"Good morning, Haggis. Did you sleep well? Let me

pee and then we'll go out in the yard and you can pee. Sound fair?"

As they pass by Jack's den, she hears him stirring. "Good morning, husband. I just want to let you know that I intend to have some serious conversations with you today. Perhaps we could start downstairs over coffee?"

"Christ, Pen."

"We need to talk."

"I don't know, Penny, I don't know."

"Of course you don't. How about I do the talking and you listen and we'll take it from there."

"Christ, Pen."

"Jack, have you any idea how ridiculous you sound?"

"I've got to get to the office."

"Husband, if you don't talk to me here, I will follow you to your office and demand that you talk to me there." At this, Jack looks up at the doorway and sees his wife standing in the hall with her hands on her hips, ready for battle. The dog is there also, panting.

"Christ, Penny!"

"Language, Jack."

She heads off downstairs before he can mumble a response. Her living room looks beautiful with the sunshine streaming in, and she notices that she needs to water the planters on the balcony. Before she does that, however, she needs to let Haggis outside. He immediately goes just around the corner and relieves himself on a rhododendron. *He is so well behaved!*

"Good boy, Haggis! What a good boy!" She is delighted as he ambles back up the porch steps and offers his head for stroking.

The day seems to hold much promise. Penny can't put her finger on the reason for this; she has no definite plans but feels excited nevertheless.

While the coffee brews she dishes out a large bowl of dog food and watches as Haggis devours every last bite. She herself doesn't know what she wants to eat. Maybe that's the problem for people. Too many choices. Maybe she should eat the same cereal for breakfast every day. Then, in the evening, the same stew. Lots of water throughout the day, lots of walking, and the odd treat if she is particularly good. She should run this diet by Heather. Call it by some ridiculous name, and when clients "hit their targets," they get a low-carb bone. It could work. Never say never.

Jack's still puttering about upstairs. No doubt waiting for his chance to slip out unnoticed. Penny feels like she can't sit still. She has this unexpected energy and needs to move.

The coffee is ready, and instead of taking a cup, she grabs one of Jack's commuter mugs and fills it to the top.

"Jack?" She is at the bottom of the stairs.

There is no answer, but she feels him listening. She can just picture him upstairs with his eyes shut tight, willing her to go away.

"Jack? I'm going out." Still only silence. "I need you to figure out how much this house is worth and how much I need to pay you out. The way things have been are no longer working for me. I would like to stay here, and since you are rarely ever here I'm hoping you can figure things out on your end." She imagines him with his eyes open now.

"So let me know your thoughts. We'll talk more. I'm very angry all of a sudden, and I should warn you that I dream of hurting you. You are no longer safe here. Don't come into the kitchen when I'm using the big knife. After all that's been happening, I don't want to hit the front pages of the *Sentinel* for aggravated assault." She hears the springs of the foldout mattress creak. "Or murder."

"Good boy, Haggis!" They haven't travelled a block before the dog produces his first turd of the day. She quickly whips out a baggie and removes the poop and disposes of it in a nearby garbage can.

Penny eats an apple and drinks the remains of her coffee. They are home in just under an hour. Jack is long gone.

"I'm going to take a shower, and then we have the whole day!" She takes the stairs two by two, astonished at her energy. She thinks she might pack a lunch and head over town to Jericho Beach. She hasn't been there in years and feels like driving with the windows down. Take Haggis over to the other side. Get a different perspective.

In the shower, she actually sings. She's never been a shower singer. She finds it weird that she is feeling so joyful, so carefree. She realizes it's the first day of September, that she survived August. Of course it is a beautiful day, and the house looks great, and the guys have let her keep the dog overnight. But she has also broached such a forbidden topic with Jack that she can't for the life of it fathom how she can be so calm. So at ease. Like their marriage is some niggling detail that has been overlooked the last little bit, and they are finally going to deal with some issue or another and solve whatever the problem may be. *Oh, honey! Then we can finally take that vacation!*

When the phone rings she is reluctant to get it for fear it is Aaron or Jimmy coming for the dog. She knows she has fallen too hard and too fast for Haggis but seems to need him by her side. *It's finally happened. I've gone quite mad.*

She lets the machine pick up.

"Hi. It's Linda."

Bless her for her straightforwardness!

Penny again looks at the dog and thinks about the lunch and adventure they were about to have. The day that looked so promising now stretches before her like some chore she has to get through. *What does that woman want now?*

Linda apparently needs to come over. She's jazzed about something or other, but Penny can't make out what it is. *I'm outta here! I'm not here!* She's so worried that Linda will arrive before she has time to flee that she grabs some sunblock and towels and the leash, a few baggies, and her wallet. Haggis, meanwhile, is quite calm.

"Okay, let's go!" Penny fumbles with her keys as she herds the dog out the front door. It's amazing how nervous she suddenly is. A grown woman sneaking off with a monstrous dog. *Not exactly discreet.* Her heart is thumping, and her hands are shaking, and she drops the keys twice between the porch and her car.

"Oops!"

Haggis senses that something is going on, but when he realizes he is going for a car ride he smiles and wags his tail, which, in turn, calms Penny down.

"You are such a good boy, Haggis!" She opens the back door for him, and he manoeuvres himself into place. Sitting behind the wheel, she takes a few deep breaths and catches sight of the dog in the rear-view mirror. Once again, the day is looking good, and she is happy all over. She doesn't know exactly where they are headed, but the fact that they are on their way is all that matters. She needs to keep moving.

And talking. For some reason Haggis makes her talk—a lot. And she doesn't edit herself or feel like what she is saying is stupid or silly. Everything that she is saying is suddenly very true and very important.

"I need to figure out what it is I want. What I need. And what I need to do in order to achieve it."

This feels like therapy. Like she's heard or read this somewhere before. She probably has, but it hasn't resonated until this moment. There is an urgency to all her thoughts. She's never been able to articulate her deepest feelings and desires, and it feels weird hearing herself speak like this.

Years back, before she went on Paxil, *or was it Prozac?* Dr. Wilcox advised her to go see a therapist. She was surprised that he would want his patients to do that.

For some reason, maybe because of his age, Penny thought he was more "old school" and didn't require her to go jump through such hoops. *She was a normal woman, for Heaven's sake! Not a crazy person.*

"You mean a shrink?"

"A therapist, yes." Dr. Wilcox was scribbling down a number and handed the card to her, which she regarded like some foreign language.

"But I just heard these drugs are quite effective. For crying and stuff." She felt ridiculous having to say this and wanted the conversation to be over. The last thing she wished was to have to go through all of this again with some other doctor. Least of all a shrink.

"Yes. I imagine they are."

Then why don't you just write out the bloody prescription!

"I just need to stop crying. It's silly, I . . ." She grabbed a tissue from his desk without looking at him. She'd been coming here her whole life and couldn't figure out what she was feeling more strongly, heartache or indignation.

"Sometimes in cases like this, it can be very helpful to figure out what is at the core of a person's pain." Dr. Wilcox has a very kind face, and Penny knows if she were to look into his eyes, she would probably dissolve into one giant puddle.

"Okay." She said it but didn't mean it, and he knew it but wrote out the prescription anyway, which made her feel very relieved and embarrassed at the same time.

"Come back in a month. It'll take a few weeks before the effects kick in, but I'd like to see you shortly after that."

She took the small sheet of paper and folded it into her wallet. "Thank you so much." She tried to keep her voice light. "Oh, my mother sends her greetings. She's settled into the Manor quite nicely."

"Ah, that's good to hear. Give Alice my regards." He touched her lightly on the shoulder and exited the small examination room, leaving her alone to collect her thoughts and blow her nose.

She remembers filling the prescription upon leaving the doctor's office, but out of guilt for the way she had acted, she didn't take her first pill until after her one and only appointment with the shrink.

It was ridiculous. He had a teddy bear.

"You want me to what?" Penny was pretty sure she had heard him.

"I want you to talk to Edgar as if he were Jack." Edgar was a dark brown bear with a blue bow tie. On the other couch was a lighter brown bear with a frilly pink necklace. She wondered what the female teddy was called.

"Pretend Edgar is Jack?"

"Yes. Tell him how you feel."

"Tell Edgar?"

"Yes."

"Pretend he is Jack?"

The therapist nodded, and she wondered what kind of success rate the guy had with this approach. Didn't other people find it ludicrous? Uncomfortable?

"I just can't talk to . . . Edgar here . . ."

"Why can't you, Penny?"

"Because . . ."

"Just tell him how you feel."

She had to close her eyes to keep it together.

"Penny? Don't be scared. Look at Jack and tell him how you feel."

When Penny felt ready, she opened her eyes only to see the therapist holding the teddy on his knee, beseeching her with the most sincere expression to confront Edgar.

Jack would never sit on this guy's knee. He wouldn't be caught dead dressed like that!

She couldn't do it. She simply couldn't play that game. She had to leave. Immediately. Problem was she couldn't remember what the therapist was called. He wasn't wearing a name tag, and of course the door was shut so she couldn't see if his name was engraved on the outside.

She recalls abruptly standing up and sticking her hand out to the man. "Thank you so much. Really. Thank you. I need to go. So sorry."

Confused, the therapist stood up too, still clutching his teddy.

"And thank you, Edgar, it was so nice meeting you too." She shook the teddy's paw and abandoned the shrink before he could entice her with any other toys.

Penny calculates that must have been over four years ago. She wonders if the therapist is still in business. If Edgar's still on the job.

And it's been ages since she has been over town and longer still since she's ventured over to this shore. Driving through Stanley Park and then into the West End, over the Burrard Bridge, past all the shops in Kitsilano, makes her feel like a tourist in her own city. And it's odd looking across the water, seeing where she lives. Penny is used to the view the other way around. It feels backward somehow.

Luckily, a camper van is backing out just as they pull into the Jericho Beach lot. She parks and they immediately head over to the concession stand. She didn't count on any bylaws prohibiting dogs on the beach, but the signs are everywhere, threatening hefty fines. She leashes Haggis up and orders three hot dogs, two without any bun, one peach-flavoured drink, one bottled water, and a large order of fries.

They find a picnic table and spread their bounty out. Penny can't remember the last time she ate a hot dog. Haggis, of course, wolfs his down, but she takes time applying the ketchup and relish and mustard.

"Haggis, be a good boy and mind your table manners." She sees a few people have taken notice of her and the dog, and she keeps one foot on the leash, as if to convey that everything is under control.

The drink is overly sweet, but she savours it as well. She hasn't consumed anything this peachy since Heather entered her life. Haggis waits patiently for his second wiener, and they share the fries, though she is pretty certain he gets the lion's share.

Lunch is over, and much as she'd like to sit and enjoy the view, Penny needs to get moving again. She doesn't know which way to walk, so she lets Haggis choose. He wants to go east, and soon the trail veers off from this beach to a small path that opens up to another beach area. Penny thinks it might be where she came for a folk festival as a teenager.

"So many memories, Haggis. So much time." She thinks of her life. Her forty years. All the things she hasn't done. The places she hasn't been. And she thinks of all the things she is going to do. All the things she simply has to do.

A number of people have come up and talked to them. Folks are eager to meet such a grand dog, and of course, they in turn chat with Penny too. Animals are such icebreakers. And kids.

"Dennis, slow down!" A lady, carrying an infant in a sling, is approaching from the opposite direction, following a running toddler.

"Heel, Haggis." He's always at Penny's side, but she says this more for the benefit of strangers, so they will know that a dog this size can be handled. That she is, hopefully, in command.

"Hey there, dog." The woman is obviously not put off by Haggis's size. Soon little Dennis is patting Haggis, who towers over him.

"He's friendly," adds Penny.

The woman chats while her son investigates Haggis.

"Nice day. Not too hot."

They talk about the weather, about school starting up. She can hardly wait for Dennis to go to kindergarten. She's almost finished breastfeeding the baby.

Penny delights in hearing this mother ramble on about these ordinary, everyday things. She feels like she is constantly making new friends.

"So, what about you?"

"Pardon?" She likes to listen, to be the audience.

"What brings you out here?"

"Me?"

"Yes, you. And your dog. Got kids? Are you from around here?" Despite the fact that the woman has been standing in one spot, talking for a few minutes now, the child wrapped around her has not stirred.

"No." Penny feels this response is adequate. That it will suffice and the conversation will come to an abrupt end. It does.

"Okay, well, nice chatting." The woman shifts the bundle at her chest over to the other side. "Dennis! Dennis, let's go, buddy. Bye. Say bye to the nice lady." And they are off.

Penny waves to the little boy, and only then does she realize that the woman is rather plump. She is wearing an orange tube top and tight-fitting white shorts. She's not much taller than Penny, but she is out here on a summer day, taking pleasure in the sunshine, her kids, strangers and their dogs. *Good for you, girlfriend. And no, I don't have any kids. But I've got this dog and I'm renovating my life! And you're gorgeous!*

It is not a scorcher, but because they have been walking some distance, Penny is hot and imagines that

Haggis is too. She takes the water bottle from her bag and drinks her fill and then pours more or less the rest of the water into the dog's mouth.

"I love you, Haggis."

He smiles up at her.

"I really do."

They head down to where the sand stretches forever. Penny takes off her sandals and exhales deeply when she wades in the shallow water. Haggis is tentative for a moment, like he is considering whether he wants to get his tootsies wet.

"Come on!"

He looks like he is really thinking hard, but when she bends down to give him a splash he charges in before she can spray him. He is off leash, and for a second she is worried that he is going to run off, but he keeps a tight circle around Penny. She counts at least five other dogs and owners frolicking in the water but is worried that if an officer were to come upon this secluded section, likely it would be Penny and Haggis incurring the fine. They stand out too much, so Penny begins to head for the shore.

Somehow this morning feels so long ago. She wonders what her husband is doing right this minute, if any part of what she said is registering with him. "It was never right from the start, me and Jack." Haggis comes and falls in with Penny's stride.

"We have been living separate lives for basically our whole marriage. What do you make of that?"

Haggis has to pee. He doesn't run but trots off diagonally to the shoreline, finds the nearest bush, and lifts his leg. She's left the sunblock in the car and is starting to feel the sting on her nose and cheeks.

As much fun as she is having, she decides in that instant that they must get going home. Walking and playing with Haggis is a diversion. But her home is across the water. That is where her life is, and she suddenly feels like she needs to face up to reality and actually attempt to make her life her own. Not a response to Jack's. Not other people's vision for a newspaper feature. Not a "before" or "after" picture. A real "here and now" fire is burning in her tummy, spurring her on.

The car is boiling, and even with all the windows rolled down, it takes a while until both she and the dog can breathe. Penny lets the warm air rush in the window. Her hair is blowing every which way. The dog has his great head out in the open air, and Penny is sure he is smiling. Inside, she is too.

• • •

Thankfully, the afternoon traffic is light, and they are crossing Lions Gate and turning onto Haywood in less than three-quarters of an hour. Jack's SUV is in the driveway, and she can tell he's been home only a short time, because the engine is making those tinging sounds, cooling down.

Penny leaves her sandals on the porch, as they are sandy and one is still damp. Barefoot, she marches into the kitchen and fills a bowl of cold water for the dog. Then she reluctantly picks up the receiver and calls the guys.

"The party's over, Haggis." And Penny really believes he looks kind of sad to be going home. There is no answer so she leaves a message.

"You know, you got a lot of nerve." Suddenly Jack is standing there, blocking the door.

"Stop sneaking up on me!"

"I am sick and tired of all this! All these people and you with your ultimatums and that dog!" Jack has clearly been waiting for her. It feels like he's started this conversation without her.

"Christ Almighty!" His voice is booming. "I should be retired! I'm sixty-two!" He is also a pacer. "I went to see the doctor last week! I am not feeling well!"

Normally Penny would tear up at this point and apologize, but the dog is cowering in the corner now, and the sight of Haggis like this incenses her.

"Lower your voice right now."

"Well, I don't like it. Plain and simple." He continues to pace, his chest visibly puffing up and down.

"And I don't care what you do or don't like anymore, Jack!"

"Christ, you're a piece of work." He stops moving for a second, and the room suddenly feels so small with him in it.

"I can't live like this anymore, Jack. I can't. I just can't breathe." She wants to open up the window wider, but it's not the moment for that.

"What? Now all of a sudden you're . . . Christ!" He has thrown his head back and is bellowing with laughter now.

"Just why are you laughing, may I ask?" This eruption has taken Penny aback.

"I knew this whole renovation thing was a mistake from the start. Look where it's gotten us."

"What is wrong with you, Jack?"

"What's wrong with me? They've turned this place into a madhouse."

"No, they haven't. They are helping me sort things out!"

"Well, I can't tell if I'm coming or going. Nothing's . . . Everything's so . . . Goddamn it, Penny!"

"It's getting better, Jack. All these changes are for the better!"

"That one with the . . . the hair . . . the weird one, she gives me the creeps."

"They all have hair, Jack."

"Always smiling like she's got a screw loose."

Penny is shaking, and it takes a long time before she finally speaks. When the words come, she speaks slowly, deliberately, one word after another.

"This is not about them, Jack. It's about us. I don't want to live like this anymore, and I don't want you to promise to change, Jack. We're beyond all that now. In fact, I don't want you sneaking around. Let's call it like it is. Hell, invite the next one over. We can do our nails, talk about fashion. I might finally have something to say on the topic."

Hearing her talk like this sucks the air right out of Jack. He's always known that she knew the score, but the rule was she never brought it up.

"Goddamn you!" He shouts with such thunderous force that his voice cracks.

Haggis is standing rigidly on all fours, emitting a low growl that Jack and Penny hear only now.

"And I want that dog out of this house!"

"Stop screaming! You're terrifying him!"

"Just look at you and that damn dog." Jack is smoothing his hair back down and wiping spittle from the corner of his mouth. "Pitiful."

"This dog isn't going anywhere."

"Over my dead body! I don't want that dog—"

"Jack, you better listen to me." There is a different look in her eyes and a tone in her voice he hasn't heard before. "This isn't about the renovation. Or the dog, Jack."

"No, we are not having this conversation!"

"Oh yes we are!" Penny reaches up and takes Jack by the shoulders. He is strong enough to break her hold, but he stands limply in front of her, his head turned to the side.

"Jack. Look at me. Look at me, Jack."

When he does meet her eyes, it is only for a brief second.

"Why do you do it, Jack? Why?"

"I don't know, Pen. I don't know."

"Why are we married? Why did we get married?"

He is shaking his head, refusing to meet her gaze.

"Why are we living like this? Jack! Look at me."

"I don't know."

"What are we doing? We pay the bills and I write that stupid column and you sell houses and I sleep in the bed and you sleep on the couch and . . ." Penny releases her hold on him and crumples against his chest. The first sob that comes out of her is like a muscle spasm. It hurts passing through her throat, but something in her is opened, and she feels like she did when she was fourteen and the Emergency doctor had just popped her collarbone back into place. The rest of the tears come silently and steadily.

"Christ, Penny." Jack puts his arms around his trembling wife. It feels awkward because he hasn't touched her in years.

"Oh, Jack. Eighteen years. It's got to stop." She can't make out his face because of the flow of tears, but she's never seen him so clearly.

"I'll stop. I will."

"No, Jack, no you won't . . ."

"I don't even want to . . . I . . ."

"I'm not talking about you, Jack. It's not about you."

"Ah, Christ, Pen. Look, I'm . . . ah, Christ." His voice is coming out all warbled now too.

For well over a minute neither of them speaks.

"I'm sorry, Jack." He couldn't bring himself to say it, but she does. "I don't know where I've been in all of this. I'm sorry."

"Ah, Penny. You didn't do anything wrong."

"Yeah, but I didn't do anything right either. I've had my head in the sand for way too long."

Penny's breath is coming out in raspy little waves, and Jack's breathing is ragged and irregular. Haggis, now pressed up against the wall and counter, hasn't stopped shaking, but he is no longer growling. When the hot steaming piss hits the linoleum, the two humans huddled in the middle of the room look over and see the giant dog, quivering with equal parts fear and shame.

"Oh, Haggis. Oh, you poor thing."

Jack watches as his wife consoles the dog. She leads him outside, all the while stroking him, telling him it's not his fault. That she loves him. That he's a good boy.

When she returns, he awkwardly thrusts a handful of paper towels at her. "Here."

"Oh, you'll need more than that." Penny is touched. It's his way of extending the olive branch that he has thought to lend a hand. "Lay those on top first and then wet some more and use that disinfectant spray. You know, the green bottle under the sink."

Next thing she knows, her husband is on all fours, cleaning up the mess.

"Thanks, Jack."

"It's okay." Minutes later he is holding a plastic grocery bag filled with the used towels.

"No, I mean it. Thank you."

"Sure. Sure."

Haggis is sitting erect, very tall. The sun is beginning to set, and the dog casts a very long shadow across the newly clean kitchen floor.

"I was thinking, Penny, that maybe you should get a dog."

"A dog?"

"Yeah. If you want. Maybe not such a big one. You sure seem to like dogs." His knuckles are red now, burning from the disinfectant and the urine. He goes to the sink to rinse them under cool water. "Wouldn't you like a dog, Penny? Wouldn't that make you happy?"

"I suppose."

"Really? I thought you'd jump at the chance. You seem so crazy about this one." Jack turns off the water and looks at his wife and Haggis.

"It's not a dog that I want, Jack."

What's your plan?
Friday, August 29
Money Makes Cents
by Penny Stevens

I was out walking with my good friend, Haggis, who loves his walks just as much as hearing a good story. I told him about the time I was eight or nine years old, when pogo sticks were all the rage.

My birthday had passed and Christmas was far off, and no amount of whining or pointing out how lucky all the other kids were seemed to have any effect on my loving, hard-working parents. My dad advised me to start saving up for one if I felt it was so important. I had just started getting an allowance, so my parents sat me down and did some rudimentary math with me. (Uncomplicated and elementary math is the best kind for finances, by the way.) After about 10 minutes of adding up numbers and multiplying this amount by weeks and months, I came to see that I could indeed afford this item. It was going to take me three and a half months.

The first and second months passed quickly and my piggy bank grew, bringing me closer to the day when I could march right into The Bay and get my very own purple pogo stick. But then, somewhere around the third month, it happened.

Something changed. Pogo-mania was still going strong, but suddenly I didn't feel the same passion for bouncing as I so recently had. Was there something wrong with me? I wondered. My parents were very proud of how I'd adhered to my savings plan, but would I buy the pogo stick because, well, that was the plan? Or would I do something else? Purchase a different toy? Or continue saving?

Perhaps it was at this moment that I began to foster the financial proficiencies that have shaped my life thus far. I don't know. What one aims for and what one wants out of life are big questions, and sometimes a person really does want a pogo stick. The next person might want a bike or roller skates. Little nine-year-old me, however, no longer wanted a purple pogo stick. Or a green one, for that matter. I had changed my mind, plain and simple.

At any rate, what this story illustrates is that before you commit to a financial savings plan or makeover, you need to ask some very basic questions.

Like . . .

Is it feasible?

How long will it take?

What sacrifices will I have to make?

And, most importantly, IS THIS WHAT I WANT?

Somewhere along my journey to pogo ownership, I realized I had committed myself to something I no longer wanted. (I ended up buying an equally ridiculous toy, if you could call a Ouija board that.)

What is important is that you do routine check-ups of your financial health. Perhaps new variables have come into play. Maybe you need to make some adjustments. And people can change their minds. It happens every day. And it's not a bad thing at all. As long as you are cognizant of your situation and are involved in the examination of your life, then all is well.

Think about what you really want before someone, full of good advice, steers you in the direction of some great new plan.

If you're going to go in for a financial makeover, be very clear about what your goals are. Not what the accountant thinks they should be, but what you, yourself, want out of this life. Don't rely on other people to tell what your goals should be. They'll do it. Everyone's got good advice. People are eager to share it, too. But in the end, it's going to be up to you. You've got to know where you're going, 'cause wherever you go, there you are!

You never know, you might end up with a pogo stick or a Ouija board and wonder what in the world ever made you think that was a good idea.

Eighteen

When does a person realize they're having the time of their life? Penny is driving in her car listening to a top-ten station and a song has come on about just that. And it has got her thinking. When she was twelve and away at summer camp, without a worry in the world, was she having "the time of her life"? Or was it earlier, when she was nine, before she realized she wasn't one of the pretty ones, when she'd run home and fly into her mother's arms, and all her pictures were beautiful, and she had the best teacher in the world? When she was invited to all the birthday parties? Was it at university? Her first job? When she got married?

It's a question that has occurred to her before, and

the more she comes to ponder it, the more she is certain that people are likely never aware that they are "having the time of their life" at the exact instant they are experiencing whatever wonderful thing they are doing. People are too busy having the fun. Enjoying themselves. They never truly grasp that they are in "the moment." A person needs retrospection for that. It is only after a time has gone by that one can stand back and see the past for what it was. Also, Penny figures, you can't say you've had the time of your life, because you never know if the best is yet to come. You don't want to jinx it. And Penny has been pinching herself a lot lately. She can't believe her good fortune. She can't believe this life she is living is actually her own. That at any moment some very important person wearing an impeccable dark suit won't reach into their Italian leather briefcase and present her with some document in triplicate explaining that "her time is now up." *Please sign here. And here. And here.*

It's been a year since she was last at Maple Leaf Garden Centre, and today for her anniversary she chooses a yellow rose bush. The colour of friendship. It took her two minutes to pick it out.

Gosh, I'm good! She's starting to love making decisions. Actually relishes going over the pros and cons and then, after thoughtful consideration, saying yes or no or I'll take this one, not that one, and not worrying about the consequences.

"Hi, Penny!" It's Annie from yoga, with an overflowing trolley of colour and leaves and clay pots and bags of potting soil.

"Hello. My, you have a lot of plants. Putting in a new garden?"

"I always get so carried away!" She is a high-energy, tightly wound redhead who has been taking courses with Lamaraya since she opened her studio. She credits the yoga instructor with saving her life and getting her off sleeping pills.

"I've done that a few times myself. Today, it's just this." Penny indicates her purchase.

"Oh, fabulous. A rose."

"It's our anniversary."

"Well, congratulations."

"Yes, nineteen years."

"Wow. Time flies."

"It certainly does, Annie. It certainly does."

A year is a handy tool to gauge your life by, Penny thinks. On this day a year ago, the Jenkinses had not yet made the fateful mistake of putting their life savings on the roof of the Oldsmobile. Penny was, as yet, "unrenovated." She weighed one hundred and fifty pounds and drank way too much Merlot. Of course, now she weighs one hundred and fifty-five pounds, but she hasn't touched a drop of wine since February.

This time last summer Jack was busy selling houses and out most every night of the week. These days the market has cooled considerably, and his social life seems to have slowed down as well. He always seems to be underfoot, asking Penny how she is, how her day was.

It's odd, Penny muses; since she gave him carte blanche he's been clinging more tightly to her. For a while there, through last fall and right up to Christmas, he couldn't seem to get it in his head that she really didn't want anything from him.

She'd come home and find him puttering around the house, looking for things to fix, wanting to know if she needed anything.

"Are you hungry? I could fire up the barbeque," he must have asked three times a week.

"I think there are still leftovers from yesterday's grill." She appreciated his efforts but couldn't eat steak and chicken and hot dogs every night.

And she constantly felt his eyes on her. Watching her. As if, by keeping Penny close and tracking her every move, Jack could somehow come to understand her. Comprehend the situation.

"Hi. It's me. Coming home early. Can I pick anything up?" If Jack wasn't preparing food for her, he was offering to go grocery shopping. It was weird.

"I think we're good." Penny would look in the fridge and hope there was something missing. She didn't want to make Jack feel unwanted, unneeded. But what could she say at that point?

"Pen, I know you're going through some changes . . ." A lot of conversations started this way.

"Jack, we've talked about this before." They discussed it daily and weekly and monthly. It took Jack a long time to come to terms with it.

"Look, Pen. I want to make sure you're not being rash. This is—"

"Rash? I'm forty years old. I've been sensible for too long!"

But Jack simply couldn't wrap his mind around Penny's new-found plans, so he kept nattering at her every chance he got. As though if he kept repeating himself and reminding her that this was a big decision and that there would be no turning back and various other clichés, Penny would wise up to her reckless ways. Things would return to normal.

Penny, on the other hand, really didn't want any input or help from him. She was going forward; she didn't want to go back. "No, Jack. Seriously. I'll sort it out on my own."

Around conversation two hundred and seventeen, in the middle of November, just after the Americans elected a black president, Jack tried a different approach.

"I would, you know, but I'm sixty-two."

"I know, dear. I know."

"But, hell . . . This is something you want, something we should have done a long time ago and . . ."

"Look, it's my thing, okay? I'm just happy to have your support."

"But you can't exactly do it all on your own, Pen. You're gonna need some help from somebody . . . and since I don't see any person in sight, well . . . What I'm saying is, and I've been thinking about it since you told me in the summer, well . . . I . . . we could do it."

Penny could see how hard it was for Jack to fathom her going ahead without him. "But we haven't done *it* in two years. No, make that three."

"I know."

"That'll pose a problem, don't you think?"

"Ah, Penny! We could do it again. We were good at it once. We could be again." He was sitting on the couch with her, running his hands through his thick white hair, seemingly believing these lines that sounded like they were lifted from bad romance novels.

"Jack, we were never truly good at anything."

It must have been around last Christmas that he finally accepted her plans. Realized that Penny was serious about this crazy idea and was going to give it her best shot. He stopped offering her hot drinks, cold drinks, or well-meaning advice.

It was also around those months that Jimmy began to show up unexpectedly with Haggis. Naturally, work had slowed for Aaron at that time of year, but Jimmy, despite being busy writing exams, came by often. He liked going for walks. It helped him sort stuff out, clear his mind. November was particularly cold and, despite the weather, Penny was happy to accompany them. She was busy wrangling her own life too. And, like Haggis, Jimmy was a great listener.

"What did the agency say?" asked Jimmy one cold afternoon. His collar was turned up and his baseball cap pulled down. The rain was close to freezing, and it was difficult to hear each other even though they were huddled under the same umbrella. Even Haggis walked quickly, eager to get back inside.

"Well, unless Jack and I make the application together and present ourselves as a happily married couple, I don't have a chance in hell. Even then they might frown on his age. Then the waiting lists. Lord!"

Penny was also facing up to the fact that she might never realize her plans. She thought she already had come to terms with that reality years ago, but things had changed. She had changed.

In early December, she found herself wandering aimlessly among the crowds in the mall. Parents and children were lining up to see Santa, and Penny was in a foul mood. She was never one to go overboard at Christmas, wearing blinking reindeer earrings and festive red and green sweaters. But she wasn't a Grinch either. Yet that day she was literally scowling at the throng of shoppers, their bags bursting at the seams.

She had submitted her column that morning and Sylvia had had to step in and help edit out her judgmental, heavy-handed tone. The economy and the fiasco with subprime mortgages and greed had spurred Penny to address the all-too-human tendency to take more than one needs.

Well, it's that time of the year again, folks. The happiest time of the year!

It being Christmas season and times being tough and money a bit more scarce, it makes me think of Joseph and Mary and no room at the inn. And the three wise guys and their odd array of gifts. Little did that trio of sage men know that their small act of bestowing a few presents would snowball into this colossal angst-ridden act of consumerism. Over two millennia later, and everybody has the odd frankincense and myrrh stashed in the back of their closets. Therefore, dear readers, I ask you to all take a moment, prior to making that purchase, and ask yourself if you really need to buy another plastic toy made in China for your kid or niece or nephew. If Jesus ever decided to visit again, I am certain we would find him in the malls, preaching, "This isn't what it's about, people! You've got it all wrong!"

"Hi Penny, do you have a second?" Sylvia never called, but that afternoon, right after reading the piece, she had phoned Penny at home. It wasn't going to fly. The theme was not right. Don't talk about greed, and avoid discussing Jesus. "I want to make sure we're on the same page. And Merry Christmas, Penny."

"Merry Christmas, Sylvia." Penny rewrote the column and then she went to the mall. As she was not in the holiday spirit, she found it impossible to purchase anything. She couldn't even bring herself to buy a few gift certificates from her favourite stores. She'd swing by the bank and ask for crisp twenties, that was the best she could come up with. Definitely not festive.

"Penelope!" She heard her name in the crowd. "Hey, Penelope!"

She swung around and searched the sea of faces. Nobody else called her by that name. There was Aaron coming out of Indigo, a bag of books in each hand. He was wearing jeans and a dark blue crew-neck sweater layered over a deep burgundy T-shirt and an olive scarf. His hair seemed messy and stylish all at once so that a person couldn't tell if he had used gel or woke up that way naturally. Everything about him looked perfect.

"Aaron!" She missed seeing him up at her home, in her garden. He had come and pruned a few trees in autumn, and she had gone to their house for dinner, but it hadn't been the same since the reno wound down. She was thankful that Jimmy and Haggis were still regulars in her life, as they met a few times a week either up at the house or down at the Ambleside dog park, but Aaron had moved on to other projects. She was glad to run into him that day.

"Hey, gorgeous, where are you off to?"

"Oh, I've got to get out of here." Just seeing Aaron lifted her spirits, but she wanted to get home.

"Let me buy you a coffee—you look like you need one."

Though Penny would have preferred wine and did protest, he managed to persuade her to have a latte at Starbucks.

"So, Jimmy tells me you need a partner." Aaron had left Penny sitting in a large, overstuffed armchair in the corner surrounded by his forty pounds of books. He had returned with the drinks and nestled in beside her. It was tight but cozy, and his cologne was a new scent, one she hadn't smelled before.

"Or I need to go on a singles cruise." Every day she was getting older, and though she and Jack had made great strides in finally accepting their relationship for what it truly was, Penny hadn't exactly made any headway in finding a willing significant other. Time was ticking. "Seriously, I think about it. Just throw myself at the first guy with good teeth and decent grammar. I'd have to book the trip to coincide with my cycle and then swoop in for some action."

"You'd do that?"

"I'd probably be the only one on board not to get lucky. I'd have desperation written all over me."

"Oh, you'd have guys after you, Penelope."

"Right. Right." She could just imagine herself luring some unsuspecting soul into her lair. Putting her legs up after sex. Making sure those boys hit their target.

"I don't think you know just how attractive and appealing you are."

"Great! This coming from a gay guy!"

A couple of weeks later, Vancouver was hit by one snowstorm after the other. It was definitely going to be a white Christmas. Jimmy and Haggis stopped by for a winter walk and quick visit before heading off to Banff, where the dog and his two dads and another couple were going to spend the holidays skiing, snowshoeing, and playing Scrabble.

"Aaron said you were talking about taking a cruise?" Jimmy wore a dark turtleneck beneath a matching Roots bomber jacket and red Olympic hat. The snow was really coming down hard, gusting sideways. It was going to be a short walk down the laneway.

"Oh," Penny laughed. She imagined the guys discussing her. For months she had been under the spotlight with Project Penny, and she had gotten used to people talking about her. With Aaron and Jimmy, however, it didn't feel like gossip or an intrusion. She knew Jimmy wasn't simply asking after travel plans. They were friends. It was all right. "Oh, I don't know. It would feel like stealing. I guess there are women out there who haven't hesitated to take matters into their own hands and to hell with the father. But I would feel so sneaky. What if the guy wanted my number? What if he just stopped by one day and there was his kid? Could I withhold that from another person? Could I let somebody walk this earth and not tell them they'd fathered a child? I don't know."

Jimmy nodded and held Penny lightly at the elbow. The snow was unbelievably fluffy and deep and fresh. His cologne was strong and musky.

"Then there's the sperm bank. At least these guys knowingly donated." Penny had begun to venture into this world but she was cautious. What kind of guy whacked off for money? Did these men have especially high self-esteem, or were they just broke? Did they think it was their duty to provide such a service? What did they look like? Were they successful? What was their background? Were they honest when filling out the questionnaire? Or were they rubbies? Liars? Desperate losers who gave blood on Mondays and masturbated on

Tuesdays? How did they spend the rest of their week?

"Well, don't you know any guys, Penny?" They had come to a stop as Haggis found a desirable bush to pee on. His bright yellow urine steamed hotly onto the crisp, white snow.

"You mean my friends' husbands? No. No. That would be too awkward. No."

"Don't you have any friends who are suitable?" Haggis, having done his deed, did an abrupt turn back toward the house. The snow was forming in small clumps all over his coat.

"You mean boyfriends of my girlfriends?"

"No. Just . . . guys." They climbed the steps to the porch and stamped their feet and wiped the snow from their shoulders. The great dog shook himself violently, spraying tiny snowballs in every direction.

"No. I don't really have any available male friends." She wrinkled her forehead while shaking out her woollen hat, mentally going through friends and acquaintances.

"You can't think of a single one?" Jimmy was holding his cap in hand.

"No, honestly. I don't associate with many men. There's Travis, the new guy in classifieds at work but, I mean, he's so young and I don't know him at all. No. I can't think of anybody." Penny brushed the snow off

Jimmy's back and noticed how it clung to the curls at the nape of his neck.

"You can't think of a single acceptable, qualified, decent fellow?"

"No." Then she saw the look in Jimmy's eyes. "Well . . . only you and Aaron and, well . . ." Somehow this wasn't coming out right. Tiny flakes clung to his long lashes. He was beautiful.

"Sure." Jimmy put his cap back on.

"I thought you were coming in for a tea. I got some of those special dog treats too." Haggis was already inside in the hallway.

"Change of plans. I just remembered I have to be somewhere."

"You don't even have time for a quick drink?"

"Sorry."

He left abruptly, taking the dog with him and leaving Penny with a heavy heart.

Yes, she remembers the fall and winter as having been pivotal months. An important time. A turning point.

Thank God for Lamaraya.

Indeed, yoga has been her saving grace this past year, much to her surprise. In that warmly lit haven guided by that long and lanky woman, Penny stretches and breathes and lifts her arms to the heavens and feels safe. In fact, Lamaraya has replaced Heather as her exercise coach. The spunky little powerhouse couldn't seem to stay motivated inspiring her pupil. She ran out of encouraging things to say to her. She wanted a commitment from her client that just wasn't coming, and finally, in the new year, Heather set Penny free.

Of course it was just around that time that Penny really began losing the weight. All those walks with Haggis and her twice-weekly sessions at the yoga studio were finally kicking in. She was down to within ten pounds of her goal weight, and she heard from Linda that Heather was fuming. It would have been such a boon to her business. Such a success story. She tried to get Penny to come back. Penny, out of sympathy, agreed, but it was like pulling teeth, and then of course Penny started gaining all the weight, and finally, this past June, Heather threw in the towel.

A whole year has passed. Twelve months. What plant did she buy Jack last year? Did it survive? She pulls up to the house and has to park on the street. Jack's SUV,

Aaron's truck, and Jimmy's Jeep are in the driveway. She takes the rose bush and her purse and hurries inside.

Tonight Aaron is barbequing a salmon he and Jimmy caught while staying with friends on Vancouver Island.

"Hello, boys! Mommy's home!"

Penny comes through the open front door, following the smell of dinner that reached her the second she got out of her car. Holding her rose bush, she pecks Jimmy on the cheek. "Where's Jack?"

"Out back getting a cooking lesson from Aaron."

"You mean he's actually letting another man operate his barbeque? Wonders never cease!" And it's true. Penny continues to be in awe at her husband's change of tune.

When she first told Jack that Jimmy and Aaron were partners, he was as confused as she had been.

"Fags, you mean?"

"Yes. They are gay."

"Poufters?"

"They are partners, yes."

"Like Siegfried and Roy?"

"Exactly. Minus the tiger—just add a large dog."

"They don't, you know, look gay." He dropped his voice even though the guys were nowhere in sight.

"Well, inside they are."

"Really."

"Yes, Jack."

From that moment on, Jack had held his tongue in check. Normally, he wouldn't have been able to hold back making desultory comments and cracking politically incorrect jokes. But with all the upheaval in their lives, Jack found himself on unsteady ground and had chosen to button his mouth. And, in doing so, had gotten the chance to get to know and like both of them.

"Happy anniversary, darling." She pecks him on one cheek and then the other.

"Thank you." He takes the rose and gives her a wink. "Are you feeling okay? Tired? Still up for tonight?"

"Of course. We can't miss it." She leans against the balcony railing, watching Aaron drizzle lemon on the salmon steaks. Jimmy has set the table outside and Jack is getting the drinks. *Me and my men.*

If she hadn't walked into that Homelife office nearly two decades ago, just fresh out of college, would she be here with Jack? If the Jenkinses hadn't left that money on top of the car, would Aaron be here? If Jimmy hadn't done well in school and got that scholarship and gone to London, and then come to Vancouver, would Penny have ever met him? If Terry hadn't brought home Haggis, would she have ever connected with her inner self and realized her deepest desires?

Dinner is scrumptious as always. "That was great, Aaron, and I am sorry to eat and run like this, but we really have to get going. It's the first class and we don't want to be late."

Jimmy and Jack and Penny begin to pick up their plates and cutlery. "Great meal, delicious, thank you . . ."

"Shoo! All of you! Get going! I know I'm just the hired help. I cook for you and I clean up." Aaron makes a big show of herding them off the balcony. "Have fun, everybody. And Jack, be nice. Jimmy, pay attention and I'll see you at home. And Penelope, just be yourself."

Penny grabs her handbag and rifles through it for a lipstick. She applies it and then produces a comb and runs it through her hair.

"How do I look?"

"Radiant. Now let's get going." Jimmy is motioning at an invisible watch at his wrist.

"Wait! Where did I put that form?" Penny is constantly misplacing things.

"I have it. I have it." Jack waves a piece of paper in his hand.

"Okay. Are we ready?" Jimmy jingles his keys, and Penny and her three men stare at each other for a moment. Nobody answers.

• • •

The class is at the local rec centre. When Penny and Jimmy and Jack arrive, everyone looks at them expectantly.

"I see you've brought an entourage." A tall woman who looks like she swallowed a basketball but who is otherwise skinny ventures to ask what no doubt a few other people are wondering. Perhaps people recognize Penny from the paper.

Penny smiles at the woman and feels all eyes turned toward her. She could play her cards close to her chest, keep them guessing. She could lay all the facts out for them. Or, as she has decided after a few conversations with all the men in her life, she can just offer up a bare minimum of facts and leave it at that.

"This is my husband, Jack. And this is my friend Jimmy."

The instructor is an incredibly delightful individual named Donelda, and immediately Penny likes her. She is straightforward, humorous, and bursting with useful information. Penny feels certain she'll learn something from this lady.

Penny glances around the room and notices that, except for the lone East Indian couple and her Jimmy, they are a homogenous group of older, upper-middle class, Caucasian, heterosexual couples. Of course, excluding Jimmy on this last point as well, she assumed that the participants would be men and women, but she didn't anticipate the age of all the women being around the tail end of their thirties. She expected she would stick out as a forty-one-year-old but thinks only two of the women to be a good decade younger. Then again, she's never been good at telling people's ages.

They take their turns around the semicircle, and she fights the urge to announce, "Hi. I'm Penny, and I'm an alcoholic." No. This would definitely not be the place to say that.

"Hello, my name is Penny, and this is my friend Jimmy, and that is my husband, Jack."

Nineteen

"Wow!" Susan leans forward, sipping her daiquiri, her eyes wide.

Penny and Susan are tucked into a booth at the restaurant that was formerly the Avalon, for nostalgia's sake. They even called to make sure Toby still worked there and was on the Thursday shift.

"I'm not kidding, this woman is amazing." She is telling Susan about Donelda and the prenatal class. "Did you have a birth plan, by the way?" Penny asks, stabbing at the ice in her Shirley Temple.

"Just the regular, I guess. Out the . . . vagina. God, I hate that word."

"I wholeheartedly agree. It is a weird word. Penis, however, I like. More straightforward. Honest. Upright."

"So, do you have some kind of birth plan, Penny?"

"In the words of my esteemed teacher, 'I can push it out, or they can cut it out.' My only concrete goal is that both me and the kid are alive at the end. I'll go into it hoping that my body'll do it naturally, but if the doctors think I need a needle or some gas or, as Donelda put it, they want to use the 'barbeque tongs,' I'm going to leave it to the professionals. Amen."

"Wow."

"Yeah, she's quite something, that lady. But I'm learning a lot, that's for sure." The most important lesson being the illusion of control.

After dinner, Susan will be coming home with Penny and spending the night—an old-fashioned sleepover. They want to catch up on life before Penny's world goes into overdrive. Tonight they are going to make popcorn, watch a movie, and paint their nails. Penny especially wants Susan to give her a pedicure as she can't bend that easily and likes having her toes painted. In fact, she's never really been the manicure type, always preferring colourful feet to painted hands.

Susan has really been there for Penny from the moment the idea was conceived. Susan has listened to

Penny and, having been down this road a few times herself, has offered advice and tips when asked. It's been fun for Penny to have her girlfriend at her side or on the other end of the phone line. They are spending much more time together, and it's made their friendship stronger. Closer.

But still they are having a very difficult time finding a film they can agree on.

"But that's such an old movie! It was made in what? 1700?" Susan is an avid moviegoer but sees only current releases. A movie from the 1980s qualifies as an oldie.

"But it's supposed to be so romantic!" Jimmy has loaned Penny one of his favourites from his extensive collection of videos and DVDs, but she is having a hard time convincing her friend.

"Well, are we agreed we want a romance?"

"Okay, but nothing in black and white." Susan must have colour in her romances.

"But you liked *It's a Wonderful Life*, remember?"

"Sure. But it would've been better in colour."

"Oh, for Heaven's sake!" It was just this past Christmas that Penny finally got Susan to watch that classic. Penny recalls how satisfied she felt when Susan produced a tear. She *had* liked it after all. It's always been one of Penny's favourites, and she thinks it's amazing

Hollywood hasn't done a remake. They seem to remake everything else.

"Okay. But let's choose a backup film. Just in case." Susan still wants to swing by the video store.

"Fine. You pick out the second choice, but I guarantee we're going to love the first one. Jimmy says it's one of the most romantic films ever made." Toby comes by with a fresh Shirley Temple for Penny and notices Susan's empty glass. She nods that she'll have another and he winks, leaving a pile of a dozen or so new coasters.

"Fine. Okay, you win. Jimmy says this. Donelda says that. And Raja Lama says something else."

"It's Lamaraya."

"Right. Right."

"What about Linda?" Susan always loves updates on Linda.

"She broke her silence and called me last week."

"She took a vow of silence? Like a monk?"

It was kind of nice hearing from Linda. She was doing a self-imposed silent retreat in the confines of her home. It was just a quick call. Linda was practising gratitude. At least that's how Penny understood it. She was meditating a lot and reading a new book that encouraged people to voice their thanks. To tell people directly. So Linda did.

"She phoned me to tell me she's thankful for the new directions in her life."

"You mean she's not mad at you? Even though your column's getting syndicated while her pilot was passed on?"

"No, not at all. She's at a crossroads and said she was just going to be open to all the possibilities. It was really . . . quite sincere, I think." The other day Penny saw a commercial in which dominos fell one after the other. She can't recall the product but was struck by the effect of all those tiles falling. Linda was the first domino, she thinks. Because Penny reluctantly agreed to the project, so much has changed. Penny remembers telling Jack that she'd probably get her hair cut and maybe get her nails done. She had no idea of the extent of the renovation. That everything in her life would change, even her career. "Money Makes Cents" is going to be made available to a number of newspapers in Canada and the United States. A year ago this wasn't on her radar, and now she's had to meet with an agent, sign forms, negotiate terms. Last week she had to get a new headshot for the byline. All of this because Linda Campbell had a vision. And so much more. "Yeah, she was really genuine."

"Hmm." Susan has never met Linda, so Penny feels responsible for the caricature of the perpetual self-help junkie she created in Susan's mind.

So if Linda needs to phone up at eight o'clock, enthused because she has been reading her dog-eared copy of the latest bestseller that is going "to change her life" and she wants to offer thanks, Penny is not going to argue or deny whatever Linda needs to say. If there's one thing she's learned this last year, it's that life is full of all kinds of people and desires and dreams, and nothing is simple. Life is unpredictable and messy and beautiful, all at the same time.

Toby appears with another daiquiri. "How are my ladies doing?"

"Very well, thank you, and getting better all the time." Susan removes the umbrella from her fresh drink and sticks it behind her ear.

"Just fine, thank you." Penny gives Toby's arm a little squeeze.

"And your husband?" He tries to conceal his smile.

"Better. Much better." *Gosh, that was a year ago!*

Penny pulls her sweater around her as a draft blows through the restaurant's double doors. It is a crisp autumn evening. The reds and oranges and yellows still cling to the trees, but the temperature has dropped decidedly this week. Soon it will be time to get out the rake and put away the patio furniture. The sun is setting earlier and earlier. The carefree days of summer are being replaced by a darker and more subdued, serious mood. So much change is on the horizon.

Susan interrupts her thoughts. "What I really want to know is what did your mom say?"

Penny finally broke the news to Alice back in May. She made herself wait just in case she miscarried. When she finally did tell Alice, it was for real.

"Mom?" Penny had dropped by on a Saturday afternoon and mustered up her courage. She was excited to tell her even if it was only part of the whole story.

"Yes, dear?"

"I have something to tell you."

"Good. What is it?" Alice was never one to beat around the bush. When Wilfred died and she called Penny to let her know, she told her daughter to stop crying and come pick her up. She could cry in the car on the way to the Manor. She was ahead of her time. A true multitasker.

"I am . . . well, I wanted to tell you months ago . . ."

"What?"

"I thought I had better wait, but . . ."

"Out with it, for Heaven's sake!"

"Mom, I'm pregnant."

"With a child?"

"Yes, with a child. What else?"

"Good. Good." Alice must have said that a hundred times. Most news at the Manor tended to be bad news. Death and sicknesses and polyps and gout. Then, as it sunk in, she was ecstatic. "Good! Good!"

And ever since, Alice has been phoning her twice a day to ask how she is. Every morning she calculates how much longer until the birth, and every night she says a little prayer for this unborn child.

"Mom is over the moon. Driving people crazy. Telling anybody and everybody that she, Alice Butler, is finally going to become a grandmother. So she's very happy."

"What did you say about Jack?"

"Nothing."

When she thinks back, she really hasn't had to say much. Even Dr. Wilcox was unfazed. When she went in that first time and discussed her plans with him, he was truly wonderful. She thought he would have been shocked or perhaps would have counselled her otherwise, fighting to hide his disapproval or restraining himself from outright objection. She even imagined she would have to find another doctor.

"So, they've been in a committed relationship for eight years?" It was early November, months before she became pregnant. She wanted to be organized, have all her ducks in a row. He was scribbling in her chart and he offered her a leftover Halloween candy. He was chewing a toffee.

"Yes." She chose a lollipop.

"And you say you've discussed all legal matters and custody and parental rights. You've seen a lawyer?"

"Yes, we have."

"And your husband is . . . ?"

"He . . . we . . . We have discussed it. He's too old to want to be a father, and more importantly . . . we're not really together."

"I see."

"He's totally supportive of my decision. A little caught off guard, but he knows what I want to do and understands. We are going to divorce after the baby is born."

"After?"

"Yes."

"I see."

They went on to discuss blood tests that the father could do either here, in this office, or at his own GP's.

Penny was taken aback at the ease with which Dr. John Wilcox talked about AIDS and its incidence in anal versus vaginal sex. They discussed the turkey-baster option and ended that visit with instructions for her to get any pending dental work done and to begin taking folic acid as soon as possible. They would have to wait a couple of months for the blood tests to come back, and then a second one would need to be performed. It was really the most normal of doctor visits, and Penny left wondering just how many others had come before her, asking the same sort of far-fetched questions. Was she out of her mind, or was this really possible?

Apparently it was and is possible.

When she considers all the months of blood tests and discussions and back-and-forth with "what ifs" and "how about such-and-suches," she is amazed that they came to any conclusion at all. They discussed it with Dr. Wilcox and went to a lawyer. When she thinks about all the couples that just jump into the sack and end up pregnant, she believes that it might be advisable that people go through some of the questions and scenarios that she has had to grapple with. Make it harder than getting a dog licence.

"What's Jack going to do?" Susan hasn't bothered until now to ask any of these key logistical questions. Who is going to live where. The finances. When exactly will they divorce? She figured Penny would offer the details when the time was right.

"Jack's not sure, and I am fine with things staying the same for the time being. There is so much change right now, a little stability is a good thing, I think."

Recently Penny has been getting a better picture of her husband and why he has consistently been one of the top realtors in the district. He is incredibly organized, down to the very last detail. He likes to make lists and has the wherewithal to achieve set goals.

Last week he was adamant that she decide between Pachelbel's Canon and *Bolero*. Donelda had told the class to choose a piece to be played during labour, and Jack was going to burn a disc for her so Penny could practise her breathing and visualize a pain-free experience.

"Are you serious?" Penny had said, as Jack stood before her with the two choices on the table before them.

"Well, as I recall, that was our homework."

"Okay, Jack. I like them both. You decide."

And he did, after much consideration. He thought the Pachelbel was too closely connected with weddings and didn't want to make that association. But then he thought *Bolero* was too taxing on a person, like a long hike and lots of trudging. He didn't like the idea of trudging, so in the end he went with the element of water and waves conjured by the Canon. He had lain on the sofa pretending he was undergoing dental surgery and had fallen asleep. This, he thought, was a good omen.

Susan and Penny order the same rice bowl. The portions are generous and they decline dessert. Just before seven they ask for the bill and then they leave Toby a hefty tip.

"Thanks, Toby."

"You ladies are off now?"

"We are indeed." Penny gives Toby a quick hug and says "just off to the loo."

"Be careful in there."

"Ha!" Penny throws her head back and heads off to the toilet. She imagines that escapade will become part of her life repertoire. A true story, filed under "hilarious."

The movie is old and wonderful—an implausible tale of a soldier returning from the Great War with amnesia. A beautiful woman comes to his rescue, and they marry and have a child. He begins to make his way in his new life only to be hit by a car, which triggers his memory of his original life but blots out any memory of his new one with wife and child. He resumes his former life, and years pass.

The plot takes impossible twists and turns. The baby dies. She becomes his secretary but never reveals their past.

But he has the key: the key to the idyllic little cottage. A small town that draws him back. Oh tragedy! Oh torment! Cue the music! Suddenly he's there, at the doorstep with the key. Cue the closeup! God, she's beautiful. Turn the bloody key!

The ending is perfect. Penny clutches her heart and Susan sobs.

"Wow. Could you have held your tongue all those years?" Susan clearly couldn't have.

"But she did it for him. She wanted him to come back on his own. She had to believe that he would. She had her hope." Penny isn't looking at Susan but staring out the French doors into the dark night, their reflections in the windows.

"She was so classy."

"Yes."

"But it must have been so hard. I mean, I really wanted her to shake him. Tell him everything!" Susan is up on her feet, stomping around.

"I know, but she had restraint. She knew who she was, and she wasn't going to let her emotions get in the way. Really, she was very admirable." Penny is fiddling with the remote and packing up the film. Haggis, who has slept through the entire feature, does a yawn and stretches into Downward Dog.

"I know, but that's just not very realistic. That's not what happens in real life."

"I guess that's why it's a movie." Penny slowly pulls herself to standing. "Then again, maybe there are people out there who, you know, have sacrificed their entire lives for an ideal."

"I dunno. I'm just glad he finally came to his senses and remembered who he was and that he loved her." Susan picks up the popcorn bowl and her wineglass and disappears into the kitchen. "When was that movie made?" she yells while turning on the tap.

"Forties, I think." Penny waddles into the kitchen carrying her cup.

"That was actually a good story. They should remake it in colour!"

"Oh Lord, not another remake!"

"This is fun," Susan says.

Penny remembers the odd time she was allowed to have a friend sleep over as a child. The late hours and the gossip. Her mother coming in to hush up the laughter. Then the unstoppable giggles followed by her father coming in, prompting her and her friend to sincerely promise to finally go to sleep.

Upstairs, the two friends wash their faces and brush their teeth. Haggis has lumbered up onto the bed and sits dead centre. He sleeps over about twice a week and knows the routine.

"It's not even midnight, but I feel so mischievous, like a . . . kid." Susan's face is shiny from her night cream. She looks younger without makeup.

"Me too." Penny takes in the dog. "Oh, you're just too big, my friend. Come here. Come on." She motions for him to get off the bed and this he does obligingly. Certainly, he has never had to vacate his spot before, and Penny suddenly feels like she is back in elementary school, when she was excluded or passed over in a group, the last to be chosen for gym class. "Oh, Haggi, what am I going to do with you? I love you, but all three of us can't fit in this bed."

"Can't he sleep on the floor?"

"You know what? He never has. God. I suppose he could, but it would feel weird." She ponders this dilemma, perplexed, thinking she ought to ask Jimmy and Aaron where Haggis sleeps at his home. This is a predicament she has never faced. Too many friends in her bed, her life.

"Jack . . . ?" An idea strikes Penny, and she leaves Susan and the dog standing at the side of the bed. A moment later she returns, towing a very dishevelled Jack in old pyjamas and a rumpled bathrobe.

"Haggis is having a sleepover with Jack! Yes, good boy! Good boy!" For a moment Susan might be forgiven for wondering just who the "good boy" is, the dog or the husband. Haggis, picking up on the excitement, is easily won over, his tail wagging. Jack shuffles into the bedroom a little less gung-ho than Haggis, but there is a hint of a smile that he cannot suppress no matter how hard he pretends he might be put out by all of Penny's antics.

"By God, Pen." He looks over at Susan and rolls his eyes.

"Oh, Jack. This will be great. He's very good, very quiet, very still. And you know he doesn't bite. He really likes to be with people. And he likes you, Jack. He does. Oh, you two will be just perfect." Penny looks at her husband and wonders if he has been waiting for this, hoping that he would be included too. Having dealt with Jack all these years, she is increasingly bewildered by her generous feelings toward this man—a person who has ripped her life apart and can still tug at her heartstrings.

"If he so much as—"

"Go on, you two, sleep tight." Penny knows Jack's

tone and sees how he scratches behind the dog's ears. She knows Jack doesn't ever want to come across as soft or easily won over. After twenty years together, she can tell.

The two women watch the man and the dog recede down the hallway. After the door closes and only a strip of light is visible, they turn and look at one another. There doesn't seem to be anything to say, and for a moment they remain there, transfixed in their own thoughts.

"What side do you want, Susan? I don't care." Penny breaks the silence. She sleeps in the middle when alone, so she is not partial to any particular side.

Without hesitation, Susan goes for the left side.

"It's so weird sleeping here with you. I'm so used to Doug."

"I know. I'm used to sleeping by myself. It's strange having someone else in the bed."

"Really?"

"Well, I told you I sleep alone." She honestly can't remember the last time she shared the bed with Jack.

"Yeah . . . ?" Susan has her head propped up on one elbow now and is grinning.

"Yeah, I sleep alone."

"But sometimes you must share the bed . . ."

"With Haggis, sure. When he sleeps over."

"Really? So no one has actually slept here? Like overnight?"

"No. Just me and Haggis."

"So, no other human being has actually climbed into this bedchamber?" Susan has pulled herself to sitting position, her knees tugged tightly against her chest.

"No." Penny is lying perfectly still, not daring to make eye contact with Susan. She stares at the ceiling and thinks that even the Shakespeare water stain looks vaguely interested now.

"Come on, Penny."

"What?"

"Come on!"

"Come on what?" It's starting to really feel like they are back in grade four. *What boy do you like? Come on . . . pinkie-swear!*

"Out with it!"

"With what?" Penny wonders how many more times she is going to say "what."

"I want details! Come on! We've been friends since forever. Cough it up."

"You want details?"

"Yes!" She is bouncing now and pokes Penny, which startles her.

"Oh!"

"Look, I want to know how you guys did it. I am your oldest friend—you have to tell me! Did he come over here or did you go to his place? Was there music playing or was it all very . . . clinical? I mean, come on!"

"Inquiring minds want to know?"

"Exactly!" She is clapping her hands at the prospect of her friend finally coming clean.

"Why?" Now Penny pushes herself with difficulty to sitting position.

"Why what?" Susan has stopped bobbing and has her hands open in midair.

"Why do you want to know?"

"Because it's amazing! I mean, it's a bit out of the ordinary, don't you agree?"

"What is ever ordinary about creating another human being?"

"Okay, don't get all philosophical on me now. Come on, Penny."

"Well, how did you guys do it? Let's start with Douggie. Did you do it doggie style?"

"Oh my God!" Susan hands fly to her mouth.

"Doug looks like the sturdy type that would be good on all fours."

"Penny!"

"And tell me about foreplay? What do you like and

what does Doug like, or do you just jump ahead to the main feature and skip the coming attractions?"

"Oh! Oh! Oh!" She is up and out of the bed and jumping from one foot to the other.

"Christ, Pen! What the hell is going on in here?" Jack has materialized from thin air.

There is a brief pause and then Susan jumps back into bed and covers herself, including her head, with the blankets.

"Sorry, are we keeping you up?" She regards her husband with his white hair sticking up every which way. Haggis's big head appears reluctantly in the shadow. They both look equally peeved.

"It's late."

"Oh, what time is it?" Penny can feel Susan giggling under the covers and fights the urge to laugh.

"It's after midnight!" Jack speaks as if it were a school night. For once, Haggis looks like he's decidedly on her husband's side.

"Okay, sorry to have woken you again."

"It's okay. But you need your rest too." He turns to leave. "Good night."

"Good night, dear."

Then, from under the covers, "Good night, Jack."

Once the door is closed, they shriek with laughter.

It doesn't subside and they have to muffle the sounds with pillows.

"Penny, you are crazy!"

"I guess I am."

She lies back down and takes hold of Susan's hand. "The thing I missed the most, that I didn't know I was missing until all this started happening, was the sense of touch. I would watch Aaron and the way he looked at Jimmy and would maybe flick a piece of dirt off his shoulder, or run his hands across his back. Or lean down and kiss him. Sometimes, when I would see them touch, I would feel a stabbing pain in my heart. I haven't been caressed by anybody."

"Oh, Penny."

"Then that dog would wag his tail when he saw me. He smiled, damn it! He loves me, and I would hug him and pet him and he would lick me. When I cried, he was there. He was there, damn it!"

"Animals are really sensitive."

"But I'm a human being. I needed to feel loved. I have so much love in me. I need . . . I need to love."

"You're going to be a great mother."

"I can't believe how lucky I am. I am going to try to be the best mother I can be."

"You will be, Penny. You will."

"And so hopefully there will be another human being who loves me. But I may never have a partner. I've come to accept that. And I don't want to bring a kid into the world to make up for the fact that I didn't pursue a relationship, you know?"

"God, you talk like you're old and withered."

"I am forty-one."

"It's not like you can't ever find someone."

"Forty-one and a single mother? Not an attractive combination."

"Oh, Penny."

She runs her hand down Susan's arm. "Do you want to know how it was?"

"You don't have to."

"Well, I told him to close his eyes and think of England."

"Penny!"

"No, seriously, I went to his house. They made me dinner. Lots of seafood and chocolate. Those are aphrodisiacs. Did you know that?"

Susan is silent now, barely breathing.

"Okay, I'll tell you, but you have to promise to never tell a soul!" Penny brushes the hair from her face.

"Pinkie-swear!" Susan touches her little finger to her friend's. As if they are ten years old again, they pull the blanket over their heads. Penny giggles and laughs and Susan is wide-eyed.

She whispers so quietly that Susan has to hold her breath in order not to miss a single word.

"Penny Stevens!" Susan is again out on the floor and jumping and shrieking.

"Then after he listened to Streisand and Cher and Bette Midler, we got the turkey baster and he went to town."

"No! No! No! Stop it! Stop it!"

"And then I did the Downward Dog and—"

"Oh! Oh! Oh!" Susan has covered her ears and shut her eyes.

They are screaming and all the covers are off the bed and Penny is making snow angels in the sheets while Susan is jumping all over the room.

"Christ . . . All . . . mighty!"

"Jack!" She freezes in spread eagle and Susan stops hopping.

"What in the name of Jesus Christ is going on in here?"

"Nothing." Penny does all the talking while Susan just looks at her feet.

"Have you lost your mind?"

"No."

"Do you want the neighbours to hear you?"

"No."

This time Haggis comes right into the room and lies down. He wants to sleep but isn't one to miss out on the action.

"Well then I suggest that you both calm down and go to sleep."

"Yes, dear." *You really would have made a fine dad.*

After Jack and Haggis leave a second time, they drag the covers off the floor and climb back into bed, then snuggle and hold hands again. They are both very tired now, but before they fall asleep Penny tells Susan what she really wants to know.

"I am very happy for you."

"Me too."

"Good night, Penny."

"Good night, Susan."

About town!
Wednesday, October 21
Mitch Williams

Was that Penny Stevens serving up steaming bowls of delicious pumpkin soup at the annual Harvest Fair? She looked radiant and is telling everyone she's "never felt better!"

At her side, her faithful friend, Mr. Haggis, sat patiently by while she ladled out bowl after bowl to happy customers.

It was a beautiful day at Ambleside Beach, and donations from this year's effort totalled over $2,000. Also on hand were the entire crew of Project Penny as well as Jack Stevens from Homelife Realty.

This is the seventh year that employees at the Sentinel have pitched in to help out Heart House, a non-profit organization providing shelter to and helping transition underprivileged single mothers.

Sylvia Langston-Peters, editor-in-chief, donned an apron for the event as well. "Though we live in a wealthy neighbourhood, we must not assume poverty is not an issue. I myself grew up with a single mother who worked two jobs. If it weren't for the generosity of friends and programs like Heart House, I don't know where I'd be today." Ms. Langston-Peters has headed North Shore's thrice-weekly newspaper for 13 years and has consistently increased readership and has been the driving force behind many charities and successful initiatives.

Speaking of which, Ms. Langston-Peters was happy to announce that Penny Stevens's Money Makes Cents financial column is going to be syndicated across Canada and in the United States. Well done, Penny! All the staff offer their congratulations to their wonderful co-worker and wish her and Jack all the best in this next chapter of life changes.

Twenty

One would think being featured in a community newspaper wouldn't be such a big deal; however, it's amazing
how many people read those kinds of things. In total,
from reporting about the Jenkinses' money to weekly
and monthly follow-ups with the reno, there were
twenty-seven articles about Penny and her home, garden, diet, exercise, and makeovers. Whether you were
an avid reader of the Home and Life section or not,
there were fairly good odds that you caught a glimpse
of Penny at some point or another. Maybe while waiting
in the doctor's office or sorting the recycling or lining
the bird feeder, her face jumped out at you. And now
people seem to recognize her wherever she goes.

It dawns on her that should she ever fall and hit her head and suffer from amnesia, as long as she doesn't stray too far from West Vancouver, she will be in good company. Somebody will always know who she is.

The public's hunger to keep abreast of "that Penny woman" doesn't seem likely to be abating any time soon. Linda will still do the odd piece on Penny when she wants to feature the season's new look, but Penny hasn't appeared in a fitness column since the summer. The life reno, nevertheless, still has legs.

And being pregnant makes any woman feel like a public commodity. Complete strangers offer up baby names. She's heard a couple of Henrys and Ethans, quite a few Emmas. No Penelopes, however.

"Thank you. I'll have to remember to jot that one down." She is always polite.

Yesterday Dr. Wilcox was running late, so she had to endure a lecture on breastfeeding from an intense young mother of three with another on the way. She, too, recognized her from the paper.

"Thank you for the information." She put the La Leche League pamphlet into her purse. She fully intends to breastfeed but finds it odd that there are websites and such passionate advocates for it. Did this most natural activity really need cheerleaders?

Many people ask her whether she intends to work post-baby, and Penny replies that she is more committed than ever to her column. It feels like her career is taking off at the exact same moment that she is finally living her life. So, yes, she will work. She wants to.

"The baby is due on December eighth and Money Makes Cents is going into syndication in January. Crazy, I know . . ."

It wasn't a question that women in Alice's generation had had to grapple with. Nowadays there are options for women, which is good. And men can decide to be stay-at-home dads. At times, however, she feels people either greatly agree with or smugly disapprove of her choice. Rarely is the question answered without judgment afterward.

"Yes, I am going to work. And I want to."

And it has been jarring to find other people, total strangers, knowing intimate details about her life. She hasn't gotten used to it and probably never will.

The other week she was at the dog groomer's picking up Haggis. She wanted him to look especially nice when Jimmy and Aaron got back from Cancun. Being the middle of November, Aaron had hung up his garden tools, and Jimmy had just finished the first draft of his thesis, so they had taken advantage of a last-minute all-inclusive holiday. They needed a break.

"I know you." The owner of a beagle was waiting to drop off her dog.

"Hello." *Here it comes.*

"You're Penny Stevens."

"Guilty as charged."

"So, what's new?"

What's new? Hmm, yes . . . let's see . . .

For a millisecond Penny considered telling all to this fine woman. Telling her that Jack is thinking about buying a few condos and then flipping them. He might keep one and live in it or sell it if he doesn't like it. They won't be ready until next fall, and in the meantime he will stay up at the house on Haywood. As for her pregnancy? No, he isn't the father. She was impregnated by a gay man. That should make for some snappy conversation at the old dog spa.

People seem to think they need to know personal details about celebrities and politicians and the like, and Penny gets that. That's why the tabloids sell. People love the nitty-gritty details of other people's lives. And even if a person is not particularly interested in these matters, it's pretty hard to avoid knowing that certain superstars are marrying or divorcing or having plastic surgery or denying having plastic surgery. Once a person steps into the public glare, their private life is up for grabs. Problem is, Penny never wanted the attention.

Every time she is in the supermarket lineup, she glances at the cover stories of the glossy magazines. If you ask a person to name the prime minister of Israel, they will likely have no idea. You ask another to point to Egypt on a map, and you'll be lucky if they know which continent it's on. But you line up with your apple pie and Cheez Whiz, and you can't help but know who's doing what with whom. Suddenly Penny feels a great affinity with these celebs.

Yes, it's true. I'm Penny Stevens. No, this isn't my natural colour. Yes, I gained weight. No, I'll be a single mother. Yes, I want this child. No, I don't do drugs. Yes, I've taken Paxil. No, I haven't done Botox. Yes, my husband had affairs. No, he's not the father. Yes, the father's involved. No, I am not a lesbian.

On the upside of all the developments in Penny's life, Jack and Alice have turned out to be the most unflappable and nonjudgmental people. As though what she is doing is the most natural thing in the world.

Alice, in particular, has really surprised her daughter. She always loved coming up to the house. Even before Project Penny got underway, Jack or Penny would pick Alice up at least once a month for an afternoon visit and early dinner. Then, with the excitement of the reno, Alice was even more keen to swing round for an update. Penny would wheel her around the garden and guide her carefully through the kitchen and tell her about every minute detail of Johnson's work. Describe the new fabrics that Linda had chosen. Penny would paint for Alice in words what she could not see with her own eyes.

One autumn evening Aaron and Jimmy joined them for dinner, and Alice was immediately besotted with them both. They cooked duck and served braised apples with red cabbage. Jimmy made his own bread and Aaron made tiramisu. Like her daughter, Alice was won over in a single night.

The next morning Penny went to the Manor, wanting to let Alice know the exact nature of Jimmy and Aaron's relationship.

"The World Trade Center shocked me. A couple of guys in love, well, I don't think that's news, dear." Alice was very matter-of-fact.

"But I assumed you'd . . ." Penny couldn't finish her thoughts. Somehow she had never imagined Alice would figure it out for herself, and Penny couldn't decide if she was impressed or put out by her mother's awareness. The fact that Penny had been initially clueless only magnified her naïveté.

"Just because I'm blind doesn't mean I don't see."

"Mom, you are so . . . cool." Penny simply marvelled at her mother.

"I know, dear. I'm old and I'm wise and I'm cool. Do you want to lick the stamps?" It was late September, and Alice was already deeply involved in the process of preparing her holiday cards. Growing up, Penny remembers, the Christmas cupboard had started filling up in mid-February. Alice always prided herself on being organized, and this year in particular she was looking forward to sending out her greeting cards accompanied by the one-page letter detailing the events of the last twelve months.

She had an arrangement with the head nurse, who would provide for someone to take dictation should Penny not be handy. The last correspondence Alice had had her daughter write was for Margaret, a cousin down in Texas, whose husband had been killed in action in Iraq back in May. In June she had delivered their son. It had been an awful letter to compose. Life and death all wrapped up together.

Just behind Alice's supply of sympathy cards was a stack of birth announcements ready to send out. Only the details were missing. As soon as the blessed event took place, Alice's system was primed to send the happy news as far away as England, New Zealand, Toronto, New Mexico, and Goose Bay. Meanwhile, at every opportunity, Alice would let the other residents at the Manor know that her daughter was expecting. That she was going to be a grandmother.

"Yes, that's lovely. You told us so yesterday, I believe . . ."

Penny would smile at these people, many of whom were reminded almost daily. The only person Alice would have nothing to do with was Mr. Miller, ever since he started flirting with somebody called Virginia. Alice assured Penny she was relieved to have him off her hands.

"How many cards this year, Mom?" Penny rarely sent out more than a handful.

"There's fifty-two ready, but I'm only sending out fifty-one. Lois Watson died last week. There goes another one off my list."

"Mom!"

"That's what happens when you live to a ripe old age." More and more often, Alice would lament that there weren't many of her contemporaries left to attend her funeral. Penny disliked these morbid conversations, but Alice was unwavering in her wish for a joyful and well-attended celebration. There was standing room only at Wilfred's service.

"And remember, I want alcohol at my party. And good stuff, too. When you get to be my age and make it to a funeral, you don't want the cheap stuff. And you definitely don't want tea."

"Yes, mother." Penny had her instructions.

"And no offence, dear, but have Aaron and Jimmy do the food. Absolutely fabulous cooks, they are. Let them cater it." Sometimes it felt like Alice really was the hippest mother ever.

Penny affixed the last stamp and then took her mother's hands in hers. For a while they were silent. Penny did not like imagining life without Alice. She loved her mother and was loved in return. And even more than that, Penny liked Alice. She often entertained the crazy idea that if she and her mother could have been children at the same time, Penny would have wanted to be best friends with Alice. Hopefully, Alice would have liked her too, though at times Penny feared she wouldn't have been cool enough.

Caressing her mother's hands, Penny looked deeply into Alice's bright but unseeing eyes. She still hadn't told her mother everything.

"I'm divorcing Jack." Penny could have sworn that Alice was looking right at her that day.

"I see."

"Our marriage wasn't really . . . real."

"I understand."

"I wanted you to know. We both wanted to tell you. We were going to tell you but it just . . ."

"I know, dear."

"I should have started a family earlier."

"It wasn't the right time, Penelope."

So life is good and continually teaching her new things. She's learning not to label people in any set, definitive way.

Jack, whom she thought she knew, certainly has had her seeing him with new eyes. Back in October, Jimmy was laid up with the flu, and Jack took Penny to the last prenatal meeting.

"What is it with you, Jack? Why have you become nicer and nicer? Why aren't you the asshole you used to be?"

"Ah, Pen. I don't know."

"Thanks for being here, Jack."

"Thanks for letting me."

Penny was grateful he was there that night, as Donelda instructed the couples to network and exchange telephone numbers. It would be a good idea to bond with another new mother, have somebody to talk to, go on walks with. The men could shoot the breeze and complain about the upheaval in their lives as well. Bemoan the sorry state of the Canucks. But at age forty-one, Penny was too shy and timid to go over and mingle with Anna and Steven. They seemed like the most suitable match—both accountants.

So while Penny sat there fidgeting with her folder, jotting nonsensical scribbles in the margins, Jack chatted up Steven and learned that they lived not two blocks away.

"What do you know! Penny, come over here."

When Anna explained which house, Penny knew exactly. The blue one with the white shutters at Gordon and 13th.

"Here, let me give you our number." Jack pulled out two of his business cards, scratched out his name, wrote out Penny's, and handed them over. The other couple did likewise, and it was all settled very simply.

Turns out Penny was wrong. She did need Jack after all.

Penny is sleeping deeply, and it takes her a long time to rise up from her heavy slumber. When she finally wills her eyes open, she can't decide if it is the dog's hot breath, the incessant rain beating at the windows, or her own cold saliva on her cheek that wakes her from her comforting reverie.

She was dreaming about Jack and Alice. They were walking somewhere. All three of them. She thinks they might have been in a hurry, but she can't recall any more of the plot. She is curled up on the sofa in the living room, and Obama is being interviewed on TV. The economy might be bad, but the future looks bright, and the President of the United States of America has a Portuguese water dog. Things are definitely looking up.

Haggis needs to pee, and he is giving Penny his doggedly patient stare.

"Oh, poor you! What time is it?" Penny wipes away her spit and checks the clock on the mantle. It's just after eight. She must have slept close to two hours. She recalls turning to the local news station after dinner.

She pushes herself to a sitting position and waits for a moment. Everything she does these days seems to be in slow motion. One of her socks has come off, and she has to root around a bit until she finds it wedged between some cushions. With Haggis in tow, she carefully waddles down the hallway, taking extra care not to slip. From the front hall closet she takes her long coat and a flashlight and sticks her feet into a pair of black rubber boots. Finally, she grabs a Baltimore Orioles baseball hat. *Bloody gorgeous, I am.*

Outside it is pitch dark and cold and wet. "Okay, puppy, do your stuff."

Haggis complies and immediately piddles and has turned to say he's ready to go back in where it's warm when the rays from a pair of headlights streak across the front lawn.

"Oh, look, it's Jack." He had said he was going to swing by the office. They remain standing in their place until the engine cuts off and he emerges from his SUV.

"Good evening, husband." She clicks the flashlight on and off.

"Good evening, wife, dog."

"So, did you sell any houses? Make any more money?" She points the light directly into his face now.

"I suppose." He smiles, and Penny wonders what he must see when he takes in this huge woman in the large coat and hat and rubber boots. The immense dog. Normally a husband would kiss his wife, embrace her, but that time has long ago passed and he has told her he doubts he will ever again be "husband" material to anyone else. In the meantime, before the whole façade comes away, he seems to be enjoying his role as Mr. Stevens, "father to be," coming home to his beautifully kept house and very pregnant wife. And ever since his sleepover with the Haggis, he really has a soft spot for the animal.

"Get inside, Penny. It's freezing."

"Yes, it is."

He holds her arm as they climb the porch steps, and inside he helps her out of her coat and pulls each boot off her feet. Haggis immediately goes upstairs.

"How are you feeling?"

"Good. Just tired. Had a long nap. Drooled all over the upholstery. Linda called earlier. She wants to get a family portrait in the paper."

"Oh. That'll be something."

"Won't it?"

For a moment they are both silent.

"Boy, she sure is one crazy dame." Ever since Linda divested Jack of his spare keys, he has been utterly perplexed by the woman.

"Oh, she's not crazy, she's just . . ."

"Nuts?"

"Jack! She's not nutty, she's very well meaning."

"Well, I don't know how people stand her. I spent five minutes talking to her, and I couldn't figure out half of what she said."

"You know what? I like her." Penny thinks Jack has met his match in Linda.

"I thought she was the one that was driving you nuts. Phoning you every day and telling you to 'get centred' and then having that nervous breakdown and screaming at you about the project. You like her now?"

"Yeah, I warmed up to her, I guess."

"Really?"

"Yeah, she's all right."

"Well, there you go. Maybe there's hope for me."

Penny takes a good look at her husband. He's tired too. There are big shadows under his eyes, and he appears somewhat smaller than before. And it isn't just because Penny has grown bigger. He's aged a lot and doesn't have the same vitality and piss and vinegar in him as before. Penny hopes he'll find someone.

"You're all right, Jack. There's hope for you yet."

Investing in long-term beauty
Wednesday, November 18
Linda Campbell and Penny Stevens

It's been months since Penny and I have spent a day at the mall. Back in June, I enjoyed helping my colleague find her way through the maze of maternity clothes. She is an expert now in picking out colours, and her hair and nails are to die for! She even taught me something! Ever frugal, Penny didn't want to invest in a large number of clothes that she would wear for just a month or two. She took me to a consignment store that had great deals and told me that swapping with friends who had already gone through maternity was a good way to save money. I agreed, and the items she took home that day looked outstanding.

So, this month, Penny and I thought we'd collaborate and discuss fashion from an investment perspective.

I have always said it is wise that an individual purchase a few wardrobe pieces that they intend to keep for a long time. Regardless of the changing fashions of the day, high-quality shoes in genuine leather will always be a good buy. The calibre of materials should not be overlooked, and you will have to pay more for expensive knits and cottons, but they will last longer and retain their shape as well. I still have a classic trench raincoat that I bought in Paris years ago. The price tag, at the time—I won't say when that was!—was astronomical, and I almost didn't buy it. I am glad I did, though, as I wear it to this day.

Which is today's topic.

"I have come to realize that buying quality clothing can be a good investment in the long run," says Penny Stevens, who would normally only scour the bargain aisles and discount bins.

"I ended up having twice the amount of T-shirts and pants, but none fit particularly well, and they ended up at the back of my closet."

Clutter buster Charlotte "Charlie" Ames gave away those items, and now Penny Stevens prides herself on being better dressed, with less junk and a closet that is easier to keep tidy.

Investments, like clothing, are something that a person wants to commit to over a long time period.

And accessories are a great way to stay in step with the fashions, without having to revamp one's entire wardrobe. When everyone was buying up paisley, all I did was find a great scarf to dress up my trusty coat.

A fuchsia belt or a pair of shoes can complement and update a basic outfit easily.

And Ms. Stevens wholeheartedly agrees. "In financial terms, I try to diversify my portfolio and research quality funds. I invest in these for an extended period, knowing that the longer one keeps one's money, the higher the interest. I tend not to invest in penny stocks as it is stressful and short-term."

So, like the basic little black dress, there tend to be solid, trustworthy articles that are worth paying a few more dollars for. And buying cheap clothing can be a gamble. How many wears will an individual get out of an item? How long before the colour fades? Before the seams rip and tear? How many painting shirts does a person need, honestly?

Look for Penny Stevens's Money Makes Cents in Friday's financial column and, starting in January, in the Vancouver Sun.

Twenty-One

When a person has a date on the calendar for nine months and it passes by without so much as a burp or a hiccup, it is anticlimactic, to say the least. December eighth arrived without any fanfare or excitement. Penny made a point of going for a few short, brisk walks, ate spicy foods, and continually checked her body for any signs of discomfort or movement.

At noon that day, Jimmy called.

"It's me. So? How are you?"

"Fine."

"Feel anything?"

"No."

Around one o'clock, Aaron called on a bad connection from Bowen Island.

"Hi, enny . . . i, it's . . . ron calliiiing. Has anything . . . arted?"

"Sorry, Aaron, I can't make out what you are saying. I'm fine, though."

"Baaad connect . . . Sorry, I'll call you late . . ." Click.

Shortly thereafter Susan called.

"Hi, sweetie! How are things?"

"Things are not happening."

"How are you feeling?"

"Oh, fine. Nothing much to report, I'm afraid."

"Well, get lots of rest, you'll need it."

So she tried to nap, but her mind raced. *I should eat something. I should go somewhere. I shouldn't go anywhere. I should call someone.*

Later that afternoon, Alice called.

"Hi, dear. It's me, your mother."

"Hi, Mom." She loves that Alice always introduces herself in this manner.

"So? Are you feeling anything down there?"

"No, not yet."

"Nothing?"

"I'm sorry to report that I am fine."

"I'll call you later, dear."

Jack has his pager on and his cellphone charged. He is making a point of staying within a fifteen-minute radius of the house at all times. He is in charge of driving Penny to Lions Gate Hospital.

So two uneventful days have passed, and a part of Penny finds it interesting that all this waiting and lack of action can be so stressful.

I should pay the cable. It's due next week. I should pay it now.

Penny gets up from her spot on the loveseat, where she has been vacantly staring into the fire. She takes three steps and thinks she feels a twitch in her stomach. It's nothing. She goes to a drawer in the kitchen to get a cheque out and finds only the empty stub.

Am I out of cheques? Then she remembers she ordered a new batch, and they must be upstairs in the den. Jack is always moving things around to places that don't make any sense. She pays the bills, so the cheques should be downstairs in her drawer, not in his den, as she has pointed out countless times to him. Alas, to no avail. *Perhaps Charlie can sort him out?*

She is about to climb the stairs when she sees the dirty-clothes hamper sitting in the hallway. She decides to take it down to the laundry and get that underway before she pays the bill. In the laundry room, while she is waiting for the machine to fill, she notices a few items that need to be ironed, so she plugs in the iron.

While she is waiting for the iron to heat up, she sees a box of Christmas ornaments hidden behind some golf equipment. These are the "good" ornaments, not to be confused with the tacky ones Jack inherited from his parents and the plastic and gaudy ones she's had for as long as she can recall. She replaced them all last year and wants to make sure they find their way onto the tree this year. That is, if he finds the time to decorate a tree at all—it's already the tenth. She hopes that Jack doesn't drag the old ones out again with that recycled tinsel and the blinking lights. She spent good money on this new look and doesn't want her child caught posing for his or her first Christmas in front of some ugly baubles and cracked Santas. No, she had better get that box out and label it for Jack. Maybe Charlie could come and help her sort through this stuff and organize it better for next year.

She is halfway through separating the contents of the old box and the new box out over the floor when she remembers the iron.

"Oh yes!" She sets to work immediately on a table-cloth and four shirts and two pairs of pants. She irons two shirts and then realizes that she needs a few more hangers, so she decides to take the ironed shirts with her all the way upstairs.

Just as she reaches the landing on the main level, the phone rings.

"Hello?"

"Hello, it's Annette from Dr. Wilcox's office calling. How are you today, Penny?"

"Fine. Nothing's happening."

"Not to worry. Often first babies are overdue. In any case, Dr. Wilcox would like you to come in at the tail end of today. Just wants to have a peek."

"Yes. When shall I come?" He explained this to her on the last visit, telling her that should the baby get to be a week overdue, he might have to induce. Somehow this didn't sound enticing, but Penny doesn't want to risk anything.

"How does five thirty sound?"

"Fine."

They hang up and Penny's stomach growls. It's twelve thirty, so she hangs the shirts on the banister and grabs a banana and a jar of peanut butter. She doesn't want any bread, so she takes out a spoon and spreads peanut butter on the banana.

She has eaten half of it when she decides she doesn't want any more. She'd like some cheese and sourdough and perhaps a pickle. The dishwasher hasn't been turned on, so she hand-washes a knife and rinses a plate. After taking two bites of this sandwich, she wants mustard on it. There isn't any in the fridge so she goes to the pantry. By the time she unwraps the plastic safety seal, she is no longer hungry, nor does she want the mustard. She's thirsty, though, and doesn't bother to rinse a glass but drinks the orange juice directly from the carton.

There.

A bit of juice has unfortunately dribbled down her front.

Darn it!

She passes by the two hanging shirts and goes directly to the bathroom to rinse off the orange juice. It looks like it's going to stain, so she heads back downstairs for the spot remover. Once again in the laundry, she sees the hot iron.

Penny Stevens!

She takes off her shirt and sprays it with the cleaner and leaves it to soak. Since she is already downstairs, she decides to iron two more shirts that she will take up in her free hands. Then she has the brainstorm to wear one shirt and iron a pair of pants as well.

Things are going smoothly, and she is whistling as she works when the phone rings again. She almost trips over a Christmas moose lying face down in the door-way.

"Hello?"

"It's me." Jack sounds like he is driving.

"Ouch!" An ornament hook has attached itself to Penny's sock.

"Are you okay? Are you contracting?" Jack knows the lingo.

"My foot. I think it's bleeding."

"What are you doing?"

"Oh . . ." She looks down at her belly protruding out of an unbuttoned blue dress shirt. "You'd be surprised."

"Well, I was just calling to see if you needed any-thing."

"No. I'm fine . . . ouch!"

"You all right, Pen?"

"I think I had a cramp."

"In your foot?"

"No."

At the front of the hospital is an inviting and attractive information desk. There are flowers and incandescent lighting, and pleasant music is playing in the background. This is where Aaron enters.

"Hi. Aaron Taylor. I'm here for Penelope Stevens. Maternity." Within seconds he is off toward the elevator . . .

At the back of the hospital is the Emergency entrance. It is still under renovation. In fact, it is always under construction. Jimmy came in this way with Penny when they did the maternity tour. There is duct tape everywhere.

"Hi. I'm Jimmy, Jim Prentiss. I'm with Penny Stevens. I'm a friend of Penny Stevens. I understand she is here. In labour. I am her friend. Oh, I already told you that. She's pregnant. Obviously. She's having the baby. Today. Or at least I hope it is today . . . that it doesn't drag on." Jimmy can't stop rattling.

The receptionist lifts her face away from the glowing computer screen to assess the rambling individual in front of her.

"Would you like the room number, then?"

"Please."

"She's up in Delivery on the third floor. Check in with the head nurse and then you'll find her in room six."

Jimmy is too impatient to take the elevator and bounds up the stairs, two at a time . . .

• • •

Susan is out in the parking lot, doing circles in search of a parking spot. She has to fight for the last stall, and in the end birth wins over death. She and a woman of a similar age in a nondescript sedan are both eyeing the same Toyota minivan that is backing slowly out.

"My friend is in there having a baby. I have to be there. She's counting on me. I can't miss it!" All this yelled out through the open windows, large breath clouds floating upwards.

"My mother, she's sick." Perhaps the woman wants to say more but doesn't.

Susan thanks her profusely and runs into the building. She has birthed four children but wasn't really present. She isn't going to miss this for the world . . .

Jack is out in the hallway, sitting on a small metal chair. Like a child who has misbehaved and is awaiting punishment, his hands are clasped and his head is lowered. He drove Penny in and called all the others.

"Are you all right?" a nurse stops to ask before going into the room.

"Fine. I'm fine." His breathing is a bit ragged . . .

• • •

In the elevator, Aaron is crammed in with a stretcher and a doctor and a nurse and people of varying ages and degrees of health. When he presses the third floor, the doctor knowingly looks at him and smiles.

"Your first?"

"Uh, yeah."

It's a bit unnerving being singled out, but if you have to go to a hospital, this is the floor you want . . .

Jimmy bursts through the heavy stairwell doors into the third-floor hallway.

"I need room number six!"

A young man in khakis is holding a small infant. "Sorry." The man doesn't know where that is . . .

Susan is billowing down the east corridor, her long cape flapping behind her as she strides to the elevator.

"Room six. Room six. I'm coming. Wait for me, Penny."

Once inside the elevator, she presses the third floor . . .

. . .

"Ah, Penny. God bless you, woman." Jack has never been one to pray, but sitting there with his hands clasped, he has closed his eyes . . .

The young nurse at the head station takes down a file from a wall-mounted divider and checks that Aaron Taylor's name is on the list.

"Ah. There you are." She writes something down and directs him to a locker where he can remove his coat and lock any valuables. There is also a smock he can put on over his clothes.

"Okay, come this way."

Like a lot of men, he looks scared and excited and totally unprepared . . .

Susan arrives just as Jimmy disappears into the change room.

"Hello, I'm Susan Fieldstone. I am Penny Stevens's friend. Here for the birth."

She is directed into a separate change room but is out well before Jimmy, who in his excitement has taken off all his clothes, right down to his shoes, and reappears in the hallway in his stocking feet.

"You'll need to put some shoes on, Mr. Prentiss."

"Right!"

Jimmy disappears into the change room . . .

"Is her doctor here yet?" Aaron asks the nurse before he enters.

"No. He called to say he's on his way." There is some perusal of charts, and then a nurse with coke-bottle glasses introduces Aaron to the other nurse.

"This is Aaron Taylor. He is one of the four people authorized to attend the event." She smiles and the other nurse smiles and Aaron smiles too.

"Oh, uh, Jim Prentiss will be here in a moment. He's on his way."

"Her husband?"

"No." Aaron notices Jack sitting hunched over, somewhat hidden by a trolley.

"That would be her husband, Jack Stevens."

At the sound of his name, Jack opens his eyes and gives Aaron a half-hearted wave. Aaron nods back at him.

"You ready, Jack?"

"Nah, I'll just stay put. I need to catch my breath." He pats his chest.

"Right then, let's go in, shall we?" The nurse gently guides Aaron by the elbow through the heavy, wide wooden door into the delivery room.

"Hi." His voice comes out constricted.

"Aaron." Penny's voice comes out small but she appears fine. She is lying under a light blue sheet and has a green hospital smock on that matches the one he is wearing. He notices her freshly pedicured toes peeking out at the bottom of the bed.

"So?" He looks about the room.

"So yourself."

"Where's the doctor?"

"He left."

"Oh."

"Dr. Wilcox is coming."

"Good."

"Otherwise I'm counting on you to deliver the baby."

"Excellent. I'll start boiling the water right away."

She closes her eyes and breathes heavily. It takes three minutes for the contraction to pass, but she is handling it well. She's been examined and was thrilled to learn she is almost fully dilated. Dr. Young told her to keep calm and continue in this manner. Every ten minutes or so he appears and congratulates her on her achievement to date. He told her she can wander the halls if she wishes, but she prefers lying down for the moment.

A team of nurses has taken her blood pressure and poked and prodded her as well. One nurse, Nurse O'Donnell, has long red hair and an Irish accent, and Penny just adores her. She is like an angel, and every time she appears, Penny feels safe.

Time is moving at an odd pace, sometimes fast and sometimes slowly, and Penny has no idea what hour it is. There is no clock on the wall, and she isn't wearing her watch.

When the most recent spasm releases her, she opens her eyes and sees Aaron's face looking directly into hers.

"Give me your hand, gorgeous. I love you. God, this hurts!"

"I thought you might be screaming like all the actresses on TV. I was worried."

"Don't write my performance off yet. I may very well do that. Where did Jack go?"

"Hallway."

"Hmm." Another contraction comes to take her mind off any further questions. Aaron's and Penny's heads are pressed together, and they are clasping hands. This is what Dr. Wilcox sees as he quietly enters the room.

"Greetings." The doctor looks taller than when she last saw him in his office. "I understand the patient is doing beautifully."

The men shake hands.

"John Wilcox."

"Aaron Taylor."

Soon another nurse enters, and Penny's temperature is checked, her abdomen is lathered with a gel, and a device is placed on her protruding tummy.

"Everything is looking great, Penny. Soon we'll have you start pushing. How do you feel about that?" Dr. Wilcox is now holding her other free hand.

Penny considers saying she'd rather not. She suddenly feels very tired and wishes it was 1950 and they would just knock her out and wake her up when the whole thing is finished.

"Okay."

"That-a-girl!" The doctor is a little too jovial at this juncture for her liking, but she supposes it's his way of lightening the mood.

She is lying with her feet in stirrups and panting heavily when Susan and Jimmy miraculously appear.

"Where have you guys been?" She feels like a bad friend, snapping at them like that. She takes a deep breath and concentrates on breathing.

"I had to help a certain person untangle his shoe-laces."

"Don't ask." In all the excitement, Jimmy couldn't work his fingers properly. If Susan hadn't come to his rescue, he would still be in that change room.

"Oh, Jimmy." Penny keeps breathing and sucking oxygen. Hopefully, she hasn't hoovered up all the air in the room, because somebody needs to think straight.

"I'm going to examine you, Penny. Just relax." Dr. Wilcox is putting on rubber gloves. She hears him but doesn't bother responding. A number of hands have already reached inside of her. *What's one more? Maybe this guy will actually find something? Like a baby, perhaps?*

Penny counts seven people in the room. Including herself, there is one doctor and one nurse and Aaron and Jimmy and Susan and another male nurse that she thinks might actually be an anesthetist, should the need arise. Seven people.

"Where's Jack? Did he call my mother?"

There is a bit of jostling since things are getting tight, but the nurse makes room and adjusts the instruments while everybody in matching green combat fatigues huddles around Penny, wide-eyed and hopeful.

"He was making a phone call about twenty minutes ago." Penny loves the lilt of Nurse O'Donnell's accent.

And Penny lies there, eyes closed, sometimes open. She feels another contraction coming on, but it doesn't seem as painful this time. Maybe it's because she's surrounded by all these people who love her, strange and beautiful and flawed people. She loves them all back.

She has been quiet this last little bit. She likes listening to the banter and conversation of the room. She drifts in and out and hears Dr. Wilcox talk about breaking the water. She hears Aaron say he'll move the car but doesn't want to do so until after, doesn't want to risk missing the moment. Jimmy is talking to Susan about having four kids. She overhears Nurse O'Donnell saying she bets the baby will be born before nine. The anesthetist seems to think the odds are after ten. She's glad Jack chose Pachelbel's Canon.

"What time is it?" Penny's question jars everybody, as though they were so engrossed in their private conversations they forgot she was even there.

"It's eight fifteen."

As far as Penny is concerned, it could be six in the evening or midnight or four in the morning. There is a shade pulled down over the window, but Penny can see that it is pitch black outside. At least she knows it's not daytime.

Just then she feels a liquid rushing out from her, and for an instant she thinks she has wet herself.

"Ah, there it is." Dr. Wilcox seems pleased. "Now I don't need to go get my knitting needle."

All the chitchat stops as the lower end sheets are removed. Then Dr. Wilcox does something to the bed, and she is lifted into a reclined, seated position.

"Your body has spoken, Penny." Dr. Wilcox puts on a fresh pair of gloves.

Suddenly Penny feels very awake and very strong. She feels the need to push. All pain has disappeared. "Yes."

Instinctively, Aaron and Jimmy and Susan make themselves very small and quiet. The doctor and the nurse move into position.

"Yes," Penny says again.

"Okay, now. When you feel you want to push, go ahead."

"Yes." She doesn't. She waits. She doesn't know what exactly she is waiting for. She is almost holding her breath. Then, something stretches inside of her and she bears down.

"Good. Good. Get your breath, Penny. Good." The doctor and the nurses are busy feeling and swabbing and waiting.

Penny, of course, doesn't notice any of this. Later when they tell her all these things, she won't remember. She was there, but she was in another world where only her body existed. The pumping of her blood, the thumping of her heart.

She hears Dr. Wilcox ask if she wants to get up more, but she feels comfortable where she is. Somebody has stuck pillows behind her, and she is in a squat position but still on the bed.

Four more times she grunts and groans and feels the need to push. Just before she pushes, she speaks.

"God!"

Dr. Wilcox answers. "Very good. We have the head. Hold on, Penny! Don't push! Hold it, please." Penny is suspended as she holds her breath, and the doctor fiddles with some tubes and suctions mucus out of the baby's nose.

"Look," Aaron says.

Outside in the hallway, Jack stands up and comes into the room.

"All right, Mother. You can push again, but not too hard this time, okay?"

Jimmy and Jack and Aaron and Susan hold their collective breath while Penny exhales and presses with all her might.

And with that, at precisely 8:24 in the evening, Penny pushes one last time, and her beautiful, healthy, and priceless child is born.

"Welcome to the world, little miss."

Love makes sense
Wednesday, December 9
Penny Stevens

Well, today is Tuesday, December 8, and my columns don't normally appear on Wednesdays, but I seem to have found a moment of time before I disappear for a few months.

As many of you can't help but have noticed, I made an emotional investment nine months ago, and I understood that the fruition date of that "term" was to have been today. I calculated, with the help of qualified experts, that on this day I could expect to cash in on my efforts. Alas, I am sad—well, perhaps not sad, but somewhat disappointed—to report that it looks like our projections and forecasts are a bit off. This often happens, so I am told.

Now, being a "numbers" person, I often rely on figures and enjoy tallying up predictions and anticipating returns on investments.

This venture, however, is going to change my life, say well-meaning friends and family and others who have gone down this very same path before me. No one knows for sure what they will end up with, how competently they will fare, how they will be able to handle the entire experience. They tell me there is peril, uncertainty, and, above all, absolute preciousness.

To somebody like me, this sounds like a risky speculation. Will the investment pay off? When will it come to term? What are the prospects?

Despite all the warnings and against all the odds, I, Penelope Stevens, who loves to save her pennies and play it safe, have decided to throw caution to the wind! And late in life too. Yes, I could have begun this project earlier, but I wasn't ready then. So here I am, 41 years old and just starting out.

I have no idea how much this decision is going to cost me—literally and figuratively. And I don't care. For once in my life, I am going full steam ahead without any reassurances or backup plans or safety nets.

I am told there are none.

I do, however, want to thank so many of you in the community who have encouraged me and supported me along this journey.

I owe so much to all of my colleagues who spurred me on and often had to prod me along in my life renovation. I truly didn't want to do it. And Linda and Heather had their work cut out for them, I can assure you all. And Charlie and Johnson and Mitch—what must you all have thought!

And Aaron and Jimmy. And Jack. What are you all thinking?

Nonetheless, here I am, a different person. Grateful. Scared. Hopeful.

I look forward to the future. I can't wait. I'm pumped!

Twenty-Two

Bringing a person into this world is quite a responsibility.

"It's okay. Sssh. Okay, okay."

Naming a child is also very important.

"Sssh, Maya. It's okay. Sssh. Okay, Maya."

Deciding what and how to feed this little being is a big and personal decision.

"Are you hungry?"

Making the choice to be a single parent has its challenges.

"Look at all these pretty outfits. Which one will we wear today?" Jimmy bought a yellow one. Aaron bought a green one, and Jack bought a two-piece pink one.

It is Boxing Day, and Maya is exactly two weeks and two days old. Thankfully, Christmas passed without incident. The highlight of the day was a three-hour uninterrupted nap for Penny followed by a four-course dinner made by Aaron and Jimmy. Jack was to have joined them but arrived late and drunk, though not unruly.

This afternoon she looks about the living room at the few boxes of gifts and is relieved nobody went overboard. Something tells her that this baby is going to be spoiled by all the men in her life and that her mother is going to have to watch that one man doesn't try to outdo the others for the wrong reasons. And there is an abundance of factors at play here that Penny and the guys never fully imagined—first and foremost being the matters of the heart.

No matter how many times she reminds herself that this was all planned and organized and decided upon, she is unprepared for how she feels. Like she said in the column she wrote just before her daughter was born, Penny is learning to stop anticipating outcomes.

She knows how Jimmy is feeling. That no matter how many times he reminds his partner that he continues to be committed to their relationship, Jimmy feels unprepared for the power and strength of this new love in his life.

She watches Aaron too. No matter how many times she and Jimmy tell Aaron they are still the same people they were two weeks ago, something intrinsic has changed. Aaron seems needy and unsure of himself.

And no matter how many times Jack tells Penny he is fine, she isn't buying it. He ended up having to wear a Holter monitor for two days, then went to his doctor to learn that his heart was functioning perfectly normally for a man of his age. He had simply been stressed. The events of that day and the previous nine months and the lead-up to that period had caught up with him. His doctor assured him that he was fine. Yet Penny knew he wasn't fine at all. Up at the club the other night, Penny learned, he even told a retired family-law lawyer, after a few too many Scotches, that he had been "jilted" by his wife of nineteen years. Jilted! Despite being the Wilt Chamberlain of West Vancouver real estate. He has screwed so many women that he has lost count, and now he says he's been "jilted."

And so the wonderful arrival of little Maya Lara has brought a lot of joy and love and happiness as well as sadness and uncertainty and confusion.

Within seconds after the birth, Jack came forward, gripped her hand, and squeezed it firmly. "Ah, Pen," was all he could say, and that summed it up pretty much.

He turned quickly away from the bedside, Pachelbel still playing softly in the background. She didn't see him again until four days later, when he arrived on his own doorstep with a bouquet of flowers and a small stuffed dog.

Within the same time frame in the delivery room, Dr. Wilcox turned to Jimmy and squeezed his hand warmly. "Ah, Mr. Prentiss. Congratulations," was all he said, and that pretty much summed it up too. Aaron, meanwhile, watched Jimmy and Penny gaze intently at the new life fussing in her arms.

Yes, everything is amazing and fabulous and out of balance. Penny is sleep-deprived but thrilled. Jimmy is ecstatic and also sleep-deprived. Aaron stays out of the way and cooks, and Jack, who is drinking a lot, is living, without the owners' knowledge or consent, in a waterfront mansion out in Eagle Harbour that he is trying to sell.

Only Maya, who is perfect in every way, seems at peace with the world into which she was born. From the day Penny's milk came in, Maya learned how to latch on with ease and has been eating and pooping and burping like a princess. Jimmy jokes that she is gifted, but secretly Penny knows this to be true.

Even her cries are the most delicate and heartbreaking sounds that Penny has ever heard. She loves to stroke her child's head and prides herself on being the one able to soothe these cries.

Most of the flowers have now wilted, and each day Penny rearranges and saves the odd carnation and baby's breath. Every day she waters the potted mums, and she plans to replant them in the spring. She wants to hold on to this time and doesn't want to lose any keepsake or memory. Her days are filled writing thank-you notes or staring at her child or looking off into space, thinking about gratitude.

"Do you want yellow or green or pink? What is your mood?" The afternoon light is waning, and soon Penny will have to put on some lamps, maybe light the fire. That always makes the room so cozy and, after all, it's Christmas. Jack never did get the tree up, and it's just as well. There are a few decorations out, but Penny is too busy with Maya and visitors to really miss the tree and the lights. She would have appreciated it, but Jack's heart, understandably, wasn't into it. There's always next year.

Looking down at her daughter, who is lying on the sofa surrounded by cushions, she still hasn't decided which outfit Maya will wear to dinner tonight. And it's an important night. Alice has reserved a private table for five, plus infant and special guest, to dine in the atrium at the Manor. Dinner will be served at precisely five thirty, and they simply can't be late.

Alice is probably dressed right now, down to her lipstick and jewellery and perfume. She hates last-minute fussing and would rather nap upright and forgo her afternoon sleep if it means being organized early and not messing up her morning hairdo.

Penny, on the other hand, still hasn't had a shower. It's almost three thirty, and Aaron has yet to call, and Jimmy is across town, standing in line to buy a flat-screen TV for a one-time "low, low, price." Penny has never understood Boxing Day sales and would rather pay double than line up out in the cold for any audio-visual equipment. But then again, she's not a guy.

It's Jack she's really worried about. Alice is expecting him, and Penny is hoping that he'll come despite his shaking of his head and saying, "Ah, Pen. Hmmm, I don't think so . . ."

"But, Jack, she'd be so disappointed."

"Ah, she won't even notice."

"But she's so . . . excited. You should have been there the other day when she first held Maya." For a solid hour she cooed and held the little bundle close to her heart.

"Ah, Pen, I don't know. I don't know."

"Really, Jack. Come." It would make Alice so happy

to have him there. She's been asking after him, and Penny keeps making excuses for him. Work and commitments and even non-existent dental appointments. Sooner or later he's got to show up.

"And the guys are coming?" he had asked unnecessarily.

"Yes, of course. Please come. It's a big deal. It'll be an early night."

But he hadn't really committed, and she's been calling him all day, leaving messages and reminding him.

"Well, sweetie. Your mom stinks. It's true. She needs a shower. Come on." Penny picks up her daughter and takes her upstairs. In the bathroom, she places Maya in a bassinet while she showers. By the time she emerges freshly shampooed, the sound of the water has lulled her daughter into a deep sleep.

She feels surprisingly fit despite the rigours her body has recently gone through. Of course she has gained weight, but she credits Lamaraya for keeping her supple and toned these last months. And even Heather's words echo occasionally in Penny's mind. When she's out she takes the stairs, and in restaurants she is very conscious of her dietary choices.

So, this afternoon, as she is getting dressed, she feels quite good about herself. She has chosen a red and black ankle-length dress that has a bit of a plunging neckline.

Her breasts are larger and firmer than ever, and she simply feels beautiful. She can't help it.

The phone rings and Penny manages to get it before it sounds a second time.

"Hello?"

"Hi. How's our princess?" Jimmy asks.

"Sleeping like a baby. How big is your TV?"

"That's a rather personal question. Bigger than most guys', if you must know."

He and Aaron had been arguing the better part of the week over the issue of size. Jimmy wanted to go for a minimum of fifty inches, whereas Aaron was aghast and appalled. He cited those monstrosities as trashy and made Jimmy promise to adhere to a limit.

"So, we'll pick you and the kid up at quarter after? Or is Jack bringing you?"

"I haven't heard from him. I called him six times, but he's incommunicado."

"He's being difficult, is he?"

"He hasn't slept here since Maya was born. Says he's living at a client's house." His condo isn't going to be ready for months, and they agreed Jack would stay up on Haywood until that time. "I don't even have the number. I guess I should just let him be, but I can't help worrying about him."

"Sure. You guys put in a lot of time, and that's something."

At ten after five, Aaron pulls into the driveway, and Jimmy runs up to the front door and carries Maya, already strapped into her car seat, out to the blue Jeep. Haggis, looking festive in a green and red collar, is sitting regally in the trunk space.

It is a bumpy and cramped ride, but Maya and her three adoring adults and dog arrive at the Manor within ten minutes. Inside, Christmas carols are playing, and the lights of the large Douglas fir twinkle; a battery-powered reindeer lifts and lowers his head as if to greet them.

"Ah, there she is." Penny catches sight of her mother sitting near a large river-rock fireplace.

Alice looks absolutely splendid. Her hair is still thick for a lady of her age, and today it is beautifully styled. Like her daughter, she, too, is wearing a red dress, revealing a pair of rather shapely legs for an eighty-five-year-old. Around her neck is a soft green scarf, fastened with a brooch. Even her fingernails are painted today.

"Wait." Penny grabs Aaron by the arm and Jimmy

stops too. She wants to savour this moment. Watch her mother across the room. Watch her waiting and listening for their anticipated arrival.

Alice's ankles are crossed demurely, and her hands lie in her lap, as if somebody posed her for a picture.

"Aaron, do you have a camera?"

"Of course." These days he has become the unofficial photographer of Maya and her entourage and the daily miracles of her young life. He is never without his digital. "It's in the diaper bag."

"Can you take one of my mom? She looks so beautiful, and she isn't aware that we're here. It would make an amazing shot."

Penny's favourite pictures of herself are candid shots, when someone took the picture without her knowing. In the other 95 percent of the photos she has seen of herself, she always has the same stupid face, and her head is constantly tilted over to one side. Maybe at one point she thought this looked good. It doesn't. However, she continues to contort herself for photos and thinks perhaps she inherited this tendency from Alice, who always opens her mouth too wide and sticks out her chest. It must be in the genes.

"Sure. Let me just set this down." Aaron is fumbling with coats and a knapsack. Jimmy is holding Maya and the diaper bag. Penny has Haggis, who is behaving with the utmost of decorum, on a short leash.

"Here, let me help you." She unzips the bag as Jimmy is standing awkwardly, holding the cumbersome seat and precious child.

"It's in the side pocket." Jimmy lifts one elbow outward so she can get at the bag with her free hand. At last the camera is produced, and the picture is taken. The light of the flash startles Alice.

"Oh." Alice blinks her blind eyes but sits perfectly still until she hears her daughter.

"Hi, Mom."

"Oh, you're here. Lovely. Hello. Hello."

Jimmy and Aaron take turns greeting Alice, kissing her cheek. Haggis moves in for a nuzzle when he finds an opening.

"Ah, Chanel No. 5. A true classic." Aaron is charming her right off as usual. Late spring, when Alice first came by the house on Haywood for a visit while Aaron was doing some yardwork, they had chatted at length about Artie Shaw and Glenn Miller and the sound of a good clarinet. Due to her limp, Alice never was a great dancer, but she and Wilfred loved to listen to the radio and cut the rug a little in the privacy of their own living room. Anyone who knew about those big bands of the

1950s was in Alice's good books. Those were great memories and good times.

"Hello, Aaron. And hello, Jimmy. And you too, Haggis."

"Merry Christmas, Alice." Jimmy is unbuckling Maya from her car seat, and Penny notices how much more confident he is in handling her. They all are easing into their roles quite capably.

"Ah, wonderful. We're all one big happy family." Alice smiles at the shadows of all the people standing about her and stretches out her arms to receive Maya.

As Jimmy picks up the child seat and bag, Aaron unlocks the brake on Alice's wheelchair. "You got a good hold of her, Grandma?"

"I do."

As they wheel down the hallway toward the atrium where a private table is set up for them, Penny watches her mother and thinks she might as well be the Queen. She waited a long time for a granddaughter and isn't going to let this moment pass without a little pomp and circumstance. Haggis adds a royal touch, and Penny thinks, if it is possible, that the dog is walking taller. A noble attendant in the procession.

Alice waves at the shapes ambling with walkers and canes. She nods to fellow travellers in wheelchairs. Mostly, though, she holds the bundle in her lap tight, kissing softly the delicate head and marvelling at the new life in her hands.

"Oh, it's beautiful, Mom." The table is set with the finest china and napkins, and each setting has its own salt-and-pepper shaker. Little poinsettias surround a stunning bouquet of red and white carnations and greenery. At either end of the table are two large red candles. "Oh, I wish you could see it, Mom."

"I can feel it." Any resident can request the room. Naturally, there is a cost above the regular monthly fee, but Alice wanted the best and never even asked the price.

"It's lovely." She gives her mom a peck on the cheek and helps position her at the head of the table. They have a perfect view of the massive decorated tree in the outside courtyard as well.

Jimmy takes Maya and sets her back into her seat, and they all take their places at the table. Haggis sits in the corner next to Penny.

"So, where is Jack?" Despite Alice's blindness, Penny feels her mother's penetrating glare.

"I don't know, Mom. He's not feeling too great. He did tell me to say hello."

"I see." Alice takes the napkin and places it in her lap and then turns to where Jimmy and Aaron are seated and chats with them.

This is a special night, and regardless of her and Jack's troubles, Penny appreciates how her mother is handling the situation. Alice told her daughter that Jack would always be family. Just because she and Jack will be going their separate ways, Alice will not be letting Jack off the hook any time soon, and Penny sees that she is disappointed.

Penny looks out into the black night and catches her reflection in the window. Then she turns and watches the people seated around the table. Alice continues to stroke Maya's arm and rocks her little seat back and forth.

A staff member enters the French doors carrying four large embossed menus.

"Oh, my." Alice receives the heavy book but passes it back to the woman. "I'll let my daughter decide." She never states that she is blind.

"Of course." The woman passes the three remaining menus around the table and promises to return shortly with wine and water.

Tonight the kitchen is offering a baked ham or a standing rib roast or, of course, a turkey dinner—likely reheated from the previous day. Normally, there is a set menu, but over Christmas week, when there tend to be more visitors than usual, residents and guests are given the choice. Tonight, everybody chooses the turkey, as last night Aaron baked a salmon. Even Alice has the same, as she loves Brussels sprouts and mashed potatoes and can't imagine eating anything else at this time of year. Haggis will be the recipient of any leftovers.

"Four turkey dinners. That's pretty straightforward." The waitress looks over at Maya. "And you are new. How old is this little one?"

"She's two weeks and two days young today," Jimmy answers.

"My, she's lovely." Then she turns to Alice. "She seems really taken with her grandmother." Little Maya is holding onto Alice's index finger.

"Yes. This is my granddaughter, Maya Lara."

"What a beautiful name."

Penny had toyed with many names over the course of her pregnancy. She knew she wanted a strong name for a boy, something like John or William or Robert. She didn't like newfangled names. But then if she had a girl, she wanted a strong name too. She didn't want anything frilly or difficult to spell, but it also had to be beautiful. One thing for certain, there would be no little Penny.

She was tempted around the eighth month, when she went in for an unexpected ultrasound concerning the baby's weight, to ask the technician about the sex.

In the end, she didn't and was glad, but she wanted to devote all her mental energies to choosing the "right" name. Why grapple with a boy's name if you knew you were having a girl? You could also tell friends, and they could buy gender-appropriate clothes and gifts.

And in terms of intuition, Penny had absolutely zero vibe on the sex of her own child. She was so focused on delivering a healthy baby that she honestly didn't care what came out. *I'll be forty-one years old. Just grant me a healthy baby, Lord. Boy or girl. Just make it healthy.*

She would go to sleep every night thinking: soon there will be a new person in this house. Soon she would walk the seawall, proudly pushing a stroller. And every night it was getting closer to happening. Her belly and breasts swelling.

Three times a week she would enter the studio on 18th Street and take her place on her mat in the far corner where the sunlight would stream onto the polished wooden floors. Lamaraya would guide her through the Sun Salutations and Twists and Warrior Poses. Over the course of the year, she got quite good at anticipating the moves, and Lamaraya helped her adapt some of the poses for each trimester. The essentials, however, didn't change, and Penny really connected to her breathing. Her body longed to stretch.

Every night, she could hear Lamaraya's voice telling her to release tension, channel her energy, and align her chakras. Some of these directives didn't make any sense to Penny, but she accepted Lamaraya's words without needing to understand them. She accepted Lamaraya as she was and focused on the work. She didn't worry if she didn't understand something, but kept moving and stretching and breathing.

She remembers a woman even cornered Penny after class one day and told her that Lamaraya used to be called Debbie.

"Yeah, I used to work for Eatons before it folded. I didn't know her, she worked in another department, but she looked totally different."

"Oh?" Penny wondered why this woman had chosen her to divulge this secret to.

"She was married back then." As if this put the matter all into perspective.

"I see." Penny could add nothing else. She turned and began to roll up her mat and then turned back to her classmate. "I'm Penny, by the way."

"Oh. I'm Claire."

"Nice to meet you, Claire."

"Likewise."

She imagined this woman contemplating her name, assessing it, sizing her up. Was Penny good enough?

Hi, Penny.

Bye, Penny.

Hey, Penny!

Except for her mother and Aaron, everyone called her Penny. Recently, though, she'd been thinking of herself more and more as Penelope. Wondering if she could dare to call herself that out loud. Maybe change her name with the launch of her new column. After all, she was a different person now.

She went home later that night and lay on her left side because Lamaraya had said something about fertility and harnessing power. She had to laugh at how important her yoga teacher had become in her life. She didn't buy into everything Lamaraya said, but whatever she was doing, it made her feel good. It calmed her down and soothed her mind and relaxed and strengthened her body. All these were good things. Maybe she would change her name and people would nudge each other as she went by, recalling that she was once Penny Stevens.

In the meantime, however, she had to find a name for her child. She settled deeply beneath the covers and laughed quietly to herself. *Maybe tomorrow I will ask Mayalara to find my child a good name. Lamaraya? Mayalara! Maya Lara.*

Penny had sat up and fumbled for a pen. She wrote

it on a bookmark because she was groggy with sleep and didn't want to forget it in the morning. Those days she was often scatterbrained.

And so, two months later, little Maya Lara is dining with her grandmother at the Manor. The thought of having a boy is now inconceivable to Penny. Of course she would have a daughter.

The same waitress is back, uncorking a bottle of white wine. Penny didn't think they allowed residents to drink alcohol, but Alice tells everyone that many of the seniors indulge daily in spirits. "Some people swear by it."

"Well, cheers!" Jimmy raises his glass and waits until everybody is ready. "To life. To love. To happiness."

"Hear, hear." Aaron reaches across the table and is the first one to clink Penny's glass.

"Hold your bloody horses!" Penny's heart literally skips a beat as Jack barges into the atrium.

"Jack! You've come." Alice tilts up her head to the booming voice.

"Of course I have, Alice. Sorry I'm late." He glances at Jimmy and Aaron but not directly at Penny.

"I didn't think you were coming." Alice grabs for his hands.

"I wouldn't miss it." He lightly kisses Maya's head and sits in the vacant chair next to his mother-in-law.

"I thought you were sick."

"I am. I was." He looks now at Penny, who just nods.

"Too busy to come by and congratulate me?"

"Sorry. I've been a bastard."

"You really have. You're lucky I like you."

"Indeed, I am lucky. I'm a lucky bastard and a fat bastard. Merry Christmas, Alice."

"Merry Christmas, Jack, and I'm glad you're here."

"Thank you."

He orders what everybody else is having, and the waitress has to open another bottle of wine so Jack can join them in a toast.

Penny looks around the table again. *So much love. So much love.* Nobody notices Penny fight back tears. They are all either fussing over Maya or talking with Alice.

It turns out to be a lovely dinner, right down to the dessert. When the waitress comes to clear the dishes, every plate is bare, thanks to Haggis, who is on his best behaviour. Only once does Maya need to be fed, and this Penny does discreetly in the corner of the room. Later, Jimmy disappears with Maya for a quick diaper change. When he returns, Marta Vanderhoerst is trailing closely behind him.

"Evening, Alice." She peers into the room. Her eyesight is excellent.

"That you, Marta?"

"Having a private party?"

"Yes, a little celebration in honour of my new grand-daughter."

"Oh, yes." Nobody in the Manor has escaped this bit of news. "So this is your granddaughter?"

"This is Maya."

"Well, she's lovely, lovely."

"Yes, thank you, Marta. Thanks for stopping by."

But old Marta lingers, hovering over the child, taking in the deep richness of her skin, the dark, tight curls, the bright, almost black eyes, and Penny recalls what Alice would always say to her as she was growing up. *Let time work its magic, Penny. Let time go by.*

And Alice was right, it seemed. Whatever Penny felt so strongly about at the moment invariably took on a new perspective as the days and weeks passed. At times she realized she was wrong to stress over certain things. At other times she learned it was her moral duty to fight for what she believed in, and on rare occasions she managed to muster the courage to do so. More often than not, however, she came to see that she took other people's opinions of herself far too seriously.

Now, having a baby with the partner of your gardener while still married to your philandering husband under the scrutinizing glare of a wealthy, ultra-conservative community is sure to evoke the odd comment or judgment.

She's the one from the paper, you know . . .

She had a baby with a gay guy, and her husband, that realtor guy, is like, still living with her . . .

I heard the husband was impotent . . .

I heard the black guy's not gay . . .

No, I think the husband's gay . . .

"Merry Christmas, Marta." Alice smiles and continues to rock her little granddaughter in her arms.

Later that night, before Penny falls asleep, the last thing she sees in her mind is Maya's little hand holding onto Alice's bony fingers.

Epilogue

"Are you holding out okay?" Margaret makes a point of asking Penny every so often. She's posed a few times and knows it can be a strain keeping still, holding a peaceful, tranquil expression while twenty strangers document every crease and crevice and curve of one's body.

"I'm good." Her breasts feel like two hard rocks. A good half-year after giving birth and Penny continues to be in awe at the wonders of the human body. The fact that she can nourish her child with milk that she produces all on her own. She's just starting to introduce solid foods into Maya's diet and is a bit reluctant to cease being the sole provider. Soon anyone will be able to feed her cereal or cut up a banana. She clings to this recent past, as it is a comfortable, warm, and solid place. The future is uncertain, but time marches forward regardless of birth and death and the time in between.

It's three in the afternoon and Penny is starving. She didn't really eat lunch, and now her stomach is growling. At first the students chuckled at the rumbles, but now they are all intently scribbling and concentrating. The class ends shortly, and they don't want to waste time. They won't see Penny for three days, and they will have to rely on their memories and imaginations if they are going to finish the piece.

Maya is having her afternoon nap in the house, and Penny is counting the minutes until she can walk out of the studio and cross the lawn and climb up to the second-floor bedroom where her daughter is sleeping. She put her down well over two hours ago, but it is a hot day and the air, even for Taos, is heavy.

They've been in this beautiful small town tucked away in northern New Mexico for almost one calendar month. And it's been just what the doctor ordered.

Nobody knows Penny here. She's just a mother of a young child. A bit quiet. There's a definite sadness to her, but she fills her days with her child, does laundry, cleans, and helps cook. She loves to take Maya into town and shop at the farmers' market. Yesterday she made jambalaya, and Margaret loved it. Even her son, Ryan, who will turn one next week, ate a good-sized bowl.

Every day the sun comes up, and invariably, at one point or another, there is laughter or tears. Ryan is beginning to walk along the edges of the furniture, and when he ventures a step or two from the coffee table he will suddenly look about the room and realize where he is, what he has done. Usually he screams. Sometimes he just plops down onto his rear end and stares in bewilderment. And Penny knows exactly how he feels.

She can't believe she is here. In New Mexico. With a cousin she hasn't seen since the fourth grade. And even then, Margaret was just an entity in a blanket. A tiny, whiny thing that everybody called "cute" but that in Penny's opinion was anything but.

Maya is breathtakingly beautiful and exquisite. Each day is a gift. Penny loves to contemplate the shape of her head, the curl of her hair, the beauty and depth of her eyes, and her perfect skin.

She knows she is living a strange life. That she is not the Penny Stevens she was a year ago is a fact. There have been so many changes, all of them unforeseen.

Especially with the passing of her mother. She didn't expect it. Alice was healthy and then she was gone. And the pain was immediate and unrelenting. Life was wonderful and then it was *bloody unfair!* Suddenly Penny was mother-less. An orphan at age forty-one. Alice had only four and a half months with her granddaughter.

Then again, as she looks back on her two score and two amazing years, she is coming to realize that she had assumed on the dock that day so many years ago, when the minister pronounced her and Jack "husband and wife" and "until death do you part," that they would go on to have a couple of kids in a perfect house with a white picket fence. That was the normal thing to do. Everybody did it, and so would she. Or so she assumed.

Life, however, had other plans.

She considers her cousin. Would Margaret still be working at the bank if Gary hadn't been killed in the desert halfway across the world? She could have stayed in Texas, where his parents live, and had help raising the baby. Would she have cashed in everything she owned so she could come to this idyllic place and start up an artistic commune? A sanctuary?

Had Alice not died, would she and Margaret have ever connected? Margaret had been visiting her parents in Seattle when Jimmy or Aaron—she can't recall who was on whose list—called to inform them of Alice's death. It was an impulse decision on Margaret's part, but she was there for the funeral, and now Penny is here.

These days it seems that Penny increasingly knows less and less. Her father used to ask her on her birthday what she knew for certain. She had to give an answer before Alice would let her blow out the candles and make a wish.

Every year she said something different. Somewhere in Alice's big albums it is recorded.

My name is Penny and I am five years old!

I think people should be kind to animals.

I think boys are gross. Except you, Daddy.

I am never getting married.

I think Andrew is cute.

I will only marry for love!

A person has to work at what they love.

I'm going to be a doctor.

Friends are important.

Never settle for second best.

I'm going to be an accountant.

I like being alone.

I'm going to be a financial planner, I guess.

"Happy Birthday to you, dear Penny! And many more . . ."

Now, all these years later, she still isn't certain what

she knows for sure. If anything, she's confident she knows close to nothing.

She lives in a world where reality shows are entertainment and half the world has too much and the other half is starving.

If her father were alive today, she would have to say that family is important. She's quite certain about it. What a family looks like, however, may not have anything to do with what she originally thought. It might not just be Mom and Dad and the kids and a dog and vacations to Disneyland.

Never in a million years would Penny think that she would befriend a gay man and have his baby. But she did.

She never thought she would be the one to leave Jack. She always assumed that one day he would finally up and leave. But she was the one to leave. She assumed he never loved her, but apparently he does. At least that's what he tells her when he calls and what he writes in his letters.

And Margaret. Did she imagine she would one day support herself through art? It was never going to pay the bills, or so people continually told her. She was going to work at the bank and then take maternity leave. Gary would be back just after Easter, and then the baby would be born. They'd have another one in a year or two.

After the twenty-one-gun salute, Gary's coffin was lowered into the ground. She was handed the folded flag and then she went home. While she waited for the baby to be born, she thought. A lot.

And now Maggie is here, hosting retreats for visiting artists and local people who want to explore the beauty and wonder of the human body.

And Penny, who was told her whole life that she was too fat, whose legs were always too short, whose boobs were too big, now reveals herself—naked, unclothed, and unrepentant.

Sometimes at night, just after writing her column and before falling asleep, she thinks her renovation went far deeper than anybody ever expected. She has to smile when she thinks of all those people back home, her friends and neighbours. What they would think if they saw her now.

And Jack's face.

He was standing on the porch with Haggis. Maggie and Penny had just packed the last bag into Penny's Volvo. Maya and Ryan were buckled into their car seats, and it was time to leave.

"I don't like this idea, Pen. I don't like it." He was

adamant that they should not drive themselves and two little kids all the way to New Mexico. In fact, he didn't want her to leave. Thought the entire idea was just another one of her harebrained schemes.

"Jack. We've talked about this already. Many times."

"Even Jimmy doesn't like the idea!"

"I know, but he's come to accept it. I'll call you all every day."

"I just don't know why you have to do this. Why now?"

"I just do. I don't know why."

She had to put some distance between herself and the three men and all the craziness in her life, people's condolences and questions and curiosity. She needed some quiet time. A refuge where she could think and be alone with her thoughts and figure things out.

Maggie and she had clicked right away. Maybe at a different point in their lives they would have remained acquaintances, but they had so much in common now that they were drawn to each other immediately. Both new mothers. Both grieving.

Thank God Alice had sent all those birth announcements. If she hadn't been so organized, Penny might never have come to know her cousin.

"So how long are you going to be away?" Jack wasn't

moving from his spot on the porch. Maybe if he came down those steps he might do something drastic and throw himself in front of the car.

"I don't know, Jack."

"Well, how long do you think?"

"I don't know."

"Well, you must have some sort of idea. What are you going to do down there?"

"I don't know, Jack. I don't know."

And she didn't. And she still doesn't. And she's been in the dark pretty much ever since. She's taking it day by day. Tomorrow, she thinks, she will make pumpkin soup. Maybe she will give Maya some. Also, she wants to buy Ryan a present. They will have a party. Then in six months Maya will have a party, but she might be home by then. But she doesn't know for sure.

Yes, amidst all the grief and craziness, there is beauty in this world. You just have to go out and look for it. And that's one other thing she knows for sure.

THE END

Acknowledgements

The following people helped me begin the book . . .

For inspiration and belief in myself, I owe so much to my women's group: Ruth Avrin, Anne Dohmeier, Jenna Jordison, Dianne Mylrea, Beverly Lock, Marilyn Leese, Marianne Pengelly, Mary Segal. I am proud to know you all.

To Ivan Coyote, an amazing storyteller and the best writing teacher I could have asked for—thanks for the classes, the writing group, and the chance to test and share my stuff.

Thanks to Dr. Joanne Larsen for medical advice.

Thanks to my father, H.P. Schneider, who always asked me what I knew for sure. I miss you. And to my mother, Christa, who made me feel like a little kid every time I brought in a chapter for her to read, thanks for believing in me. I am so glad you finished reading it before you left us. This is for you.

These individuals helped me finish the book . . .

Shannon Leggett for reading ten chapters of the first draft and then promptly setting out a very clear path for me—all the way from Prague! Thank goodness I listened to you so that I can also thank Terri Harker, who put the book into Leo MacDonald's hands, who then opened the door at HarperCollins. I am very aware that I have angels with me on this journey. *Merci.*

From here my thanks go to Jennifer Lambert, my editor. Thank you for taking me on and guiding me through the polishing and rewriting of this book. As painful as the editing sometimes was, the novel is so much better for it. Every time a package came to the door it was like Christmas.

And many thanks to friends . . .

Gillian Dew and Brian Polydore, for the Dominica Stones Commodore 64 (was it?) that you put into my hands all those years ago. Yes, technology helps. To Leslie

Buchanan, for wanting to publish my work just because she knows me. That's unwavering support. To neighbours Jackie and Bruce Coupland, who listened to me. Thanks for your encouragement. To Marilyn Leese, for reading the entire first draft in record time. Your enthusiasm and belief in the book has been wonderful. To Megan Johnston Saul, my best friend. Thank you for reading the book. I am stronger knowing you stand behind me.

Finally, I want to acknowledge two people in my life, without whom this story would never have been written.

First, my daughter, Thalia, for being the kind of kid who inspires a parent to act upon what they are trying to instill. Thanks for always having your homework done and being more organized than me. I am so lucky you chose me as your mom. It is a joy to see you grow up and sheer pleasure to watch you dance and put yourself out there. See, kid, it is true.

Second, my husband, Robert Crymble. I love you. A lot. More than fifty dollars. When Ivan said a writer needs an "ogre" and you volunteered, I really think that sealed the deal. Thanks for equal parts encouragement and harassment. I am lucky to share my life with you. Really lucky.